ALSO BY A. J. TATA

Double Crossfire

Dark Winter

Direct Fire

...ged (*Publishers Weekly* Top 10 Mystery/Thriller of 2017)

Three Minutes to Midnight

Foreign and Domestic (2016 Barry Award Finalist)

Reaper: Drone Strike (with Nicholas Irving)

Reaper: Threat Zero (with Nicholas Irving)

Reaper: Ghost Target (with Nicholas Irving)

Mortal Threat

Hidden Threat

Rogue Threat

Sudden Threat

CHASIN

THE LIG

Besi

CHASING THE LION

A. J. TATA

ST. MARTIN'S PRESS
NEW YORK

First published in the United States by St. Martin's Press, an imprint of St. Martin's Publishing Group

CHASING THE LION. Copyright © 2021 by A. J. Tata. All rights reserved.
Printed in the United States of America. For information, address St. Martin's Publishing Group,
120 Broadway, New York, NY 10271.

www.stmartins.com

Designed by Jonathan Bennett

The Library of Congress Cataloging-in-Publication Data is available upon request.

ISBN 978-1-250-27048-1 (hardcover)
ISBN 978-1-250-27049-8 (ebook)

Our books may be purchased in bulk for promotional, educational, or business use.
Please contact your local bookseller or the Macmillan Corporate and Premium Sales Department at
1-800-221-7945, extension 5442, or by email at MacmillanSpecialMarkets@macmillan.com.

First Edition: 2021

10 9 8 7 6 5 4 3 2 1

To my buddy, Snowy,
who patiently accompanies me when I write

CHASING THE LION

1

STILL REELING FROM MELISSA'S death, I closed my eyes and recalled the simple phrase she would repeat to me when the chips were down: "Good wins."

With my faith already shattered by losing my wife too early, the notion of goodness in general seemed remote as I stared at the cave mouth of a suspected mass grave in the Iranian high mountain desert.

Major Sally McCool had landed our MH-60 Pave Hawk in a narrow defile less than ten miles from the village of Tabas, or Desert One, where Operation Eagle Claw had ended in a giant fireball in 1979.

I walked toward Master Sergeant Joe Hobart, my senior operative. We were wearing our new Integrated Visual Augmentation System, or IVAS, that displayed the terrain in front of us like a video game. The outline of Hobart's body looked like that of a high-definition avatar. Normally a man of composed indifference, Hobart was rhythmically tapping his right thigh, his nervous energy compelling the entire situation to move more quickly. He knew we had precious little time on the objective area.

To Hobart's right was the dark, inverted U-shape of the cave mouth.

To his left was a soldier named Randy Van Dreeves. These two men were my longtime teammates and best operators.

I was proud to be a member of this small team. If I had known ahead of time any of what was about to transpire, I was certain I would have made different decisions along the way, but we did the best we could with the information we had. The moment never waited—you either commanded it or it commanded you, and even when you owned it, everything could go wrong.

The ghost of the failed American raid to rescue our hostages over forty years ago in this same province hung in the air like spent gunpowder. As prepared as ever, I reached Hobart, who nodded, whispered, "Boss," and then turned to Van Dreeves, who was scanning in the opposite direction from a rock crevice like a parapet on a medieval castle. He tapped Van Dreeves on the shoulder and said, "Masks."

We all removed and stowed our IVAS devices, then donned our protective masks, the large eyes and circular metal filter making us appear as if we emerged from a World War I trench in Verdun after a heavy German artillery barrage. The mask focused me inward instead of outward. The rubber smell, the mechanical voices, and the amplified breathing created an illusion of claustrophobia. Our masks had sturdy rubber tubes running over our shoulders into small oxygen tanks. It was not that we didn't trust the filters the army provided, but after the COVID-19 outbreak, we were prepared for any virus, bacteria, or chemical that could wilt a standard protective mask filter. We followed Van Dreeves into the dark cavern, flashlight beams crisscrossing in the blackness.

The night was crisp here in the Eshdeger Mountain Range of central Iran as we transitioned from arid to damp in a matter of seconds. Hobart and Van Dreeves shined their lights as my Pave Hawk crew, Sergeant Jackson and Corporal Brown, secured the mouth of the cave. They had left McCool and her copilot, Chief Warrant Officer Jimmy Rogers, in the idling helicopter.

As we journeyed deeper into the cave, Van Dreeves's Polimaster chemical agent detector, a small handheld device, suddenly lit up like a million-dollar slot machine.

"Picking up chemicals, but not identifying them," Van Dreeves said.

"This way," Hobart said. His uncharacteristic use of more than one word made me want to smile in the darkness, but the heavy weight of the mission and Melissa's death were constant reminders of life's fragility. While on these missions, I took comfort in the teamwork and camaraderie, like a basketball team that could do behind-the-back passes and alley-oops without discussing the plays beforehand.

We were traveling in a diamond wedge now. Van Dreeves was on point with the Polimaster, Hobart to my right front, holding his M4 carbine at the ready. Jackson, a former NFL linebacker, ducked to avoid scraping his head along the cave ceiling to my left front. Brown, behind me, was ready to ward off anyone chasing us from the rear. Our breathing collectively sounded like Darth Vader on steroids as we sucked in oxygen through the tanks on our backs. The rubbery taste and odor of the mask replaced the dank smell of the cave.

Van Dreeves was still winning millions in Vegas as the Polimaster's blinking red lights gave way to a steady red glow. I stepped forward and looked over his shoulder, noticing that the meter simply read: Unidentified Agent.

Van Dreeves had reached a dead end. Our flashlights were dancing on a textured wall that was inconsistent, flat, whereas everything around it had contours, ridges, spines, impressions, bumps, and grooves like a bas-relief.

"Fake," Hobart explained.

"Here," Van Dreeves said. His hand found a seam in the wall and slid open the thin divider, which was a sheet of heavy, lead-filled cloth—like an x-ray vest—painted gray to blend into the tunnel walls.

As Van Dreeves stepped into the dimly lit area to our front, Brown quietly said from behind me, "Movement." I continued staring into the expansive cavern beyond the divider, not only because I trusted Brown to handle the problem but because the piles of dead bodies were beyond anything that I had ever seen. Twisted forms, frozen by rigor mortis, with grotesque grimaces, arms eternally reaching as if praying to an elusive god. There must have been over five hundred bodies stacked in deepening layers at the far end of the cave, maybe fifty meters away. Near my feet there were three women, mouths open, silent screams ringing in my ears. They were gray with death, maybe two or three days dead, an image seared into my mind.

The cave floor was littered with mobile phones. Some of the dead bodies were still clutching phones held high, as if taking postmortem selfies.

The entire landscape was barren of life. It was a scene that could make a person lose all faith in mankind, the depressing escape of hope and conviction replaced by the brutal reality that mankind was evil. The pre-briefing intelligence had been accurate in one sense. It was a mass grave, but it was also more than that. These people had not been buried. They appeared to have made a pilgrimage here, climbing over one another toward the opposite end of the cave, all the while holding their phones like compasses.

"Movement," Brown said again.

I turned with the rest of my team to notice a man crawling. He was one with the ground, arms outstretched, clawing the shale. I debated whether he was coming toward us or following the pilgrimage to whatever altar lay at the far end of the tunnel.

The man was wearing a ripped protective mask, gray with dust. The eye coverings were a hanging flap, making his face clearly visible. I knelt down and put a rubber-gloved hand on his face not only out of compassion but because I recognized him.

I was surprised to find my friend Dr. Ben David crawling toward me, perhaps beyond me, in a cave full of bodies in the middle of the Iranian desert.

The events that have unfolded since are well known today; the ghastly story behind them, not so much.

2

I FIRST MET MOSSAD agent Ben David fifteen years from when I found him in the cave in central Iran. I had been in a small Israeli Defense Force command center near the Gaza Strip, and he had just exfiltrated through a mile-long tunnel connecting a cement factory in Beit Lahia to a small kibbutz near Shikma Reservoir.

He credited me with saving his life that day, but it was actually the Israeli soldiers at the command center who chose not to fire that prevented his death. I had traveled from Anbar Province, Iraq, through Jordan, and into southern Israel for discussions with the Israeli Defense Forces. We needed to ensure they understood the nature of our surge of forces in Iraq in 2006 and how it was intended to revive the moderate Sunnis, who were necessary to establishing what was characterized as peace in the Fertile Crescent.

Remote ground sensors had detected movement near the Walid Cement Factory west of the Gaza boundary fence. The radar indicators were a pattern of eight pulses followed by a pause and then followed by another eight pulses. This pattern had repeated itself enough that I knew it was not random movement; rather, it was a code of some sort. It certainly wasn't Morse code, not that I was an expert in that cipher, but it was a message, nonetheless.

The Israelis were lying in wait, weapons trained on the fence a mile away. David told me later that he was thankful for that distance, because it gave me a few minutes to realize that he was transmitting Eli Cohen's Mossad code name. After checking on the radar analysts, I followed the outpost commander, Colonel Itzhak Begin, to the roof of the observation tower, where a mile of flat, uninterrupted land spread out before us. Through the binoculars' magnified lenses, there was considerable "Hamas movement," as my guide referred to it, into the cement factory on the opposite side of the border. The eighty-eight code still swam in my head as I processed what was happening.

The colonel ordered two drones—primitive by today's standards—into the air to monitor the situation, all the while not realizing that the threat was burrowing beneath us. I found it odd that dozens of Hamas soldiers poured into the factory, but none seemed to come out. It was a grander version of the old-fashioned game of cramming a phone booth.

Only the Hamas soldiers *were* funneling—into the tunnel they had drilled into Israel in pursuit of Mossad agent Ben David, a man of many faces and languages. What ensued was nothing short of artful.

I said to Colonel Begin, "Do you know of any Mossad agents in Hamas?"

"Why do you bother me with such questions, Colonel?" he replied.

"Because I don't want you to kill one," I said. That got his attention, most likely as he considered the career consequences of doing so.

"Explain," he demanded. Sweat trickled down his neck, an obvious sign that he was feeling the pressure of an uncertain situation that could take several paths, none of them spectacular for him except maybe one.

"If you had a Mossad agent in Gaza, is it likely he or she would know where the ground radars are located?"

"*If* we had one there, yes, they would know everything about our defenses so that they could report to us where we might be vulnerable."

"Then maybe repeating two eights, side by side several times, is a way of telling us 'Eli Cohen' is there," I said.

Begin scoffed but then caught himself, again perhaps considering the severe implications of not remembering Eli Cohen's deep-cover call sign in Syria when he had been masquerading as Kamal Amin Thaabet, the merchant. From 1961 to 1965, Israeli hero and spy Eli Cohen had been deep within the Syrian government's inner sanctum and was subsequently captured and executed for "treason." One country's traitor was another country's hero. Today, Eli Cohen was lionized and revered in Israel. Was it likely that Israel now had a deep-cover asset in Gaza? It was certainly possible, and Begin seized on that thread of probability to warn his men of the likelihood that a "friendly" element may be attempting to escape.

Within ten minutes of Colonel Begin issuing clarifying instructions to his team, David came pouring from the mouth of a tunnel no less than fifty meters from our observation post. The ground seemed to produce David as if he were appearing from a trapdoor on a stage. The Israelis had no idea the tunnel existed, and to this day, I am amazed at the restraint shown by the soldiers who, judging by the puzzled look on Colonel Begin's face, had been surprised by the tunnel. Covered in grime and white, chalky dust, David stumbled and ran toward the Israeli soldiers, who, thanks to Begin's guidance, did not whittle him to shreds with a fusillade of machine-gun fire. David shouted, "Eighty-eight, eighty-eight, eighty-eight!" as he reared up from the hole in the ground.

I had felt satisfaction in helping Begin and his outpost recover David, who had found the Hamas tunnel during one of his resupply missions. In a moment of excitement, he had snapped some pictures of the tunnel from his phone and was detected doing so by a garden-variety Hamas fighter, who had been suspicious of him. He killed the soldier and fled.

And so it was a situation that seemed to make sense to the crack IDF troops peering through their sights.

Unfortunately for the Hamas soldiers who stumbled out behind David, the Israeli soldiers had shown no such restraint, placing accurate and withering fire onto the mouth of the tunnel. The IDF defenses held against twenty or so Hamas militants, to include a woman who appeared to be the first out of the tunnel behind David.

My stunned tour guide Colonel Begin immediately called Mossad headquarters in Tel Aviv and relayed the results of his initial interrogation of David, who was theatrical, if not convincing. Because of my status in the Joint Special Operations Command and responsibility for several dark sites—a euphemism for prisons, dungeons, or chambers—Colonel Begin allowed me to witness the combination debrief and interrogation. Bound and haggard, David relayed an incredible account of four years behind enemy lines in the Gaza Strip and beyond.

David was an Iranian Jew whose Arabic and Persian skills were unparalleled. He was able to mimic Anbar Province's dialect to avoid suspicion as he served as a logistics officer in Hamas, shuttling supplies between Jordan, Egypt, and Iraq, with the occasional venture into Palestinian territory. He had graduated as a medical doctor from the Ben-Gurion University but had ditched that degree to serve the highest of Jewish callings—the Mossad. Passing himself off as an Iranian special forces soldier, David operated under the nom de guerre Xerxes, an homage to the infamous Persian warrior of the empire era.

During the interrogation, David/Xerxes was visibly upset as he recounted that he had been smuggling people and supplies between Iraq, Jordan, and Egypt. He would disappear into the souks of Basra and reappear in Iran, providing his ersatz masters there enough intelligence to remain in their graces. During his tenure, he gravitated upward in the chain of command and was ultimately responsible for delivery of all weapons and ammunition from Iran to Hamas. He had expressed feelings of remorse over supplying the means of warfare to Israel's sworn enemies, but his frequent contacts with Mossad agents in Baghdad had allowed him to assuage the guilt.

At some point during the four hours we were in the command bunker near Gaza, the director of Mossad, Gabriel Dymond, appeared out of thin air, or more likely arrived from Tel Aviv. We were all dismissed, and Dymond ushered David away personally.

At his request, I next saw David a few months after his escape from Gaza, in a café near the Ritz-Carlton south of Tel Aviv. When I approached, he was looking into the Mediterranean Sea, its waves rolling in and making me think of Van Dreeves and his surfing. It was a clear, sunny day with a comfortable temperature and gentle sea breezes wafting over the rock jetties. Given my liaison duties, it was not uncommon for me to travel to Israel. My commander at the time told me to see if David had any intelligence on Iran and their wicked improvised explosive devices we called EFPs—explosively formed penetrators.

"Colonel Sinclair," he had said, looking at me with distant eyes.

"Please, Doctor. It's Garrett." I offered my hand, and he half stood and shook it as I sat in the chair across from him.

"Okay, Garrett, but please call me Ben. Medical school was for my parents," he said.

"Isn't it always," I said.

"This life," he said, "is what I want."

Even then he had a wizened, weather-beaten look. The years on the rat lines between the Persian, Arab, and Israeli worlds had worn on him. He was ten years younger than I was but looked ten years older. Thin and wiry, David nursed a small cup of espresso, which looked pretty good given my lack of sleep at the time. Chipped, perpetually dirty fingernails spun the tiny white porcelain demitasse, a metaphor for the contrast in David's life. Refined in Israel and soldierly in Iraq and beyond.

I ordered the same, and David ran his hands through his thick, black hair, flecks of gray highlighted by the sunlight. His olive complexion was still deeply tanned from years in the heat and sun, though it looked darker without the Gaza tunnel dust covering his face and body.

"I learned that you convinced Colonel Begin not to shoot me," he said. "I wanted to thank you in person."

He spoke Begin's name as if on an ordinary day the man may actually choose to shoot him.

"It was smart of you to send that message," I said.

"I ran nearly a mile from the radar to the tunnel. It had only been six months since my last meeting in Baghdad, where I reviewed the Gaza defenses. I knew that we had no clue about that tunnel. When I was discovered, I did what I had to do."

"I'm glad you're okay. You led many Hamas fighters directly into an ambush," I said.

He nodded, looked out to the sea again, obviously something on his mind.

"Yes," he whispered. A cloud passed across his eyes. It was impossible to know what he was thinking so I took a guess.

"You're going back?" I asked.

His gaze never left the Med, but his lips turned up in a slight smile.

"Aren't you burned?" I continued, giving him an out for not having to tell me something that he most likely was forbidden from doing.

"They've checked everything. Anyone who suspected me was killed at the mouth of the tunnel. I'm usually gone for three months from Iran and three months from Gaza. It's time for me to go into Baghdad and make my way."

"You need a ride?" I asked jokingly.

"Yes." Not joking. "I need to infiltrate with you and disappear into Anbar so that I can get back to my routine."

Seeing the obvious upside for our intelligence-gathering efforts, I made plans to leave that evening by way of my favorite route through Jerusalem into Jordan and then Anbar. We shared a meal of hummus, fish, and salad before embarking on a two-day journey through Israel and Jordan, moving between safe houses using CIA burner automobiles and fake passports. At six foot two inches with dark skin, I can pass for Arabic with the right headdress, which we had. Of course, David was a polyglot, and his Persian lineage allowed him the freedom to claim any number of nationalities.

DURING THAT TRIP, we bonded and told war stories, and for the first time, I felt that I had made a true friend that could relate to my years as a JSOC soldier. Which made it doubly difficult to see his body on the floor of the cave in front of me tonight.

I leaned down and opened his tightly balled fist. He was clutching a medallion, what soldiers in the U.S. military know as *challenge coins*. This coin had Farsi characters and the black-and-gold Quds Force insignia: an outstretched arm and fist clutching a combat rifle superimposed on a globe framed by a laurel leaf.

It was a fitting symbol for a global terrorist organization fueled by religious extremism. I flipped the coin over and saw what I feared—the one-star emblem of Brigadier General Dariush Parizad, the heir apparent to Qassem Soleimani, the infamous Quds Force leader that we had recently killed.

Parizad only gave his coin to his most trusted operatives. I nodded in admiration at David's inert body. He's still in the cave. Best to delete location. He had made it into the inner sanctum of Iran's Islamic Revolutionary Guard Corps.

As bad as Soleimani was, Parizad was far worse. For him, the long war with America was personal.

3

McCOOL'S VOICE CAME THROUGH our earpieces: "Radar shows two Hind helicopters inbound."

"Let's move," I said.

Hobart motioned to Jackson and Brown, who slipped on rubber gloves and lifted Ben David's body as Van Dreeves, our resident combat lifesaver, tested his pulse with a small biometric probe into the mouth.

"Heart rate depressed," he said. He retrieved the probe and then used pliers to pick up a small vial, which he double secured in two sealable pouches, then placed the pouches in his cargo pocket.

"Boss?" Hobart asked.

"Exfil," I said.

Just then, David's lips started moving imperceptibly. He was whispering something none of us could hear. Curly black hair was matted to his forehead. His face was white with chalky dust, and his lips were pink and parting slowly. I leaned forward so that I could feel his breath on my ear. The mechanical breathing noises from my protective mask and oxygen tank competed with the words he was saying. Finally, though, I understood him.

"Naomi," he whispered.

Figuring Naomi was his wife or partner, I logged the name away and squeezed his shoulder with a gloved hand. His utterance seemed to be all the effort he could muster.

I led the team out of the cavern and into the night. The helicopter blades were whipping fifty meters away. We returned to McCool, ducked beneath the blades, and placed David in a body bag to contain whatever contaminants he might have been carrying. It wasn't perfect, but better than anything else we had. We removed our masks and dumped them in a hazmat bag, which Van Dreeves sealed and stowed beneath our seats. As soon as we were seated, McCool powered up, nosed over, and sped away. Joining us were two AH-64 Apache attack helicopters, which we would need immediately.

We split two mountain peaks like a football through the uprights and dipped below the next ridge. The Apaches spun around so that they could ambush the Iranian Hip and Hind helicopters buzzing through the spires. Two bright explosions momentarily whited out my IVAS screen. In a flash, blackened pieces of the helicopters were trickling down from the sky. I was all for playing the rabbit in an ambush, but we still had 150 miles to the "safety" of Afghanistan, where a slightly smaller army wanted to kill us.

The one thing that CENTCOM commander General Fred Fillmore told me before executing this mission was, "Don't fuck it up." I always appreciated broad guidance, and my plebe-year West Point roommate knew that was all I needed.

Fillmore and I remained close throughout our careers. While I played baseball, Fred was a miler on the track team. He had ascended quickly through the ranks because of his professional acumen and intelligence. I was happy for him and his wife, Diane, as he was now being considered for chairman of the Joint Chiefs.

Fred had provided me the undivided attention of the CENTCOM

chief of operations, Vice Admiral Tom Rountree, who was monitoring our status. Even though we were a Special Operations Command asset, we were in Central Command's area of operations, and they had airplanes, missiles, and troops to assist, if necessary.

"Frogman, this is Dagger, over," I said into the mouthpiece on my headset.

"Frogman. Go, over." His voice was crisp and authoritative on the net.

"Dagger green. One additional friendly pax. Unidentified chem. Possible sample. Red pursuit on exfil."

"Copy. Anything further?"

"Negative, out."

There was a pause on the radio. He knew what I was doing. If we didn't make it, he at least had the information and, knowing Tom, code name Frogman, from operating together on multiple combat missions, I was sure he was marshaling airpower in Afghanistan and the Persian Gulf. He had probably even directed some type of feint or provocation in the west to aid in our escape to the east. It was what I would have done for him if the roles were reversed.

We made it to the first wet wing refuel stop about seventy miles from the border. The MC-130 Combat Talon's propellers were spinning. The hoses were laid out in the desert fifty meters behind the workhorse airplane. To avoid another Operation Eagle Claw mishap, we stayed in the air as the Apaches landed one at a time and refueled along the dirt road. Brown dust billowed up like an explosion, and for a long moment, I couldn't see the airplane or the Apaches. The second Apache lifted from the dust, allowing my heart to start beating again, as they positioned in the air for us to land.

McCool crept the Beast into the refuel point, and the fuel handlers came running out, crew helmets, goggles, and kaffiyehs covering their heads and faces. We refueled for a few minutes and were shortly back up in the air, nosing over to the east.

Our return was surprisingly uneventful, always a good thing, and we landed at Forward Operating Base Farah, where I said, "Good job, Cools."

"Roger that," she replied. Just another day in the office.

We carried David in the body bag to a decontamination site, where we all went through an extensive hosing down. The medical team was on hand to clean and tend to David, who miraculously was still alive. Somewhere during the flight, Van Dreeves risked slipping an IV into his arm, and I was glad he did.

He handed over the pouch to the joint weapons of mass destruction analysis team, led by a portly FBI analyst named Rogerson. They were all dressed in crisp hazmat suits, and we were in soaking-wet T-shirts and briefs. Holding the pouch at arm's length, Rogerson and his two helpers waddled off to the container that housed the lab.

The five of us dug through our kit bags about the time McCool and her copilot, Jimmy Rogers, walked up.

"Pushing the envelope, General," McCool said to me.

"What else would you prefer I do with it?" I replied.

She smiled and said, "Not a damn thing."

After everyone had washed off the residue of the mission, we gathered in the Sensitive Compartmented Information Facility, or SCIF, which was a container within a container where we could discuss classified information. We rehashed the operation, and everyone decided that while we could have done some things better, overall it had been a successful mission built upon teamwork, training, rehearsals, and coordination. That old bit about the plan not surviving first contact with the enemy was untrue. Good plans always provided a foundation for response. The best plans had already thought through the multiple contingencies that could take place. The wet wing refuels, Apache helicopters, and F-35 jets were all derivatives of the planning-and-rehearsal phase.

The one thing we didn't plan for was finding Ben David nearly dead in that cave.

"We knew about the possibility for chem but didn't plan on handling POWs who had been exposed," Van Dreeves said.

"Valid point," I replied. "Good job improvising with the body bag."

A similar complex and daring raid had not been contemplated since Operation Rhino in Afghanistan, and this mission had been a hard sell to a reluctant outgoing president. The West Pointers, including Secretary of Defense Jim Tharp, Secretary of State Kyle Estes, and CIA director Samantha Owens, were eager to amass evidence that Iran was violating international law and should be, perhaps, invaded to make them see the error of their ways. Further, in the wake of the COVID-19 outbreak, their military was weakened. Iran was vulnerable.

General Fillmore had tried to be the voice of reason, arguing that perhaps it wasn't a brilliant idea to invade a country twice as large as Iraq with a warrior culture embedded in their DNA.

Outside of the West Pointers, I didn't know anyone who thought this was a good idea. Most of us who survived Operations Iraqi and Enduring Freedom understood that politicians with no skin in the game were happy to put their ideology to work through the likes of me and my troops.

As we were finally dressed and ready for a hot meal and some rack, I received a secure text message from Rountree advising me that General Fillmore would soon be contacting me. First, though, he needed to brief me. He asked me to move to a SCIF, which I did. I was back inside the metal container that was itself an insert within a double-wide trailer sitting on temporary concrete block footings. If twenty years of involvement in Afghanistan was "temporary," then we truly had lost all perspective.

"Dagger here," I said into the landline handset.

"Frogman. Okay, we've got Fillmore here about to blow a gasket."

"He misses me?" I asked.

"That chem you collected from the cave? The FBI already has a match."

That was news to me. Having been the ones to retrieve said sample, it would have been nice for Rogerson and his geeks to let me know what we found if for no other reason than to understand the hazards to which we might have been exposed.

"That was fast," I said instead of bitching, which never did any good.

"Yes. It's a supercompound, but it's not what you think. It had similar properties to a nerve agent, but it affects the brain in a more direct way. Naturally, everyone was concerned about another COVID deal. This is worse."

"You're confusing me, Tom. What was it?"

"It's new. They've given it a name—Demon Rain. Optical gas sensors are indicating what Rogerson is saying, that it's a combination between LSD and nerve agent. Makes you batshit crazy and chips away at your central nervous system."

"Mind control?" I asked myself more than Tom.

"Possibly. Were you exposed?"

"Take me to your leader," I quipped.

"Not funny. This stuff can be aerosolized and is highly potent."

I thought of the mass of dead bodies in the cave. Going into the mission, we assumed Iranian soldiers had herded them there and then slaughtered them using some type of poison, like a gas chamber. I still was not convinced, having seen the orientation of the bodies, clawing in one direction, looking upward, as if God's hand were reaching down to them.

"We completely decontaminated, Tom. We're fine. Got new uniforms and everything. The question was, why didn't Rogerson tell me?"

"Fillmore had this on his PIR," Rountree said.

Priority intelligence requirements. When soldiers in the field discovered a clue that addressed one of the commander's PIRs, it was "wake me in the middle of the night" type of information. Given the time difference, for Fillmore it was more like "interrupt my golf game." One of Fillmore's PIRs was: any indication of new nuclear, biological, or chemical weapons manufacturing capability in Iran. Rountree and I developed those requirements, but they were nonetheless "his."

"That's still unusual. They should have let me know so I could put it in context for him. What if it was COVID?"

"It's not, but I don't disagree. Fillmore now wants you to return to CENTCOM HQ and have a conversation."

"What's wrong with VTC?" If Fred wanted me to return to Tampa so soon, there had to be a good reason. If it were urgent, though, I would have preferred video teleconference.

"Direct orders. I don't like it, either, but he wants an in-person meeting."

"Is he sending one of his fancy airplanes?" I doubted he would send a Gulfstream unless there was one already in theater, which was unlikely. I sensed the smile in his voice when he said, "Yep. The rotator C-17 is en route now and will conduct two in-flight refuels. No layovers, brother."

"Shall I bring our contaminated friend?"

"No. Rogerson and team are dealing with him."

His voice was different when he said this, as if his mind took him to another place as he spoke.

"Will he stay here?"

"The boss was having discussions with all the alphabets right now about that."

The alphabets were the three-letter agencies, such as the CIA, FBI, DHS, DNI, and so on. Basically, the Intelligence Community, which had both served and betrayed the country in the last several years. I was left wondering which version of the story Ben David would receive.

"Roger that," I said and hung up the phone.

When I went to roust my Dagger team out of their bunks, I found Jackson and Brown sound asleep while Hobart and Van Dreeves were cleaning their weapons. Aviators and infantry. About right.

"Let's go, guys," I said.

"Airborne," Hobart, a former paratrooper with the Eighty-Second Airborne Division and Rangers, said.

Airborne could mean anything from "awesome" to "oh shit." Hobart's inflection indicated something in the middle, like, "We just got here, but we do what we're told, so okay."

It was a language unto itself, understood by the fortunate warriors that earned the privilege to immerse themselves in the paratrooper ethos. While my team was packing, something to which they were accustomed and did rapidly, I walked a hundred meters across the gravel beneath the black night to the FBI trailer, which was surrounded by chain-link fencing and razor wire. A guard called out to me, noticing the three stars on my uniform, but I stopped him before he saluted me.

"No need," I said, reaching out and blocking the upward movement of his hand. "Just need to see the results of our efforts." He was about six feet tall, square jawed, brown eyes, uniform salty and stained from sweat and hard work with the faintest whiff of body odor, which was the norm for soldiers here in Afghanistan.

"Sir, I'm not allowed to let anyone in," the private said.

"First of all, what's a paratrooper like you doing guarding the FBI facility? I don't remember signing any authorizations for this."

The soldier smiled and said, "They pulled me out of my squad patrol to stand here."

He was wearing an Eighty-Second Airborne Division patch on his left shoulder. He was a paratrooper like me, Hobart, and Van Dreeves. His name tag said BOONE.

"Any relation to Daniel Boone?" I quipped.

"Sir, I get that all the time. It's my nickname by now, so I just roll with it. Probably ought to officially change it."

"Hell, I'm in charge. If you have some paperwork, I'll just sign it. Make it official." I was smiling. He was smiling, and I could see the "to hell with the FBI" look on his face. Eyes darted to the left toward the gate.

"Think I'm going to take a smoke break, sir," he said.

"No need, unless you really want one. I'm in charge here, and there's an old saying, 'When in charge, be in charge.' This is me being in charge. Keep up the good work, Airborne."

I patted him on the shoulder and walked through the gate, up the steps, and into the trailer. It was dark, save a light at the end, which I pursued. I turned the corner and opened the door, behind which were metal steps leading downward, unusual for a temporary structure on an FOB. I descended into the dank tunnel, filled with musty smells of freshly dug earth and drying concrete. I turned a corner and saw two men huddled at the end of the corridor, which was flanked on either side by concrete block cells with metal doors.

I walked toward the two men, one of whom was Rogerson. He was blocking the man with whom he was speaking. A loud moan emanated from the second cell on my right. Through the barred window of the door, I saw a thin man with a long beard placing his hands on the walls, holding them there until he removed them and continued staring at the wall as he made a low, guttural sound, as if he were amazed. He definitely saw something that I did not. This individual appeared to have been in his "room" for several days or weeks and was not Ben David.

"General!" Rogerson barked as he came barreling toward me. I tried to look beyond him to gather the identity of the second person, but Rogerson's hazmat suit, sans headgear, made him look like the Michelin Man, filling the narrow corridor. A door clicked behind him, undoubtedly someone slipping away. Rogerson's background indicated he served as a senior advisor to the FBI director, making him about the same rank as I was, but in a civilian status. I had been told he wore his ego on his sleeve and had thin skin. My only concerns here were the fate of Ben David and what type of chemical my troops might have been exposed to.

"What are you doing here? No one is allowed!"

He was my height but twice as wide. I stared at him for a moment. He looked worried, eyes flitting to his right. He was holding a tablet of some sort, not an iPad but something that used an Android operating system.

"I could make the argument that this trailer belongs to me, Rogerson. What is it that has you so concerned? And who just slipped out the back, Jack?"

"What, now you're General Paul Simon? Never took you for a music guy," Rogerson said, avoiding my question.

"What is the status of the man we brought to you, and what kind of chem did we find?"

"He's quarantined at the clinic, and we are still studying the samples your team retrieved."

Ever since the COVID-19 outbreak, every FOB was required to have a quarantine area to house confirmed or suspected cases of individuals with the virus.

"That's not what I heard."

"I'm unconcerned with what you hear, General, and I don't work for you," Rogerson said.

I looked over my shoulder to make sure we were alone, save the imprisoned subjects. This was not a detention center; rather, it seemed to be an experimentation lab. I considered my options. It was probably not a good idea to beat Rogerson into submission, though I was sure paratrooper Boone would vouch for me. I could, of course, accept his defiance and depart, as I was sure he wished for me to do. But my preferred course of action was to engage him, get him talking enough to make a mistake.

"That's a poor attitude for an interloper in this war," I said.

"My attitude is irrelevant. My job is to identify threats that no one else can," he said. "I helped break the COVID-19 viral code, and now I'm going to figure out if there's anything to what you may or may not have found. I'm good at my job."

"I'm decent at mine, as well. My job is to defeat those threats and protect my team, so how about a little teamwork here?"

"General, my security level is Q. I'm not sure what yours is, but I know everyone who is cleared for the compartmented program that I run. You provided me information I need. Now I simply ask that you let me do my job."

Rogerson's eyes narrowed, and sweat ran down his neck into his space suit. He was speaking louder than he needed to, and I had the impression he was mostly talking to some unseen person.

The man in the cell behind me started shouting again. "Oh my God. It's true. It's true!"

Rogerson's eyes darted to his left. He wanted to get rid of me but probably realized he had used up the bulk of his bravado. The man in the cell reminded me of the long-haired men and women in those 1960s films with their flowing shirts and bell-bottom pants, tripping on acid and saying, "Far out, man."

"Do not mistake my calm demeanor for weakness, Rogerson," I said. "My men just risked their lives to gather the intelligence we provided you so we can do more missions to protect our country. Besides your captives, it's just you and me in here, and if I'm cleared to gather the intel, I'm damn well cleared to know what the hell we are dealing with."

Something in him broke, and he said, "You do have a certain reputation for coloring outside the lines."

"A euphemism if I've ever heard one. I think a better one might be 'Shoot first, ask questions later.'" I rested my hand on my pistol.

He nodded and spoke rapidly. "You're not supposed to know this, but it's an aerosolized synthetic quinuclidine benzilate, known as BZ, with LSD in a mix we call Demon Rain. There are sarin properties, also, but I suspect Admiral Rountree already gave you a heads-up."

"Purpose?" I was thinking of the bodies crawling over one another. Perhaps they were climbing away from the gas, trying to escape out the opposite end of the cave, which we didn't have time to inspect. Van Dreeves had taken some pictures, but I doubted any of them would prove useful in identifying what the people might have been moving toward. If Rogerson was telling the truth about some type of supergas, with a comic book moniker of Demon Rain, then maybe they were going crazy, feeling claustrophobic, needing oxygen. But still, the dead bodies didn't support what Rogerson was telling me.

"Purpose?" he asked.

"What does it do? How does it kill?"

He paused, considering his answer. "The best we can tell is that it opens the mind to visual manipulation while impacting the nervous system in some way. Think kids staring at their phones all the time. Content is a kind of mind control. Demon Rain stimulates dopamine to crave a particular type of image or content. The subject is seeking direction or is at least open to it. Whoever inhales the gas becomes a single sheep in a flock seeking some kind of guidance, image, or content. You ever play any of those brick breaker or word games on your phone?"

"No," I said.

"It's like that. Addictive, but we don't know what it is that they are addicted to, and that's all you're getting from me, General."

I stared at him for a long moment, trying to understand the connection between a mind control drug and the gruesome scene we had just witnessed. Were they convinced they were sick and the cure was in the far corner to which they were climbing? A thought hung in my mind, something to do with the COVID-19 outbreak and how much of the world's entire population obeyed their governments' directives to shelter in place. Was it really that hard to control minds?

I logged the thought away. Never wanting to create a bureaucratic rival where I didn't need to, I asked him, "Do I need to sign a waiver?"

He hesitated. "I'm going to trust you not to repeat anything. If you do, I'll just deny it or say you pulled rank on me."

"You'd know if I did that, Rogerson. One last question, though. Are you FBI . . . or CIA?"

Rogerson regained his composure a bit, smiled, and said, "Ever think if what you're doing is worth it, General? The risks you take? All your time over here? Away from your family, friends?"

I deflected and set up my exit by saying, "As a friend of mine once said, 'I'd rather die a hero than grow old.'" One of my operators, Jake Mahegan, was a Native American who had that Croatan proverb quote taped on the inside of his locker in a team room.

He nodded, most likely not understanding the sentiment of my response. I exited, patted Boone on the shoulder, and took my time finding my way to my bunk, where I grabbed my gear and met my team at the airfield. Jackson, Brown, Hobart, and Van Dreeves were standing with their kit slung over their shoulders looking like a band of mercenaries ready for their next mission. I stepped around the hangar as the C-17 was taxiing toward us. As we boarded, McCool and Rogers were tending to the Beast with its blades already folded and shoved into the C-17 cargo hold.

"What's up with the REMFs?" Hobart asked. *Rear echelon motherfuckers.* It wasn't an official acronym.

Up toward the nose of the airplane was a gaggle of soldiers, most of whom were probably headed back to the United States for discharge or other administrative reasons. Some were in civilian clothes, and some were in uniforms.

"You're spoiled," I said. We normally had our own transport to avoid operational security issues. "Just keep the team here near the ramp."

"Roger that," he said.

My team laid out sleeping bags and immediately took advantage of the opportunity to catch some rack while I tried to focus on whatever the next mission might be. I couldn't shake Rogerson's question, though.

Ever think if what you're doing is worth it, General? The risks you take? All your time over here? Away from your family, friends?

Until fifteen months ago, I had never questioned my mission or my family, but now it was a daily struggle to see the purpose. Melissa's death took something from me, and as the wheels clunked into the chassis of the Globemaster cargo airplane, I laid my head against the red webbing of the seat, wondering about the trade-offs. The killed-in-action soldiers, missed birthdays and baseball games, dead civilians, and not being able to make it to my wife's side before she passed from cancer.

We had been at a remote Turkish airbase in the middle of the mission to kill Abu Bakr al-Baghdadi when Fillmore had called me and told me that Melissa didn't have long and that I should return immediately. Because he was one of my closest friends, I wrongly suspected he was being overly cautious. The rotors had been spinning on the helicopters. I'd stood on the runway, jet fuel burning my nostrils. Missions such as these were what I'd lived and fought for. I had been surprised by Fillmore's urgent call, and I kicked myself now for not giving him more credit. But only hours before, I had spoken with Melissa and was convinced there had been more time, that there was even some glimmer of light that she would beat the disease.

"Roger," I had said to Fillmore. I hung up and boarded my command-and-control Pave Hawk helicopter. The mission was going to take three hours, max, and it would take an hour or two for the air force to get an airplane to Incirlik Air Base in Turkey with a crew prepared to fly to Washington, D.C., so I was trading maybe an hour of travel time. The mission was a complete success. Three hours later, I was on the C-17 out of Incirlik, twelve hours away from Bethesda's Walter Reed National Military Medical Center, where Melissa had been admitted to the executive wing.

Upon landing, a driver picked me up with the chief of army chaplains in the back seat of the sedan. He informed me that Melissa had passed an hour before I landed.

After twenty-nine years of marriage, I never got to say goodbye.

Killing al-Baghdadi was no consolation.

4

I MET MELISSA BROWNLEE Sinclair when I was at E. E. Smith High School in Fayetteville, North Carolina. She was the daughter of a paratrooper command sergeant major and elementary school teacher. We met at church, where she was working as a Sunday school teacher while still in high school.

We both called home the historic Haymount neighborhood of Fayetteville, adjacent to the U.S. Army's Fort Bragg. As much as anyone in the military can call anyplace home, we both were essentially raised there. My father was the commanding general of XVIII Airborne Corps, and my grandfather before him had commanded a special airborne task force under General James Gavin in World War II. They were West Point grads like I was, and so it was a minor miracle that I'd actually lived in one place long enough to label it "home."

Melissa, on the other hand, had been born and raised in Fayetteville. Her father was an enlisted man who had risen from private to sergeant major in the Eighty-Second Airborne Division with a few intermittent tours in Korea as an infantryman and Fort Benning as a drill instructor.

A decorated war veteran of Vietnam, Grenada, Panama, and Iraq, Command Sergeant Major Brownlee was a legend on Fort Bragg and in Cumberland County until he passed away three years ago. Melissa's hard-nosed mother, my mother-in-law, had kept their children firmly planted in the neighborhood, church, and school system while their father fulfilled his military duty away from Fort Bragg when necessary. It was a talent and ethos she'd passed to her daughter.

Melissa was tall, five foot ten, and had auburn hair and green eyes. She was the only woman that I ever truly loved and probably the only one I would, which was fine. By my assessment, few people enjoyed the type of relationship Melissa and I had, despite the fact that it was cut woefully short. I had looked forward to retirement with her, maybe somewhere along the North Carolina coast that we enjoyed so much. Wrightsville Beach, Topsail Island, and Cape Hatteras were all options we had been considering. We had saved as well as possible when raising two children on an officer's salary, which was to say that we lived sparingly but had most of the things a family could want.

One day while we were still in high school, I caught up with Melissa after my long conversation with the preacher about going to West Point. I was being recruited by NC State and UNC–Chapel Hill to play baseball, along with a few other colleges in Virginia and South Carolina. The pressure from my mostly absent father to attend West Point was enormous but didn't compare to the expectations of my mother. The traditional officer's wife, my mother was beautiful, regal, and conniving. Her motives were pure—her methods less so. And so I turned to our pastor for advice. My baseball coach had already tossed his hands in the air, not wanting to face the wrath of my mother.

There was a lot of appeal to attending a school in North Carolina and playing shortstop for a Division I contender. Coach Jernigan, the West Point baseball coach, was putting the soft sell on me knowing that my mother was the closer throwing ninety-five-mile-per-hour fastballs at me every night. I loved my mother, no doubt. Fiercely loyal to everyone that returned the favor, she ruled the family with a white-gloved iron fist. My sister, Katherine, had run away to the Peace Corps for fear that my parents were going to send her to West Point, also. Kat appeared every now and then seemingly out of nowhere, announcing she was working for a new, different nonprofit to save some aspect of the planet. She rebelled enough for both of us, I presumed.

After a long conversation with Pastor Paul, I saw Melissa, who was cleaning up from class in the rectory. Her hair was radiating in the sunlight that shined a spotlight on her as she swept up some construction paper clippings in the hallway.

"Need a hand?" I asked her.

"No, thank you. I'm just fine," she replied.

Not accepting the brush-off, I reached for the dustpan and knelt down to allow her to scoop the debris, which she did.

"Thank you," she said. Her voice was dispassionate, uninterested.

Just then, Pastor Paul truly changed my life.

"Garrett," he called from the end of the hallway in his hellfire-and-brimstone voice, as if from above. "Good luck on your decision between Harvard and West Point."

Now Harvard had never really been an option, though I suppose if I had ever thought about it, it might have been. Catching his quick wink as he turned away confirmed to me that the pastor was doing me a solid by tossing me an icebreaker or perhaps a life preserver.

"Harvard?" Melissa said, taking the bait.

Not wanting to get off on the wrong foot with a whiff of dishonesty, I shrugged and said, "Probably West Point."

No fool, Melissa's eyes narrowed. "Wait a minute. You're the general's son. You're definitely going to West Point, and I'm not sure you're smart enough to be going to Harvard."

She was nothing if not blunt and honest, and correct.

"Well . . ."

"Don't get me wrong," she continued. "I'm sure you're smart, but I'm in all the AP classes and haven't noticed you gracing our presence. Too busy on the baseball field, I think." She tapped her lips in a thinking pose that made my heart leap. Her hair flowed over her shoulders. Her green eyes were clear, innocent, and knowing at once. Her attire was a proper mid-calf Sunday school dress revealing nothing but the contours of a tall, slender, athletic body beneath. She wore practical pumps and carried a three-ring binder like everyone used to carry back before iPads and smartphones. The label on the binder's spine read SUNDAY SCHOOL. There was a yellow smiley face sticker at the bottom.

"I do well enough in school, but I'm certainly not as smart as you," I said in my failed attempt at self-deprecation.

"I know that," she said. "But Harvard is a bunch of snobs anyway, right? I've heard a little about you, and it's not all bad." She smiled. "Plus, you've been here awhile, unlike a lot of the transients. Not that the transients are bad, but it's hard to know the depth of someone without understanding their roots, their background, their faith, and so on. And you're reasonably good looking, not that you should let that go to your head."

I was simply going to ask her if she wanted to grab a doughnut, but here we were in a deep philosophical discussion about life, partnerships, and potential mates, which I soon learned was Melissa's approach to life. She was simultaneously enjoying the moment while advancing her cause, that of her community, and that of the country in general. There was never a more solid or devoted patriot than Melissa Sinclair.

"I'll take 'reasonably,'" I replied.

"A tad generous, but it *is* Sunday," she said, smiling.

"Thank God."

"Indeed. And here we are meeting in church, another positive."

Melissa's mind was an amazing synthesizer of information, environment, and potential pros and cons. She was a rock-solid decision-maker, and anyone fortunate enough to have been in her hemisphere of influence, from family readiness groups, which helped family members of combat units, to friends and family, was better off today because of her.

"It would be proper of me to offer to carry your books—or book, in this case."

"It would," she said, smiling again.

For a moment, I was confused but understood where she was leading me, where she would always lead me . . . to do the right thing without preamble.

"May I carry your book?"

"Good job," she said. "But you were right the first time."

She led me around the corner into the classroom, where she had four boxes of religious textbooks ready for movement to the hatch of her dated Jeep Cherokee. These were thick hardcover books, and each box weighed at least thirty pounds.

"You're clever," I said, ferrying the boxes to her car.

"Aren't I, though? But I'm also fair. I'm buying at Bell's."

We eventually grabbed that doughnut and Coke at Bell's Feed and Seed, which she paid for, and spent some time getting to know one another, which consisted mostly of her talking and me listening, a positive harbinger of our courting, marriage, and life together. She shaped our life by bearing us two children, raising them to be wonderful, if not occasionally obstinate, kids, and providing me support and love like I could have never experienced with anyone else. As with all Melissa did, she loved me wholly so that I could focus on my tasks as a soldier and leader of combat warriors. It was one of her many ways of serving our country. No one leads soldiers without support, and the best leaders I know have firm encouragement that gives them the unfettered focus on the mission in front of them.

We learned of Melissa's cancer together, me holding her hand in

Dr. Winthrop Blankenship's office at Walter Reed in Bethesda, staring at the opaque monochromatic mammograms with the visible lumps that had appeared out of nowhere so suddenly. Dr. Blankenship was a civilian cancer expert who had invested much of his career at the National Cancer Institute. He had been newly assigned to executive patients at Walter Reed, and we were hopeful that he would have new ideas and treatments to prolong our time together on earth. I stared at his impassive face, rectangular wire-rimmed glasses, slicked gray hair, and protruding jaw. He looked aristocratic, his Harvard medical degree hanging on the wall behind him.

Melissa was typically stoic when Dr. Blankenship said, "Malignant." Her hand squeezed mine, and I felt fear like never before. When I've wrestled Al Qaeda terrorists in knife fights, I didn't feel a whiff of the dread that washed over me when Dr. Blankenship began speaking. I realized that Melissa's hand squeeze was not her flinching—she never did—it was a reassurance to me that I would be okay. As strong as I appeared to all the men and women in my command, our allies with whom I coordinated, and to our nation's enemies, I realized at that moment the source of my strength was Melissa's wellspring of love and determination. Ever since that first day in our church, she swept me into her magical world of home and family, knowing that I would be an utterly lost mercenary without her grounding.

"No!" I shouted at Dr. Blankenship, who undoubtedly had heard it before. He handled my fear and rage like a consummate professional by nodding warmly, but I persisted. "There's got to be a mistake."

They just stared at me, waiting for me to realize that there was no error, that the doctor would never make such a diagnosis without triple confirming the data. On the ride home, Melissa said, "It will all be okay. I'll do the treatment, and we will figure it out from there. We will discuss it with Reagan and Brad and make arrangements going forward."

She continued to lay out a methodical plan for our family to handle her treatments and the disruption that they would cause to the rhythm of life that she had created for us.

"Reagan knows enough that she can work with family readiness groups . . . Brad can take a lighter load if necessary at Chapel Hill . . . You've got a deployment coming up, so we need to make sure you're set for that . . . Your mother will want to help . . ."

In typical fashion, she discussed everyone but herself. She was selflessly mapping out the legacy she had created: her family. More than anything, she wanted her family to not only survive but to thrive. Minimal disruption. Like a magician, she was able to leave her incredible power and force behind in her wake with no visible effort apparent to the casual observer, though as her husband, I saw the strain reflected in her weakened eyes, the crow's-feet diametrically making her more beautiful yet showing the weight she carried for all of us. Now her presence was tangible to me every day. Perhaps it was the harrowing guilt that I carried, but I was so fortunate to have her present in my dreams.

Melissa died the way she'd lived, gracefully and with dignity. My children, Brad and Reagan, were by her side, loving and comforting her.

And I had been merely on the way.

The plane droned on, the four Pratt & Whitney engines moaning softly, lulling me back to sleep. Melissa's face floated in my mind as I drifted. I recalled the letter waiting for me, penned by her weak hand as she lay dying and I was fresh off the al-Baghdadi kill.

> *My dearest Garrett,*
> *Time seems to be spinning faster, and I'm afraid I won't see you*
> *again before I slip away, as you paratroopers like to say. I've loved*
> *you madly since that day you pretended to have a shot at Harvard.*
> *You're the knight in shining armor that every young woman hopes*
> *one day will arrive; I'm glad you were mine. No, you didn't save*
> *me, and I didn't save you, but we lived life as life is intended to*

be lived. My prayers are with you and Joe and Randy and Sally as
you make our world safer. My sadness related to missing you now is
replaced by years of happiness having you by my side. We produced
two wonderful children with Brad and Rea. Continue to guide
them as we've done. I'll no doubt be reaching down and reminding
you to not give Brad a hard time about his music and to support
Rea in her efforts to—in her own way—follow in your footsteps.
Continue to be kind, gentle, and firm.
   Always seek. Be Brave. Be True.

                                                  Yours forever, Lissa
                                              P.S. Steadfast and Loyal ;)

I had memorized every word of her deathbed letter, its strength and
directness affirming our selection of one another as life partners. The last
sentence about seeking, bravery, and truth was an uncharacteristic note,
but I attributed that to the fact that death's door was opening slowly, confronting her. *Brave and True* was the motto of the West Point class that
graduated a year prior to us. Ours, *Steadfast and Loyal,* was how Melissa
and I often ended our letters. I assumed that given her friendships with
several members of the preceding class, including Jim and Donna Tharp,
that they had visited and as her mind was winding down, she mentioned
both mottos.

Melissa's face appeared in my beta sleep state of mind. "Naomi, Demon
Rain, and True Bravery," she whispered in my hallucination. The words
scattered to the back of my mind, but her image hovered vividly. Her lips
pursed and moved softly, her gentle smile pushed up her cheeks, and her
eyes glistened, reminding me how her death had so entirely crushed my
spirit that it was nearly impossible to move forward.

SOON AFTER WE LANDED, I was sitting in the MacDill Air Force Base office of General Fred Fillmore, one of my classmates—*Steadfast and Loyal*—and someone I considered a friend.

The floor-to-ceiling windows had a majestic view of Tampa Bay, a C-suite corner office if there ever was one. The other three walls had dozens of pictures, awards, and shadowboxes highlighting Fillmore's career. Pictures of dignitaries with Fillmore dotted the wall with the occasional images of mountains and farms. I cooled my heels in the soft leather sofa that faced his gigantic desk and considered whether the bad guys could predictably target this office with a drone from a random takeoff point nearby and fire a few missiles in the window.

It wasn't that I wished harm on Fillmore or anyone else in the building. Calculating risk was just how my mind worked. Over decades of combat, my brain was mapped to assess my environment, check for immediate threats, and then consider possible creative enemy courses of action and solutions that might counter them.

Sitting just outside the open door was Fillmore's executive officer,

Colonel Luke Hodgins, who looked like a gym rat with his muscled arms and blocky chest. He sat in an adjoining office that controlled access to Fillmore's digs. On the wall facing Hodgins's desk were the usual plaques and mementos that every officer collected over the course of their career. Evidently, he was a military police officer, with his Criminal Investigation Division plaques prominently displayed. I couldn't see any combat tours reflected in his gallery; perhaps Fillmore had hired him because they had that in common. It was difficult for me to conceive how someone could have not deployed to Iraq, Afghanistan, or Syria in the last twenty years, but there were some that fortune passed over. As for Fillmore, he had served in remote headquarters in Kuwait and the UAE, but never in the trenches of combat.

Fillmore entered the office and said, "Enjoying the view?"

"Impressive," I replied.

"We've come a long way since graduation," he said.

Fillmore was six feet tall, wiry, and had a nose too large for his face. His body was sleek and angular, his face narrow and acrodynamic, as if he were built to be a track-and-field athlete. He was wearing his army-blue uniform with short-sleeve white shirt, showing his lean, muscled biceps and forearms.

"Still running?" I asked.

"Every day," he said. Then, after a pause, "Good job on the mission, Garrett. How are you holding up?"

His simple question was loaded with memories packed so tightly it was explosive. He had encouraged me to return before Melissa died. I had chosen to take the extra time to conduct the mission. Fillmore had disagreed, urging me back. And while his question was genuine, how *was* I holding up? Not too fucking well, at all.

He sat across from me and leaned his elbows on his thighs in a compassionate, friendly pose.

"You know the deal, Fred. Life sucks without Melissa. Period."

"I can't begin to imagine, though she was dear to all of us who knew her."

"Yes, she was," I said quietly.

"I know we could have teleconferenced this meeting, and I apologize about having you come back."

"Never apologize," I said.

He nodded and continued. "I wanted to give you an out on the next mission if you wanted it. Things may get tougher from here forward. Not that there was anything easy about your Iran raid. After the COVID struggles, the president isn't taking any chances, nor do I suspect the president-elect will, either, and I know things have been . . . different since Melissa's passing."

"What's the mission?"

"This is probably the most sensitive, important op in our lifetime, perhaps since World War II. Iran is off the charts with Soleimani dead. The COVID scare has given rise to new concepts of operation and attack."

We had been on a roll, killing terrorist leaders at will, seemingly. Soleimani, al-Baghdadi, Hamza bin Laden, Osama bin Laden's son and heir apparent. Before that, we killed Osama himself. Iranian Quds Force, ISIS, and Al Qaeda leadership had been knocked into the dirt. We were feeling good about our intelligence and operations. But the coronavirus outbreak had added another layer to everything.

"Biohazard? Pathogen?"

"Close. I got the report from Rogerson on your friend Ben David. Then I checked with Mossad. The Israelis are being very cloak-and-dagger about him. They're not sure whether he's gone native with the Iranians or is still loyal to Israel. He *was* an Iranian Jew, after all."

"Still is, but he's loyal. You can worry about the rest of the world. I know Ben David."

"I'll take your word for it. I trust you. You trust him. That works. But you should know that he escaped."

I stared at Fillmore a moment. Escaped? It would be just like him to do that. Rogerson was no match for a healthy Ben David. But why would he escape instead of providing us with critical intelligence?

"Any idea where to?"

"We are assuming back into Iran, but really that's just a bullshit guess."

I stared at the rippling water of Tampa Bay, the sun's reflection looking like a million diamonds twinkling, thinking of Ben David and churning through scenarios of why he left, or even *how* he fled, given his condition. Nothing took hold.

"Are we looking for David?"

"In Afghanistan, yes. The Iranian military is on the border, so our cover is blown there."

"Did Rogerson make any progress?"

"No. Rogerson couldn't get anything out of him, and David was gone by the time you landed here," Fillmore said.

I nodded and changed the topic. "Rogerson is an interesting character. We chatted some in Farah. Said this op was beyond my pay grade."

"He could be right, but I know that you've got a special relationship with President-Elect Campbell. In a couple of days when she's inaugurated, you'll be cleared for everything," he said.

KIM CAMPBELL, A former schoolteacher, won her historic presidential election in November. On the campaign trail, she singled out our actions during the al-Baghdadi raid as something exceptional. Hobart, Van Dreeves, Jackson, Brown, and I were all in on that action and at the time she had flown to Fort Bragg to meet with us as well as attend Melissa's funeral during her campaign. Until now, I didn't know of anyone who had leaked that information. I was glad for my men that a presidential candidate would personally thank them for their actions. She never sought any publicity; rather, she talked with the troops for about thirty

minutes and with me for about two hours. We sat in a nondescript windowless room along Pope Field at a gray metal table in two ratty chairs
from the property disposal yard and discussed Middle East policy, defense budgets, family readiness groups . . . and Melissa.

But our relationship long predated that meeting behind the fence at
Fort Bragg. Kim and Melissa had been college roommates at Raleigh's
prestigious all women's university, Meredith College. They both aspired
to be teachers and make an impact on generations of students. Kim's
career took her into an impassioned run for the North Carolina state
legislature, followed by service as the state's second female governor and
finally to the brink of the presidency after a bitterly contested race. She
was now awaiting her inauguration less than a week away.

While I was dating Melissa, I knew Kim as just an athletic girl with
blond hair and ice-blue eyes who liked to drink beer with us and her
then boyfriend, a young man named Peter Ducoix from Duke's Fuqua
School of Business. On my breaks from West Point, Melissa and I would
spend a fair amount of time shuttling between Fayetteville and Wilmington visiting friends and families. The Campbells had a large home
on Wrightsville Beach, near Wilmington. When Kim told us about her
presidential ambitions, Melissa and I joked with her that we knew too
much about her beer-drinking days. Now, thirty years later, she had married, divorced, and remarried, finding marital bliss, served one term as
governor, and become president of the United States.

We shared a common grief in the loss of Melissa. At the funeral in
Fayetteville, she had approached me, the tears in her eyes as genuine as
the friend she'd been to Melissa. "I'm terribly sorry," she said. "I miss her
so much."

"Me, too," I replied. I had received thousands of calls, texts, emails,
and visitors after Melissa's passing and remained relatively stoic throughout it all, yet Kim's simple gesture produced a lone tear cutting a solitary

path down my cheek as I stared at her. In her eyes, I saw resolve, empathy, and determination. In mine, she most likely saw an utterly shattered human being trying to reassemble his life.

"We need soldiers like you. Leaders like you, who know not just the price of war but the cost. When I win, I'll be counting on you."

Most often, senior leaders, whether they be generals or CEOs, had few people with whom they could genuinely share thoughts and emotions. Just like people wanted to believe their doctors and priests were of divine origin, the fifty thousand troops you command in a combat zone *needed* to believe you to be Conan the Barbarian, not someone with shattered emotions. The truth was I was both.

And her own empathy was heartfelt. There wasn't a political utterance in our conversation. I was not naive enough to think she wasn't there to shore up her military family support credentials with the election a year away.

Based on Kim's and my longstanding friendship, the television pundits briefly speculated that I was the lead nominee to be her national security advisor, but I put an end to that by never answering the media's phone calls.

However, before leaving Melissa's funeral, she had handed me a smartphone. "Keep this," she'd said. "You may need me. I may need you. If I don't answer, don't leave a message. I'll know it's you and will call you back if I've still got the phone. You respond, or not, however you wish if I call you. Could be two friends just needing to talk. Could be how to stop World War III. Remember, if I win, I'm going to ask you to be chairman until you say yes."

"You know what they say about friends in Washington, D.C.," I replied.

"Yes, get a dog. I've got two, and you don't live in D.C."

I nodded and said, "And you'll have a whole bunch of people leading you into World War III as they're telling you how to avoid it. Watch those West Pointers."

She smiled and stuck a slender finger in my chest. "Exactly. Keep the phone."

I pocketed the phone and had not used it, nor had she. Part of the reason was my deference to the chain of command. I was always a leader who dwelled within the organization, not one that looked outward from it, seeking my next thing.

SNAPPING BACK TO the moment, I said to Fillmore, "Kim and I go back to college, but she was really Melissa's friend."

"President Stone and President-Elect Campbell are being briefed on this mission. You are the commander of the task force leading it. If you need to give anyone a heads-up, feel free."

Because the mission could span the transfer of power, Fillmore was giving me an opportunity to discuss the mission with Kim, but I deferred to him.

"That's your lane, boss. I don't need a million people listening to my conversation with the incoming president."

"True, well, here's the deal. Rogerson said that the chemicals we found in Iran can be traced to a lab in Germany. The national command authority wants us to investigate it, and they want the same team that did the Iran mission to go to Germany."

"Germany? This is Demon Rain?"

Fillmore nodded and rubbed his face, something he did when he got nervous. "Yes. There are two schools of thought. The FBI is thinking this could be about mind control. The CIA is thinking this could be a superspreader chem-bio combination—a manufactured virus that has chem properties. Think COVID-19 mixed with sarin mixed with LSD."

I thought of Ben David's face contorted in horror. "Worst case, we have a highly infectious virus that can attack your respiratory and nervous systems?"

He aimed a finger gun at me and collapsed his thumb like a hammer falling. "But with mind control mixed in there."

"COVID got everyone to stay home. What more mind control could you want?"

"That's what we're concerned about."

I nodded again, rubbed my chin, and asked, "Do we have a location in Germany? A timeline?"

"We do. Near Heidelberg. Old CIA testing site. Intel shows Iranians are trying to improve the lethality of the corona family of viruses and are conducting testing on human subjects. Giving them the virus or exposing them to the drug and then testing their reaction to the . . . elements. Burning them to see how much heat is too much, freezing them to determine when the body becomes hypothermic, boiling them, bleeding them, and gassing them. It's barbaric."

He shuddered, and I nodded. Yes, barbaric, but we only had to look in the files of our very own Fort Detrick to reveal previous research done by Nazi and Japanese doctors and scientists that the United States spared from the war criminal tribunals and hired in a misguided attempt to collect all the "talent" associated with mind control research. The wild, feral eyes of the dead in the Iranian cave seemed to suggest they were desperate to escape more than death, whatever that might be.

"Anything to add to our files?" I asked.

"You're a hard man, Garrett." Fillmore sighed.

"It's no secret that the CIA and FBI were as bad as the Nazis back in the day. No need to sugarcoat it, but I'm skeptical that this is about mind control," I said.

"Why?"

"The whole concept seems so . . . unrealistic," I said.

"Dulles, Gottlieb, and the whole lot at the CIA got close. That was as real as it gets."

"It did give us LSD and the Beatles."

"Yes. Think about it. With artificial intelligence, the combination of mind control through subliminal messaging is the new frontier. Apps that listen to your phone calls and read your texts and emails, then show you what advertisements are most suited for you. Do you not think that similar technology could be leveraged to manipulate the mind? Instead of telling you what you need based on your conversations, it can influence your conversations and then your needs," Fillmore said. "There's a virus that can kill you. Stay home. That's COVID. What's the end state of something that can either control your mind or kill you? For the enemy, it's a win-win."

I said, "They're two different things. We're developing vaccines to the coronaviruses out there. The mind control experiments in the '50s and '60s had both tactical and strategic aims. Tactically, we were interested in interrogation techniques, getting Russian spies to divulge nuclear secrets. Strategically, there was a belief that mass mind control could occur, mostly spurred by twenty-two American pilots defecting to Communist China after the Korean War. That one incident catalyzed the mind control race more than anything else because our intelligence geniuses actually believed that it had occurred and that the Commies had the secret."

"They were close," Fillmore said.

"Close to what? The MKUltra program was vast with New York City suicides, San Francisco brothels, and impromptu LSD parties run by a clubfooted, polka-dancing husband and father of three. Gottlieb was an actual Dr. Jekyll and Mr. Hyde. The family man who raised goats and chickens while dispensing acid to unwitting subjects."

"They had to try, though. And I've missed debating with you, classmate."

I remembered the cell phones in the cave. The stiff hands of long-dead bodies clutching the phones as if their lives depended on them. Were the Iranians working on a combination techno-drug for mind control?

"The one thing that could change it, now that I think about it, would be modern technology."

"Yeah, how so?" Fillmore asked.

I wanted to be careful about how much I said, but I had to bring him up to speed.

"Our report shows that there were cell phones with the dead bodies in the cave," I said.

"I saw that but interpreted it to mean it was just a bunch of people with cell phones."

"It could still be, and I don't want to make too much of this, but we should consider other possibilities."

"Maybe Dulles and Gottlieb were before their time," Fillmore said.

"Maybe," I said. "Shut down in the '60s and then Gottlieb destroyed most of the evidence in the '70s. Still some remnants of the program, I'm sure."

"We may need to dust that off in the wake of COVID-19. Scary to think about what's possible today."

"Yes, it's really about fear, when you get right down to it."

Fillmore leaned back and tapped his index finger against his lips, humming slightly.

"Speaking of fear, our intel says Dariush Parizad is running this show," he said.

And there it was—the reason I was sitting here in the office. Parizad, my longtime nemesis, was in charge of a chemical or biological program aimed at attacking the United States on the heels of the COVID recovery. The mention of Parizad's name changed my entire view of this mission.

If Parizad was involved, this was worse than any pandemic. He was the deputy Quds Force commander in title only. In reality and on the ground, he was the leader of the most lethal state-sponsored terrorist organization in the world. Demon Rain, whatever it might be, in the hands of Parizad could be disastrous. Whatever Parizad had in mind would be strategically targeted, not a random community spread.

As I stepped outside, the burner the president-elect had given me buzzed in my pocket. I looked at the phone as Hobart and Van Dreeves waited by an armored Suburban in the turnabout by the CENTCOM flagpole.

The text message read: *Call me.*

6

I HAD NEVER USED my hotline to the president-elect and was half expecting to be put through several functionaries and aides until finally receiving a message that she would call me back.

Instead, Kim said, "Garrett."

"Madame President, nice to speak with you again. To what do I owe the pleasure?"

"Don't get ahead of yourself. I still have a few days before I'm sworn in."

"Well, congratulations. Melissa would be proud."

"Yes, she would," she replied, her voice trailing off. "Can you talk?"

The president-elect of the United States was asking me if I had time to speak with her. I appreciated her humility.

"Of course, ma'am."

"I've received a ton of briefings from the Intelligence Community, and all these ring knockers are worried about you," she said.

I looked at the phone, knew it wasn't secure, and said, "Perhaps I could come to Washington, D.C., to discuss this, ma'am."

"I'm not giving away state secrets here, Garrett. I saw something in

46

the briefing book this morning that unsettled me. I can't put my finger on it, but when I saw your name, I wanted you to know that you can call me anytime, anywhere. I'm not sure who I can trust, and given that Melissa and I were best friends . . ."

Her voice trailed off again. I imagined her staring out of the Blair House onto Lafayette Square.

"I understand. You can count on me," I said. "Something big *is* in the wind, I know that much. I'm receiving a briefing from Secretary of Defense Tharp this afternoon."

"I agree. Come through D.C. when you're back, or better yet, I can meet you somewhere in North Carolina away from all this nonsense. The beach," she said wistfully. The sigh on the phone told me that she missed the simplicity of swaying sea oats, roaring surf, and gentle sea breezes.

"Roger that," I said. "But I think you're going to be limited on your beach trips."

"You might be right. Be safe," she replied and hung up.

All these ring knockers . . .

Those would be Secretary of Defense Jim Tharp, CIA director Samantha Owens, and Secretary of State Kyle Estes, whom the media had begun referring to as the Ring Knockers, a sometimes-affectionate euphemism for West Point graduates. This power juggernaut had been leading U.S. foreign policy for four years, sometimes to good effect. I imagined their real concern was whether they would stay in their positions and, if not, how much time did they have left to propel forward policies they hadn't achieved. It was like washing your car before you sell it.

"Boss," Hobart said. Van Dreeves was at the wheel.

I stowed the phone, nodded at Hobart, and said, "Back to the compound. We've got a mission."

As Van Dreeves steered through Tampa to Saint Petersburg, I thought about the origin of our mission and what the ultimate play for my West Point peers might be. When Fillmore mentioned Parizad, I had two points of triangulation. Ben David had been pursuing Parizad on behalf of Israel, and we'd found Parizad's commander's coin clutched in David's hand in the cave. There was no mistaking that symbol, especially in Iran. I took these two clues at face value: Parizad was central to the activity at the cave. Why else would Ben David be pursuing him, and why else would he be in possession of Parizad's commander's coin?

Perhaps there was no person in the world who understood Dariush Parizad better than I did—as far as that was possible.

I FIRST MET Parizad in a safe house near Basra, Iraq, in 2001. It was August, a month before our geopolitical landscape would forever change with the attacks of September 11, 2001, and the deaths of several thousand Americans. I had flown from our joint operations center, or JOC, in Bahrain to Basra based on an Iranian request to meet with the Americans intent on dueling with Saddam Hussein. Once the Bush administration came into power, with Vice President Dick Cheney and Secretary of Defense Donald Rumsfeld, there was renewed interest in assessing methods to eliminate Hussein as a thorn in the side of the international community. Iran was, at the time, the enemy of our enemy, Iraq.

I had flown at night in a Pave Hawk with two Apache attack helicopters escorting me along the Persian Gulf coast and up the Euphrates River until we landed southeast of Basra. It was a risky mission, but the neocons were all about finding a path to Baghdad, even if it meant accepting help from Iran, which was notoriously unreliable. The Pentagon's misguided notion that Iran would be friendly to us if we confronted Iraq was just as insane as the idea that rose petals would be showering American soldiers as we paraded into Baghdad.

The Iranian special forces were technologically advanced. Their landing zone team used infrared lights to guide our pilots into position. We flew a nap of the earth, or low-altitude course, along the desert. The lights of Basra winked to our north as we hooked south off the river and sped toward a nondescript latitude and longitude on the ground. Any minute, I was expecting a rocket-propelled grenade up the exhaust, but it never came. I was escorted into a small qalat, or adobe house, where I was frisked by two guards speaking Farsi. My three-man security team, including Hobart and Van Dreeves as young Rangers, waited outside, not liking any of it.

Inside, a dim light bulb hung from a piece of twine and shined weakly on a man with a nose broken so many times it zigzagged. He was about my height, maybe an inch shorter, and solid like a weight lifter. Black hair fell over his ears and low across his forehead. He had a scar running the length of his left cheek, and he had disfigured skin on his neck beneath his left ear, burned by shrapnel at a young age.

The dossier my intel team had prepared showed that Parizad was born and had been raised in the small town of Tabas, Iran. His father had been a local businessman, providing agricultural equipment to the farmers in the region. Parizad Sr. had been called out one memorable night in 1979 to retrieve a disabled John Deere plow that had stalled about twelve miles from the Parizad homestead. Senior had worked through most of the night and into the early morning to retrieve the machine. It was a decent payday to fix the worn-out engine for the conglomerate that planted most of the wheat for the Yazd Province bakers.

Young Dariush awoke to loud buzzing, like airplanes, followed by deafening chopping sounds he couldn't place. *Hammers in the sky,* he thought. Unsure what was making the noises, he scurried to the barn and began his chores: milking the cows and goats, selecting the best eggs, and feeding the horses. He'd never really fallen asleep, upset his father had not taken him along on the repair journey, but nonetheless, he was eager to please his father by tackling his duties. The barn being on the south side of the property and up on a ridge, he finally heard the big tractor his father was using to tug the broken equipment back to the repair shop, which was next to the barn.

Dariush was excited because he enjoyed watching his father, a big man, work on the farm equipment, repairing it and making it right. He marveled at his father's mechanical acumen and strength, the way he used his large hands to make things work for other people.

Distant voices were muffled by an idling bus just below the ridge. It was the regular route that carried workers to the mines and farms. But on this night, airplanes buzzed, and hammers banged at the sky. The hammers were loud and obnoxious, echoing for miles across the valley floor. Sand billowed into the black sky like a shamal, but thinner and unnatural, man-made.

Dariush ran to the ridge and saw machines moving along the road that ran from south to north into their village. To the east, he thought he recognized his father based upon the two tractors, one pulling the other. More machines arrived, more hammers in the black sky, banging away at the black night, kicking up more sand, billowing high like a small explosion.

Only once had the Iranian military flown airplanes and helicopters near their remote region. Maybe it was a practice of some sort? The noise was deafening, and his seven-year-old mind thought that the government should have told them about this, because the animals were scared. Regardless, he stumbled down the hill, running at breakneck pace toward his father when the night lit up and a second later a shock wave and boom knocked him into the hard shale of the ridge. Flame licked at his face and back, singeing his shirt, and shrapnel whizzed into the slope, sticking like ninja stars and slicing his face in lines of blood.

Gaining his bearing, he saw that his father's two tractors were close to the explosion and not moving. He scrambled to his feet and sprinted the remaining four hundred meters to his father. As he approached, Dariush smelled gas, what he would later know to be jet fuel, something that he would become intimately familiar with on his chosen path.

But this night, he was a kid, watching the man he loved and idolized roll in the dirt with futility in a losing effort to douse the flames. His entire body was an orange blaze, soaked with gas.

Men were running around shouting at one another, speaking a language that wasn't Persian or Farsi. Dariush had a friend in school who had spent a year in an Iranian community in London, England, who spoke some English. While he didn't understand any of what these uniformed men were saying as they shouted and screamed, the words sounded similar to what his new friend said when he was teasing them with English.

Dariush sprinted past the wreckage and arrived at the sputtering tractor towing the defunct machine. He heard his father scream a type of primordial wail that came from somewhere deep inside. Something primal that he had never heard before. Not from his father or anyone else. It was the high screeching sound of unbearable agony. Dariush stiffened as his father transitioned from wildly thrashing to frozen in place like a piece of modern art on the valley floor. He was burned to a crisp, teeth bared against melting lips. It was horrifying.

"No!" he screamed.

Nobody heard him above the cacophony of chaos behind him. More loud machines had arrived and departed, and suddenly all that was left were the smoking remnants of American helicopters and an airplane. He saw movement on the ridge above him. More people from the village had come to inspect what all the commotion was about.

Dariush Parizad never forgot the image of his father burning alive at the hands of the American invaders who had with precision chosen his village to conduct their military operation. Nor would he forget the sound of crackling skin. The banshee wail of pain.

Even as a kid, he was sure that the planning had included all kinds of maps, radios, calculations, and weighing of options, whereupon the American generals pointed at a map directly where he was standing that morning in 1979 and said, "Land there."

He had stayed with his father, whose body smoked until the sun rose and the Americans were gone. His mother and sister arrived initially more curious about his location and the commotion, then adding to the howls of anguish once they saw Dariush kneeling and rocking next to his smoldering father.

Once his mother and sister relieved him of duty, Dariush walked among the charred wreckage, seeing similar shapes to that of his father. Gray smoke rose from the black ashes, collecting on his tattered, melting *giveh,* his shoes, produced in Yazd Province and made of thread and rubber soles. As he traversed from the airplane to the helicopter, he stepped around black skeletons in the desert like photonegative chalk outlines at a murder scene. The short trek gave his shoes enough time to cool off and not burn his feet. He walked through the second charred remnant and then looked at his family fifty meters behind him.

He stepped out of the black residue and stared at the sky. More hammers, echoing loudly along the valley. This time, the men that poured out of the helicopters were Iranian military, speaking his native tongue. He watched them bark orders and take up security positions, looking for stragglers left behind, he presumed. One of the men came running at him, and they exchanged a greeting, which, given the tense atmosphere, could have been a lot worse. He explained to the man that his father had been burned and walked him to his grieving mother and sister. He watched the soldier inspect the scene and then call over a radio. Suddenly, two men appeared, one of whom was a doctor, though it was clear there was nothing that could be done.

The doctor did help with Dariush's burns. The other man was an imam, who consoled them. Dariush stood in the black ashes of the tractors, its tires still spewing black smoke. Soon, more helicopters began arriving, filled with state media reporters and cameras. They flooded the scene, taking video and still pictures from above and the ground. He remained stoic and determined, unflinching amid the chaos.

It was only later that he realized a picture a reporter had snapped of him standing above his weeping mother and sister and next to his charred father would become a symbol of the revolution. A young boy. A dead father. Weeping women. All at the hands of the Americans.

By the end of the day, it seemed all of Tehran arrived in the small village of Tabas for his father's funeral. They made a large spectacle of the entire process. Soldiers helped him process his father for burial, a ritual that had to be completed within twenty-four hours. They buried him without a casket, consistent with tradition. Many of the soldiers, who happened to be local national guard from Yazd Province, attended and checked on him and his family. There were over five hundred people at his father's funeral, which he found overwhelming.

Later, standing by his father's grave behind the barn, he watched the politicians and soldiers board the helicopter to leave and at that moment decided instead of a mechanic like his dad, he was going to be one of them—a soldier. Not just any soldier but the best kind of soldier. A special operations soldier.

One group had not yet departed as he stood above the freshly tilled dirt. Dariush had only seen pictures of Ayatollah Khomeini, the tall, bearded figure that was the face of the revolution. The ayatollah was in Tabas, at his father's funeral and placing his hand on Dariush's shoulder. Standing next to Khomeini was a twenty-two-year-old lieutenant with gray eyes, black hair, and a friendly smile. Parizad didn't realize it then, but the soldier was Qassem Soleimani, the bodyguard of the ayatollah.

"You've suffered a great loss," Khomeini said. "No child should lose his father so early. The Great Satan took him from you, and now Iran will be your father."

Dariush swallowed and nodded.

"Eighty years ago, Iran's last Persian lion was killed by Zionist poachers, just as your father was killed today," the shah continued. He turned to the assembled throng of fifty or so villagers remaining after the funeral. "But the Persian Lion has returned today in the form of Dariush Parizad . . .

"Lion of Tabas."

THAT NIGHT IN Basra when I met the Lion of Tabas, I was prepared to encounter a hardened, vacuous man with a grudge against the United States. I intended to give him no quarter, no concessions. I was there to get information and understand his perspective. While the man I met was hardened, he was neither vacuous nor appeared to have any ideological bent against America. This, of course, was not the case, but Parizad turned out to be a master magician with a poker face worthy of a Vegas World Series tournament.

"Colonel," he said. Parizad stuck out his fist and opened it to a baseball-glove-size hand. I shook it and gave him the same response. We were equal in rank, both lieutenant colonels in our respective militaries.

The air was damp and smelled of dead fish. We were close to the river or one of its tributaries. We sat in two old, filthy chairs facing one another, and I got the impression that this was where Parizad held court.

"I must say that it is troublesome to me that my government has asked me to sit across from you, a ghost of a man who has created so many problems for my country, my people, but they recognize you as the man on the ground who can convey the message properly," he said in nearly perfect English.

I nodded. The idea that Parizad was troubled by anything was laughable. His black eyes glistened in the dim light. His voice was deep, matter-of-fact, without pretense. The scar on his face buckled when he spoke. He wasn't playing a game, at least it didn't appear so at the time.

Calling me a ghost, however, may have been accurate. In 2002, very few people knew who I was, because I remained a quiet professional behind the fence at Fort Bragg. Even today, I had no social media accounts, per se, though there were some pretending to be me. The Department of

Defense scrubbed all the images of me from the internet, not that there were many to begin with. Much to the chagrin of my kids, I never posed for family selfies or provided anything that could contribute to facial recognition algorithms on Facebook, Google, and Instagram. I didn't have a Twitter account, and the only email account I used were my DoD classified and unclassified as well as a self-erasing program created by the CIA that had been licensed out to a few special operators. My team was fully functioning on this cloud-based program called Alphmega.

Parizad had no idea what I might look like and whether or not I was actually the real Lieutenant Colonel Garrett Sinclair. Maybe they had snapped an old copy of my West Point yearbook, or *Howitzer,* photo. There were a few pictures of me playing baseball, but even the online version of the yearbook had been altered to have my picture blacked out. Melissa and my wedding photos were old-school, in a scrapbook, nothing online. Any promotion or award ceremonies were always small affairs in closed rooms with no cameras. Changes of command were done discreetly, out of the public eye. My time as an Army Ranger and paratrooper was equally discreet with missions from Panama to Desert Storm all being conducted with precision and away from those that sought the glory. I had known what I wanted from the moment I graduated from West Point: to be my version of a professional athlete getting paid to jump out of airplanes and lead men on the battlefield as a team, earning the only victories that counted. Accordingly, the Department of Defense was continuously in the process of redacting my life in the name of national security.

"Your government has become very interested in Iraq," Parizad began.

"We've always been interested in Iraq," I replied.

"Not like this," he said quickly. "Jets, helicopters, scouts are all coming into the no-fly zone. Basra is as much Iranian territory as it is Iraqi. The Shia population here identify more with Iran."

"Your point?"

"Should you invade, the Shia will be a big problem for you. My government has asked me to convey to yours that any such incursion is not welcome, and while Iraq and Iran are enemies, we will do what is necessary to protect the people of Basra."

I nodded, and he continued. One of his guards was holding a small flip phone by his side, attempting to take a picture. I turned my head directly before the click.

I stood and walked toward the guard, saying, "Seriously? There's not enough light in here to take a decent picture." The man froze as I snatched the phone from his hand, snapped it in two, and tossed it through the open window, next to where my men were standing.

"Colonel, this is not necessary," Parizad said.

"You don't see my guys taking pictures, do you?"

He looked over his shoulder. "How do I know what your men are doing? In the Iranian military, we have a saying: 'If you aren't cheating, you aren't trying.' Are you surprised?"

"No pictures," I said, sitting down again.

He nodded and got back on track. "As you know, the boundaries in the Middle East were drawn primarily by the West. We live with these tortuous lines, but what you see on a map and experience on the ground are two very different things."

"I understand," I said. And I did. The Durand Line in Afghanistan was a prime example. It separated that country from Pakistan and split all the primary tribes in half, leaving the east-west migratory and trade patterns in a problematic cross-border status. Instead of halving the power of these tribes, the Brits had managed, in a way that only they could do, to multiply their influence, having major ramifications for our twenty-year effort in Afghanistan.

"I know you do," Parizad said, smiling. "And I know you will convey to your country that any attack on Iraq will invite Iranian assessment and reaction."

"Anything else?"

Parizad shook his head and smiled. "We shall meet again," he said. "Your government is stupid, arrogant. Men like us will be required to confront each other on the battlefield. It gives me no great pleasure, but we each have our duties."

"Roger that," I said. I stood and departed, the whipping helicopter blades drowning out any sound and creating that perilous moment when you lose a key sensory capability on the battlefield. I boarded the helicopter, and we nosed over the river back toward our facility in Bahrain.

Into the headset piece, I said to a young Sergeant Hobart, "You get the phone?"

"Roger that. Got pictures, too."

I nodded, thinking about the rule of threes. This being the second time I had seen Parizad, there would most assuredly come a third.

7

WHILE THE FIRST TIME I had met Dariush Parizad was in Iraq, the first time I had *seen* the Lion of Tabas was when he was sixteen years old, fourteen years before that brief encounter in Basra.

A newly promoted first lieutenant in the army, I was serving in the Rangers, and we had been deployed to the Republic of Korea to patrol the outskirts of Seoul and search for North Korean infiltrators that might try to attack the 1988 Seoul Olympics.

Every day, I mapped out new missions for my thirty-five men. We wore civilian clothes, carried the U.S. Army's newly adopted sidearm, the Beretta 9 mm pistol, tucked away under our windbreakers, and had access to our long rifles should we need to conduct quick reaction force duties.

We were given instructions to pay particularly close attention to the Iranian contingent. They had boycotted the 1980 and 1984 Olympics, and this was their first foray back onto the international stage. The intelligence briefings ranged from believing that they were going to be rank amateurs at everything from athletics and spy tradecraft to the notion that they had been preparing for World War III, were ten feet tall, and were the vanguard of the Soviet Army.

On top of all of that, South Korean students were rioting, protesting that North Korea should be cohosting the games, even though their country was still technically at war with the hermit kingdom. Ethiopia and Cuba boycotted the games to support North Korea. And, ironically, this would be the last summer games of the Warsaw Pact nations under Soviet rule.

The entire picture painted by the intel geniuses was a little better than a "we're mostly sure." As we'd been trained to do, we created priorities. I determined we would watch the South Korean, Iranian, and Israeli contingents. I had three observation teams, and we focused on fixed locations to determine patterns of behavior. I placed an observation team, who just happened to have an M24 sniper rifle and spotter's scope, on the high floor of a building under construction that gave us clear lines of sight into the Iranian Olympic residence. It was a small contingent of wrestlers, tae kwon do martial artists, cyclists, and one boxer, Dariush Parizad.

We watched and took pictures as the men ferried back and forth between the residence and the sports venue in a white van with no windows. I was reminded of the Palestinian massacre of eleven Israeli athletes, wrestlers and coaches mostly, at the 1972 Munich games. Only sixteen years removed from that tragic event and a very public liaison between the PLO and Iran after the shah's deposing in 1979, tensions were still high.

My teams reported on the three compounds from different locations. I rotated my time between the high-rise looking onto the Iranian facility, the two-story residence we borrowed to watch the South Korean athletes, and the office building from which we monitored the Israeli compound, which was fortified and secured better than Fort Knox. I also walked patrols with my men, all of which gave me a good feel for the vibe of the city and the tensions.

During my rounds, I found myself spending more time with my team observing the Iranian residence. Through the spotter's scope, I could see the courtyard, where several of the twenty-seven athletes would warm up, stretch, or practice their moves. Day after day, a young, powerfully built teenager was sparring barefisted with other men his size but older by maybe ten years or more. His routine was to drink a few cups of coffee, in rare supply in an embargoed Iran, and then train aggressively for a few hours.

Parizad's fighting style included shuffling his feet and connecting on every left jab or right cross. He had a wicked left jab/deep fake right cross/left hook combination that seemed to fool the partners even though they knew it was coming. His fists were a flurry, as if working on a speed bag and not a sparring partner's face. This was no gratuitous effort by opponents to make the contender feel better. Day after day, Parizad would suck down what seemed like a gallon of coffee, face new sparring partners, knock them all down, if not out, and then sit down and drink more coffee.

Three days before the competition was to begin, I was in the high perch with my sniper team watching a display of boxing skill and thought that this person actually had a chance at beating Ray Mercer, the American heavyweight boxer whom we were all behind. Mercer was an active-duty army sergeant and the son of a Fort Benning mechanic.

"Might want to wing this guy before he gets to Mercer," Sergeant Harlen Tackberry, our best sniper, joked. Tackberry was from Pensacola, Florida, and actually knew Mercer from basic training.

"Mercer would come after you if you did," I said, running with the joke. "He wants a fair fight, and he's still steaming from that Félix Savón match, so I'm not worried about him." Mercer had defeated Cuban boxing champion Félix Savón, but, in a microcosmic display of geopolitics, the Soviet referee stopped the match before Mercer had a chance to finish him off.

Corporal Johnnie Wright, Tackberry's spotter, said, "That guy's a machine. We watch him every day, and he just crushes people."

I watched through the scope. Parizad drank his usual five cups of coffee, steam rising from the porcelain mug. We joked that his bladder was the toughest part of his body. After he set down the cup, a large man dressed in a black T-shirt and white gym trunks walked out. He looked formidable. Parizad stood, wearing his traditional white T-shirt and black shorts. He and his equally powerful doppelgänger began brawling. The two were throwing and landing punches with a flurry. Parizad's signature combo wasn't connecting as it had on previous opponents. They continued for several minutes. There were no referees or clocks to monitor the fight. A couple of coaches seemed to be watching. As the fight progressed, the other athletes in the yard stopped their own preparation and watched.

The brawl continued for a full fifteen minutes. This was some warm-up. Suddenly, Parizad connected with three powerful uppercuts and a right cross that would kill a horse. The opponent dropped, lights out.

After a few seconds, one of the coaches knelt next to the man on the ground and began waving his hands and shouting. Tackberry and Wright were sharing the sniper rifle's scope.

"Fuck," Tackberry said. "That dude is dead."

The medical team arrived, and they tried several different maneuvers. Heart paddles, mouth-to-mouth, but to no avail. The man was indeed dead.

Parizad was standing by himself next to the fence that separated the Iranians from the streets of Seoul. His nose looked broken. His white T-shirt was red with blood. His fists were still clenched, biceps rippling in the morning sun. Heavy breaths escaped in misty explosions.

When they carted the dead man away, Parizad raised his arms in victory like Rocky on the steps of the Philadelphia Museum of Art.

Word leaked quickly that there had been a death in the Iranian athletic camp. It was impossible to hide when the doctors transported the body to the hospital, which was being monitored by the Olympic committee for athlete injuries and drug testing. As a rule, the International Olympic Committee tested Parizad for drugs, finding caffeine. In 1988, eleven athletes were disqualified for drugs, five for furosemide, three for stanozolol or propranolol, one for pemoline, and two for caffeine. Blood thinners, blood pressure medicine, attention deficit disorder drugs, and, evidently, alertness, were not allowed at the Olympics. I later heard from the Ranger commander that the decision to disqualify Parizad came after the other ten had already been ruled upon. The American official with the IOC had interrupted the normal evaluation process, complained about Parizad, secured a new vote, and had cast the deciding ballot in a 6–5 decision to expel him.

The next day, Parizad walked into the courtyard, sat at his usual table, drank his coffee, then stood and walked to the fence, looked up at our position, pointed at us, and nodded as if to say, "I'm coming after you."

Of course, Parizad had no idea who we were specifically or that we were even there. Iranian counterintelligence must have spotted us. Regardless, if you combined the American nightmare at Tabas in 1979 and the American judge's ruling in Seoul in 1988, I could understand his hatred of America, which was why I had been anticipating a scornful man back in Basra in 2001.

Ray Mercer went on to win an Olympic gold, and I wondered to this day how a Mercer-Parizad fight might have progressed. Mercer was a powerful technical fighter. Parizad was an unstoppable force with an intense hatred of all things American.

I was left to consider that if the Lion of Tabas had beaten Mercer then, would he have quenched his thirst for revenge and allowed us to avoid the horrors that subsequently unfolded?

8

PARIZAD FOLLOWED HIS PASSION in boxing, winning all his matches in Iran and becoming the Iranian national champion by the time he was seventeen.

He tapered his boxing interests, though, in pursuit of his goal to be a soldier. Given his size, strength, and intellect, and the fact that he was the ayatollah's chosen one—the Lion of Tabas—Soleimani had mentored him as a young soldier and throughout his tenure, first against Saddam Hussein in the Iran-Iraq wars, then against Israel, teaching and coaching Hamas and Hezbollah to defeat the Jews.

Parizad was commanding special operations units throughout the 1990s and early 2000s, when he had successfully overseen the production and importation of the explosive formed penetrators (EFPs)—six-inch copper discs seated inside the lip of six-inch PVC piping, which was stuffed with urea nitrate or any explosive—that had maimed and killed so many of our soldiers in Iraq. Soleimani assigned Parizad primary responsibility for Hezbollah operations in Lebanon in the Beqaa Valley, where his protégé began to experiment on the creation of new, more nefarious improvised explosive devices. In 2000, Parizad led the training and equipping of Hezbollah in southern Lebanon and armed them with experimental rockets and explosive devices that ultimately drove the Israelis from Lebanon. Soon thereafter, duty called in Iraq in the spring of 2003, where Parizad, then a lieutenant colonel in the Iranian Quds Force, led the import of the devices he had styled in the Beqaa Valley and used the EFPs to great effect throughout Basra and southern Iraq against American soldiers.

He had been true to the words he had spoken to me in the 2001 meeting in Basra. Iran was attacking American soldiers.

Everywhere Parizad deployed, Iran succeeded. It didn't matter if it was overt combat or supporting a counterinsurgency, Parizad was viewed by the Iranian cabinet as a rising star not only in military circles but potentially even in the harsh political warrens of Tehran. Those that favored Parizad liked the idea of a military man with impeccable credentials who had been endorsed by the ayatollah himself.

Those that opposed Parizad's ascendancy were quick to come around or die. Young Dariush was not only proving himself a worthy combat commander, he also was becoming adept at organizational maneuvering. He had teamed with a fellow boxer and soldier, a man named Mahmood, who was slightly taller and broader than Parizad at six and a half feet tall and over two hundred pounds. Mahmood had the misfortune of being one of Parizad's sparring partners after the 1988 Olympics, and in part because he had survived, the two remained close throughout their respective military careers.

After the Iraq War officially ended in 2011, Parizad pressed the Iranian advantage to deploy his clandestine special operations forces throughout western Iraq, turning many Iraqis to support the network he had created. Persian-Arab relations had always been tenuous, but in this part of the world, that old saw of the enemy of my enemy being a friend was ruling the day. The Sunnis and the Shias wanted the Americans out, and Parizad exploited that sentiment to Iran's advantage.

Ben David and Parizad likely had overlapped during this transitional phase, but it had been a long time since I had spoken with David. Until two days ago.

Only in hindsight was I able to reverse engineer Parizad's movements and put together how his plan unfolded. He was methodical and kept meticulous records, first in notebooks and later by spreadsheets, and even later via saving his picture, video, and audio records in the cloud, much of it recorded by smartphones and computers.

Forty-two years after the infamous Eagle Claw mission at Tabas, Iran, thirty-three years after he was denied a shot at Ray Mercer because of a bogus doping ruling, and at the same time as I was leaving Fillmore's office in Tampa, Florida, Dariush Parizad stood in the observation room offset from an interrogation cell in a cinder-block building on a remote compound near Heidelberg, Germany.

Inside the cell was a man holding a smartphone in the air as if he were taking a selfie. He took a few steps in one direction and then stopped.

"The hack is effective on both the iPhone and Android. It invades apps like TikTok, Instagram, and Twitter to then take over the camera. When the subject has Demon Rain in his system, he sees images that aren't really there. Those images can be manipulated remotely. We can even do deepfake videos," Dr. Abdul Noora said.

"How does it work?" Parizad asked.

"The people in the cave, for example," Noora said. "We gassed them with Demon Rain near the village of Tabas, and as they were trying to call for help with their phones, we projected an image onto the screens of Allah leading them to the cave. By the time they huddled inside, the sarin had worked on their nervous systems. It is a one-two punch. We can control their minds and kill them. It just depends on the impact we want to have."

"Good work," Parizad said. "But why my hometown?"

Parizad had moved his mother and sister to Tehran when he joined the Quds Force nearly thirty years ago. He had little connection to Tabas other than the emotional tie of where he lost his father and the place that the ayatollah had named him the Lion of Tabas.

"These were prisoners that had been released during last year's COVID-19 outbreak. The police gathered them, unfortunately some with their wives and children, and bused them to the mountains about ten miles from Tabas. I chose that location based upon its remoteness, not even thinking about it being near your hometown."

"That's okay. If what you've developed and tested there has the effect we want in America, then maybe everything will have come full circle."

Noora coughed and looked at Parizad. "All the experiments combined indicate that you should be able to achieve the effect you seek."

They walked to another cell along the cinder-block corridor. Inside was a man pawing at the wall, drool running out of the corners of his wide-open mouth. He looked like a street mime pretending to be locked in an invisible cell. His hands pressed against the block, and then he removed it, staring at the spot where his hand had just been.

"We can batch Demon Rain so that it has more hallucinogenic properties or go the other way and scale more sarin into it. This is a variation of the Demon Rain hallucinogenic combination," Noora said. "Watch."

Noora opened the door and walked in, Parizad following. Noora tapped the shoulder of the man, who had been oblivious to their entry. He turned toward them with wide eyes and a smile. The black beard on the man's face was an inch long. His white teeth bared in an open-mouthed smile as if he were experiencing some type of wonderment that only he could see. He was sweating profusely.

"Name?" Noora asked.

"I'm Daniel," the man said in a perfect American dialect.

"Where are you from, Daniel?"

Daniel huffed his chest and said, "I'm from Virginia in the United States."

Noora handed him a phone and said, "Tell me what you see."

The man stared at the phone and lifted it up toward the ceiling as if he were taking a selfie.

"Jesus," the man said.

"What is he saying to you?"

"That I'm to kill you," Daniel said. He giggled slightly as if he'd just spilled a secret.

"Who can you tell about this mission?"

"No one," Daniel said.

"Then why did you just tell us?"

His faced screwed into a puzzled knot as his eyes widened, still looking at the smartphone screen.

"I wasn't supposed to," he said.

"Correct. What are you to do if you accidentally tell someone about your mission?"

"Kill myself," Daniel said.

"Can you show us how you would do that?" Noora handed Daniel a pistol.

Daniel grabbed the pistol without breaking eye contact with the screen. "Yeah. Just like this."

He put the pistol to his head and pulled the trigger. The explosion from the gun boomed in the small room. Red mist sprayed onto Parizad's face and black tactical clothes. The bullet bored through Daniel's head and smacked into the wall. Daniel slumped to the floor, dead.

Noora turned toward Parizad and said, "So we've still got some work to do."

Parizad smiled. "Yes, but not bad."

"He was just a somebody I had coffee with the other day. Spiked it, and he followed me here."

"Interesting," Parizad said.

"One more," Noora said.

They exited and walked along the hallway until it opened into a larger cell with a plexiglass viewing area directly beneath them. There were fifteen rooms off the larger common area. Parizad and Noora were looking down through the clear flooring like looking into a barren terrarium filled with pets. The common area was the size of half of a basketball court. Noora pushed a button on the wall, which opened the doors to each of the fifteen cells. The subjects stood, held up their phones, and started walking, following the images on their screens. Their necks craned as they lifted their phones and moved slowly toward Parizad and Noora above them.

"This is a better example. The mass effect of the technology and drugs. The combination creates a type of swarming. The Americans have been testing drone swarming for twenty years now, as have we. Given all our testing, I reverse engineered it into something that might work on humans. It's hypnotic."

The men and women in the cell were now climbing over each other, their faces misshapen, contorted, as if in agony. They formed a sort of unorganized human pyramid that resulted in one person climbing to the top, pressing his face against the plexiglass as if seeking oxygen. Breath fogged the pane beneath their feet.

"Interesting," Parizad said. "Based on what Gottlieb and the CIA did seventy years ago?"

"Mostly," Noora said. "The CIA conducted thousands of tests on unwitting Americans. In many ways, it was worse than what the Nazis did in Germany."

The subjects continued to claw like zombies.

"Among other things, I'm wondering why they're drawn to us."

"They've been in isolation for days, maybe weeks. They are completely broken. They're seeing what I choose to show them on their phones."

Noora turned, opened a door to their left, and entered a small control room, where a young Iranian man was typing on a keyboard.

"They're seeing you, Commander, standing above them and waving them forward as you promise them release."

Parizad stared, looked at Noora, looked at the computer monitor again, smiled, and said, "Well done, Doctor."

Below, the subjects continued to claw their way toward them, climbing over one another, mouths open, drooling, eyes wide, silent screams frozen on their faces. Noora spun a dial that released a gas, and the people crawling over one another froze in place, dead, phones held outward, fixed in their rigid hands.

"Also very effective," Parizad said.

"Yes, so we have some options," Noora said.

"We have options but no time," Parizad said.

"Of course," Noora said. "Which is why the product is already in America with Mahmood at the farm."

9

AS PARIZAD WAS TESTING Demon Rain and other concoctions, I was in our team house stretching for a run as my teammates got a rare moment of relaxation. We had spent enough time in Tampa that JSOC had purchased a Spanish-style, six-bedroom home on Carolina Avenue in the Venetian Isles community of Saint Petersburg, across Tampa Bay from MacDill Air Force Base. The house saved money in the long run and turned out to be a decent investment for the government, which purchased the property back in 2012 at the market low. Instead of staying in hotels and eating in restaurants, we were able to crash here when in town and eat healthier meals. While I approved the decision, it was for the troops, who appreciated the ability to have some modicum of normalcy when not deployed. It was one of the few genuine perks I've seen in my career.

Standing in the backyard next to two palm trees painted white around the trunks—something to do with rat control—I thought of Fillmore's office a few miles across the water. Hobart and Van Dreeves were spotting one another on the bench press in the corner while Jackson and Brown were drinking beer and shooting the shit in the pool.

When Sally McCool came walking out of the house, all heads turned in her direction. Probably the most physically fit member of the team, she was wearing a Swiss Army one-piece racing suit that left little to the imagination. She smiled and said to Jackson and Brown, "Don't let me interrupt your workout." Then she shook her head, tugged a race cap and goggles on, dove into the twenty-meter pool, and began a workout.

I turned around, walked past them, and said, "One hour. SCIF."

I jogged onto Carolina Avenue and threaded through the bayfront community at a decent clip. As I ran, my mind circled back to my team of handpicked warriors. Over the course of a career, any leader has the opportunity to choose those he wishes to mentor along the way.

MY FIRST OPPORTUNITY came along the banks of the Sava River separating Bosnia and Croatia, in December 1995. I was a major in the Eighty-Second Airborne Division about to transition back to the Rangers when the U.S. Army Europe commanding general asked for help deploying a force that had for fifty years been training primarily to defend Germany against the anticipated Soviet horde.

"Give me your special operators. Your rapid-deployment guys," I'm told the commander in Europe had said to the Airborne Corps commander under whom I served.

I was in Heidelberg, Germany, a day later and spent a month helping the First Armored Division command team figure out how to "rapidly" deploy across the European continent into Bosnia. I was the only soldier wearing the airborne signature maroon beret, an Eighty-Second Airborne Division patch on my left shoulder, and a First Ranger Battalion scroll on my right shoulder, which signified my combat experience in the Panama raid to free the Panamanian citizens from the vise grip of then dictator Manuel Noriega's criminal enterprise.

After bouncing between Wiesbaden, Bamberg, Heidelberg, and Grafenwöhr, I was summoned by a general to "pack my shit" and head with him to Županja, Croatia, the border village where the army had chosen to cross the river into Bosnia. We landed in a helicopter on a snow-covered hill overlooking the engineer base camp that had been swallowed by the annual flood of the Sava. The genius commander had placed his unit inside the dike of the river, because it seemed like an easier place from which to do their job of building a ribbon bridge across the Sava. The technique was to use downstream bridge erection boats pushing against interlocked bridge sections to counter the current of the river and hold the bridge in place.

The flood's carnage of the base camp was complete, though, and there was no ribbon bridge. Tents floated downstream beneath remnants of the existing Route 55 bridge, which had been destroyed by Serb missiles. Previously, the mile-long bridge had connected Županja, Croatia, and Orašje, Bosnia.

The tops of large shipping containers poked above the silty brown water like rocks in a stream. Humvees drifted with the current. Bridge pontoons were askew, spinning in the rapids. Random firefights between the Serbs, Bosnians, and Croatians sparked in the distance. It was a shit show of the highest order, and the fiasco was being dutifully captured by an attentive media set up on the remaining chunk of bridge that spanned maybe a third of the river, like a scenic overlook, before some sawhorses and yellow tape identified the jagged, shorn edges of the bombed-out bridge deck.

Soon, a lieutenant colonel appeared, eyes downcast, as he moved to salute the general. I reached out quickly and shook his hand to prevent him from the single worst combat zone faux pas, which was saluting a man who might be in a sniper's scope a mile away. The colonel looked at me as the general said, "Thanks, Sinclair."

We were wearing combat gear, including helmets and body armor, and carrying weapons and ammunition. I had an M4 rifle and a Beretta pistol, standard issue back then, and a Fairbairn-Sykes fighting knife, or dagger, which was not standard issue.

The general's two-man security detail carried M4s, as well. They were privates, who had disembarked from the whirring chopper, which inexplicably remained in place atop this hill in the middle of an unfamiliar combat zone.

"Pardon me, General, but this helicopter should leave," I said.

"We'll only be a minute," he said.

In my experience, that was all it took to kill a bunch of soldiers.

"I'll be right back," I said and walked to his security detail.

"Fucking airborne guys," the general muttered.

Both security soldiers were on one knee outside the arc of the chopping helicopter blades. They wore new battle dress uniforms, the black-and-dark-green patterns in stark contrast to the white landscape upon which we had landed.

I shouted, "Follow me!" and we jogged fifty meters through the snow until we reached a good vantage point on the downward slope of the hill, and I said, "Use this rock as cover, and watch for snipers across the river."

I looked at their name tags for the first time as they prepared to scout.

"Roger that," Private Joe Hobart said.

"River is a mile wide," Private Randy Van Dreeves added.

"Look over there, too," I said. To the west, the river turned south, where some boats were struggling against the current.

"Any reason you can think that boats would be in this water?" I asked.

"Scoop up army shit floating down the river, because that dumbass colonel made a stupid decision," Van Dreeves said.

"Attack," Hobart said.

Even as an eighteen-year-old private, Hobart had a keen eye and a penchant for brevity. Both men could have been right, but Hobart's assessment was my concern. The Serbs weren't happy with the Dayton

Peace Agreement, which imposed a temporary cease-fire on their pillaging of Bosnia and Croatia. From what I was seeing so far, the war was still raging. What better way to nix the deal than to stuff the American army at the river in a flare of incompetence?

I nodded and said, "Van Dreeves, you watch the town across the river. Hobart, you watch the boats."

"Some already across," Hobart said.

Between our position and the boats that were struggling against the floodwaters was the bridge full of journalists with cameras. There were about fifty engineers walking through the mud a quarter mile to the north.

"Rocket!" Hobart said.

I knelt next to them and looked through my binoculars. A Serbian wire-guided missile was smoking from a hidden position across the river in our direction. We weren't the target, though.

I bolted back up the hill as the missile exploded into the helicopter and a fireball ballooned outward and into the sky. The heat licked my face as I dove to the ground and rolled down the hill. Spinning to one knee, I ran back up to find the flames too hot to penetrate, but the general and colonel, as well as the helicopter crew, did not make it out of the explosion.

Hobart shouted, "Taking fire!"

The boats on the river had fully crossed to the Croatian side and had disgorged Serbian infantry that were moving toward the bridge with the journalists, who were caught in the dilemma of recording the helicopter explosion and reporting on the attacking infantry.

"Stay low," I said. "Provide cover. I'm grabbing those guys." I pointed at the engineers who were now all looking up at the burning chopper.

"We've got this," Van Dreeves boasted.

"Just be ready," I said and ran toward the engineers. A downtrodden captain covered in mud looked up at me and started to salute. I snatched his wrist and asked, "Are these your men?"

He looked over his shoulder and said, "Yes, sir. What's up with the chopper?"

"Serb attack. Rally your men now," I directed.

He turned and pumped his fist up and down, shouting, "Close in!"

His troops responded promptly, and soon we were surrounded by the peering eyes and weary faces of the bridge company, muddy M4 carbines slung over their shoulders.

"Serbs are attacking to overrun what's left of the base camp and maybe take the journalists hostage," I said, speculating.

"Fuck, they can have the journalists," one soldier said from the rear to some muted laughter from the troops.

"I've got a security team observing from the small hill near the burning helicopter. Captain, take half your men and attack them from north of the hill, and I'll lead the other half from the south. Don't shoot us."

He acted quickly, dividing his platoons, and tore off through the mud behind the flaming helicopter. The soldier who had commented about the journalists was actually the company executive officer, a lieutenant, and I said, "Have your men follow me."

We jogged past the hilltop where Hobart and Van Dreeves were already firing their weapons at the rapidly moving Serbian infantry. A small group was reaching the bridge as we neared it.

I knelt, shouldered my rifle, and fired as a two-man Serb team ran up the asphalt ramp onto the bridge. They both dropped. The men behind me seemed unsure of what to do. I expected that none of them had experienced combat. The Bosnia mission was being billed as a peacekeeping endeavor, but it appeared that we needed to establish some peace to keep.

Return fire popped over our heads, the first time most of these men had heard a shot fired in their direction.

"That group right there," I said to the company executive officer, pointing at a gaggle of ten Serbs. "Have your men kill them."

"Kill them?"

"Yes. They're trying to kill us, so let's return the favor."

He looked unsure, but turned and said, "Supporting fire on the enemy. Just like the rifle range."

I jogged up the hill and got the attention of Hobart and Van Dreeves, who were taking heavy fire. Under my direction, they backed off the hill and joined me at the base. We jogged behind the engineers and ran along the clay bank. The elevation of Route 55 and its asphalt road provided us cover as we approached the bridge. The journalists were taking cover, but their camera operators were filming us until we got beneath the bridge and to the opposite side. We came in from behind the enemy and found the Serbian commander kneeling with a radio handset stuck in his ear. He had a perfect vantage point to observe the bridge, the hill with the flaming helicopter, and the engineer base camp.

We snaked through tall grass until we were ten meters away. I pointed at Hobart and his target and then Van Dreeves and the man I wanted him to kill. They aimed, I dropped my arm, and they fired. The commander looked at his two dead security guards as I tackled him and drove my dagger through his neck. We searched the makeshift command post and found some maps and hand drawings of the engineer base camp. I took the radios, and we gathered the weapons and ammunition.

The engineers finally got organized and began to overwhelm the Serb infantry, who were retreating toward our position into the withering fire of Hobart and Van Dreeves.

"Let's go," I said. "They've got this." We exfiltrated out of the back of the Serb command post and walked for about a mile through the woods until we decided to cross the main highway into the north part of Županja.

Only then did Van Dreeves say, "That was a righteous kill with the dagger."

"Dagger Six," Hobart said. *Six* was the suffix that identified a commander.

While I wasn't their commander, it was the highest compliment that Hobart could pay me.

I nodded. "You guys did well. Let's grab some chow." We found a First Armored Division convoy, traded the Serb weapons and maps for some MREs from a fellow soldier, leaned our backs against the giant tire of a parked truck carrying an Abrams tank on a flatbed trailer, and talked about the future.

A day later, the engineer company commander and lieutenant were recognized by the First Armored Division commander for saving the base camp and the journalists. A thankful press lionized them, and the engineers were grateful for the change in journalistic tone.

Hobart, Van Dreeves, and I caught a ride to the First Armored Division headquarters, where I called back to Eighty-Second Airborne headquarters and said, "Hey, I've got two guys for you."

THAT WAS TWENTY-SIX years ago, and Hobart and Van Dreeves have been by my side ever since.

I finished my run, went to the master bedroom, showered, changed, and then waited in the SCIF. The team arrived, muttering that they wanted more time to work out.

"Me, too," I said. "But duty calls."

McCool was dressed in black jeans, a Grunt Style T-shirt that said BEAUTIFUL BADASS, and Doc Martens boots. Her blond hair shaded toward brunette when it was wet, as it was now. Hobart and Van Dreeves hadn't changed from lifting and were in running shorts and T-shirts. Jackson and Brown had cleaned up and were wearing their uniforms, anticipating a mission.

"Where's Rogers?" I asked of McCool's copilot.

"He's got wife issues in Orlando, so I gave him some time. He's on his way back," she said.

"Okay, here's the deal," I started. They sat down, and I switched on the monitor in the small room. Dariush Parizad's face looked down on us with his broken nose, facial scar, and flat, black eyes.

"Fuck," McCool said. "Parizad?"

"You've done your homework," I said.

"Biggest badass bad guy in the world right now. ISIS, Al Qaeda, the rest of them can't keep up," she said.

"General Fillmore tells us Parizad has taken over a safe house in Germany. We can't go to the Germans because this is one of those off-the-books CIA formerly OSS safe houses where we hired Nazi doctors to continue their experiments into mind control back in the late 1940s and through the '50s and '60s."

"Fun Fred," Van Dreeves said. "Mind control. Good combo."

"That's *General* Fun Fred to you, VD," McCool said. She smiled and winked. I always suspected a connection between these two, but if they had anything going on romantically, they managed to keep it out of my sight. McCool was attractive with her focused eyes, crooked grin, and girl-next-door appeal. Van Dreeves was a classic surfer boy and looked the part. I'd first noticed the spark between them when I caught McCool glancing at Van Dreeves at a Halloween throwdown at the "compound" here when he had worn board shorts, OluKai sandals, and a curly blond wig to go with the boogie board he was carrying around.

I ignored them and continued. "Evidently, Parizad has converted whatever substance he found into something that can be deployed to disable masses of people. He has experimented with it and had some success in operationalizing this compound. Unclear if it's nerve-center-based or psychological. SOCOM and CENTCOM intelligence are concerned that he's moving quickly from an experimental to weaponized formula. Our task is to gather intel and stop him."

"Where in Germany?" Hobart asked. His eyes were intently focused on Parizad's face. He had a ruddy complexion and thinning, wavy black hair. After twenty years of operating together, I couldn't recall having seen him smile.

"Outside of Heidelberg. This was a CIA deal, and they wanted to be close to the small airport there for clandestine flights."

"Plan?" McCool asked.

"Minimal footprint on location. Team will fly on a C-17 into Ramstein with the Beast. You and Rogers will stay there on the air force side of the airport with Jackson and Brown. Hobart, VD, and I will go to Heidelberg. We'll observe, develop patterns of life, make sure this isn't some head fake, then take down the target."

"We solid on if Parizad is really there?" Van Dreeves asked.

"Reports have him there, but only one way to find out. We thought we had al-Baghdadi a hundred times until we did," I said.

"Why can't the Germans do this?" Hobart asked. "Or U.S. Army Europe?"

"Too sensitive, and the Germans would try to embarrass us," I said.

"Picture of the house?" Hobart asked.

I punched a button on the keyboard and an aerial image of the compound appeared.

"Damn. You said *house,* not *castle,*" Jackson said.

What was on the screen was actually something beyond a regular house and below a standard German castle. It was U-shaped with a small courtyard in the middle. A rectangle of fence that appeared to be fifty meters from the main structure enclosed the compound. I clicked a button, and a street-level view showed the fence to be black wrought iron and about ten feet high with spear tips as finials. Another click on the keyboard produced a second aerial photo that showed the compound in relation to the small Heidelberg airfield. There was about a football field's distance between the back gate, indicated by the open U shape and the runway.

"Might need Cools to get us in there," Van Dreeves said.

"Or out of there," I said. "Like always, we will sketch out an initial plan and modify once we get on the ground with eyes on."

"I got it," McCool said.

"Two points of intel?" Hobart asked. He was drumming his fingers on the conference table around which we all sat, which was about as much emotion as Hobart might show.

"Fillmore didn't let on. I've got some sources working it, but it's all just a sketch right now." For each of our missions, we strove to have two sources of confirming intelligence.

"Or sketchy in general," Van Dreeves said. That got a few chuckles from the team. Even Hobart had a slight turn of one side of his mouth.

"Okay, pack up. We leave within an hour," I said.

We broke the huddle and were on the way to the airfield at MacDill in less than thirty minutes. We walked into the back of the C-17 aircraft, which had the Beast inside, its blades folded back atop one another. The Beast was McCool's very own Pave Hawk MH-60 helicopter. She walked up, rubbed its nose as if she were greeting her thoroughbred, which in a way she was. It was our steed that we rode into battle and she had saved our asses more times than we cared to recount.

The ramp snapped shut on the setting sun over Tampa Bay. We powered down the runway and took off for Ramstein AFB, Germany, just another U.S. military milk run to Europe. As we leveled out over the Atlantic Ocean, I stood and walked to the back of the aircraft, leaned against the left paratroop doorframe, and thought of the many jumps I had performed from this door on this model aircraft. Hundreds?

I felt a presence behind me and turned. Hobart stood there, arms crossed against his chest, eyes boring into mine.

"This changes everything, boss," Hobart said.

He was right, but I wanted to hear what he thought. "How so?"

"We're chasing the lion," he said.

A moment passed between us, understanding fully the risks and dangers of pursuing the Lion of Tabas.

"Weaponized drugs. Mass deployment. It's different from your standard chem/bio threat we're always prepping for. Chem and bio can only deploy a few ways on a mass scale—like COVID—most of which are recognizable, stuff we deal with routinely. We're trained to find dirty bombs, artillery shells, anything with urea nitrate. We've got the sensors for gunpowder, anthrax, and sarin gas, but not for some drug that only becomes a weapon when it's mixed with another. Like coronavirus. It just showed up," Hobart said.

Hobart was one of the smartest soldiers with whom I had the privilege to serve, which was why I had chosen him out of a competitive group of prospects nearly twenty-five years ago.

"That's why it's important to find him before he can scale this thing," I said.

Hobart nodded. After a moment, he said, "What else, though? Something's eating at you."

"Nothing serious," I said.

The thing about Hobart was that he didn't let go of anything until he had properly resolved it in his mind. His eyes were lasers that locked onto a target and released only when he was satisfied.

I looked at my watch and held my wrist up so that he could see it.

"Melissa gave me this watch a long time ago. She had it inscribed, 'Good wins.' She knew there was evil in the world but always urged me to embrace the goodness."

"Nothing good about a chem/bio threat."

I nodded. "She also knew the two things I truly care about are my family and my soldiers. We've been back here less than twenty-four hours, and neither of us got a chance to see our families, except maybe Rogers, and his marriage might be headed for divorce."

Hobart nodded. The plane yawed beneath our feet. The loadmaster stared at us from across the cargo bay.

"Bothers me, that's all," I said.

"You gave us our creed: quiet professionals," Hobart said. "We do our job and don't brag or bitch."

That had been my reigning maxim for three decades of combat operations, my rallying cry for my soldiers in battle.

"Quiet professionals," I replied. And that was the entire conversation, longer than usual with Hobart, until Van Dreeves showed up.

"Planning World War III?" he asked. We were dressed in black cargo pants, long-sleeve polypropylene shirts, outer tactical vests, and black tactical boots.

"Something like that. Figured you'd be sleeping and dreaming of California girls," I said.

"Something like that," Van Dreeves replied with a smile. "Plan?"

The engines whined as we churned over the Atlantic Ocean. I had executed hundreds of combat missions with these two men by my side. Our conversation felt as natural as a Yankees 6-4-3 double play.

"Just discussing how I drive you guys too hard," I said.

Van Dreeves looked at Hobart with a serious face, then turned back to me. "Bullshit. Hobart wouldn't entertain such a conversation. I, on the other hand, might, and while we do spend more time downrange fighting the bad guys, it's what we signed up to do, and there's no one better at it than us. I mean, what else would we be doing? Scoring hot babes, drinking cold beer, hanging at the beach? Please. Killing bad guys beats that."

"Got to have balance," I said.

Van Dreeves lost his smile and looked at Hobart and then back at me.

"This is about Melissa. Boss, we miss her, too. Nowhere near the way you do, but she was family, and we know it hurts."

As I said, we knew each other well, and there was no hiding my emotions sometimes. It had been over a year, and the giant hole Melissa's absence had left in our lives was reflected now in my countenance. Nothing I could do about it.

"She always said that the good guys win, and we haven't proven her wrong yet," I said. I patted Van Dreeves on the shoulder and walked to my rucksack on the red webbing next to the Beast's nose.

Everyone else was asleep, my soldiers knowing to rest when they could. Van Dreeves and Hobart chatted for a minute and then laid out sleeping bags on the floor of the aircraft. I followed suit and dreamed of Melissa, Brad, and Reagan during happier times when the kids were young and Melissa was alive.

But it was Hobart's words that echoed in my mind.

We're chasing the lion.

THE SOUND OF THE aircraft wheels lowering from the fuselage woke me. The entire team was stowing their gear, mission ready, mission focused. We landed and secured a black SUV the CIA had left for us at Ramstein, a Cold War holdover that converted to a power projection platform for the Balkan and Middle Eastern wars that ensued after the Soviet empire had crumbled.

McCool, Rogers, Jackson, and Brown handled the Beast while Hobart, Van Dreeves, and I began our trek toward the target. In the back of the SUV was a Sting Ray cell phone jammer, four Black Hornet personal reconnaissance drones, and some other toys the CIA gadget shop had decided to include.

We pulled out of the airfield hangar with Van Dreeves driving, Hobart in the shotgun seat, and me in the back checking my weapons. Hobart studied the drones and had the controller in his lap. Van Dreeves drove us along a major artery from west to east. The lights of Kaiserslautern, Mannheim, and Heidelberg punched into the sky ahead of us. We arrived after ninety minutes of careful navigating by Van Dreeves.

"Tennis courts on one side and aggregate yard on the other. This being January in the middle of the night, I doubt anyone will be playing tennis. Could use that parking lot," I said.

"Roger," Hobart said. Then, "Here."

We nosed into the parking lot for the tennis courts, which were blocked by twenty-foot-high fences covered in ivy. Van Dreeves shut the lights, and we exited the vehicle with our equipment. The target house was a hundred meters away in a thick, two-acre copse. As we rounded the tennis courts, the military airfield runway and control tower were visible. I had previously flown out of this small airfield on King Air C-12s, and the operators had to block a road every time we took off or landed to give the aircraft enough runway. The wooded area with the former CIA compound, now owned by a German businessman, was visible to the west. During the flight, CIA director Samantha Owens had her operations officer provide confirmation that the German businessman was actually an Iranian oligarch, who had close ties to the ayatollah.

We knelt as Hobart had the first drone in the air. The night was cool but not freezing for winter in Germany. We had donned lightweight black Gore-Tex jackets prior to leaving the SUV. I huddled over Hobart's shoulder as Van Dreeves studied the terrain around us, covering our flanks. The control display for the Black Hornet showed the path of the seven-inch-long, two-ounce kit. It buzzed silently along the tennis court fence, crossed the fifty-meter open area, lifted over the wall of trees that hid the fifteen-foot protective fence, and then dipped into a search pattern. Hobart flew the drone in expanding circles until he found a small brick structure separate from the main building. It was the size of a post–World War II home you'd find in any city in America. The drone's thermal camera painted the display with green, black, and white shades.

There was a ten-meter-wide warning track around the interior of the fence, no doubt monitored by cameras and guards. The Black Hornet zipped around the northeast corner, which was adjacent to the airfield hangars. The usefulness of this compound was immediately apparent given its proximity to the airfield and densely forested area. The thermal camera showed a break in the fence, which was most likely a gate leading to the airfield.

In my earpiece, McCool said, "Beast ready, standing by, blades turning."

"Roger, stand by," I said.

As the Black Hornet mapped out the compound, it discovered four guards manning fixed points at each right angle of the rectangular fence. The guards didn't appear to stray too far from their appointed corners, which meant they were augmented with additional observation and communication means.

Our operating maxim was always to move as swiftly as possible once we had sufficient intelligence to accomplish the mission, which, in this case, was gathering intelligence on Iranian chemical and biological warfare developments. That we were in Heidelberg, Germany, was not a complete surprise, remembering that Mohamed Atta and several of the 9/11 attack plotters holed up four hundred miles to the north in Hamburg, Germany, for two years as they mapped out their scheme.

"Okay, four external guards. Do we have hostile intent?"

"We're cleared hot to take all necessary measures to gather intelligence on a possible virus, bacteria, or chemical weapon. Intel leads us to believe that the number-one terrorist in the world—Parizad—is in there. So, yes, we have hostile intent. We may also have pathogens more contagious than coronavirus in there," I said.

"Roger. Okay, the best way in appears to be that we penetrate at one corner and disable one, then the others. Work outside to inside then penetrate at the garage connection," Van Dreeves said.

"Too sequential. Anything quicker?"

"We could each go in a separate corner, then convene at the fourth," he said.

"How about we go in one point for ease of breach, then each go to separate corners to disable guards. Hobart and I convene at the garage, use the Hornet to watch the fourth point while you disable him, then follow us in?"

"That's good," Hobart said.

"Roger," Van Dreeves agreed.

Van Dreeves moved the drone so he could watch the far southwest quadrant of the compound. The guard was typical of most guards late at night: lax and semi-observant. Hours, days, weeks, and months of no threat or activity dulled any guard's combat edge. He sat in a metal folding chair looking inward toward the front gate, which opened to the street. The drone inspected each corner, finding a guard at each post. Two were standing, one smoked a cigarette, and one was seated. Each carried HK long rifles that in the darkness looked like the 5.56-caliber MR556A1 with their sawtooth top rails and prominent vertical iron sights.

"Go in using the tree branch and then fan out from there. Keep the drone on the southwest corner. Take down the guards as soon as you get to them. I'll go south, you two go north, hit the northeast corner together, and then VD sets up the drone controller while Hobart takes the northwest corner. If I can get a quiet shot on the southwest guard, I will. You guys should do the same. VD, keep watching him with the drone, and let me know if anything changes. The mission is to find Iranian general Dariush Parizad and indicators of development of weapons of mass destruction or mind control."

"Roger, boss," the two men said.

"I've got Cools on standby," I said.

We moved along the tennis court's outer fence, darted across a small opening, looking for sensors and cameras, which were no doubt there. A heavy branch from one of the large walnut trees hung over the fence like a muscled arm. Hobart tossed a rope over the limb and secured it near the ivy-covered fence. We climbed the rope without touching the fence, mostly because we were concerned about motion detectors. Hobart was first. He leaned over the thick limb and helped me up. My Black Diamond Crag half-finger gloves gave me extra traction as I scaled the rope and grabbed Hobart's forearm. Hobart shimmied toward the trunk as I helped Van Dreeves, who scampered up the rope using only his arms like a ninja. Van Dreeves secured the rope and stowed it as we all crossed the top of the fence and climbed down the base of the thick tree. Hobart stood rock steady as I put a boot on his shoulder and jumped silently to the ground. We both eased Van Dreeves from the tree; then we knelt, listening to our environment.

The heat pump hummed lightly in the distance. A faraway siren wailed in distinctive European duotone fashion. A musty aroma of earth and tree sap hung in the air as a small animal, probably a squirrel, jumped from limb to limb high in the trees. A red fox shot across the lens of my night vision goggles as I snapped them into place.

I tapped Hobart and Van Dreeves, pointed at my chest, then pointed at the southwest corner, my target, about fifty meters away. Each man gave me a thumbs-up, and I moved in a low crouch to the south. The large home in the center of the compound was to my right. It was two stories with a steep, pitched roof of dark shingles. The façade was stucco, sporting tall, rectangular windows framed by wide boards, most likely brown. The ridge of the roof ran from east to west, perpendicular to my movement, which indicated the home was wider than it was deep. Some of the windows on the first floor showed light deep within the interior. I continued to pick a path among the deadfall, groomed shrubs, and trees that minimized noise.

I stopped at the base of a spruce tree, its low branches forming a solid skirt that hung three feet above the ground. Low crawling beneath the tree, I saw the shiny eyes of a fox glistening at me. They belonged to another fox. There was probably a family on the premises, the groundskeepers allowing them to stay to help control rats and mice.

As I nosed out from under the leafy needles, I had a clear view of the guard in the southwest corner. His cigarette glowed brightly in the goggle retina with every drag. I had two basic options, close for the kill or use a silenced shot from my pistol. The shot would create more noise than I wanted, making the Blackhawk knife on my outer tactical vest the best option. I imagined that Hobart and Van Dreeves were also about to close on their targets, as well.

I continued to low crawl and move silently toward the guard. I was exposed now, completely out from beneath the tree with about fifteen meters to go, my pistol still on my hip, my knife now in my dominant right hand. The grass was a type of well-manicured fescue with thick, broad leaves that retained moisture and wet my face as I slid forward.

A billow of smoke encompassed the guard's head, and I imagined him enjoying a brief nicotine high, perhaps even closing his eyes. I bent my knee and wedged my boot toe in the soft soil, then sprang to my feet, charging the man as he relished his fix. Immediately before I was upon him, he looked in my direction, no doubt feeling the breeze from my movements. His eyes widened as I plunged the knife in the side of his neck and covered his mouth simultaneously, catching the weight of his body as I dragged him into a waist-high hedge.

After about a minute of struggle, his mouth quit moving against my hand, reminding me to remove my knife. I took a deep breath and let it out slowly as I knelt and wiped the bloody blade on his clothes. The foxes would be on the scent soon enough.

I searched his body, found a pistol, long gun, and smartphone. The screen was unlocked to a scrolling series of messages indicating the guards checked in with one another every fifteen minutes. There were five different numbers on the group text. I touched the wireless communications device in my ear and said, "Clear."

"Clear," Van Dreeves said. "Stand by."

A minute later, Hobart said, "Clear."

With three guards neutralized, I retraced my route back to the tree where I found Van Dreeves kneeling and controlling the drone. The tablet screen showed the last guard sitting in the metal chair, looking at his phone. A bright light reflected upward into his face as he worked his thumb and forefinger on the screen.

Hobart said, "Going to number four."

"Roger," I confirmed.

The drone backed away in time to capture Hobart moving like a zephyr until he closed with the guard. Hobart swiftly disabled and killed the man, retrieved his gear, and returned to our position.

"Five on the group text," I said.

"Roger. Saw that," Van Dreeves said.

"Penetrate through the basement level?" I asked.

"That's the plan. This hedgerow leads to a small basement window," Van Dreeves said.

"Looked like a first-floor window was open," Hobart said. "West side about a third of the way."

They looked at me.

"Okay, path of least resistance. Fly the drone in there, and let's check it out."

Van Dreeves manipulated the tiny aircraft through the fluttering drapes, revealing a long dining table framed by a dozen high-back chairs. A wide hutch filled with china loomed over the table from the near wall. The room was minimally lit by a lamp in the adjoining room. The drone scouted the next room that had bookshelves stacked from floor to ceiling. A desk, sofa, and wooden chairs. A high-pitched ticking noise emanated from somewhere inside the house.

The drone made a loop through a grand foyer, along the hall, passed a door on the right, and then hovered in the kitchen. No activity.

"Okay, keep it watching from the point of entry, then go downstairs," I said. Then to McCool, I said, "Beast execute."

"Roger," McCool said in my earpiece. The plan was for her to fly from Ramstein to the Heidelberg airfield in twenty minutes unless I told her otherwise. We would have fifteen minutes to capture Parizad and collect intelligence.

"Let's move."

We scooted along the hedgerow and climbed into the window with no issues. Inside, we knelt behind the dining room table and covered each other until Hobart was at the hallway door.

He tried the knob, and it was locked. He pulled his lock pick set from his tactical vest and opened the door thirty seconds later. Hobart and I funneled down the dark stairway, stopping at the first landing as Van Dreeves recalled the drone and deployed it, the quiet rotors breezing past us with a whisper.

In the basement, the drone's thermal camera proved invaluable. The main hallway led between two rows of barred windows and doors like a prison. The drone hovered, turned, sped to the next, hovered, turned, and repeated the process the full length of twenty cells on each side. At the end of the hallway, two men were standing with their backs to the drone as they stared up at a large monitor.

"Audio," I whispered to Van Dreeves. He touched a toggle on the control panel.

"—compare notes with Yokkaichi."

"We know it works. Why waste time?"

It had been nearly twenty years since I had heard Parizad's voice, but it was unmistakably his Farsi inflections emanating through the drone's microphone and into my earpiece. The drone's camera was so powerful that it picked up the slightest movement of Parizad's hair, tossed by the whirring blades. *Not good,* I thought. We needed to move. Hobart and Van Dreeves looked at me. I nodded and pointed with an outstretched hand to the two men. They were maybe forty meters away at the far end of the basement.

As we stood to move, three things happened all at once, none of them spectacular for us.

Parizad and his companion turned and saw the drone. A second passed, and Parizad made a movement with his hand, whereupon the doors to each of the cells opened. A moment later, the door at the top of the steps behind us opened.

Hobart fired twice at the guard coming down the stairs, who fell and tumbled into our position. Van Dreeves fired a nonlethal weapon at Parizad, rubber bullets smacking into his torso. Parizad was reaching down to grab something on the table, but Van Dreeves's fire was intense, and the rubber bullets *could* kill a man. We had chosen this option because we needed Parizad alive to tell us how far along he was with his plan. Van Dreeves's weapon coughed in three-round bursts. Hobart's fire, on the other hand, was lethal, and he felled three guards as they clumsily spilled into the basement.

"Parizad!" I shouted.

We were up and moving along the corridor with the open cell doors. A man ran from one of the cells into the hallway, screaming at the top of his lungs and disrupting our movement, no doubt Parizad's plan.

"Fire! Fire!"

He was a disheveled lunatic with wild eyes. His gray hair was matted. A dingy beard framed a hollow face. He was naked and had wires connected to his testicles. Hobart shoved him back in his cell and ripped the wires away before closing the door. More people had flooded into the corridor, though, and most were naked.

Van Dreeves changed magazines on the move, dodged the cell dwellers who were filling the hallway, and maintained a high rate of fire at Parizad and his comrade. They continued to try to dismantle something on the table, but ultimately, our proximity and Van Dreeves's aim convinced them that discretion was the better part of valor, and they escaped through a door to our right.

Dodging the human subjects in the basement became problematic. They were a heartbeat away from being zombies, but in reality, they were guinea pigs for the most lethal synthetic chem/bio/viral hazard being developed, provided our intelligence was right. We emerged from the opposite end of the corridor and saw a door slam shut. All of us noticed a MacBook tethered to an HDMI cable, the treasure that Parizad had been attempting to secure. Hobart scooped up the MacBook while Van Dreeves recovered and stowed the drone in his outer tactical vest.

"Blow the door and—" I stopped.

The horde of inmates was crawling toward us, looking upward, above our heads, and holding phones as if each of them were making a video of the exact same thing at the exact same time.

"See anything?" Van Dreeves asked. We were all looking up in the same general direction.

"There," I said.

A pile of bodies was frozen in death at the end of the hallway, where a common room opened up. Above us was a plexiglass ceiling—like an observatory platform.

The ceiling began to hiss. Some kind of gas.

"Masks?" I barked.

We fumbled with our protective masks and secured them. As operators with limited time on the objective, we weren't inclined to look at anything but the exit; however, comparisons to the cave in Iran were impossible to ignore. Van Dreeves had rigged the door with an explosive charge. With surprise no longer an issue and a fog beginning to rain down upon us from a sprinkler system above, we were loud and proud. We huddled behind a wall, the explosion destroyed the door, which hung by a hinge, and we poured through, the captives now ignoring us and climbing into the corner atop one another.

"Parizad is the target," I reminded the team. Everything else was a distraction.

We scurried along a dark tunnel, hooked a left and a right. The walls were damp brick, and a kerosene-soaked torch seemed appropriate. Instead, we used the Maglites on the ends of our weapons as we peered through our mask eyepieces. The beams crisscrossed, painting the black corridor with light. Footsteps gathered behind us, most likely Parizad's security team.

We rounded a turn and found a locked wrought-iron gate, which Van Dreeves made quick work of with the bolt cutters. A faint light beckoned in the distance. Bullets chipped at the bricks behind us. Hobart spun around me and fired into the void along the perpendicular tunnel we had just traversed.

"Outside," Van Dreeves said. He'd found a path out of the basement.

I carefully spun to the right behind a brick wall as we spilled onto the back courtyard. Outdoor tables and chairs surrounded an unlit fire pit atop flat stone tiles. We were exposed to three sides from the two-story mansion in a literal U-shaped ambush. Our masks limited our peripheral vision, so we removed them.

Glass crashed to my right as we dashed into the backyard toward the gate. Gunfire chased us into the darkness. Security lights flooded the backyard suddenly, as in a prison breakout. An aircraft propeller spun loudly as a small airplane darted into the sky and banked south. Almost immediately, McCool said into my ear, "Bogie headed south. We are on final approach. Status?"

"One hundred meters to your three o'clock. Hot LZ," I said.

"Roger. Will come to you."

Van Dreeves had already disabled the back gate on our way into the compound as we swept the guards. The random gunfire told me that Parizad had taken personal security with him and what was left was an unorganized group of guards. Perhaps the alpha security guard had gone with Parizad.

The Beast crabbed toward us as we ran behind some low-slung airport hangars. We found a hose and sprayed one another quickly, doing a field-expedient decontamination. McCool landed in the grassy infield about fifty meters from us as we closed the gap. Jackson and Brown opened the doors, and as soon as we poured into the aircraft, it was lifting away and banking hard back toward Ramstein Air Force Base.

"Status," I said.

"Up," Hobart said.

"Up," Van Dreeves said.

"Up," I said. No injuries. All equipment on hand. One MacBook secured.

"Just like the cave," Van Dreeves said.

"My thought exactly," I said.

"Drone?" Hobart added.

"We can look at the video back at the base," I said. Then to McCool, "What was that flying out as you came?"

"King Air. Got it on gun tape. Will download it when we get back. We can watch the movies," she said.

"Hit the CIMR tech," I said. Ever since the COVID-19 outbreak, I had Continuous Infectious Microbial Reduction (CIMR) machines emplaced in the Beast and our SCIFs worldwide. These "air purifiers" produced a steady mist of hydrogen peroxide and other patented compounds that killed all known viruses. So far, we had avoided biothreats, and perhaps we needed the technology now more than ever.

Jackson flipped a switch on his crewman's console, and a light fog poured into the cargo bay where we sat. The mist was cool on the skin, and I hoped it was working its magic.

Jackson and Brown manned their respective crew positions at the port and starboard machine-gun posts, respectively. We landed at the massive Ramstein AFB runway and quickly ferried into a hangar. As the crew took care of the aircraft, Hobart, Van Dreeves, and I took the time to further decontaminate all our clothes and equipment, including the captured computer. We walked through another CIMR "car wash," as we called it. When we were done with showers and had changed into new clothes, we moved into a small SCIF in a basement beneath the hangar. It had a large monitor facing a gray metal conference room table and matching metal chairs that at one time had been padded. Now they were cracked, showing yellow stuffing.

Van Dreeves set up the charging station for the drones, snapped them into place, and then retrieved the computer he had secured from the objective and plugged in a DGI cable, projecting onto the large-screen TV above us.

He moved the mouse around, clicking his way through several irrelevant folders. Hobart started cleaning his weapon, breaking it down on the table, in effect saying, "Let me know when you've got something," but of course, being Hobart, without saying anything.

I hadn't fired my weapon but broke it down and wiped it clean anyway. Done with the rifle, I retrieved my Beretta pistol and was about to disassemble it when Van Dreeves said, "Boss."

Both Hobart and I stopped and looked at the monitor. Van Dreeves had a grainy black-and-white video on the screen. Parizad stood above a hooded individual sitting in a chair. It was easy to distinguish Parizad's broken nose, pinched eyebrows, facial scar, and matted black hair. The person in the chair was slight, possibly a woman. The hands were bound to the arms of the chair. Another man, perhaps Parizad's companion tonight, was standing over the subject in the chair, listening to the prisoner's heartbeat through a stethoscope, but quickly stepped out of the picture.

My arms began to tingle. There was something familiar about the hostage in the chair. The hands wrapped around the armrest were slender. The shoes were the same kind of running shoes Melissa typically kicked around the house in. Even the sandbag-covered head had Melissa's signature tilt, as if wondering something or on the verge of asking a question. I immediately thought of Reagan and Brad, my children. Was Reagan a hostage? Her physique mirrored that of her mother's, except she was taller by a couple of inches.

Parizad held a syringe as he knelt in front of the captive. He smiled and looked at the camera as he slowly removed the black hood and handed the prisoner a cup of water. His body blocked the face.

When he stepped away, Melissa stared at the camera. She had a dreamy look on her face, maybe even a smile. Parizad unbound her arms, and she stood, her gaze fixed on a faraway spot that we couldn't see on the video. She stepped from the chair; eyes cast upward into the far corner beyond the cameraman.

"What's the date of this?" I asked, my voice breaking. I had seen her dead body. Buried her. As much as I wished and hoped she would come back to me, there was no way this was real. Maybe it was some kind of technology where a doppelgänger could completely replicate someone and fabricate their existence, like a deepfake video. With virtual and augmented reality, it wasn't a stretch to believe that was possible. But why?

The video stopped. It wasn't lost on me that Melissa had the same distant look in her eyes as the cave and basement people we had discovered.

"Fifteen months ago," Van Dreeves said.

"Before she died, obviously," I said.

After a long pause, I directed Van Dreeves to show the video again. And again. In total, we watched it five times before I couldn't take it any longer. The subsequent viewings didn't reveal anything special. The room was nondescript. It could have been in the mansion we'd just raided, or it could have been the basement of our home in Virginia or my family home in North Carolina. Behind her on the wall were some faint markings, like someone counting the days with perpendicular lines and a horizontal slash.

"You okay, boss?" Hobart asked in a rare display of verbosity.

I nodded. "Just need to step outside. You guys study this. Figure it out. Where were we when this was shot? Where was that video made? Any chance she was in that place in Heidelberg? Then look at the drone video. Try to figure out what everyone's looking at. And when McCool gets down here, review the gun tape. Find the King Air. Then see if there are any connections."

"McCool is here," she said, strutting into the room. I brushed past her without acknowledging her and climbed up the steps into the hangar, then stepped into the cold German night.

It was quiet, save a few random work trucks puttering around at the distant end of the airfield. The sky was black, millions of stars shining down, one of them Melissa burning brightly in heaven.

I thought back fifteen months. I was in Syria with my team. We were a few days out from the ultimate al-Baghdadi raid. I was ferrying between Ankara, Aleppo, Baghdad, Kuwait, Tel Aviv, and a dozen other shitholes in Syria proper, gathering intelligence. Until recently, it was the last time I had seen Ben David. I would never see Melissa alive again. I remembered it all very well.

How had Parizad and Melissa been together in the same place? He was an international terrorist on the United States' most wanted list. There was no way that he passed customs anywhere. The U.S.-Mexican border? Canada? Somewhere else with some other nefarious method?

We were close tonight and would get even closer in the near future, but the video of Melissa and Parizad in the same room had changed everything. I wasn't thinking of national security now. I was thinking of lifelong commitment and killing Parizad.

The worst thing Parizad could have ever done was to involve Melissa in whatever he was doing, because at that very moment, I knew that I would find him and kill him slowly, making sure he felt every ounce of pain I delivered.

11

WHEN I WENT BACK into the basement of the Ramstein hangar, the entire team was there, including the helicopter crew with McCool, Rogers, Jackson, and Brown. They fell silent, out of deference for what I might be feeling, but also because some of them were close with Melissa before she passed.

"Okay?" Hobart asked.

"Fine," I lied. They were standing around the conference table flicking their eyes between me and the frozen image of Melissa sitting in a chair with her hands bound. "Before we release this information to anyone, we need to have a conversation about what the fuck we think is happening."

Van Dreeves stared at me, probably wondering why I'd dropped the rare F-bomb.

"There's more," he said.

We all sat down at the table, and he manipulated the controls to show other images of subjects in the same chair as Melissa over time. None of them were speaking, all just staring with that same glazed look.

"Demon Rain," I said.

"Parizad has been experimenting on people for more than a year," Van Dreeves said.

"But Melissa hadn't been in Germany for a long time and certainly not fifteen months ago," I said.

"The only conclusion is that Parizad was in the United States," Van Dreeves said. "Someone had picked up Melissa and fed her the drugs, maybe Demon Rain, in that chair."

"She was at Walter Reed, for Christ's sake," I said.

"You know that Walter Reed doctors have been involved in the CIA mind control experiments to this day, right?" Van Dreeves said.

I paused. "I wanted to believe that the mind control nonsense stopped with Gottlieb and Dulles. But this opens a new possibility."

"What's that?" Hobart asked.

"That someone killed Melissa."

"We were thinking that," Van Dreeves said. "But didn't want to go there until you arrived at that yourself."

"But why?" I asked. "Why kill Melissa?"

"Because we all loved her," Van Dreeves said. "To get to you, us." He pointed at me and then waved his hand around the room.

"To what end? Stop the al-Baghdadi raid? Rock my world?"

"Maybe all of the above," McCool added. "Maybe she was the soft target they could get at to make us feel exactly what we're feeling. Shitty, guilty, angry, everything."

"To just generically decrease our effectiveness? I'm more focused and angrier now than before. While I still didn't see her before she passed, now it's possible there was an accelerant."

"Who's the doctor?" McCool asked.

Van Dreeves backed up the video and played it again, first in regular time and then in slow motion. Long, wavy black hair hung over a lab coat collar. The hand holding the stethoscope to Melissa's neck and chest had weathered fingers, but that was about all we could see. There was a flash of white across the person's left hand, but the image was fleeting, on the screen for maybe a second.

"Unclear. Checking her heart rate. He's not in any of the other videos with the other subjects, either," Van Dreeves said.

We were mulling this over when Fillmore called the SCIF landline phone. Hobart answered and passed it to me, but I motioned for him to put the call on the monitor.

Fillmore appeared from the CENTCOM SCIF in Tampa. The army and CENTCOM insignia were in the background, framing his serious face.

"Status?" he asked.

"We just returned. It's too early to tell," I said. I wasn't even thinking of who had combatant control at the moment. We were in the European Command theater of operations pursuing a terrorist from a Central Command nation, and I of course worked for Special Operations Command.

"How did it go on the objective?" he asked.

His face was expressionless, sullen eyes and lips pressed thin in concern. His executive officer, the muscle-bound Colonel Hodgins, leaned into the camera also.

"We were in and out in fifteen minutes," I said.

"Any computers, hard drives, flash drives?" he asked.

"As I said, we're just huddling up and inventorying the take."

"Okay, let me know ASAP."

"When we do these missions, we have to get our equipment ready for the next one. We've been prepping the helicopter and cleaning weapons. We just began analyzing what we've got. I can call you when I know more," I said. "We plan on going back into the compound tomorrow in daylight. There is a lot more there to see, I'm sure."

After a long pause, he said, "There's no time. We've got a track on Parizad. His plane is headed to Tokyo."

"He was on a King Air. It doesn't have the range."

"He switched to a private jet in Mannheim. They're in a Dassault

Falcon 50 over Ukraine right now with a refuel stop in Kazakhstan's Nursultan airport. The flight plan shows Tokyo, but I'll send the details for what we think they're doing."

It was unlike Fillmore to be this operationally involved tracking the Iranian Quds Force commander, but I did appreciate the assistance.

"Roger that," I said. Fillmore pushed away from his chair and exited the screen with his executive officer. Admiral Tom Rountree sat down, waited a second until we heard a door close, and said, "Just wanted to see your smiling face, Ranger."

"Good to see you, too, Tom," I said.

He lowered his voice and said, "The military police at Camp Farah found a dead airman smoldering in the burn pit the day before yesterday."

"This concerns me how?"

"All his credentials were missing. He was shown as having been on the manifest of the rotator flight. His wife called and said he never showed up and we didn't think it was a big deal until his body was found . . . in Afghanistan."

"Somebody took his place?" I said aloud.

"Maybe. We're checking video footage now."

I paused, processing what Rountree was telling me. Suddenly, the screen went blank. I tried calling the number a couple of times, but we must have lost our satellite connection, a common occurrence.

"What was that last part?" McCool asked.

I shrugged, but there was something there. I couldn't place it just yet. Had someone taken the dead airman's place on the flight? Or had a crew chief mistakenly submitted the preprinted manifest?

"Unusual level of interest from General Fillmore, don't you think?" Van Dreeves asked.

"I do, but given what we've seen here, I would like to nail Parizad down."

My voice must have cracked, because Hobart said, "Boss?"

I looked at Hobart, who was staring at my right hand, which was gripping my freshly oiled pistol. My hand was white from the pressure. My trigger finger was inside the trigger housing, but there was no magazine in the well or round chambered. Still, it was an unconscious, amateur thing to do. If Parizad's intent was to attack my psyche, then it was evidently working. I opened my hand and placed the pistol on the table. The inside of my palm was filled with red and white checks from the textured grip. My hand was shaking.

McCool came walking back into the SCIF and said, "Airplane is ready."

"Okay, let's go. We can finish this in the C2 pod in the C-17," I said, my voice cracking again.

We collected our gear and everything we had seized at the Heidelberg compound. I was happy for the diversion from my anxiety. I slipped my rucksack over my right shoulder and carried my kit bag with my left hand. Almost everything I needed in life was in this balanced load. As I walked onto the tarmac with my team, I thought of Brad and Reagan, not much younger than Jackson and Brown. They'd had their mother snatched away from them. Was it by cancer or Parizad?

Strapped in and ready to go, we bumped along the runway and lifted into the sky in pursuit of Dariush Parizad.

As soon as we leveled out, I stood and entered the command pod that had a small conference room table with four chairs. Hobart, Van Dreeves, McCool, and I sat facing one another. With the door closed, the engine noises were muted.

"My first question," Hobart said. "Why was Parizad at a U.S. CIA safe house?"

"General Fillmore told me it was a former safe house and that the German government took over a couple of years ago," I said.

"Why would the CIA just hand over a black site? The DNA. The history. Who knows what the hell happened in there?" McCool asked.

"When she takes office, President Campbell will be all about cleansing the CIA of its 'abusive past.' I think that's how she put it. Not sure if she'll keep Samantha Owens," I said. It was true. Like Jimmy Carter had done, Campbell had pointed at a history of CIA missteps and deliberate abuses that had led to chaos, not greater world peace or increased national security. "I'm told she wants to give up about five compounds or black sites."

"It'd be good to know who *really* owns that place," Van Dreeves said.

"Dig into that, Randy," I said.

"Roger. So what was Parizad doing in there?" Van Dreeves asked.

"Good question," I said.

The phone on the console buzzed with an incoming call.

"Well, well. As if we conjured her ourselves," Van Dreeves said.

CIA director Samantha Owens had graduated from West Point a year ahead of me. She was first captain of her class, which is to say that she was in charge of the cadet chain of command. She had daily duties to perform, as well as her classwork and athletics. We all knew that someday she would be running the world, and that day had arrived.

"Yes, ma'am," I said, punching her call onto the video screen.

Owens had short gray hair, a lean face, and serious eyes. Her forehead pinched into a single crevice in the middle above her nose. She was wearing a navy-blue blazer over a light blue shirt as she sat at what I imagined to be her desk in her office.

"Garrett, hello. I see you've got your team there with you."

"I do. No secrets here."

"That may be, but I need it to be just you and me."

I nodded at Hobart, who ushered the team out of the command and control pod.

"Okay, go ahead," I said.

"Fillmore called and said you hit the Heidelberg house. What did you find?"

"As I told Fred, we are still sorting things out. He mentioned something about Japan. There are still people in there, subjects Parizad was experimenting on."

"Yes, it seems some former CIA properties we sold have been purchased by an Iranian holding company, allowing Parizad to move clandestinely from Germany to Japan."

"That answers my first question," I said.

"Glad to be of service," she replied.

"History tells us that Germany and Japan are countries we want on our side," I continued.

"True, but no one else knows about this. I have an asset that had reported on the Heidelberg house, but the defenses were too strong, so we deferred to Defense, which is how this got to you. Now to remain consistent, I'm giving you what I've got on Yokkaichi. Gottlieb and his bozos ran a 1960s mind control lab there, and we sanitized the place a few years ago. It sold for about $2 million, and nobody thought anything of it. Now our intel shows that Parizad has been experimenting in the Heidelberg and Yokkaichi compounds."

"To what end?"

"We think Parizad is preparing to attack the United States. You know as well as anyone that every time we do a change of command, someone is going to test us. Well, there is no bigger change of command than a presidential inauguration. This one will be massive. First woman president."

"He's testing mind control to be able to do what? All the possibilities on that were debunked," I said.

"Until now. There is some evidence that this cocktail we are calling Demon Rain is able to produce the effects of LSD but also open the mind for manipulation. That was the holy grail that Gottlieb never got to. Technology seems to play a role."

"Okay, so he controls the mind of someone or a group of people, and they do what?"

"Kill the president. Kill me. Order your team to attack friendly military bases. The list is limitless if it can truly be done. Like *The Manchurian Candidate,* only more sophisticated."

"My team?"

"The whole idea of mind control is that there's no way to tell who has been infected, so to speak."

"What evidence do you have that you're not sharing?" I asked. I was thinking about the dead bodies in the cave and tunnel that had all been searching for the same thing and likewise the people in the basement all doing the same.

"I've shared everything. Rogerson from the FBI ran some samples. We believe that the compound is most effective when injected directly into someone, but it can be aerosolized, also, and keep its properties."

"Any update on Ben David?"

Owens looked away briefly and then returned her gaze to the camera. "Nothing concrete. He's a slippery bastard."

I processed for a moment that the CIA and FBI had lost control of a Mossad agent in Afghanistan. If Ben David had escaped, that was David Copperfield–level stuff, but something was scratching at the back of my mind. David was the best spy I knew. I tucked away the notion and focused on the task at hand.

"What are the indicators that Parizad is going to attack the United States?" I asked.

She looked away again briefly. Maybe someone else was in her office.

"The Quds Force has hunkered down in Iraq and Syria. No activity. Our station chiefs in the region report that the ranks have thinned. Parizad has been shuttling between Japan and Germany, evidently working on this poison. Iranian subs are aggressively patrolling in the northern parts of the Persian Gulf, chasing oil tankers. Being a general pain in the ass. Add in the mix that we've an inauguration coming up. It's that time of year."

"Has Parizad been in the United States?" I asked. Without sufficient time to process what I had seen, I wasn't prepared to confront Owens about Melissa just yet.

"I certainly hope not!" Owens snapped. If she was an actress, she was a good one, because her reaction seemed authentic to me. "Why would you ask such a thing?"

"Germany and Japan were the two focus areas of the Marshall Plan," I said. "Maybe there's a connection."

She wrinkled her brow and said, "And here I thought you were just a jock at the academy."

As if that explained everything. I may have been an athlete, but I did know what the Marshall Plan was.

"I was, Director. I also have been boots on the ground for the last twenty years while you've been printing money."

Before becoming CIA director, Owens had ascended to the presidency of a large midwestern bank after serving her five-year commitment in the army. She had graduated from West Point as a Finance Corps officer, a controversial pick seeing how most top-tier grads chose combat positions, not support. Worse, she had spent her entire career at the burgeoning base in Northern Virginia named Fort Belvoir, formerly the home of the U.S. Army Corps of Engineers and now the home to several agencies, including finance, that had consolidated into one location. From there, she doled out the cash.

Don't get me wrong; we all enjoyed receiving our meager paychecks and were glad that a sharp mind like Samantha's was at the helm cutting paychecks, but it seemed like such a waste of talent.

"Garrett, there's no doubt you're the right man for this job. Get to Japan. See if you can find Parizad. I'll have one of my teams link up with you."

"Roger," I replied. "Meanwhile, Director, please get boots on the ground in that German compound. By now, there are probably dozens of dead people in there, most likely exposed to whatever this Demon Rain thing is you're talking about."

"We've got a team in there now with the German BND. Everyone you saw down there was likely injected with Demon Rain. Like I said, there's some kind of virtual reality aspect to this we don't quite understand yet. When you get to Japan, spend more time on the objective. See what's happening with these groups of people." The German BND was the equivalent of the American CIA.

"How long have you been tracking Parizad?"

"Forever and a day. Why?"

"I mean recently," I said.

"Intensely for about eighteen months," she said.

It was quite possible that she knew about Parizad interrogating Melissa, or maybe, to be generous, she knew he interrogated a woman. I kept my cards close to my chest for the moment.

"What other sites are there?"

"Parizad's been operating in Yazd, Heidelberg, and Yokkaichi. That's what we know about," she said.

But she knew more. Had to. Melissa hadn't been within five thousand miles of any of those places. Parizad must have been in America unless the video was a deepfake, which I hadn't fully discounted.

"Anywhere else?"

"What are you getting at, Garrett?"

I paused before answering. I knew when someone was working me, and Owens certainly fit that profile. Succinct answers. Deflection onto the target. Vague generalities.

"Nothing, Director. You've been very helpful," I said.

"Brave and True," she said, signing off with her class motto.

I looked down at my worn West Point ring, dulled by years of constant wear. I had never taken it off, primarily because the wedding ring Melissa had placed on my finger was welded on the inside, keeping Melissa and West Point both close to my heart.

Steadfast and Loyal.

I slid my thumb across the dulled class seal and rubbed the wedding band.

"Lissa," I whispered. My voice caught. "What did they do to you?"

After taking a deep breath, I opened the door to the pod. McCool, Hobart, and Van Dreeves reentered.

"Did you ask her about Melissa?"

I looked at McCool and shrugged. "Not ready to give up that information just yet."

Hobart leaned forward. McCool leaned back in her chair. Van Dreeves looked at the door to the pod.

"You think our government is in on this?" McCool asked.

"I'm not sure what to think. I'm sitting here trying to hold everything together and objectively develop a plan, after seeing a video of my wife being interrogated by an international terrorist. We are following direction from the National Command Authority to get eyes on the former CIA safe houses, because, as Owens just put it, with the inauguration coming up, it's that time of year."

"Tactically, we executed the Heidelberg house operation near flawlessly," Van Dreeves said.

"It was almost too easy," Hobart added.

"My thoughts exactly. We got in, found that laptop, and escaped," I said.

"Think the laptop is a ruse? Could the video of Melissa and Parizad be like photoshop but in a video not a picture?" McCool asked.

"Deepfake?" Van Dreeves asked. "More and more hackers are using artificial neural networks to superimpose images and voices into videos."

"I get that technologically it's possible, but in this case, why?" McCool asked.

I had an idea but found that my understanding of any situation grew if I let the team hash out their different perspectives.

"You see it all the time on Facebook, Instagram, Twitter, all that bullshit. There's a video of Campbell talking to a group at a town hall meeting. Is that really her? Did the meeting take place? Is it all bullshit?" Van Dreeves said.

"Are you sure it was Samantha Owens on the video call?" Hobart asked, serious.

"It's a secure line, so I'm guessing we're okay. What we do know is that we found my friend Ben David in a cave in Iran. We found Parizad's coin in his pocket. And I had a live conversation with General Fillmore."

"Everything else could be real or could be bullshit," Hobart added.

"I think the crux of the matter is that we potentially have a dead Israeli spy and some kind of testing of mind-altering drugs. The promises, such as they were, of LSD never panned out. The intent was to tactically get a prisoner to tell the truth or influence a few people, and the holy grail was to control large numbers of people. The CIA, Nazis, and Japanese were able to develop sodium pentothal, scopolamine, and other drugs that loosen the brain and nudge the victim's mind toward being open and frank."

"Dirty bombs, chemical attacks, and nukes all create mass casualties. Psychoactive drugs are meant to control individual minds. Isn't it more likely that Parizad's intent is to control a single mind to execute an attack that has the impact of a WMD?" McCool asked.

I stared at her a moment, thankful for these three warriors around me. Not only their incisive calculations but also their camaraderie.

"You may have a semi-decent thought there, Cools," I said.

She took the compliment as intended. If I praised too highly, they knew they were in trouble. If I jokingly minimized the action, it was high praise indeed.

"I'll take semi," she said.

"What about the gazers?" Van Dreeves asked.

That was a good term for the people we had seen dead in the cave and in the Heidelberg compound.

Hobart was leaning back in his chair, thinking. He looked at Van Dreeves and said, "I have a thought on that."

It was almost as if he needed to explain that he would say more than a couple of words.

"Let's hear it," I said.

"Two groups of dead people climbing on top of each other like they couldn't breathe and needed oxygen. If Rogerson is right, they inhaled this Demon Rain drug. Maybe the drug makes your mind want one single thing so badly; like you need oxygen to stay alive, your brain craves x just as severely."

"Any thoughts on what x might be?" I asked.

"There's all kind of research on dopamine. Drug addicts, booze, exercising, et cetera. Maybe this drug creates a need that is just as vital as oxygen, and if they don't get it, they die."

The plane hit turbulence, and we jostled around for a few seconds. I looked at the flight map and saw we were over Kazakhstan, most likely fighting the brutal low-pressure systems that created minus-forty-degree temperatures this time of year.

"Okay, but to what end? What's Parizad's purpose?" I asked.

"This is the time of year for crowds, right? The director mentioned inauguration. NFL playoffs. Any number of targets if you can aerosolize it," Van Dreeves said.

"Yes, but why? Just to land another blow against the Great Satan? Parizad's a bigger thinker than that. A garden-variety terrorist attack seems . . . beneath him, or at least he might view it as such. Besides, we're so divided now that another attack will just get us pointing at one another," I said.

"Especially if it's made to look like one side did it to the other," McCool added.

I leaned back, took in her steely eyes, the hard angles of her face, and nodded.

"We always talk about feeding into vulnerabilities. That's our weakness right now. Divided loyalties. Two camps lobbing digital grenades at each other. This Demon Rain thing could do something there, maybe escalate it to a civil conflict," I said.

"Like civil war?" Van Dreeves asked.

"Makes more sense than just another random attack that will be forgotten in a few weeks. Parizad's in this for the long haul. He believes we have forever altered his life; he wants to do a generation of damage, if not more," I said.

"So what is the catalyst? How do these piles of dead people factor in?" Van Dreeves asked.

"Demon Rain," I said. "Control enough influencers' minds and the rest will follow. Program them to fight each other."

Everyone remained silent, soaking in the gravity of what I'd just said. The thought had not occurred to me previously, but listening to my team brainstorm had crystallized my thoughts.

"Makes sense, boss. Who are the targets? What's the cue?"

"Maybe Japan will help us figure that one out," I said.

"Speaking of which, I've got a diagram of the compound," Van Dreeves said. He pressed a button, and the monitor showed a rectangular structure with a long sidewalk leading to it from the road frontage. Behind it was a stream that wound to the south. Across the stream, the terrain rose steeply and was thick with Nikko fir trees.

"Okay, walk us through it," I said.

He used a pencil to point at the different features. "Here you've got the first gate with the traditional posts and overhang that looks like a Rakkasan symbol. Here is the approach—looks like sandstone. There's a second gate surrounded by ceremonial guardian lion-dogs, all which lead to the sacred fence."

"Sacred fence?"

"Yes, this place was some type of palace," Van Dreeves said. "Evidently, it was the best place to conduct torture during and after World War II. Anyway, inside the fence is the compound, which has the curved, tiled roof you might be accustomed to seeing in the movies. Through the front door, you have a standard layout, and then there are two basement levels accessed by this stairwell or this elevator." He pointed at the stairwell on the left side of the house and the elevator on the right side. "The suspicion, I'm guessing, is that the two bottom floors are where we might find the Demon Rain victims. It's built into the side of a mountain."

We spent another thirty minutes discussing our plan and then decided to retire to our sleeping bags for some rest. I wolfed down an MRE and lay down on the cool metal floor of the C-17 inside my sleeping bag. Using a rolled-up pair of pants as a pillow, I thought about Melissa, Brad, and Reagan.

Did my two children know anything of what Parizad may or may not have done to Melissa? I liked to think not, because I was almost certain that one or both of them would have told me something. Then again, Parizad was a crafty operator and might still maintain some type of leverage on them. I drifted to sleep thinking about how an Iranian madman had violated the most personal sanctuary of my life: my family.

Was he somehow blaming me for the failed mission in Tabas over forty years ago?

If so, I saw no way for this to end well, and maybe that was his point. Both Parizad and I had lost the most important people in our lives and had only revenge to live for. For me, it wasn't a bitter, hateful emotion. Rather, Melissa's death, and Parizad's potential involvement in it, had removed all uncertainty from my life.

I intended to kill everyone who had anything to do with involving Melissa in the Demon Rain project. Little did I know how difficult it would be to kill so many, so close to home.

12

WE LANDED AT YOKOTA Air Base north of Yokkaichi and off-loaded the Beast in a U.S. Air Force hangar on the south end of the runway. We taxied into the hangar, two plainclothes airmen lowering the door behind us as soon as the tail cleared the entrance.

I had Admiral Rountree from CENTCOM to thank for this support. During the flight, I had given him the mission of finding a safe haven for us. There was always a shit storm of activity at Yokota, so a random C-17 wouldn't raise any suspicions.

As McCool and team readied the Beast for action, we made final plans. There was one road leading into the compound, which was carved into the side of the Miyazuma Gorge overlooking the Utsube River. Van Dreeves's map recon showed that the only way to get in and out with any element of surprise was vertical envelopment. We decided that we would fast rope onto the back side of the hilltop and then infiltrate into the rear of the compound that backed up to the terrain. We packed 120-foot ropes because the slope appeared to be severe.

We waited until midnight, passing the time by cleaning weapons, sleeping, and eating. Hobart sharpened his knife. Van Dreeves flipped a pen through his fingers as he stared at the map, divining routes in and out, perhaps. McCool and her crew turned wrenches on the Beast. Eventually, we conducted a walk-through rehearsal of the plan, again, with Hobart, Van Dreeves, and me reviewing in detail executing on the objective. We made sure we had ropes, rappelling equipment, protective masks, oxygen tanks, and flex-cuffs.

As midnight fell, McCool had the rotors spinning. The wind was up, and a cold front was moving through, sweeping down from the mountains in the west and lowering the ceiling, which created suboptimal conditions. We knew there was a chance of weather, but McCool had the latest avionics in the cockpit. She always told me that she would never fly faster than she could see, but she was on the margins tonight. Rain lashed at the windscreen. Winds buffeted the aircraft with sudden invisible punches.

As she hovered over the target landing zone, the Rolex Melissa had given me read 0034 hours. The flight from Yokota to our landing zone had taken thirty-four minutes. Jackson dropped the thick rope, and we slid down onto the hilltop a half mile behind the compound. We were over the landing zone maybe for fifteen seconds, and McCool made a series of false insertions on the way into and out of the objective to mask our actual insertion point, in case anyone was watching.

We rallied in the trees as the sound of chopping rotors and whining engines was replaced by stillness and quiet, save the wind rustling the treetops. The rain had moved north. We donned our IVAS night vision sets as we performed our customary five-minute listen-and-learn waiting session to get acclimated to our new environment. Animals grunted in the forest, probably smelling us.

"Bear or boar?" Van Dreeves whispered.

Hobart finally stood, put a hand on Van Dreeves's shoulder, and nudged him toward the objective. We broke brush until Van Dreeves found a narrow trail through the thick forest. Tall pines towered above us. Low ground cover grabbed our legs and ankles. Spiderwebs hung between trees in perfect symmetry. One of the benefits of the IVAS was the high-definition picture and thermals, but the heads-up display, built-in compass, and Terminator-like optics were truly next generation. We were walking on a 208-degree azimuth toward the objective when Van Dreeves found a set of power lines angling toward the back of the compound. We walked along the edge of the forest, keeping parallel to the relative open terrain to our left. There was a grove of small trees beneath the power lines, and every hundred meters or so, large metal towers climbed into the sky, supporting the drooping cables that hung above the trees. A creek meandered through the right-of-way. Two wild boars bounced along a trail and stopped, most likely noticing our scent. They grunted and ambled to the northwest, upstream. A bear growled in the distance like a muted foghorn carried by the wind. The treetops rustled and swayed, scratching at the sky.

Once the pigs cleared away, we veered away from the power line easement and crossed the creek, stepping on large stones across the ten-meter-wide run. After another fifty meters, we were staring over a cliff at our target. It was fifty meters below our position, the only real access being from the front. Van Dreeves retrieved a rope from his rucksack and looped it around a thick tree trunk twice, cinching two half hitches tightly against the base. He fed the rope over the lip of the overhang while Hobart and I secured our rappelling seats.

We took a minute to outline our plan, study the compound, and send a quick communication to McCool, who had recovered to our airfield thirty miles north. She was standing by with blades turning. Once again, our time on the objective was going to be restricted. We had not alerted Naicho, the Japanese equivalent of the CIA, and there was good reason for this. During the Iran nuclear deal negotiations, Iran's Ministry of Foreign Affairs had wisely paraded Parizad, the Lion of Tabas, through all the meetings. He had become central to the negotiations and accordingly was well received in the West as a champion boxer, soldier, and diplomat. The future of Iran. Accordingly, he had many friends throughout the intelligence communities around the world, including Japan, one of the largest would-be benefactors of the economic expansion in Iran. Given the level of graft and corruption involved, there was no shortage of intelligence operatives ready to sell information to the Iranians and who might give up an American or two.

We studied the compound's entry points, which were guarded with cameras, lasers, and sensors. The twenty-foot-high fence was wired with electronic motion sensors, given away by the white plastic snaking through the ivy-covered chain links.

"Would have been better to just fast rope into the compound à la the bin Laden raid," Van Dreeves said, joining Hobart and me.

I ignored his comment and said, "Randy, we discussed neutralizing the sensors. Can we jam them?"

"I see a junction box and wires coming into it, so it's hardwired, not wireless. This was the intel we didn't have. There were two options. Brute force through a soft point or call Cools for backup and fast rope into the courtyard, as Van Dreeves had just suggested."

While fast roping was a preferable solution, I didn't think we had the time to redo everything, and the weather was shit. If an attack on the United States was imminent and Parizad was in the compound, which was unclear, then we had to act immediately.

"The fence is only ten meters from the cliff, if that. Can we reposition the rope on that branch and swing over the fence by pushing off the rock wall?"

"We can try anything, boss," Van Dreeves said.

"That should work. Let's try it," I said.

Van Dreeves untied the rope, shimmied up the tree, and secured it on a thick branch hanging over the expanse between the fence and the cliff.

Since it was my idea, I threaded the rope through my snap hook and rappelled down the face so that I was about ten feet above the top of the wall, which I could now see had thin spikes at the top. The rope wasn't positioned all the way beyond the top of the fence, so it wouldn't naturally swing me to the other side. A suitable outcome would result from a combination of athleticism and timing, neither of which were what they once had been when I was a hard-charging captain.

I held on to the rope above my head while I opened my snap link and removed the rope from its loop. My right foot found a tiny crevice to support my weight as I balanced between the rope and the ledge. I needed to swing with enough momentum to clear the deadly finials atop the fence while also not allowing the rope to land with any force against the fence, triggering the sensors.

I gripped the rope and pushed away with my legs like a swimmer making a turn in the pool. When my momentum reached the nadir of the rope's arc, I released and flew across the fence into the backyard, executing a parachute fall by keeping my feet and knees together and rolling like a gymnast, popping up and lifting my rifle against any guards who might be pouring into the area.

None appeared.

"I'm in," I whispered. "Watch out for the spikes on top of the fence."

"Roger. Hobart coming."

Soon, Hobart landed like a ninja next to me, rolled, and popped up to one knee, scanning.

"Coming in," Van Dreeves said.

Above us, the sound of cloth ripping broke the silence. Van Dreeves let out an oomph as he landed and rolled. He came to one knee next to Hobart, then rolled on his back and swatted at his leg, as if killing a stinging bee.

Through the IVAS, it was clear that his leg was cut and bleeding.

Hobart opened Van Dreeves's rucksack and retrieved the medical kit he carried for the team. He cut Van Dreeves's pant leg with a pair of surgical scissors. Opening an alcohol wipe, Hobart cleansed the wound then wrapped it tightly using gauze and tape.

"You'll live, Ranger," Hobart said.

The look on Van Dreeves's face concerned me. The cut seemed minor, something I had seen him shrug off a hundred times. He'd been shot and stabbed and appeared less concerned than he did now.

"Good?" I asked.

"I'm good," he said.

He reached into his rucksack, removed the cell phone jammer, adjusted the frequencies he wanted to block, and switched on the handheld device. We moved to an outbuilding that looked like a small pagoda. Perhaps the CIA interrogators and torture chamber operators had come out here to pray after experimenting on humans.

"Back patio entrance looks best," Van Dreeves said. He winced as he spoke.

We moved in a tightly packed triangle. I still relished the adrenaline rush of conducting operations. The breeze in my face, the uncertain outcome, the unpredictability of it all. The heavy weight of my responsibility to my team outweighed any childish exuberance that attempted to creep into my thoughts. At the moment, I had a nagging concern about Van Dreeves's minor leg cut. Infections could happen, but he seemed to be powering on, as usual. A thought scratched at the back of my mind, remembering what our CIA had once done at these facilities: made the deadliest poisons in the world and tested them on unwitting societal ne'er-do-wells.

Approaching the back patio, we veered toward the back wall of the compound and raced up a set of steps that led to the top floor. Van Dreeves pushed open a sliding glass door that was unlocked. So far, so good.

We entered a small bedroom, which was vacant. The room smelled musty and unused, which made me wonder why the door had been unlocked. I heard a distant whirring noise. When things were too easy, there was a good chance you were in trouble. It was a truism that I had seen proven too many times on missions. There was always a balance between pursuing good fortune by not letting self-doubt get in the way of success and blindly stepping into a well-laid trap by believing you were a genius planner and executor.

It wasn't that everything had been easy. The bad weather. The improvised entry. The spiked fence. Van Dreeves's cut. But overall, it shouldn't have been this easy to gain entry to a former CIA compound owned by the Iranian Quds Force, who were conducting clandestine human experimentation labs.

Were we standing in a snare about to be closed?

"The basement," I said.

Van Dreeves led, I followed, and Hobart watched our backs as the three of us moved in unison into a dark hallway. The house seemed empty, with no signs of recent life, though there were also no cobwebs or indicators of prolonged disuse.

The landing overlooked a gathering area fronted by a large fireplace, Western influences on the inside of a decidedly Eastern exterior. We swiftly and silently moved down the stairs and through the large room, finding the door to the basement, which was open.

A light shuffling noise came from a room adjacent to our position in the hallway. It must have been the kitchen, based upon the diagram we had reviewed. Hobart's pistol coughed twice, followed by a thud on the floor. Another sound preceded a booming gunshot as we filed down the stairs.

"I'm hit," Hobart said.

With Hobart, that could mean he was missing a limb or had a flesh wound. As I was turning to check on him, Van Dreeves's pistol fired twice, and bullets pocked the wall next to my head. Two dark forms were fleeing through the only exit we knew of in the basement.

"Status?" I asked Hobart, keeping my pistol gripped in both hands, held low until I had a decent target.

"Okay," he said. There was something in his clenched-teeth response that told me his wound was on the serious side of his considerable pain spectrum. As we moved, the faint whirring sound oscillated, sometimes louder, sometimes softer. It was the same sound we had heard in Heidelberg and the Iranian cave.

Van Dreeves pursued to the left as I spun to the right and shot a man lifting a weapon toward me. He dropped, and I pushed into the room opposite Van Dreeves. Stepping over the dead man, I cleared to the far wall, found a door, and said, "Door."

Hobart was struggling behind me, but he was there.

"Roger," he said.

"Opening," I said. I pulled the heavy wooden door, which opened into a long hallway with doors evenly spaced on either side like a prison. Like Heidelberg.

A man at the far end of the hallway was holding something in front of him, like a crossbow. Before I could fire, I felt a pinprick against my thigh. My pistol bucked in my hands as the target dove behind a wall at the end of the corridor. I turned toward Hobart, who was limping, and pulled him with me to the protection of the near wall perpendicular with the hallway.

Hobart's leg was bleeding. The wound appeared to be on the outer part of his right leg, away from the critical femoral artery. Still, it looked like a serious wound from a large-caliber bullet.

There was a dart protruding from my pant leg. I reached down and tugged at the feathers, but it felt like the tip was barbed as it ripped my muscle. Nonetheless, I grimaced as I removed the device and stuffed it in my pocket. The pain was searing, almost blinding. I clenched my teeth and stifled a scream. Taking a quick peek around the corner, I saw no one, but heard moans coming from the cells. Low groans and some mumbling.

"Status?" I said.

"Coming your way," Van Dreeves whispered.

Momentarily, he was kneeling beside me and getting to work on patching Hobart's wound.

"You're bleeding, sir," Van Dreeves said.

"I know. Crossbow got me," I said.

"Crossbow? What the fuck?"

He took a minute to clean and wrap Hobart's leg. Our time on target inside the compound was at seven minutes. We had eight minutes to conduct sensitive site exploitation and retrieve any evidence. Naturally, I was motivated to see what other indicators of Parizad's interrogation of Melissa might be on hand, but primarily, our focus was stopping Iran's much-rumored attack on our homeland.

The sounds in the cells became more pronounced as my hearing seemed to intensify. Fingernails were scratching at the walls. Chains were scraping against the concrete floor. Fans were whirring loudly, their metal blades brushing the manifold.

"Ready?" Van Dreeves asked.

I nodded, but my eyes followed a light in the ceiling moving along the hallway. I stood and began to walk slowly until Van Dreeves pulled me back as machine-gun fire echoed in the small space, sounding like a hammer on a metal trash can lid.

"Sir?"

My eyes continued to fix on the small bead of white light like a laser pointer, moving along the ceiling, beckoning. For a moment, I was oblivious to the danger posed by the bullets ricocheting along the walls.

"Let's move," Hobart said.

"Boss has lost more blood than we'd thought," Van Dreeves said.

"No," I managed. "We have to open the cells."

"That's the last thing we need. A bunch of zombies coming after us. There's a computer room on the other side. That's our target."

"Requested ETA," McCool said. She was listening over our secure high-frequency radio communications platform, Alphmega. Her voice was tight, packed with concern.

It was my job to call McCool for pickup, but I couldn't manage to formulate the words. My mind was drifting from its normally tight focus on executing the mission. Insects were scratching inside the walls. Hobart ratcheted his rifle, chambering a round. Van Dreeves muttered loudly, "Sir!"

Time spun away from me. My mind swirled as if I were moving through molasses. I felt Van Dreeves lift me onto his shoulders, and we began moving slowly toward the stairwell, but my eyes followed behind him. Hobart fired his silenced long gun, which sounded like a small firecracker with every shot. I was watching the floor, and the white beam of light kept appearing and pulling my eyes toward the ceiling. Van Dreeves's rucksack bored into my abdomen. Metal scraped against fabric. Loud swooshes rattled my eardrums until I couldn't hear anything at all. The floor began to spin. Hands waved in front of my face. I landed on the floor. Bright lights washed over me. Someone was dragging me. Fragments of time came and went like a strobe light. One second I was there, another I wasn't.

Hot prop wash blew over me. My nostrils filled with the smell of aviation gas. I had no control over my limbs. I felt another pinprick, this time into my shoulder.

Clusterfuck was the last word I heard before passing out.

I AWOKE ON A stretcher in the back of the same C-17 aircraft that had carried us to Japan, though I had no idea where we were other than somewhere in the air. The turbulence rocked the airplane. A fire extinguisher sprung loose from its hold and landed with a loud clang on the metal floor.

When I opened my eyes, McCool was standing over me, her hand on my arm, fear in her eyes, her voice rushed and low.

"Sir, can you hear me?" she asked.

I managed to nod.

"Hobart? Van Dreeves?" I muttered.

She looked away, a tear in her eye.

"Tell me," I growled.

"Hobart is going to be okay. Randy's hit bad. Jackson, too."

"How bad?"

"We had to leave them in Japan. Randy wasn't okay to fly. Two shots to the abdomen. Lots of bleeding. Jackson . . ." Her voice trailed off.

"Van Dreeves . . . carried me," I muttered.

"Yes. Randy got you to the helicopter. We took heavy fire. We unloaded two cans of ammo into that place."

"The others?" I asked.

McCool looked away and started talking, but I couldn't concentrate on what she was saying. Her voice was much louder than normal. I listened, but all I could think about was that Van Dreeves had saved my life. He openly risked his own life to get me to the helicopter because I'd became a liability during the mission.

The jet engines whined with piercing authority. Medicinal smells of alcohol and antiseptic permeated the air. The normally dim lights in the C-17 cut through my eyelids like razors. Every inconsistency in the medical litter poked into my body like needles. When I swallowed, I tasted copper.

"Sir?" McCool said. She had been talking to me. "Did you hear me?"

"Come again?" I croaked.

"On exfil, Admiral Rountree sent us a report that five Iranian Akula-class submarines left the Persian Gulf a week ago," she said.

I struggled with the information. The Akula submarines were Russian stealth technology first sold to India and then, we suspected, to Iran after Iranian coffers were flush with the $50 billion from the Iran nuclear agreement. Not being a politician, I had no opinion on that deal or its reversal. There were consequences either way for military personnel and our nation. My job was to assess the threat and prepare to handle it.

"Akula?" I said.

"Right. More than we thought they had."

I tried to sit up but couldn't elevate. McCool put her hand on my chest and nudged me back down. I was able to catch a glimpse of two men in suits standing at the foot of the litter.

I tried to lift my hand to motion McCool closer to me but couldn't move my arm. It wasn't that it was heavy; rather, it felt like someone had tied my arms down. My injuries must have been worse than I'd thought given that I was secured so tightly to this stretcher. I motioned with my chin for McCool to lean over me, which she did. The smell of sweat and hydraulic fluid blasted my nostrils as she placed her face near mine.

"Who are they?" I whispered, my voice hoarse and dry, the coppery taste still present.

She looked toward the two men and then leaned into my ear.

"CIA," she said.

She slipped something into the side of my combat boot as the two men abruptly nudged her away and stood on either side of my litter like guards. I was too exhausted to tell them that McCool was one of mine, I was on a friendly airplane, and I didn't need security. Whatever poison the dart might have carried, I felt better today than I did during the first moments after being struck. My main concern, as usual, was the status of Hobart, Van Dreeves, and Jackson, but apparently, my condition was worse than I'd anticipated, because they weren't letting me up.

To emphasize the point, a third unfamiliar man pulled a surgical mask over his mouth and nose, leaned over me, and shined a light in my eyes. He had the youthful appearance of an actor with his disheveled brown hair and three-day beard. He continued inspecting me with latex-glove-covered hands, squeezing my leg around where I'd extracted the dart. His face zoomed in and out as he pushed on the wound. The pain rocketed through my body, causing me to flinch and release a slow hiss through my teeth. The rushing air through my mouth caused the roots of my teeth to ache. Every nerve in my body was exposed.

Not responding to my wince, the doctor shoved a needle in my arm and pumped something into my body. Then he turned to the two CIA men, nodded, and walked away. The CIA men looked at me and then at their watches. McCool was nowhere to be seen.

Before long, I drifted in and out of sleep until the sound of landing gear releasing from the fuselage jolted me awake. I was slow to focus, my arms on fire. My eyes followed a distant white dot for a moment, then it faded. I faintly remembered the brilliance of the dot shortly after the dart had penetrated my leg. In contrast, what I was seeing now was something less stark, more of the starburst people see when they take a shot to the head and the optical nerve is rattled.

When the plane landed, my body ached at every juncture. The entry wound seemed to explode with pain, and my eyes flashed with a galaxy of stars. Normal conversations, for a moment, sounded like people shouting directly in my ears.

"The car is waiting for us!" one man said.

"I'll link up and then help you move them!"

To my disappointment, the shrill voices dimmed as the first man said, "Take the captain and . . ."

They were talking about McCool. While she could handle herself, I was paternally concerned for her. She was like family. Hell, she *was* family. I had spent more time with McCool and the others in my team than I had with Melissa, Brad, and Reagan. I assumed that "them" meant Hobart and me, since McCool had told me he was on another litter.

When the airplane stopped taxiing, the engines wound down, the whine of the turbines was replaced by the loud rattle of a garage door.

"I'm going with him!" McCool shouted. Then, "Don't fucking touch me!"

There was a struggle that I couldn't see, but given the size of the two CIA men and even the doctor that I had seen, I wasn't hopeful that McCool, as talented a fighter as she was, would be able to subdue them.

Feet banged on the floor of the aircraft with loud slaps, as if she were being held by her upper body but not her legs. McCool had just been awarded her first-degree black belt in Brazilian jujitsu, and I interpreted the sounds as her fighting off two or three of the goons. While I had worked extensively with the CIA, including Director Owens, I was struggling to resolve why these men might be aggressive with McCool. Ostensibly, Hobart and I were being evacuated due to wounds received during an authorized combat mission, albeit one that had to be denied and hidden from the general public. We conducted these missions routinely, often with men and women getting wounded, and had protocols in place to evacuate, cover our tracks, and make our presence no more than a zephyr.

After a minute, the sounds subsided, and the two hulking CIA men returned. They undid some latches and lifted the medical litter to carry me off the airplane. As they shuffled along, I caught glimpses of the Beast, riddled with gray bullet holes pockmarked along the exterior of the aircraft. The skin of the left engine housing was charred as if it had caught fire. Snippets of the exfiltration rocketed through my mind.

I remembered Hobart shouting, "Go, go, go!" A bright burst followed by Van Dreeves saying, "I'm hit! Watch the boss!" The Beast yawing wildly in the sky.

But I couldn't replay the entire video in my head. I was only able to grab scenes for a microsecond here and there.

As we descended the ramp, the ceiling of the large hangar came into view. A large black SUV was waiting with its hatch lifted. The two men slid me in the back before I could say anything, and then the man I presumed to be a doctor leaned in and punched another shot into my arm. The hatch closed, and I felt the weight shift twice on the SUV as we began rolling.

I didn't see McCool or Hobart and suddenly became concerned that my wounds were worse than I'd thought. I presumed that these men were whisking me to Walter Reed in Bethesda and that we had landed at Joint Base Andrews.

I presumed wrong.

14

AS MY MIND WAS drifting into its fugue state, Brigadier General Dariush Parizad was finalizing Iran's attack plans on the United States.

Perhaps there was no better Iranian to lead the effort against the Great Satan than the Lion of Tabas, forged in the literal fires of Operation Eagle Claw. The United States had executed that mission at the peak of its military incompetence and simultaneously at the debut of the still-surviving theocracy that had propelled Iran to become a major geopolitical power and nevermore a puppet of the United States. Rising from the ashes of the global coronavirus pandemic, Iran—hit particularly hard because of its close ties to China—was following Parizad's strategy of attacking an opponent on the ropes.

The record shows that Parizad spoke calmly with the ayatollah and President Rouhani in the humble confines of the Office of the Supreme Leader, which was appointed with a mahogany desk, four wooden chairs with bad white-and-gold-flecked upholstery, and an oversize chair covered with the likes of a bedsheet. Parizad and the president sat in the wooden chairs facing the ayatollah in the oversized chair. A large brown hutch with assorted gifts from Chinese, Russian, Syrian, German, French, and other world leaders stood above them along the wall.

"The submarines are free. The commander reported that he escaped the Persian Gulf and is now following our plan," Parizad said.

The grand ayatollah nodded. "Detected?"

Parizad shrugged. "We think so, but now they are deep and alone making their way to their targets."

The ayatollah nodded and spoke. He made subtle motions with his hands and spoke softly through thin lips covered with wisps of his gray-and-black beard.

"When my mentor and predecessor, Grand Ayatollah Khomeini, named you the Lion of Tabas, he placed great responsibility on your shoulders. He foresaw that one day our people would require visiting the shores of the United States and collapsing the evil empire from within. The Americans came to your village and killed your father. Everything that has happened until now has been in preparation for this, setting the stage for your action. With the cowardly strike on Soleimani, our preparations have not been in vain. Now we must show strength after this plague."

"We will achieve the complete revenge and more," Parizad said. "The plan is fully in motion. We are wounded, but a wounded animal is to be feared."

The ayatollah was the head of the Iranian state and commander of all military forces, not unlike the American president is the commander in chief in addition to the country's highest executive. Parizad's rise to power was accelerated by the American drone strike that killed Major General Soleimani, the former leader of the Quds Force and Islamic Revolutionary Guards Corps.

The ayatollah nodded and asked, "The American?"

Parizad remained silent for a moment, then said, "The American is reliable."

"The Jew?"

"The spy escaped. We should have contact with him soon."

"The testing?"

"Complete. Everything works as our doctors said it would."

"The electronics?"

"The application works. Everything will come together at the right time."

The ayatollah spread his arms in welcoming satisfaction.

"I will leave these matters to you, General. While I am your commander, I do not pretend to have the battlefield skill that you possess. Since you were a young lieutenant, you have succeeded in bringing honor to your homeland, and I am convinced you will continue to do so."

"Thank you, Supreme Leader," Parizad said.

"Your travels will take you abroad for a long time. We will await your return and provide for you a fitting hero's reception."

"Supreme Leader, I am not one for recognition. Everything I do is for my country and my mother and sister. Please," Parizad demurred.

The ayatollah looked at the president, a small man in an oversize suit, and said, "Very well. Provide General Parizad all the support he requests, nothing less."

With that, the meeting adjourned, and Parizad visited the technical services department of the Ministry of Intelligence where he was outfitted with the necessary equipment. He then departed Tehran on an Iranian jet to France, where he changed planes at Paris Charles de Gaulle Airport and was lost in the crowd.

It wasn't long before I saw him again.

15

I AWOKE IN A sterile room still strapped down, but this time fastened to a large metal gurney that was fixed in the middle of the floor.

A bank of fluorescent lights screwed into the ceiling shined down on me. The intensity of the light was not as severe as I had expected, given my last several memories. While the skin on my arms tingled, it did not seem to be on fire as I had experienced in the airplane.

I lifted my head and felt a mild ache, but not the throbbing pain I had previously experienced. Whatever medicine the doctors were giving me seemed to be working. Water was dripping somewhere behind me, but the *plink, plink, plink* was muted, not harsh.

My immediate concern was for McCool, Hobart, and Van Dreeves, as well as the rest of my crew. Two men stood outside the door, half of which was a wire-mesh window. I appreciated their concern for my safety and welfare, but honestly, I thought this level of protection was beyond what I needed or deserved.

"Hello," I called out.

A voice came over the intercom speakers above me.

"You don't need to shout, General. We can hear you."

I swallowed and said, "Okay, thank you. Is there anyone who can tell me the status of my team?"

A long moment ensued before a different voice said, "Someone will come in to speak with you shortly."

I listened carefully to the inflection in the voice, the words, the tone, and something gave me pause. I wasn't sure just yet. I'd been wounded and obviously drugged both with some kind of poison dart in Japan and then an antidote—a simple EpiPen—that Van Dreeves had injected followed by whatever the doctors were giving me. My senses had been impacted in a way that distorted reality, or maybe I was experiencing actual reality without the filters our bodies provided us.

The door opened, and a tall man walked in. He had shaggy brown hair that fell over his ears, a hawkish nose, and narrow eyes. His forehead was pinched tightly as he looked at a tablet and then at me over wire-rim glasses.

"General Sinclair, how are you feeling today?"

"Better, I think. Can you tell me about my team? Their status?"

He pursed his lips and said, "We are still researching that. You have people spread out everywhere."

"Randy Van Dreeves is who I'm most concerned about. He and Sally McCool and Joe Hobart. I think Rogers, Jackson, and Brown are okay." But something clawed at the back of my mind about Jackson.

"What makes you think that?" he asked.

I was annoyed he wasn't directly answering my questions. I never pretended to be entitled to respect or information at any rank, though as a commander of soldiers, I had a responsibility to my troops, and I needed answers to make decisions about their welfare.

"Let's try answering my questions, and then I'll consider answering yours," I said.

His lips turned up in an arrogant self-assured way that reinforced the scratching in the back of my mind.

"Yes, well, I'll see if I can get some information for you, but first I need to diagnose you."

"You're a doctor?"

"Yes, I'm a doctor."

"Am I at Walter Reed?"

"Again, I'll answer your questions in due time. It's important that I speak with you while your mind is fresh so that we can help you and your team."

"Who is 'we'?"

He huffed and smiled as he smoothed his pant legs and sat in a chair next to the gurney. "We're going to start with you telling me about what you saw in Japan, then in Heidelberg, and then in Tabas, where it all began. Now who authorized your mission in Yokkaichi?"

"Why don't you tell me who the fuck you are," I said. I couldn't imagine too many people that had the authorizations, clearances, and contacts that I did, though I was sure they existed. "But first, unstrap me from this gurney."

"You're not leaving the gurney, General, until you answer my questions."

He sat patiently, waiting.

"I doubt you're cleared to know who authorizes me to take a piss," I said. "Get me out of here."

"I'm sure it is uncomfortable for you to not be in control—we've heard this about you—but you either trust me or it's going to be a difficult road for you, I'm afraid."

"What are you talking about?" I was incredulous. "I just got wounded on a mission of the highest importance to national security. Why are you treating me like the enemy?"

The penny dropped into the cone of my mind and began circling around slowly toward the center.

Why are you treating me like the enemy?

I always operated by the principle of Occam's razor, the simplest explanation being true, which in this case meant that if they were treating me like a prisoner, then they most certainly *viewed* me as one.

But why? I wondered. What had I done to deserve this type of confinement and questioning? I reviewed the pieces of my shattered memory as best I could. Japan, Germany, Iran, other missions. Nothing seemed to resonate. All of it was executed with professionalism and as much precision as humanly possible.

Iranian helicopters chased us from Yazd Province, but casualties were minimal, and it had never been mentioned in the news. In Heidelberg, we killed four guards outside and had some scrapes inside but found a computer and confirmed Parizad's location. In Yokkaichi, well, everything went to shit when we were in the basement. I was unsure if we retrieved anything of value, but I sure wasn't going to reveal anything to this stranger, who may or may not be CIA.

"I'll ask you again: What happened in Japan?" the man said.

"Let's start with my questions. I can do this all day. I'm the one who has been locked down here. Haven't you read anything about prisoners? They have all the time in the world," I said.

In Afghanistan, Iraq, and Syria, I had interacted with more than my fair share of detainees—enemy prisoners of war—captured on the battlefield. Once they knew they were locked down, they tried to escape, settled in for the long haul, or did both.

"What makes you think you're a prisoner?" he asked.

I got the impression he might be a psychiatrist of some type. He kept asking questions in a patient and practiced manner with the underlying threat of harm just beneath the surface. My protestations were BBs bouncing off a tank. He didn't care. He had an objective in mind and multiple strategies to achieve his desired outcome. On the other hand, I had little reliable information other than what my drug-induced mind could absorb. The gurney to which I was still strapped. The isolated room. The guards. The binds across my legs and arms.

I recalled when we had captured Abu al-Ghazni, a Haqqani affiliate in Afghanistan. He had been wounded in the kill/capture mission, and we had secured him in almost precisely the same fashion as I was bound.

"Well, I'm strapped to this gurney, that door is locked, and there are two armed goons on the outside guarding the door."

"Is that what you think? They're guarding the door?"

"Why don't you tell me, Doc?"

"Do you believe I'm a doctor?"

I changed my mind. "With all these questions, I think you're probably just some jerk-off sent in here to fuck with me."

The arrogant smirk returned, as if he were a tolerant parent enduring a petulant child's tantrum. Granted, these emotionally driven outbursts were not my typical style. While entirely reasonable, I was more prone to retreat inward and silently outmaneuver whoever this might be. The thoughts and memories came fluttering to my consciousness like a flock of sparrows from a barn, darting in every direction. Hobart, Van Dreeves, McCool, the Beast, Japan, Germany, Iran, al-Baghdadi . . . and Melissa.

"Melissa," I whispered.

Her face hovered in front of me as I willed myself to retreat inward, riddled with pain. At her graveside I had been stoic, strong for my children and those that loved her. While Reagan and Brad had wept in my chest with my arms around them, I'd stood there like the rock that they had needed. A tear never found its way onto my face. The pain was swallowed inside my soul, now an underground lake of sorrow and guilt.

But now, in front of this nameless man with no title, I felt tears stream across my cheeks.

"Melissa," I whispered again. "I'm so sorry."

The image of her being interrogated by Parizad flittered through my mind, one of the darting sparrows from the barn. What had happened? How?

"Tell me about Melissa," the man said quickly, sensing an opening, I presumed.

I turned my head away. I would rather share state secrets with this man than divulge the sorrow and guilt I felt for Melissa to him.

"Fuck you," I said instead.

"Why are you sorry?"

"Because I'm in here with you and not with her," I unwittingly said. I was off my game. Something had unhinged my normal thought process. For a brief second, I'd thought a snarky reply actually made sense. A moment later, I realized it came off as petulant.

He seized the opportunity.

"You'd rather be dead? Your wife is dead, and you'd rather be with her, correct?"

I turned and looked at him. "Yes."

"Is there anyone else you want to kill other than yourself?"

It was a bold leap to go from assessing that I wanted an afterlife with my wife to believing I wanted to kill someone, even myself, but it gave me insight into what he was thinking. I could see the chart now: Suicidal ideations, possibly homicidal.

When I least expected it, Melissa's face hovered in my mind, penetrating through the swarm of sparrows—no, becoming the swarm, the whole of my existence, all the memories captured in one place. This flock formed into Melissa's loving face. Her soft smile with the barely discernable dimple. Radiant green eyes. Smooth skin. Wisps of reddish-brown hair over her forehead. She did what she always did. She gathered the scattered, harrowing memories and absorbed them as if she were a black hole, her love capable of devouring evil and producing good.

Good wins.

I felt for my watch by shaking my left wrist. It was somehow still present. If my watch was still there, my combat boots might also still be. I twisted my ankles and felt them covered by something, not risking a glance.

Melissa hovered in my mind and spoke to me as only she could.

"Garrett, haven't you got the patience to let this man feel important so he'll leave sooner?"

"Yes," I whispered.

"Good. Then close your eyes and your mouth and wait him out. He's not got your best intentions in mind, that's clear. Remember that good winning requires skill and some luck, it doesn't just happen. There's too much evil in the world. And quit your crying. I know you love me and miss me."

"Who else would you like to harm?" the man asked.

Like that, the image of Melissa shattered into a million pieces in my mind, but her message poured into me like molten steel. I understood what she was saying, and this moment, however powerful, made me miss her much more tangibly. I did as she directed, though, and closed my eyes as I turned my head away.

Sometime after I did so, I heard the chair scrape backward, the door open, and a few mumbles before the door closed. The man I had presumed to be a psychiatrist had left. I had spent an entire adult lifetime trying to figure out what our nation's enemies were attempting to do to our country, our allies, or my soldiers. Part of that assessment included a belief that, for the most part, my government was one of the good guys, an unwieldy if not supportive bureaucracy. Now it was time for me to reassess that assumption, as any good commander should do, especially given the likelihood the shrink was an unspoken member of the U.S. government.

As always, my thought revolved around my mission and my family. I still had information about potential attacks on our country that someone needed to hear, and I personally needed to resolve Parizad's interrogation of Melissa.

With those two guideposts, I began to consider whom I could trust. Certainly not the man who was just in here questioning me as if I were a prisoner. My list included my team, Admiral Rountree, and my children—though they could be obstinate, they were loyal. I had some friends, but working through this short list in my mind made me wonder about friendships and relationships in general. I had been a gentleman to most everyone I'd ever met, prioritized my time for my country and my family, and naturally interacted with the vast social network created by Melissa, but all of that, *all* of it, amounted to exactly ten people I could trust. Notably not on the list were either of my parents. I trusted my mother to an extent, but I couldn't trust her to handle the situation I was potentially facing. Her meddling in my career, attempting to "improve upon" my assignments always resulted in embarrassing back-channel calls that required me to politely urge her to stand down her well-intentioned efforts. Mom and Dad were living in Pinehurst now, where my father, retired lieutenant general Garrett Sinclair II, played golf at Carolina Country Club every day with all the other retired generals in the area. While I had reached the same rank as my father, my endeavors as a special operations soldier had been too unconventional for him. He tolerated my path but was clear that his more conventional route to flag officer was superior.

My list assembled in my mind—my two kids, six teammates, Admiral Tom Rountree, and Israeli spy Ben David—I then had to determine a path out of my current predicament. I had missions to accomplish. The straps across my arms, chest, and legs were tight, and I suspected that any effort to wriggle free, other than being pointless, would be recorded by cameras that had to be monitoring the place. Several years ago, Reagan had been all agog about a televised talent show where a magician who was bound and dumped into a vat of hot oil, had been shot out of a cannon and landed in a pool of water, where he came free of his binds before drowning.

If that guy could do it, I could. Of course, that was a made-for-television production not involving the CIA or FBI, so I figured my chances were better given the government's penchant for lowest-bidder materials.

There was a needle poking into my arm, which I assumed was an intravenous feeding tube. I had no concept for how long I had been without solid food. My best guess was between twenty-four and forty-eight hours. I felt fatigued but not weak. Tired but not exhausted. The morphine, or whatever painkiller I was on, was probably catching me up on sleep I'd missed over the last twenty years of nonstop combat.

"Guard!" I shouted. After a few more shouts, the guard opened the door and looked in.

"Sir?"

He was a different guy from the previous two. Short and stocky, he looked like a college wrestler. His hair was buzzed on the sides into a Ranger haircut, which gave me some optimism that he was prior military and may have a sympathetic bent toward my predicament, whatever it may be, precisely.

"I haven't eaten for some time," I said. "Is there any way to get some chow?"

He looked at the hall and then at me before stepping in and closing the door. As he walked the ten paces toward me, he glanced at the top right-hand corner behind me, which meant the camera was up there. He set the appropriate stoicism on his face and leaned into me.

"I'm not here to feed you, General," he said.

As he hovered over me, I caught a scent of soap and laundry detergent. His clothes were freshly cleaned. He'd come for the next shift, so I would be seeing him for the next eight to twelve hours, I figured.

"I know that. What's your name, soldier?"

"Sergeant Carson, sir—wait a minute. How'd you know?"

He didn't seem pissed off, thankfully. Guard duty sucked no matter who you were guarding or for how long. It was typically a static and universally despised mission. I thought of Corporal Boone from the Eighty-Second Airborne guarding the FBI trailer at FOB Farah in Afghanistan.

"You don't look like those other tools. Military haircut and bearing are different. I was in Farah a few days ago and ran into Corporal Boone from the Eighty-Second. They'd given him guard duty on the FBI compound. He was enjoying it about as much as you are," I said. "Know him?"

"It's a big army, sir. I'm Rangers. He's Eighty-Second. Two different worlds."

"Good to meet you, Ranger Carson."

He pressed a button on the side of the gurney, causing it to lift past forty-five degrees.

"More comfortable?" he asked.

"Yes, thank you. If you're Rangers, then you're JSOC. My command."

He nodded. "Roger that," he said.

"Why do they have Rangers guarding this place, wherever we are?"

"Figured you'd know, being the boss man and all. I'm just a sergeant."

"Just a sergeant? You're a god to your men," I said.

"Well, I did save Admiral Rountree and his Navy SEALs one time," he said, leaning forward over the rail of the gurney. He slipped something in my right hand. I did the geometry in my head. The camera in the corner was blocked because he raised my bed. Whoever was watching might suspect something, but they certainly wouldn't be able to see whatever he put in my hand. It might have been a key or a cyanide pill, though I wasn't sure why the second thought crossed my mind.

You'd rather be dead, is that correct?

I wasn't suicidal. I could long for my wife and yearn for the day we are reunited without wanting to slit my wrists, a point the shrink seemed to have missed.

"Did the good admiral say thank you?" I asked.

Carson chuckled. "Rountree is as hard as woodpecker lips. All he knows about is moving on to the next thing. All kind of shit going down soon, and I'm hoping to be out of here, ASAP, if you understand what I'm saying."

I nodded as his hand rested on the gurney near my right hand, which was strapped with leather binding as if I were a psych patient, which maybe I was.

"Yeah, me, too. Doubtful that they'll be letting me out anytime soon," I said.

"No. I expect not." He paused. "Listen, I'll see what I can do about your food. Might be an MRE."

I laughed. "I'd devour an MRE right now."

"That hard up, huh? Okay, I'll get right on it."

He turned to leave as the shrink and the two goons came barreling into the room.

"What is going on in here?" the shrink shouted at Sergeant Carson.

"The general asked for some chow. I told him I'd see what I could do. He hasn't eaten in days," Carson said.

Days. Had I been in here days?

Iranian submarines floating around the ocean practically undetectable. A new mind control gas called Demon Rain. A deeply divided country. Inauguration. Super Bowl. So many high-visibility events on the calendar, though with social media today, everything every day was high visibility, one of the reasons that the general population had been desensitized to actual threats. Daily outrage wore down the spirit like water on a stone.

"You are to guard the door! Nothing more, nothing less," the shrink said, poking his finger in the chest of Carson.

"Understand, sir. My bad," Carson said. "He tricked me using his general's voice."

I didn't mind him throwing me under the bus. My guess was that Carson was perfectly capable of holding his own, but he wanted to present a less confident image to the men who had just barreled in.

"The audio wasn't working. Did you turn that off?"

Carson shrugged. "I wouldn't know how."

That wasn't a no.

"Get out of here," the shrink said. "You two, back on guard."

"Let the jarhead do it," one of the two big guys said.

"Not a fucking marine," Carson shot back, a hint of anger in his voice, interservice rivalries being what they were.

"Do as I say," the shrink directed.

One of the universal truths in the military, CIA, and FBI was that professional positions like doctors, lawyers, and clergy were always part of the team but didn't really hold much sway over the operational personnel unless they had been placed in operational roles. The shrink, then, probably wasn't a shrink. Maybe he had read a book about it, but in my four decades of service, I had never seen a doctor boss around two operators, especially armed ones, with the heft of these two thugs. Which led me to wonder whether this was the CIA or some other entity altogether.

The door closed, and from what little I could see through the wire-mesh window, one of the big guys stayed behind while it looked like the others walked to the left. I unclenched my fist and removed it from beneath the covers. As I slid my arm along the sheet, I had more room to maneuver than I'd expected.

Ranger Carson had done me a solid by discreetly cutting the leather strap securing my wrist. I glanced down, cognizant that the cameras and sound were now most likely operational again. The camera, though, I imagined, was one of those wide field-of-view home security things looking more for large movements than subtle shifts in my body position. My left hand was still restrained. Carson had done what he could, leaving the rest up to me.

He had slid into my hand a seat belt cutter that had become an essential part of every soldier's equipment kit after Parizad's predecessor, Soleimani, and others had begun using the lethal EFPs, which were so debilitating, each blast left soldiers inside burning vehicles with melting seat belt fasteners. Our troops had been literally locked in the burning Humvees, and the only solution was to create a device that could safely cut a seat belt without injuring the trapped soldier.

I slowly slid my right hand out of the cut leather strap and lifted the sheet with the back tips of my fingers, crawling my hand over both of my legs, and then placing the opening of the plastic-encased blade on the leather. The device was made to be yanked briskly across the seat belt, but my governing principle here was to avoid detection by the camera. I felt the blade bite into the supple strap. Over the next several minutes, I worked it back and forth, making millimeters of progress with each subtle move of my hand.

The door opened, and two guards stood outside the open passageway. "What are you doing?"

I looked at the guard, who had turned around to answer the question asked of him by the shorter of the two men.

"Video's out still. Just checking the camera," the taller guard said.

"We're not supposed to be in there, man."

"Duh. The camera's broke, dick. Who's going to know?"

I quickly slid my hand into the cut leather strap. I couldn't get it to fit perfectly because it required another hand to make the two leather pieces appear seamless, but it would have to do.

The two men talked for a minute outside the door, but the taller guard kept the heel of his foot in the door. Not wanting to waste time as they argued about the broken camera, I slid my right hand underneath the sheets and ripped down on the seat belt cutter, leaned forward and cut the straps on my legs, removed the IV from my arm—all as quietly as possible—slid out of the bed, felt weak in my knees but didn't buckle, and closed the distance to the back of the man with his heel in the door. My head swam with the morphine, but I powered through the effect of the drugs.

During their first visit with the shrink, I'd noticed the tall guard carried a pistol beneath his coat and one on his hip, specifically a Glock 19 with a magazine in the well. My guess was that he had a round chambered; most law enforcement personnel did, but politically correct culture had infiltrated all government agencies, and it was anyone's guess what agency, if any, these people worked for. For all I knew, I was the captive of a rogue band of government contractors.

The advantage to being in a closed room with only a small window was that the tall man's body blocked the only line of sight inside. He began to pull back from his now-whispering conversation, pushing back on the door with his elbow and creating a wedge between the door and his body.

The gun was right there in a clip-on holster.

My movements from this point forward had to be precise. I clenched my fist and released, keeping the blood pumping through my arms. He was less than two feet from me. I reached into the holster and snatched the weapon out. Metal scraped on plastic as the man jerked back and turned, but his coat snagged on the door handle. He stared at me for a brief second until I hammered the butt of the pistol into his forehead. A second blow sent him crumbling to the floor, serving a useful purpose as a doorstop.

I had the pistol in the face of the shorter guard, who was fumbling for his weapon.

"I'm two seconds from pulling this trigger," I said.

He raised his hands slowly, discretion being the better part of valor and all. Because he could escape laterally down either hallway, I stepped closer to him, wedged my back into the door, and pushed it backward to create more of an opening for him to pass through.

"Step over your buddy and drag him to the far corner," I said.

He kept his hands up, put his chest out, and kept his back to the opposite side of the doorjamb as he scooted through maybe three feet from me. He got a healthy look at my steady aim and the black bore of the pistol.

He moved on me quickly. I dropped the hammer of the pistol, which, if it had been loaded, would have drilled a 9 mm bullet through his forehead. However, political correctness—or maybe he wasn't a gun guy— left the chamber empty. I parried his awkward lunge as he stumbled over his unconscious taller partner, providing me an opening to jack him across the nose with the butt of the Glock. Blood sprayed everywhere, and the wall looked like a modern artist had thrown red paint at a canvas. He tripped to one knee, a red stream pouring from his nose.

"Motherfucker," he muttered.

I had been having success with the pistol, so instead of kicking him in the teeth, which I was perfectly poised to do but was unsure of my leg strength, I hammered the lower back of his skull, a notoriously perfect spot to kill or knock a man unconscious. He fell across the taller man already on the floor, which created a predicament for me. I had been counting on one man carrying the other while I propped the door, as I was quite certain it locked when closed. There was no keyhole on the inside of the door, so I removed the shoe of the top man, a basic leather Bass toe cap that needed shining, and used it to prop the door as I dragged the two men completely inside the cell, which was how I viewed the room now. I ensured they were tucked out of line of sight of the window behind the gurney and in the dead space of the camera, if that should ever come back on. Then I rumpled the sheets of the gurney. With the back jacked up, I hoped it would take a few seconds to recognize that I wasn't there.

A few seconds could make all the difference in the world.

I was still dressed in my boots, black cargo pants, and black long-sleeve shirt, but my outer tactical vest had been removed. I smelled like dry sweat, and my mouth tasted like the tall guy's shoe smelled. I scoured each man for smartphones and weapons, resulting in one iPhone and one Android, two knives, and a second Glock 19. I unlocked both phones with the thumbs of each man, quickly went to the auto-lock feature of each—a skill we had honed over the past twenty years of raiding terrorist hideouts—and hit Never on each one, which would burn more battery but ensure each one remained unlocked unless I got stupid and pressed the Screen Off button on the side.

I also found two sets of keys and car fobs, which could be useful. I stuffed their wallets in my left cargo pocket, put the phones in my right one, and checked the magazines of all three pistols: full. I jacked a round into each chamber and put one pistol in my left pocket while carrying the other in my right hand.

I kicked the guard's shoe out of the door and wedged my back against it as I peered around the corner in each direction. The hallway to the left was longer than to the right. Thankfully, both directions were vacant. There were two closed doors to the left and what looked like an exit door to the right. I wondered about Hobart and the rest of my team. My first duty was to them, so I tested the keys in the lock while I still had cover, found the right one on the fourth try, and then pulled the door shut. The lock clicked as I moved into the hallway. I tested the doorknob, and it was locked.

Moving to my left, I tried the key on the next room's door, and it worked. Opening it slowly, I saw a similar arrangement, but the room was vacant. Realizing that the hallway and each room probably had cameras, I moved swiftly to the next room and found the same setup. Gurney, bed, camera, but empty. Stepping into the hallway, I stopped. Something caught in the back of my mind. I looked back into the room and stared. Two chairs. Cinder-block wall. Dim light. A small pattern on the wall— like writing that had been painted over.

I couldn't recall what it was that was bothering me or why it was important, so I closed the door and continued to the last room, which was different from all the others.

It was vacant but had a table with four chairs on either side, two iPad tablets propped up on collapsible keyboards, assorted papers, and a coat-rack. There were two long winter coats, a watch cap, a tweed flat cap, and a scarf. I snagged the longer of the two coats, the beanie, and the scarf. Each of the iPads had portable USB ports with flash drives. I snatched each of the portable drives and pocketed them as I shrugged the coat over my shoulder. I looked at the iPad screens—both warning me that I had improperly removed the flash drives—and took the one with the video surveillance camera feeds, all of which were blanked out. I checked the Wi-Fi indicator at the top ribbon and saw it had an exclamation mark through it. I pocketed both on the hopes that one contained archived video feed of exactly who had come and gone. My pockets laden with a trove of intelligence and weaponry, I redistributed my haul in the large wool coat's pockets, both interior and exterior. Lastly, there was a six-pack of orange Gatorade bottles on the table, so I snatched two from the plastic rings and stuffed them in my pockets while guzzling a third on the spot as I peered into the hallway.

The people that had come into my room had seemed to exit to the left. I walked the remaining twenty meters to the door, which had a wire-mesh window and a standard crash bar running horizontally across its length like an auditorium exit that typically declared, "Alarm Will Sound."

No such sign existed here, yet there was no guarantee that neither alarms nor sounds would be activated if I pushed on the bar, if they hadn't already been. Through the mesh screen, I saw a concrete pad and stairwell that led upward. The entire setup reminded me of a school or abandoned public building of some type. Even where I had been placed was the size of a classroom. Everything seemed familiar while simultaneously unnerving. I struggled to reconcile the competing emotions, and when I failed, I wrote them off to the drugs. But still, something nagged at the back of my mind.

I didn't have time to consider the matter anymore, because as I pushed on the bar, an alarm clanged loudly above my head. It was an old-style round metal disc with a striking mechanism inside. Being so close to it, the high-pitched pinging pierced my eardrums.

I bolted through the door.

Sunlight. The sun was low in the sky to my left, southwest. The air was damp and heavy. A creek babbled somewhere not too far away. The gunmetal sky was foreboding, and the temperature was slightly above freezing.

There was a parking lot to my right. A wooded area sloped down to my left. Another building straight ahead was connected to the one I was exiting by a corrugated metal overhead cover and a cracking concrete sidewalk. Definitely an old elementary school.

There were two cars in the parking lot. I fumbled with the keys and pressed the button on the Toyota RAV4. It beeped twice, and the lights flashed on and off.

The *This is too easy* warning began to flash in the back of my mind— who was Carson, and where had he come from?—but I countered it by convincing myself to seize the opportunity and to go with the momentum. Sprinting to the mini SUV, I did a cursory check under the wheel wells for tracking devices, found none, slid into the driver's seat, and pushed the Start button. I pulled away from the parking lot and studied the building.

There was yellow tape all around it with some chain-link fencing that appeared to be in mid-construction. The building was single story with a flat roof and red bricks.

In the opposite direction about a mile away there was a water tower and a cluster of buildings. A field—almost like a pasture—separated me from what looked like a village.

In the distance, two police cars began to race toward the building with lights flashing. I turned out of the parking lot in the opposite direction, casting a glance back at the sign fronting the building.

FORT DETRICK CHEMICAL TEST FACILITY

16

AS I WAS TRYING to figure out how I had gotten to Fort Detrick and, more importantly, why I had been there, the forensic data showed Dariush Parizad was traveling first class to Princess Juliana International Airport in Saint Martin and then to Inagua International Airport on the Bahamanian island of Great Inagua. By definition, practically every flight to this southernmost island of the Bahamas, juxtaposed between Cuba and Haiti, was international.

The runway had been hardened in 1994 when the United States was preparing to invade Haiti. The U.S. Army had over fifty Black Hawk and Apache helicopters that had self-deployed from Homestead Air Reserve Base to Great Inagua, the most remote and uninhabited island of the Bahamas, and were ready to pick up the three thousand paratroopers that were jumping into Port-au-Prince's airport and an offset drop zone.

Today, Great Inagua was still a sleepy hollow, but the airfield contributed to a small and growing wildlife adventure industry. Fly fishing, hiking, bird-watching, and treasure hunting were the main attractions on this seashell-encrusted bump in the ocean floor.

Another attraction was that it was off the radar for almost every customs official and a perfect place for Parizad to fly under an assumed name—Raj Kameen—who claimed to be a treasure hunter. Ever since the Spanish galleon *Infanta* and its $20 billion in gold and silver had been discovered by treasure hunters off the coast of Great Inagua three years before, the small island's popularity had been increasing.

Parizad spent a day diving through a local service, using a captain named George Hamilton, who incuriously read mystery novels while Parizad was exploring the reefs. After the dive, Hamilton didn't notice that a doppelgänger had boarded instead of Parizad himself, who had swum a half mile to a waiting forty-two-foot Hatteras deep-sea-fishing vessel. The doppelgänger was an Immortal cell team member who had infiltrated to Orlando seven years ago. His appearance reasonably passed for Parizad, and the two men swapped boats as a method of infiltration for Parizad to enter the United States undetected.

Under Soleimani's tutelage, Parizad had engineered the infiltration of Immortal teams into the United States, mainly through Venezuela and Central America. There were seventeen Iranians who had been living in America for over three years, all in preparation for a time when they would be activated. They owned homes and had jobs, even though special bank accounts had been established for them to maintain a reasonable lifestyle.

Parizad had chosen the name *Immortal* based upon the nickname the Greeks had given the heroic Persian fighters who had helped Darius I conquer India in 520 B.C.

The underwater tap in and tap out went smoothly. The boat had been chartered out of Miami, and so there was no suspicion when it came back on its regularly scheduled time at 5:00 p.m. the following day from its departure. Safely in Miami, a man named Arshad picked Parizad up from the Dinner Key Marina and drove him to an Iranian safe house in the Olympia Heights neighborhood west of Miami.

The house was a single-story, four-bedroom rambler with beige stucco and a white picket fence that framed the entire yard, including the drive-way. Houses were modest, yet in the $300,000–$400,000 range. It was a perfect place to blend in. Arshad owned a bakery and small farm five miles away. The farm was twenty acres, sporting a thriving mix of toma-toes, oranges, broccoli, and strawberries. Monthly, the urban dwellers of Miami made a pilgrimage to Arshad Farms, where they picked whatever was in season.

The beginning of Soleimani's plan to infiltrate the United States, Ar-shad had been in the country for twelve years. He had arrived with a bank account flush with a never-ending supply of $8,999 deposits and a starting balance of $950,000, which allowed him to buy the land next to the Everglades and the house, both when the prices were half their value of today's.

Arshad was forty years old, a man of medium height with thick black hair, a dark complexion, and black eyes. His hands were nicked and calloused from farming. His arms and chest were muscled, and he was physically fit. He had been in the United States long enough to establish citizenship, which allowed him to purchase any number of AR-15s and Sig M400s, which were M4 knockoffs. The back room of the house was an armory, filled with assault rifles, pistols, and ammunition. Parizad didn't believe he would need any of the weapons—someone else was tasked with doing his bidding—but it never hurt to be armed and ready to go.

In the second bedroom was a collection of small, lightweight drones. There was an assortment of DJI and ARRIS drones uniformly lined up.

"I trust your crops are doing well?" Parizad asked.

"Business is thriving," Arshad replied.

"Good. We cannot have any disruptions in your services."

"In January, all we have are broccoli and cabbage for picking and har-vest," Arshad said.

"And the bakery?"

"My staff is on top of everything, but I will continue my routine."

"My car?" Parizad asked.

"Your car is the gray Buick Enclave. I've put less than two hundred miles on it. The plates are registered to me. No tickets."

"I would prefer your name not be involved."

"Likewise, but there is no option without raising suspicion. If I get a friend to do it, that is someone I have to kill. If I use a cutout name and identification, it's possible that could be uncovered. Once the mission is complete, we can see what the blowback is, if any. I can handle it. It is important you obey the speed limits and traffic regulations. Here is your phone, also registered to me. Your Apple ID and password are typed into the notes function. Memorize it and delete it. I've placed a backup battery on it for you. It works. I've been using it for about a week to establish a pattern of use. Helps with blending in. I've paired the Bluetooth with the Buick. On the back of the phone is a pouch with your driver's license, which is your picture on my information. As you instructed, I have kept my Instagram and Facebook accounts family oriented, showing neighborhood parties and my businesses. The app is active on this phone. Same username and password. The Immortal teams check their accounts every day, awaiting your word."

"I have become you," Parizad said. "And you will suffer the wrath of the aftermath. That was not my intention."

"Yes, but I knew that when I accepted this assignment ten years ago. It is no matter. The events of the last year have convinced me now more than ever that our time is now. I am prepared for whatever comes next." Arshad motioned toward the arms room.

Parizad nodded, took the keys, and loaded what he needed into the Buick, which required him to lay the back seat flat to carry everything required for the mission. He laid a blanket over the equipment and backed out of the driveway as Arshad held the white picket fence open for him.

As he shifted into drive, he buzzed down the window and said, "Be ready when I call you."

"I will," Arshad said.

Before he reached I-95, the smartphone chirped with a call from Arshad. "I've just received a message that Sinclair has escaped."

AS PARIZAD WAS BEARING down on the greater Washington, D.C., area, I sped away in the RAV4, wondering what the hell I was doing at Fort Detrick, Maryland, home of the U.S. Army Chemical Corps and, I suspected, still a few deep black CIA drug experimentation operations.

The GPS steered me toward a gate, which of course was welded shut and had concrete dragon's teeth guarding both sides as if this were the Maginot Line. For my purposes, it might as well have been. The gate appeared not to have been used in years. With the sirens growing louder, I backed up, spun around, and pursued a two-track dirt road that dipped north into the woods. Many bases cordoned off areas for hunting, and this had the feel of a protected area. An unreadable brown sign was on the right as the road dropped into a tunnel of trees.

The RAV4 bounced through a stream, nearly bottomed out on the rocks, and then climbed up the far bank where the two-track ended at a chain-link fence. This was not a hunting area, rather a green buffer between the main base and the free world. I shifted the RAV4 into low and spun the wheels against the bank until they caught firm terrain and rifled me through the gate, metal, glass, and fiberglass all crunching and squealing.

I popped out into the backyard of a two-story house with a perfectly manicured fescue lawn. The RAV4 tires made it less perfect as the wheels spun through the damp turf. I angled the car along the side of the house and noticed two kids barreling onto the back deck as I sped along the narrow side yard. They had their phones up in true twenty-first-century fashion, video recording an army general stealing a Toyota, without looking up from their smartphones.

Another thought scratched at the back of my mind as I spun the RAV4 onto the road and followed it to the left, which my sense of direction told me was west. Hooking a right onto a county highway out of the subdivision, there was a sign for a state park, which I followed. But I couldn't shake the image of the kids holding up their phones and how similar they were to the dead bodies in the cave and Heidelberg basement. We never got far enough into Yokkaichi to see if there were similar subjects there, but I was sure there must have been.

I sped through another tunnel of trees, their bare branches bony fingers reaching out for me in the diminishing light. There were enough mountain pines interspersed with the deciduous trees to provide at least concealment from any observers, such as drones, airplanes, or helicopters. By the time I reached the park, darkness had enveloped the road. The headlights pierced the blackness twenty meters to the front. I snapped the wheel and avoided a deer staring at me from the narrow shoulder.

I took a corner too tightly, and the SUV tilted onto two wheels before it slammed down and rattled the chassis. I slowed from eighty miles per hour to about sixty and pushed forward. The GPS showed the road looping in a semicircle from where I entered to a northern point about five miles away. I crested a hilltop and passed through a brief clearing, which showed two police cars with lights flashing at the bottom of the hill to the east, maybe three miles away near Fort Detrick. They could be responding to the stolen car, the break in the fence, or my absence. I doubted that they were coming after me directly. Whatever the CIA was holding me for had to be off the books, and they wouldn't risk going public with it by involving local cops or even military police.

I did, however, need to ditch this vehicle and find somewhere I could make a phone call using one of the two phones I had lifted from the guards. It would be risky, but I had already felt my pocket, and my Campbell burner was missing. As the north exit to the park approached, a helicopter chopped in the distance. It was impossible to tell whether it was a CIA or a Frederick Police Department helicopter. The blades slapping against the sky reminded me of McCool and the rest of my team. If there were ever a time I could use their support, it was now. Van Dreeves was critically wounded. I was unsure about Hobart. McCool had been the only teammate I had actually seen after returning from Japan.

Thinking of the arrow made me cognizant of the sharp pain in my left leg. Whoever had patched me up on the scene must have pulled the poison out. Van Dreeves carried a rattlesnake bite kit, and I briefly remembered seeing it flash in my periphery. My mind sparked white hot. I saw the distant white dot for a brief second and then refocused. Whatever mind control combination Parizad was concocting dealt with the optical nerve in some fashion. Having studied Gottlieb and his misguided efforts, I had little confidence that actual mind control was possible, other than in a debilitating sense.

The rotor blades grew louder, so I pulled the RAV4 off the road onto a minor two-track that led sharply downhill. The vehicle bounced and jarred every nerve in my body, my senses still on high alert. At the bottom of the hill was a clearing with a sign that read CUNNINGHAM FALLS STATE PARK.

I pulled the vehicle into a roundabout with trail markers heading in four different directions. On one side of the circular gravel drive was a steep, rocky drop-off protected by a split-rail fence, its designers likely trying to keep the area consistent with Frederick's Civil War roots. I checked the vehicle back seat and found a backpack, which I snared and emptied and stashed my cache of weapons, knives, phones, Gatorade, and electronics.

I slipped the backpack over my shoulder and spent less than a minute moving the split-rail fencing to create a gap, and then pushed the RAV4 over the ledge. Steel and glass shattered all the way down as it pinwheeled and dropped about a hundred meters, shrieks of metal piercing the night. It was hissing, and a faint whiff of burning electronics wafted in the air like toxic perfume.

I replaced the fence—nothing to see here—and took off in the other direction, breaking brush and following any path I could find, most of which were deer trails. I rambled across deadfall and beneath bare limbs. My cover and concealment ranged from negligible to significant as I followed the contours of the land to the northeast.

I paused at a large rocky area, maybe two miles from where I had pushed the vehicle over the ledge. I breathed heavily for a minute as I checked my surroundings. Rapid mists of condensation billowed in front of me. I hadn't realized how fast I had been moving. Everything was working, though. I was sweating beneath the long coat and watch cap. My senses were all firing perfectly. I took a deep breath, filling my nostrils with the crisp winter air that carried with it a combined scent of leaves decaying atop the moist earth and a fish odor. A stream babbled on the opposite side of the rock. Most likely a trout creek or river. Each tumble of water was a shrill tinkle like bells ringing. The waft of the helicopter circled a mile or two away. Police sirens cut through the night, ebbing and flowing along the major arteries a few miles in the distance.

The wind was light, rolling downhill to the east. The boulder to my right was shoulder high with a slight curvature that allowed me to huddle in the small cave behind it. I risked turning on the phone and flipped on the flashlight to make sure I wasn't about to cuddle with a black bear. While vacant, the spot was definitely an animal haven. The two-toed deer hoofprints crisscrossed among the much larger bear prints and what looked like some type of feline, maybe a bobcat.

I took my turn in the den and knelt as I opened the backpack. I stuffed a pistol in my pocket to defend against anyone who might be pursuing me on foot. I studied the two phones, one iPhone and one Android. The Android had 78 percent battery power, and the iPhone, whose flashlight I had been using, was already at 54 percent.

Some small animals rustled in the trees, their paws scraping loudly against the leaves. My hearing was acuter than I could ever remember. A bear roared in the distance; its baritone growl tumbled across the forest much the way a lion gave notice on the Serengeti. Knowing that bears might have the best sense of smell of all the animals, I wondered if my sweat would attract or deter. I quickly downed a bottle of Gatorade and put the empty in the backpack.

I reached down to tighten my laces, thinking about what my next moves might be. My priorities conflicted between finding out why Melissa had been talking to Parizad and warning the National Command Authority about what my team and I had seen. If the CIA was blacklisting me, we had to have uncovered their participation, either witting or unwitting, in the scheme. It would not be the first time the CIA knowingly had involved the United States in questionable activities and then attempted to make the issue go away with their extreme powers.

Importantly, I had key information about Parizad, who had been in both Germany and Japan. He was experimenting with a mind control drug or poison, or both, that he could deploy either on a specific target or in mass, as we had seen in Yazd, Heidelberg, and Yokkaichi. Their preparations seemed . . . far along. But to what end? I remained convinced that Parizad was a more strategic thinker than your garden-variety terrorist.

My hand scraped the outside of my right boot, reminding me that McCool had slid something in the pocket. While my fingers were frozen, I managed to rip the nearly seamless Velcro apart. There was a small plastic container with a SIM card snapped inside and a paper clip tucked next to it.

McCool's starter kit for communication. I imagined that she trusted that I would escape and find a phone. She was right so far. Perhaps she had sent Carson? I guessed that she wanted me to put the SIM card in the phone and call her.

I spent some time studying the notes function of both phones as the animal noises around me intensified. The focus was good for me, though. I was thinking logically, searching for anything that might indicate a four- or six-number pattern for unlocking the phones in the event that changing the SIM card shut it off. It was five minutes wasted.

I fumbled around with the paper clip and extracted the SIM card from the iPhone and placed McCool's chip inside.

Damn.

The phone powered off. I pressed ahead, regardless. After a minute, the phone rebooted, and after another minute, the lock screen appeared, showing a voice mail from a number I didn't recognize.

This could work as long as the number displayed was the one McCool wanted me to call. I dialed all ten digits displayed, my cold index finger starting to shake as I pressed the last few. My excitement got the best of me, though, because I had my rucksack open and the pistol in my pocket. Normally, I would be packed into one tight ball ready to respond, but I was too focused on the one task of pursuing this lifeline.

As I stared at the phone, an image of a smiling man walking toward me appeared. The background in the phone was as if I were looking through the camera. The trees. The black night. The crescent moon. I held the phone up, moving it back and forth, realizing that I was doing exactly the same thing as the cave people and Heidelberg subjects. The man was large and wearing a brown Carhartt coat. Though there was something slightly off about his movements, the man's smile was friendly as if he were about to say, "Hey, buddy, I'm here to help."

It took some willpower, but I closed my eyes and opened the phone app to press Dial on the missed call number.

As I did so, a man charged me from behind a large oak tree maybe ten meters away.

The phone rang once before it was answered.

As I was drawing my pistol, President-Elect Campbell said, "Garrett! Where are you?"

18

THE MAN CHOSE TO rush me, which was a mistake for him.

While I was confused, tired, hungry, and weak, Melissa's face replaced the image of the man who was now physically attacking me. She hovered in my mind, urging me forward, reminding me of my task and purpose. Melissa, as usual, would forever be the strength upon which I could rely to avoid peril.

My attacker's face was twisted into a vulpine snarl, and for a brief flash, I wondered if he was an animal, but the pistol in his hand removed all doubt. Wanting to avoid any type of gunshot that could alert others to my location, I leaped at him, and we collided in midair like two mountain rams locking horns. My movements weren't as fluid as I'd hoped. The duster was cumbersome, but I managed to pull his outstretched right arm and slide to my left, avoiding the bulk of his considerable mass. He tumbled headfirst into the large rock I had been using as cover. He scrabbled up from the fall as I kicked the pistol from his hand and landed a boot heel in his face, followed by the butt of a pistol to the back of his head.

He dropped flat, unconscious.

Where there was one, there were typically two. I immediately scanned in every direction. The man's erratic breathing prevented me from hearing much beyond my immediate space.

"Garrett!"

Someone was calling my name. Melissa? Was she my refuge and purpose? Of course, she always had been in life; why not in death?

"Garrett!"

The smartphone lay on the ground near the attacker's head. I remembered that a minute ago I had been calling President-Elect Kim Campbell.

I stepped away from the rock and inspected the tree behind which the man had been hiding and then walked the ten meters back to rummage through his clothes, finding a wallet, pistol, knife, and phone. I pocketed the first three and used his thumb to unlock the phone and repeated the process to keep the screen unlocked.

Only then did I kneel and lift the phone to my ear without looking at the screen and all the while keeping my eyes on the horizon, turning slowly in each cardinal direction.

"Yes?" I said.

"Garrett. What is going on? Where are you?"

"You tell me, Kim," I said. I dropped all pretense of respect.

While I didn't suspect Campbell had anything to do with my situation, I couldn't be too careful. A day out from inauguration, she would have been in position to influence my captivity.

"What do you mean?" she asked.

"I was taken to Fort Detrick and detained," I said. "I'm thinking such an action would have to be sanctioned at the highest levels."

"I have no idea what you're talking about, Garrett. I'm not president yet. We're friends," she said.

It was nearly midnight, and she had answered my call amid preparations for a historic inauguration.

"You're in all the briefings. You're president in thirty-six hours."

"But I'm not in charge. Is that why you're calling from a different phone?" she asked.

"Yes. I escaped," I said.

"You escaped? What are you talking about?"

"Why was Melissa interrogated by Dariush Parizad?" I asked.

"Garrett, are you okay?"

"I'm definitely not okay," I said. "I'm being chased by government goons, and I'm wondering about the status of my team. Melissa's dead and gone, and Parizad may have had something to do with it."

"We need to meet," she said.

"I don't think that's a good idea."

I continued to assess my surroundings by slowly turning in a circle. The man at my feet coughed and twitched. I kicked him in the head to help him sleep better.

"I'm the president-elect. You're a general. I can play that game if you want," she said.

"I'm too busy playing a different game, ma'am," I said.

"What game is that?"

"What did Melissa know? Why was she interrogated?"

"Melissa was my best friend. My roommate. She died of cancer, Garrett. I'm sorry. I know nothing about a meeting with Parizad—"

"She didn't *meet* with Parizad. She was in captivity. I saw the video," I growled. My voice was angrier than intended, and for a moment, I forgot I was speaking with the president-elect of the United States. Did Melissa know a secret that could have impacted this election?

"Garrett? The anger. I'm your friend, too. And it sounds like you may need all the friends you can get," she said.

I looked skyward, frustrated with myself for this unrecognizable emotion that had me treating her like an enemy. She was right.

"I'm sorry, Kim. I'm trying to figure out what's going on," I said.

"I can help. Where are you?"

"I'm not exactly sure. Somewhere near Fort Detrick. In the woods." I looked down at the unconscious man at my feet. "People are chasing me."

"Whatever for?" She sounded perplexed.

"What did Melissa know?" I asked.

The phone was silent for a second longer than it should have been. Her other responses were immediate reactions. Repeating the question had made her think.

"You're acting very strange, Garrett. I told you to call me if you needed help, and I'm glad you did. I'm going to send some people to get you to the hospital, where it seems you belong."

Had she done the same for Melissa? A governor has pull. Melissa was living in Fayetteville when she'd been admitted to Walter Reed.

I hung up, staring at the darkness, my mind reeling and replaying the events of Melissa's death. The "best oncologist" at Walter Reed. The "best staff" in the exclusive executive wing. While we hadn't known any of her health care staff prior to Melissa's diagnosis, we had been appreciative of their professionalism and service. We'd had no suspicions then, and until now, I had no reason to question anything about her cancer or death.

One thing I did know was that Melissa was dead. I'd kissed her and held her when I returned from the al-Baghdadi mission. She had still been in the hospital. I was an hour late. An hour to say goodbye. I hadn't asked for much in this life, but it seemed a sharp price to pay to have her stolen away from me before I could return. And now, I questioned the entire process. Had she even had cancer? Was there something she knew? She and Kim Campbell had been like sisters when they were roommates at Meredith College. They were going to tackle the world, separately and together. Their paths had veered, however, when the army moved us from base to base all over the world. We had served at Fort Bragg, North Carolina; Fort Benning, Georgia; Schofield Barracks, Hawaii;

and Fort Drum, New York. The constant shuffle wore on relationships, both within the family and among friendships. We had survived our one dreaded Pentagon tour.

Throughout our careers, though, there had only been one time when the subject of Melissa's relationship with Kim Campbell had come into question. Melissa had never been a big drinker in college, nor was she a prude. Kim had a reputation for going on the occasional binge, exploring the Raleigh, Durham, and Chapel Hill bars, depending on what mood she was in. Kim's childhood friend Lorie Wesson would sometimes join, though Melissa didn't care for her much. Melissa recounted for me one time when Kim had come back upset, eyes red from drugs or crying or both. She had plopped on the bed and passed out. The next day, they learned that Lorie had died in a drug overdose in an upscale home inside the Raleigh Beltline, home of the upper crust and not far from Meredith College. I'd never pressed Melissa on the matter. For one, I had been at West Point at the time. Second, I knew her well enough that if she had anything she wanted to share with me, she would, and if she didn't, that was okay, too.

While every couple wanted to believe that there were no secrets between them, that was a naive construct. I could not imagine a more trusting, loving relationship than ours, and I knew that we both harbored things we didn't want to share with each other, however short the list. In my case, my hidden secrets mostly revolved around combat deaths. Soldiers I had lost. Some I would discuss with her; others I just couldn't. I didn't want to expose her to the raw brutality and carnage of war. She was a tough woman, but she was also my girl. From a purely chivalrous place, I liked the idea—and so did she—that I could somehow shield her from the horrors of our chosen profession.

I utterly failed in that mission in the end, and it was probably the height of naivete to believe I could succeed. There was something important hidden here, within this stream of consciousness following hanging up on the president-elect, but I struggled to pin it down.

A groan from beneath the rock brought me back to the moment. My would-be assailant stirred on the ground. One thing I learned from combat was to never waste a good prisoner. I removed his belt and laced his ankles together and then used his boot laces to tie his hands behind his back. Using one of the Gatorade bottles, I splashed his face and slapped it until he pulled out of his boot-induced slumber.

"What the fuck?" he asked.

"That was my question," I said, kneeling in front of him. My back was to the rock, and I had positioned him about three feet in front of me. I rifled through his wallet and phone, avoiding looking at the screen. He was a private detective who carried a Veterans Administration card, which meant he was prior military service. Mike Denuncio. DENUNCIO PRIVATE SPY: FOR ALL YOUR PRYING NEEDS. Catchy.

Why was he following me, and more importantly, how had he found me so soon? The two thugs that I had disabled back at Fort Detrick might have worked with Denuncio. Maybe the CIA contracted the guards. I was mildly insulted by the thought. Denuncio was dressed in dungarees, a long-sleeve rugby shirt, a Carhartt jacket, and brown hiking boots. He was soft and overweight. His eyes carried no light, as I liked to say. There was no apparent wisdom in them. My guess was he was a low-level pawn, though he didn't appear that much younger than I was.

"Denuncio," I said. "Where did you serve?"

"Not talking to you, traitor," he said.

Traitor?

"You have me mistaken for someone else. But I have a few options here. We can have a civil conversation where you answer my questions, and then I release you into the wild, so to speak. I can apply my four decades of combat experience and many of the interrogation techniques I've learned—I believe they're called *enhanced*—or I can open some of the food in my rucksack and smear it on you and be on my way. I'd choose the bear over the bobcat, if you get the choice. Kill you quicker. So what will it be?"

With wide eyes, he registered his predicament.

"What do you want to know?"

I was glad this guy was out of the army. Caving this quickly to a disheveled general in the middle of the woods wouldn't portend well for his fellow soldiers if he fell into enemy hands.

"Good decision. First, who are you?"

"You've got my wallet," he said.

"Right. I do." I paused, waiting for him to answer.

"Mike Denuncio," he finally said, exasperated.

"Who hired you?"

He shook his head, his left cheek touching the dirt. "Okay, there's this guy. He comes around to my office every once in a while and gives me a job. I'm in Frederick, and I guess you were close."

"Who's the guy?"

"I don't know. He works on the fort. He gives me a job and pays me cash. Jobs are usually quick and easy."

The cash part was true. He had ten hundred-dollar bills in his wallet. Easy grand to bring in an old general, he must have thought.

"How's that working out for you?"

"Fuck you. I always hated generals," he said.

He knew who I was, which told me the "guy" had given him specific information.

"How did you know where to find me?" I asked, though I was almost positive that he was tracking one or both of the phones.

"The phones."

I nodded. "Where did you serve?" I wasn't trying to bond with him; rather, I was interested in any connections I might have previously had with him.

"Did my time. Military police. Germany, D.C., a couple of other places."

"Where in D.C.?"

He paused, and again, I knew what he was going to say.

"Fort Belvoir," he said.

Criminal Investigation Division, which was the army's premier law enforcement and detective service. I could see why Denuncio was washed out.

"No combat time?"

"They needed MPs at the home stations," he said.

"Yeah, we needed them in combat, too," I said. "What's the name of your contact? Where's he work?"

"He goes by Tom Brokaw, you know, the newscaster guy. I don't know his real name. Like I said, always pays cash, and jobs—until now—have always been easy."

"Such as?"

"He's had me watch some houses and report. Maybe follow some people and observe and report. That kind of thing."

"Did he ever have you transport anyone?"

"No. Nothing like that," he said. Denuncio had not been looking me in the eyes primarily because it was difficult for him to do so. Still, the tell was there. He was lying. "You're lying," I said. "All the goodwill you built up being forthright? Vanished. And I've got about a minute before the black helicopters come in here looking for me. So give me something useful, or I'm leaving you for the bears."

"You can't do that, man. I've told you everything I know."

"When were you at Fort Belvoir?"

"That was thirty years ago, man. Got nothing to do with anything," he said.

I stowed that useful piece of information away as I stood and scanned my surroundings. The sun would be rising in a couple of hours, and I needed to move. I flipped Denuncio over and removed the SIM card from the iPhone and restored it to McCool's nifty plastic protective sleeve, which I returned to my boot pouch. I smashed the Android I had used to call Campbell and tossed it into the woods, and I did the same to the iPhone. I still could use Denuncio's phone for the next few hours, so I disabled his tracking app and stuffed it in my pocket. Luckily, no ghosts appeared as I briefly looked at the screen to navigate my way through the device.

I put Denuncio's knife in his bound hands.

"Don't hurt yourself," I said.

I packed my rucksack tightly with Denuncio's additional weapon and another empty Gatorade bottle and took about fifty steps away to reacclimate my hearing, though Denuncio was shouting.

"Hey, motherfucker, you said you were going to let me go!"

"I lied," I whispered to myself. If he had any skill at all, he would be able to cut through the shoelaces in a minute.

I broke brush for another fifty meters and listened again. Two helicopters buzzed in the distance. I needed to get to the small town north of here, find a room using the money I just took from Denuncio, and think about what I had just learned.

The most intriguing piece of information to me was that Denuncio had been based at Fort Belvoir during the same time that CIA director Samantha Owens was there serving her finance officer tour of duty.

A coincidence?

Or a thirty-year connection between a young finance officer and a special investigator?

19

AS I WAS DISTANCING myself from Denuncio and the Catoctin forest near Frederick, what I didn't know then was that Dariush Parizad was
driving the speed limit on I-95 in North Carolina.

When he crossed the border of Virginia, he pressed ahead and crossed
the Rappahannock River, then the Potomac, and followed the signs to
I-70 and passed Frederick, where he exited the interstate and followed a
series of state and local roads to a five-hundred-acre cattle and corn farm
on the Maryland-Pennsylvania border.

Parizad rolled over the cattle grate and followed the gravel road up the
bucolic hills for another half mile until he crossed a bridge, climbed out
of a riverbed, and crested the plateau where the large stately mansion was
perched on the left and a quarter mile away two red barns and three silos
dominated another hill. He pulled into the open garage, having sent a
text that he was five minutes away.

His Immortal team appeared from the rear barn and greeted him. The
four-man team was led by his longtime associate, Mahmood, who had

infiltrated the United States through Canada two years before. Parizad hugged him and said, "My brother."

"My commander," Mahmood said.

Mahmood's charges stayed a respectful distance behind, allowing the two men a moment of privacy after so many years apart. After a few minutes, Mahmood turned to his men and introduced them. They were all competent and capable fighters, big men with a solitary focus of supporting their commander's plan. Parizad shook their hands and measured each man by looking him in the eyes and gauging his ferocity. He was pleased.

"The others will be here throughout the day and night," Mahmood said. "We have been tracking the communications of our host, who is on the way here to meet with you."

"The host violates so many protocols, but we must indulge to determine what he knows," Parizad said. "What do we believe he knows about our operation?"

"He believes I am the only one staying in the garage apartment. He has not seen the communications architecture, and he's curious about the pigs."

Parizad smiled. "The pigs are in the corral?"

"Yes, one hundred and fifty of the filthy animals."

Pigs were central to Parizad's plan because they shared pathology, physiology, body size, and anatomical relevance with humans. How pigs responded to specific biological or chemical pathogens and threats would predict how humans might respond.

"The captives?"

"In the basement. No one lives in the house. I go in once a day and rough them up, slide them some food and water, and check their medical condition. Weak, but alive."

Parizad nodded. "Excellent. I'll check on them after I deal with our host. Receive the incoming teams in the back barn, and prepare them for tonight and tomorrow."

"Yes, Commander."

Parizad walked around the forward barn and up to the mansion that dominated the hilltop. Catoctin Mountain rolled away to the north in gentle contours, merging with the Blue Ridge Mountains, all part of the greater Appalachians. The air was cold and damp, different from Iran, where it was warm and arid. There was nothing pleasing about this environment other than his mission. He waited impatiently as the black SUV drove slowly up the driveway.

"I'm taking a huge risk meeting you here," his host said after stepping from the vehicle. They walked inside the main house through a connecting breezeway between the home and the garage. They stood in a large family room with an atrium ceiling and a brick chimney crawling up the western wall. The fireplace was large enough for the tree trunks that were stacked against the hearth.

"The entire operation is a huge risk," Parizad said. "Here in the final hours, a face-to-face meeting is much better than anything that can be traced digitally or electronically."

"Even my presence here can be traced," his host said.

"I would think that your expertise would involve making sure that doesn't happen?"

"I've taken the necessary precautions. We've got five minutes. What do you have?"

"Sinclair has escaped," Parizad said.

"I know. There are people chasing him. Demon Rain injection makes him a threat to the country."

"Does he know our plan?" Parizad asked.

"The assumption is still that his wife told him."

"Well, we took care of *that* issue, anyway."

"Yes, I did. The kids may know. We might have to do something about that."

"You're calling the shots," Parizad said. It was actually a toss-up between Parizad and his host as to who was in charge. It was a fluid operation.

"Anything else? This was all about Sinclair?"

"No. I wanted to show you the plan," Parizad said, bluffing.

"No one wants to know," his host said. "As long as it is enough to do the trick."

"Fine. Another matter is the breach in operational security," Parizad said. "I trust we have no more of those?"

"No. We've tightened the circle and eliminated the leak."

"And General Sinclair?"

"He's handled, as well. No issues."

"No issues? He *escaped*."

"We've got him in our sights."

Parizad nodded, noted the security cameras throughout the home, and walked to the expansive back window that provided a west view of Catoctin Mountain.

"Okay, I have a lot of work to do," Parizad said. "If everything is back on track, then I think we're fine. Any questions for me?"

"What did you shoot Sinclair with?"

Parizad smiled and looked at his watch. "He's got about twenty-four hours before it kicks in."

"Then what?"

"Our tests have shown that he becomes quite homicidal with the right cue. He will need to be put down, you know, after," Parizad said.

"That's a big ask."

"The success of the mission will hinge on Sinclair responding to the drug and then us responding to him."

"The mission is still limited in scope, as discussed, correct?"

"So you want to know about the plan now?"

"No. Forget I asked that."

"Everything is as discussed for the past two years," Parizad said. "You give me access. I give you access. Mutual assured destruction applies to more than just nuclear weapons. We've developed a trust and bond over the years, correct?"

"Yes, of course."

Parizad walked his host to the door and watched the SUV drive away. Then he walked into the basement, where he opened the two cells that had been retrofitted into the large space, like saunas, but not as relaxing. Both held hostages huddled into the corners. They looked alive, which was good enough for him. He locked the door and walked up to the main floor, through the breezeway, and into the garage, where he opened the SUV hatch, unpacking the contents. He spent the next few hours monitoring Mahmood and his men as they assembled the remaining small commercial-grade quadcopters. Once that task was complete, he finished the setup of his command and control center in the four-room suite above the garage.

Parizad spent an hour erecting the monitors, plugging in cables, and aiming the satellite dish at the secret Shadow Commander reconnaissance and communications satellite that the Iranian Space Agency had discreetly punched into space last year. Named for Major General Qassem Soleimani, the satellite floated unencumbered in outer space, circling the globe in geosynchronous orbit waiting for today, the day when the Lion of Tabas would be on American soil to exact revenge for his father and his mentor, Qassem Soleimani, both killed by the American military. He would execute the sweeping plan that would force America to a tipping point of economic and psychological collapse.

He pressed a button, and the operational indicator turned green, showing a secure connection between his communications platform and the satellite, which gave him access to the entire Iranian network scattered throughout North America and beyond: sleeper cells, sympathizers, logistics networks, and even the submarines, five of which were steaming through the Pacific, Caribbean, and Atlantic Oceans.

To Parizad, though, Soleimani and the ayatollah had it wrong. Territorial conquest fueled by hatred of Israel and the United States was analog. True victory today was not even digital but IoT, AI, and machine learning. Google, Facebook, Twitter, YouTube, and thousands of other similar platforms all controlled the thoughts of hundreds of millions through smartphones, websites, and apps. People staring down at their phones as they walked on sidewalks and in the street were commonplace today. Information was malleable. A subtle omission here, a minor word change there, and suddenly, the meaning of something was altered. The anchor for factual data had lifted from the seafloor of truth. The old saying that the victors wrote history was no longer true. Everyone wrote history. Whichever mob could swarm the Wiki page, search engine, or social media platform would elevate that version in the rankings.

History and facts were now the domain of popularity. The footnotes required on Wiki were simply "news" articles that carried the version of the truth that best supported the desired position.

Parizad knew that warfare today still required physical and mental tenacity, but technology had added this ever-complex and evolving requirement of being able to visualize a multidomain attack. While the cyberdomain was critical to victory, it was the synchronization of all the levers of warfare that an asymmetric adversary had to apply to even hope to scratch the behemoth. Just as the chariot had changed warfare two thousand years ago, so had artificial intelligence and machine learning today. Whereas his namesake, Darius the Great, could stand on a hilltop and command his forces to victory, today, Parizad could sit in a loft with four computers and a satellite to launch the most asymmetric attack the world had ever witnessed.

Parizad was focused on the realities confronting him. The variables were plenty and risks enormous. The United States was as divided as it had been since the Civil War. Parizad saw the opportunity to attack on the heels of the coronavirus pandemic, to further weaken the U.S. economy and push it into a depression. His own form of sanctions.

Just like Google, Facebook, Instagram, and Twitter were listening to every conversation in every household around the world and presenting an advertisement for a new exercise regimen for back problems five minutes after a husband complained to his wife about his aching back, Parizad's legions of coders had developed the ultimate artificial intelligence.

Demon Rain opened the mind for manipulation while the Iranian deepfake application presented the subjects with a dopamine fix for the one thing they needed most, whatever the algorithms determined that to be at the moment. The application was able to collate the recorded conversations, search histories, and text messages to determine the precise fix at the exact time. If people needed hope, they were shown a messenger of optimism. If they craved evil, they were provided with a messenger of, or even a pathway to, death.

This was the end state of Gottlieb's research, Parizad realized. Gottlieb had opened the mind through LSD but had never been able to convert on the opportunity. With smartphones and applications, and a more potent form of hallucinogenic, Parizad had realized Gottlieb's dream of mass mind control.

To make matters worse, while Soleimani may have physically operated within the tight confines of Southwest Asia, he had the unfortunate foresight to put Parizad in charge of the sleeper cells, Parizad's New Immortals. Over the past ten years, Parizad had used Venezuela as a pivot point in the Western Hemisphere to move Immortal teams up through Central America and across the border into the United States.

The monitor in front of Parizad showed every Immortal asset scattered across the globe. Some were at the border in Mexico, but they were facilitators. Others were scattered across the Southwest and Midwest of the United States located at specific targets. Commanding was all about resourcing. He learned early that if he had the tools, he could accomplish anything, and so he had resourced his forces deployed throughout the country and world.

He retrieved Arshad's smartphone and placed his thumb on the Instagram app. Stored in the phone was a picture of the nondescript crossroads where Operation Eagle Claw had taken place in his home country. The Eshdeger Mountains abruptly poked into the pale blue sky in the background. Windswept desert was in the forefront, sagebrush dotting the tan landscape for miles. The brown adobe walls of Parizad's home were in the far distance.

He pressed on the upload function on the picture, added no filter, and typed in the words: The Lion Once Roamed This Desert.

20

AS PARIZAD WAS IN northern Maryland establishing communications for his forces, Secretary of State Kyle Estes, Secretary of Defense Jim Tharp, and CIA director Samantha Owens were all traveling by separate vehicles to a compound in Great Falls, Virginia, overlooking the Potomac River. General Fillmore had previously flown into Reagan National Airport, where he eschewed his CENTCOM driver and security team to secretly rent a car to conduct "personal business" for two days in the Washington, D.C., area.

Meanwhile, I was hunkered down in a roadside motel known for being packed during the autumn leaf season and anytime that Gettysburg, Pennsylvania, had a reenactment of the penultimate battle of the American Civil War. One day before the inauguration of Campbell, I was expecting all sorts of Secret Service activity searching for terrorist cells operating proximate to Washington, D.C. This was the first safe haven I could find, and I needed a few hours to consolidate, refine intelligence, and refuel before I physically shut down.

With neither of those events on tap in mid-January, the place was vacant, and the millennial behind the registration desk never removed the AirPods from his ears when I slid two hundred-dollar bills across the desk to pay for two nights plus a generous tip. He was lanky and thin, wearing a gray Shippensburg University sweatshirt with a hood hanging beneath his long brown hair.

"I'm Chad," he said, handing me an old-style key on an oblong key chain.

"I'm nobody. I'm not here," I said, sliding him another of Denuncio's hundred-dollar bills. It took him a moment to understand, but I saw the concept register in his innocent eyes.

"Like spy shit," he said. "Cool."

I walked away and used the key to enter the end room of the motel. It was farthest away from the road and nearest to the forest, which was thirty meters down the hill.

Two sagging full-size beds sat on either side of a single nightstand. A credenza with a semi-modern television was to my right as I squeezed through the narrow gap between the beds and the credenza. I checked the bathroom to make sure I was alone, which I was.

I dumped my haul on the bed nearest the bath and took inventory: a respectable HK VP9 from Denuncio plus an unlocked iPhone with 97 percent battery power, having apparently drained its outer battery sleeve; two Glock 19s from the guards at Fort Detrick; and one iPad with an assortment of flash drives and recharging cables. The iPad had 17 percent battery power, and I was reminded of today's modern soldier in combat, where we spent a significant amount of time ensuring battery resupply for all our equipment. If there was a single point of failure for today's networked army, it was battery power, which was why we trained the basics: hand-to-hand combat, close-quarters combat, and physical training. A sharp body made for a sharp mind, and the only recharge the physique needed was a minimum four hours of sleep a night, which I had not had, though to be fair, I had been drugged and knocked out for an indeterminate amount of time. I needed to charge my electronics to mine what little data I had at my disposal.

First, I took a quick shower and ran the water almost at full-throttle hot. I emptied the shampoo and body wash and scrubbed crevices that hadn't seen soap in days. I was weary and weak, needing sleep, but instead toweled off and pulled on the same cargo pants, shirt, socks, and boots I'd been wearing before. I pocketed the Glock 19, because I had fired it and knew it worked, pulled the watch cap and duster back on, and strode to the check-in office again.

"Hey, man," Chad said. His voice was high-pitched. He was maybe twenty years old and made me think of Reagan and Brad. He rocked forward in his chair, perhaps anticipating another payday. I pulled another hundred-dollar bill from Denuncio's wallet and said, "I'll buy that iPhone charger from you."

"Dude, it's yours," he said. He unplugged the white cord and adaptor from the wall socket and slid it across the worn check-in desk. He placed his hand on the hundred-dollar bill and said, "Are . . . are you still not here?"

"I was never here," I said. The look on my face must have been convincing.

"Okay, well, I just thought you should know I've got one reservation for tonight, so you know, if you're not here, that might be good to know."

"Put him at the other end of the hotel," I said.

"He's a she, but yeah, okay," he said. "I get it."

"Can you order some food and drinks, have it delivered here, and then call me?"

He looked at the hundred-dollar bill and said, "Out of my money?"

I began to tug the bill back. "Four hundred dollars of my money for two nights in a shitty room. You'll pocket no less than three hundred, so order me some chow. A pizza and you can eat half of it."

"Chow," the kid said.

"Food," I said. "Call me when it's here." I released the money and walked across the barren parking lot to my room. I plugged in the iPad, connected the recharging cable, and began reviewing the hard drive of the iPad and the contents of the flash drive.

After fifteen minutes of mindlessly reading files, I found my first hopeful sign. It was a PDF of a long handwritten list of names. The writing was in block letters, not cursive, and appeared masculine. I hit the document search function and typed in:

```
Melissa Sinclair
```

My heart leaped as the document moved to her highlighted name.

```
Sinclair, Melissa; Secret
```

I stared at the words, mulling their potential meaning in my mind. *Secret* was typically a classification, but the way it was written didn't seem to indicate a stratification of security clearance. Rather, it seemed to be a noun: Secret.

What secret? About President-Elect Campbell? If anyone knew any secret about Campbell, it would have been Melissa.

The words below read:

```
Admitted to National Cancer Institute / October 25
      LTG Sinclair / Syria / Al-Baghdadi
```

That date was two days before the al-Baghdadi mission. I had been told she'd been rushed to Walter Reed, but this information placed her at Fort Detrick, where the National Cancer Institute maintained a research campus. Two days before she died? Why? Was this a last-minute treatment regimen that was kept off the books? Had then governor Campbell pulled strings to get Melissa the best health care the government could provide? Or was something more nefarious at play?

A car pulled into the parking lot as I began a search for her name through all the files, to no avail; however, I did see another reference to Fort Detrick.

Project Naomi

As a car door slammed not far away, my mind cycled back to Ben David in the Yazd Province cave when he whispered, "Naomi," in my ear through the hanging flap of the protective mask he had been wearing. The document read:

```
MKUltra chemical experimentation in the 1950-1968
time frame was NOT halted as CIA reported. Sidney
Gottlieb destroyed most records, but others have
been found indicating Ultra's predecessor, Naomi.
Naomi first pursued mind control through any means
necessary as a weapon of mass manipulation. Prom-
ising new developments have led State and CIA to
resurrect Naomi to achieve non-kinetic effects in
warfare using a drug called Demon Rain in Build-
ing 57. Intel fusion from AT&L and CyberCom shows
significant smartphone shipments from China to Iran
and application development for camera modification.
MTF. Techno-drug development possible.
```

AT&L was shorthand for Acquisition, Technology, and Logistics, the Department of Defense activity responsible for tracking global supply chains. CyberCom was the acronym for U.S. Cyber Command, the four-star functional command that monitored global cyberactivity. An analyst in the Intelligence Community had flagged the two separate threads of intel as possibly having some correlation, suggesting mind control impact derived from a combination between a hallucinogenic and smartphone technology.

Interesting.

It could have been psychosomatic, but my optical nerve spasmed, and a starburst of white light exploded in my eyes like fireworks. Fillmore and Owens had told me that the Iranians were developing Demon Rain. Now someone's records indicated that both Melissa and Demon Rain had been at Fort Detrick. I had seen Dariush Parizad in Germany and Japan at former CIA safe houses. I steadied myself by sliding off the bed and standing, hands against the wall. I walked to the door and cracked it to let in the cold January air. Despite the chill, I had cold beads of sweat sliding across my face.

Through the crack in the door, I saw a shiny black Porsche Cayenne SUV park at the front door. A woman walked into the office and came out two minutes later as an older rust-colored Toyota Camry eased into the spot next to her. Suddenly, this was a busy place. The Porsche driver had kinky blond hair that fell past her shoulders. I instinctively retreated into the room and quietly closed the door before I could see the driver of the second car. I stuffed the pistol in my right pocket and my knife in the other.

The ringing landline phone startled me. I lifted it, and the voice said, "Dude who is not here has food that is not here."

I hung up, shook my head, tried a weak smile at the bad joke, and managed to shake off the bit of nerves I had developed from seeing Melissa's name on the flash drive. I watched through the sheer curtain of the dingy window spotted with road dust as the woman parked at the opposite end of the motel. She unpacked a small rolling suitcase that could fit in the overhead compartment of an airplane. She was dressed in a gray suit with crisp creases in the pants and narrow lapels on the blazer.

Her white blouse appeared sheer, and I wondered why she wasn't wearing a long overcoat. It was maybe forty degrees outside. She lifted the suitcase with no effort and strode confidently into the room. I had the impression she was a former college athlete.

An image blurred to the right on the opposite side of the window a second before there was a light rap on my door. The face on the opposite side of the peephole surprised me to the point that I opened the door without hesitation.

My friend Ben David stepped through, saying, "Quick, Garrett, close the door."

"What are you doing here? How did you find me? Are you okay?" I asked. I was tired, hungry, and weak, but his presence provided a jolt of adrenaline that focused me.

David was dressed in black jeans, black combat boots, an olive Gore-Tex coat with the initials IDF on the upper-left breast, and a black watch cap not unlike the one I had stolen from Fort Detrick.

"Garrett, you've got to keep moving," he said. His hands were pushing me back into the room as he closed the door behind him.

"Slow down, Ben," I said. His eyes darted left and right, assessing the room, then focused on me. "How did you know where I was?"

"Heard about the breakout from Detrick. IC is lit," he said. That the Intelligence Community would be searching for me was no surprise; that David found me, and so quickly, was. "I started thinking about logical hideouts within an escape radius. Some private eye reported to the IC that you left him for dead in the park near here. You're on foot. This is logical. I've spent thirty years avoiding VAJA, Mukhabarat, GID, and even IDF."

VAJA was the Iranian intelligence agency, while Mukhabarat was Iraqi, GID was Saudi, and the IDF, of course, was Israeli.

"Wasn't planning on staying. Just needed to regroup," I said.

"If I can find you, they can find you," he said.

"Who exactly is 'they'?"

"The CIA. You're a threat, Garrett. They've got something planned. Mossad got me out of Afghanistan and into the U.S. to pursue it," he said.

"In forty-eight hours? That's quick, my friend," I replied. My voice sounded more suspicious than I'd intended.

"*Friend* is the operative word," David said. "I'm here. I'm warning you. I'll be around. Use this," he said, handing me a burner phone still shrink-wrapped in its packaging as if he'd just purchased it from Costco.

He turned, opened the door, and slid through the gap, evaporating before my eyes, which seemed to be his specialty.

I stared at the phone in my hands and checked the packaging, which seemed airtight, but it wouldn't be a stretch that Mossad had made this phone, planted a tracking chip, and packaged it perfectly. It was Ben David, though, and my trust factor was high with him. If he or Mossad were tracking me, I assumed it would be, worst case, to paint a better picture for Mossad of what was happening. Best case, David wanted to protect me.

I stuffed the phone in the backpack and repacked all my other loot, waited ten minutes, and slipped out the door in my watch cap and duster. I walked behind my room while hugging the wall, found the military crest of the slope, and circled behind the office, which looked like a pillbox even from the back. My math told me it was twenty-four feet by twenty-four feet. Efficient construction, where twelve sheets of plywood laid in three rows of four dictated the building floor plan. I entered the office from the opposite direction, keeping the small building between me and the motel.

"Dude! I was just watching. Where'd you come from?"

When I came in, Chad was staring at my room through the window. A pizza box sat on the counter. I opened it and offered it to him first. He grabbed two pieces and placed a roll of paper towels on the counter.

"Damn. Me and the spy eating pizza."

"Shut up," I said.

He stopped chewing, his eyes grew wide, and he swallowed. "Sorry, man."

"What's her name?" I asked.

He looked at the register, the computer monitor, and through the window.

"Um, not really part of the complimentary pizza package, man."

I said nothing.

He kept talking.

"Look, man. A few days ago, the cops came around checking to see who had reservations. All about the inauguration. Told us to watch out for suspicious characters." His eyes shifted to the Kim Campbell campaign bobblehead doll on the counter.

"Do I look suspicious to you?"

"No. Totally not. I mean, maybe to others you might, but definitely not to me. You're like the least-suspicious-looking character I've seen today."

"So that's a yes."

I grabbed another piece of pizza and slid another of Denuncio's hundred-dollar bills across the counter.

"Name, address, everything you've got on her."

He pocketed the cash and typed into the computer keyboard.

"Chloe. Ha. Love that name. Chloe Kardashian. Just kidding. Chloe Collinsworth. Pretty good name right there."

"Job?"

"We don't get that info, man."

"Google her," I said.

"She's pretty hot. Stalkerrrr." His voice hit a high-pitched octave as he drew the last word out. Damn. Professor at University of North Carolina. Teaches dendrology."

He started searching for the meaning when I said, "Trees. She teaches about trees."

"Right. I knew that."

I also knew that a common undercover legend for CIA or FBI field agents was serving as a professor, journalist, or photographer.

"Keep the rest," I said, pushing the pizza toward him.

"Heading back to the room?" He raised his hand as he spoke.

"Where else would I be going?"

He was young and careless. He didn't deserve to die, but neither did I. The stack of bills he had accumulated was significantly larger than the five hundred dollars I had given him. Someone else had paid him off.

As soon as he lifted his hand, I dove to the floor, and a bullet passed through where my head had been and slapped into his neck. His carotid artery sprayed like a geyser as he spun around, shouting, "Ohmygod, ohmygod!" I would have helped him if I thought it would do any good, but he was going to bleed out in less than a minute.

I dove through the window as a car rammed the front door. Spinning to one knee, I leveled the Glock on two white men in plain clothes with high-and-tight haircuts. They were either private military contractors or CIA assets. They aimed at me. I shot them. Sometimes it was as simple as that. They might have been half my age, but I was twice as quick.

I rolled to my right and felt the sniper's bullet wash past me. It cracked overhead and singed the wool of the duster as it flared upward. The ground was hard and cold, crunching beneath me as I low crawled down the slope to the woods. Confident I was over the ridge, I stood and ran into the protective cover of the trees. Two more shots snapped overhead, crackling through the branches. At the nadir of the terrain was a creek that ambled from the mountains in the west to the east, toward Fort Detrick.

I splashed into the cold water, crossed to the north side, climbed up the steep bank, found a power line right-of-way, and sprinted for at least a mile until I felt safe enough to slow down. Reaching a road running north and south, I eased back into the trees that hugged the creek bed. I retrieved Denuncio's phone, considered using David's shrink-wrapped gift, but instead inserted the SIM card in Denuncio's and used the iPad to call the number in the voice mail. I avoided staring at either device, though my eyes sparked as my optical nerve flared.

"Garrett, where are you?" Campbell said.

"Why did you send Melissa to Fort Detrick?"

She paused a beat, which I took as a tell. "What are you talking about? I was governor. I had no sway to send Melissa anywhere. Garrett, I'm concerned about you. Tell me where you are."

I suspected she might already know. "What secret did she know?"

My voice choked as I spoke and considered the improbable but increasingly possible scenario that Melissa knew something that could have impacted Campbell's election.

Secret

I was watching the road fifty meters to my front from behind a thick oak tree, its barren branches tangling to create a lattice canopy above the creek. The Porsche Cayenne with the blonde—Chloe Collinsworth—drove slowly over the adjacent bridge. She might have been studying trees, but I doubted it. While she didn't look like a sniper, I had learned a long time ago to never be deceived by appearances. Bursts of mist puffed with every deep breath. My lungs ached.

"Secret?" Campbell asked.

"Never mind."

I punched off the iPad, removed the chip from the phone, and placed it back in my boot, secured in the plastic sleeve. I then smashed both the iPad and Denuncio's phone and tossed them in the water, leaving me with David's phone if I needed to contact anyone.

A helicopter chopped in the distance. A black Cadillac Escalade dipped through the river and climbed up the hill about one hundred meters behind the Porsche. Once they were both out of sight, I checked what we call a *linear danger area*—a road—and darted across, racing along the power line right-of-way again and separating myself from my pursuers.

Campbell's denials weren't convincing. I had once considered her a friend, and now I determined that if she had anything to do with Melissa's death, she was a mortal enemy, president-elect or not.

My optic nerves flared again as I slowed. I attributed this to my wounds and exhaustion. I considered for the first time that I had no idea what drugs the CIA—or whoever they were—had administered at Fort Detrick in my lockdown cell. Maybe they had given me more Demon Rain, if that was what Parizad had shot at me.

Regardless, the anger I felt toward Campbell began to boil into a murderous rage, which was unlike any emotion I had ever felt. Even when chasing al-Baghdadi or Soleimani, I was objectively above the fray, always focusing on the tasks at hand.

I slowed again, maybe two miles from the road, my lungs feeling like they had been perforated by ice picks. I was soaked with sweat as I slid back into the trees. I leaned against a tall pine, its needles the only green against a brown-and-gray backdrop of trees and mournful skies.

I looked at the ground and coughed out a sob, then lifted my head and shouted, "Melissa!"

Time seemed to stand still. Crows stopped pecking at feed in the adjacent farmer's field. Squirrels halted their scampering in the bare limbs above. The crystallized particles of exhalation hung in front of my face like a motionless cloud.

Then I remembered.

Be Brave. Be True.

She had ended her deathbed letter to me with those words. *Brave and True* was the West Point motto of the class prior to my graduation: the one that had produced Samantha Owens, Kyle Estes, and Jim Tharp, the current CIA director, secretary of state, and secretary of defense.

Was she cautioning me against them? I had dismissed her warning as an errant inconsistency provoked by the grim reaper. Never before had I underestimated her. In my grief and without her reassuring nudge, I had missed this clue.

But what did it mean?

I needed to talk to Reagan. Melissa had confided in our youngest child when I wasn't there. While Reagan had gone through her doting-daughter phase with me, my intermittent presence had forged an immutable bond between her and Melissa. Brad was exceptional in many ways and almost always respectful, but he carried an air of immaturity with him that gave Reagan the slightest of advantages when it came to any sort of edge in parental relationships.

A freshman at the University of Virginia, Reagan was now entering her second semester. I decided not to use the phone yet, though. If it was a Mossad device, I didn't want them listening in to my conversation with either of my two children. I unfroze myself from the moment and powered forward by sheer determination and, as always, Melissa's guiding hand.

Before I stepped to cross the road, another car drove slowly to the north. I followed the car with my eyes. Ben David was driving a late-model white SUV. He sped up the hill before I was able to race out and flag him down.

21

INSTEAD OF PURSUING BEN David, I continued east, where I reached the chain-link fence of Fort Detrick at about 4:00 p.m., though the low cloud cover and mountains in the west created a layer of darkness that gave the illusion of nighttime. As far as I knew, I had not been detected. I knelt in a copse of pine trees about a quarter mile away, the air becoming increasingly cold and bitter, winds beginning to lash like the erratic crack of a whip's popper.

Fueled by both a need to have an unmonitored conversation with my daughter to unravel Melissa's cryptic note and my anger at Campbell's possible role in Melissa's death, I lay on the ground. Fifty meters to my left was a strip mall with a nearly vacant parking lot. There were about ten stores linked together by a sidewalk fronting the mall. A set of rusted green dumpsters was situated in the corner nearest me, their black lids askew, some open and some closed.

Inside the fence, a military police car patrolled an inner road like a baseball field warning track. Two Black Hawk helicopters ferried into and out of the base, landing on the east side and staying on station less than ten minutes. It was impossible to see who, if anyone, boarded or disembarked from the aircraft. Traffic ebbed and flowed on the road opposite the strip mall. It was a normal day with less than twenty-four hours until inauguration.

I thought about the threads of clues and what they might mean:

Melissa's presence at Fort Detrick immediately before her death.

Her warning about the previous West Point class.

Dariush Parizad's involvement in Demon Rain, a U.S. program, not some nefarious Iranian drug, as Fillmore had briefed me.

The huddled groups of people all looking skyward. Could they have been experiencing the same optical nerve damage that had been giving me sporadic issues?

Ben David in the cave and now in the United States warning me. Following me? Perhaps he knew I was in trouble and was here to find me and help me navigate my way out of the confusion. Had he, too, been injected with Demon Rain by Parizad?

How did all of this come together, if at all?

If Demon Rain was an American program, why have us raid the compounds in Heidelberg and Yokkaichi?

I needed my team here to help me figure out these questions. Not only was I worried about them, they were indispensable to me.

The military police car stopped at the fence and idled. Another showed up and parked about fifty meters behind it. A third came from the opposite direction and positioned fifty meters from the original car. The drivers simultaneously switched on spotlights and shined them on the fence where I had been considering crossing.

A camera had to have captured my image somewhere, though I had been cautious to avoid any obvious locations. There was no discounting that if they deemed me important enough, Tharp or Owens could order a Reaper or Predator drone to do a quick "training mission," which would include searching for a fifty-year-old man in a black watch cap and gray duster, wandering somewhere between Camp David and Fort Detrick. Between the upcoming inauguration and heightened terror alerts, the mission might have already been planned.

As I was processing this information, the Cadillac SUV nosed around the corner from the far side of the mall. Either these guys were excellent at reconnaissance and basic cloverleaf search patterns, or I was still transmitting from some device. There was always the possibility that while in custody, someone had stitched a tracker into my clothes, but I had done a thorough search after my shower earlier and found nothing out of the ordinary. The more likely scenario was that a drone had found me.

If that were the case, the Cadillac guys had a proximate location, not a specific one; otherwise, they wouldn't have given me the early warning they did, or so I thought. To my right, I heard the crunching of pine straw in time to roll to my left and lift my pistol.

A man dressed in black peeked from behind a tree and aimed his long gun at me. It was a standard issue M4 with a silencer screwed onto the muzzle. It spit twice as I rolled behind the tree, realizing my flank was exposed to the Cadillac that had distracted me, if only for a brief second. With the military police spotlights at the fence, I was in the center of a triangle.

A second man rushed under the cover of the man with the long gun. They had gained a flank on me through the very creek that had been my protective cover for the last several hours of exfiltration. The Cadillac's bright lights shined in my direction, and the operator continued to crawl the vehicle forward while the military police lifted their spotlights, aiming them directly at me.

This was a coordinated attack. It occurred to me that it wasn't the first and that this tactical action was the result of months of strategic planning for some grander event. I was a threat to someone, and thanks to Melissa, I had an idea of whom these people might be working for, but all the knowledge in the world right now wasn't helping me. There was no McCool coming to the rescue as she had done so many times.

I held my fire and slid into a small drainage ditch, which would afford me more cover and a few more seconds to consider my options. The rustling of pine needles alerted me to the tightening of the noose they had placed around me. They had been smart, waiting until I was back-stopped against the fence line of Fort Detrick. Whoever was corralling me had the authority to order the military police to work in concert with the commandos outside the wire. Lights washed over my position as the Cadillac closed in. Footsteps got closer, which I used as an opportunity to low crawl about twenty meters to the south.

"Still got him?" a voice asked.

"Scanning," another said.

This was encouraging to me, so I followed the ditch another twenty meters and turned in their direction. Now, they were highlighted by the Cadillac lights, backlit like rock stars at a concert. They spun in my direction, realizing a second too late they had been outflanked. I didn't hesitate to fire. The pistol was loud against the night that only seconds before had amplified stealthy movements.

Pop. Pop. Two shots and both men fell. I doubted either was dead, but I used the window of confusion to bolt west through the very woods from which they had flanked me. Shots cracked behind me, and I wasn't sure if they were coming from the Cadillac, the military police, or the wounded flanking team.

I was tripping on exposed roots, clawing at the ground, and rolling forward, never letting my momentum subside as I angled toward higher ground, where I could make better time. The problem was that the clearest path ran parallel to the parking lot, though the Cadillac's lights were well behind me and didn't seem to be in pursuit. They were most likely tending to the wounded, which lengthened the window of my escape.

I circled back toward the Cadillac, correctly betting that the driver had left it momentarily unattended. Racing through the parking lot, I slid behind the SUV and jumped into the driver's seat, closed the door, and sped away, turning hard toward the road. As I had the vehicle on two wheels, turning south, there was another SUV in the far corner near the road about a quarter mile away. I didn't have time to assess exactly what model it was, but I had to account for the possibility of a chase car.

I found Route 15 heading south and left my unanswered questions about Fort Detrick at the fence. I powered ahead to find my daughter, whom I hoped was still alive and could unlock the mystery of why Melissa was at Fort Detrick.

22

AS I WAS TRYING to stay undetected from drones and spies on Route 15 south of Leesville, Virginia, Dariush Parizad was monitoring the activity at Fort Detrick through the Iranian Shadow Commander satellite in the above-garage apartment of the expansive farm straddling the Maryland-Pennsylvania border.

Four forty-inch monitors were arranged side by side on the wall above the desk where he sat. The cursor was set in quad mode where he could effortlessly move from one monitor to the next. On the far-left screen, he tracked the Iranian Warrior submarines, their class so named after the ayatollah that had anointed Parizad as the Lion of Tabas. Construction on the nuclear submarine, modeled after the Russian Akula-class missile-launching subs, had begun in 2015, with three crews working twenty-four hours a day to deliver five subs by the summer of 2020. Built in Russia and paid for by Iran, the ayatollah, at Parizad's urging, had re-named the class of submarine, "Warrior-class." The submarine crews had been trained at the Leningrad Naval Base, conducting maneuvers in the Baltic Sea in months of left seat–right seat rides, where the incoming team first learned from the trainers and then "swapped seats" and took the controls while the trainers observed.

Because the United States had a strategic gap in production of sonobuoys—the devices that helped detect submarines in wide swaths of ocean—ten years before, Parizad had encouraged Soleimani and Aya-tollah Khamenei to invest in a strategic capability that could extend Iranian reach beyond the Persian Gulf, which the Conqueror-class subs were currently patrolling.

The five Warrior-class subs had redundant communications capabili-ties using floating antennas, buoy systems, and radio masts that allowed for the transmission of data to the *Shadow Commander* satellite.

A month before, each had exited the Persian Gulf on different days and moved silently on separate axes into the Atlantic Ocean, Caribbean Sea, and Pacific Ocean. Each was armed with one hundred Kh-55SM cruise missiles that could travel over six hundred miles. These missiles had been effective in the strike on Saudi Arabia's largest oil refinery in a successful training exercise for what Parizad had in mind for the United States.

Why continue this strategy of death by a thousand cuts? The United States had proven itself resilient in the wake of the 9/11 attacks, using those as an excuse to invade Iraq with two hundred thousand soldiers. The close fight on the Arabian Peninsula needed to become a supporting effort in the deep fight against America.

The only way to successfully do this was by attacking on every con-ceivable front in an asymmetric way using all the elements of Iran's na-tional power. Just as how he boxed, Parizad's plan struck the United States at every level from strategic to the tactical and even the individual, targeting the U.S. Army Joint Special Operations Command. Indeed, one country's terrorist was another country's hero and vice versa.

At the moment, the five blinking GPS indicators on the left-hand display showed two submarines off the coast of California five hundred feet deep in the waters off the Cortes Bank, one hundred twenty miles from San Diego. Another two submarines sat in four hundred feet of water in the Sigsbee Deep, a hole in the middle of the Gulf of Mexico about fourteen thousand feet below sea level. The fifth submarine hovered fifty miles off the coast of New Jersey, sitting six hundred feet deep. All were trying to avoid detection from the aggressive patrolling of the U.S. Navy.

The strategic gambit included an attack on the oil refineries of the United States. Over the past five years, Immortal cells had precisely pinpointed each of the major refineries, allowing Parizad and his team to narrow the mission to Port Arthur and Baytown in Texas and Baton Rouge and Garyville in Louisiana, each location responsible for processing over five hundred thousand barrels of oil per day. Those four targets would receive fifty missiles apiece, nearly double the amount used in the Saudi Aramco oil pumping station attack, which had also included drone strikes.

The West Coast submarines lingering in the depths of the Cortes Bank were programmed to launch at five targets, raining twenty-five missiles at refineries in El Segundo, Carson, and Torrance in the south and Richmond, Martinez, and Benicia in the Bay Area. These attacks were intended to disrupt another 1.5 million barrels per day of processing capacity.

The lone East Coast submarine was targeting the nearly five hundred thousand barrel per day capacity in New Jersey.

Upon initiation of the attacks, the submarines were to speed into the harbor channels in San Diego, San Francisco, Houston, New Orleans, and Manhattan, where they would detonate themselves, creating a nuclear wasteland at the entry points to the major ports of the United States.

With the finding of the Khuzestan oil fields and its fifty-three billion fresh barrels of oil waiting to be drilled, Parizad and the Iranian leadership had developed this multifaceted plan not only to decimate the United States' economic and military capacity and throw the arrogant American citizens into poverty and violence but to also dominate oil production across the world. On the heels of the coronavirus pandemic, this one-two punch would send the American economy reeling while also shattering the hope proffered by the first female president.

The objectives were to destroy 40 percent of the country's daily oil processing capacity, block five major ports with nuclear subs that would contaminate the surrounding area for decades, and decimate the leadership of the country, throwing the United States into a dizzying maelstrom of confusion, all while boxing in their special operations commander.

The crews of the submarines monitored Arshad's Instagram account and began to move to battle positions when they saw the picture of desert and mountains. Likewise, the Immortal cells took note and began preparing for execution of their asymmetric attacks.

It was a brilliant plan that in hindsight, like the 9/11 attacks, U.S. intelligence should have caught, but the inward focus on political campaigns and corruption had distracted the Intelligence Community from missing the obvious big-muscle movements. There had been a couple of analysts shouting about Iranian subs and drones, but no one had given them much credence. One even noticed that Parizad had been spotted at Paris Charles de Gaulle Airport, but the French were slow in informing the United States, as senior officials were too busy jockeying for powerful assignments in the new administration instead of keeping a watchful eye on the world at the most vulnerable time in any democracy. The inauguration machinery was in full gear, and no one was stopping the party.

Parizad was confident in his plan, having rehearsed it several times on computer simulations in Tehran. His confidence now allowed him to focus the bulk of his efforts on finding and dueling with his nemesis, General Garrett Sinclair.

23

I RACED SOUTH ON US-15 and connected with US-29 in the stolen Cadillac Escalade, knowing full well that whoever was orchestrating the operation to kill or capture me was following me from the sky, the ground, or both.

A distant set of headlights popped in and out of view of my rearview mirror, but I couldn't be certain it was the same vehicle. It was most likely the SUV from the parking lot, which was almost certainly Chloe Collinsworth's Porsche Cayenne. I wasn't slowing down to confirm, as I had little time to waste.

I stayed below the speed limit to avoid any type of police interaction. I didn't look the part of an army three-star general with my watch cap and duster, nor did I have any credentials to prove my identification. Rather, I was driving a stolen vehicle with no license and multiple stolen firearms. If the police weren't looking for me, they should have been.

The Android phone in the center console was most likely the driver's device. It rang no less than a dozen times on my three-hour drive to Reagan's UVA dormitory off Alderman Road near Scott Stadium.

The Bluetooth was connected, and I saw a variety of names pop up on the Cadillac's monitor, but "Hodgdog" appeared six times. The name sounded familiar, but I couldn't place it. There was a tiny circular picture above the name, though I didn't stop and study it. By looking at the vehicle's onboard display, I hoped to be avoiding whatever issue had occurred previously by looking at the phone. My eyes still buzzed with frayed optical nerves, causing me to see stars. Nonetheless, I was able to drive and focus on the task at hand.

I arrived in the parking lot at about 7:00 p.m. still checking the rearview mirror. Driving slowly past the dorm, I saw a few students milling about and huddled against the biting wind and cold, heads down and feet trudging up the steps. The students were wearing so many jackets, scarves, and beanies, I wouldn't have recognized Reagan if she were staring at me.

It was a gamble coming here to her. I could be putting her in danger, but at the same time, the people chasing me knew where she and Brad lived. I had to warn them regardless, and I wanted to stay off the phones as much as possible after what had happened in Maryland. Plus, Reagan would not be trusting or forthcoming if I simply called her.

Pulling out of the parking lot after a slow pass, I was glad that Reagan lived in a well-populated dorm with tight restrictions and ironclad security. I had helped her move into her room the previous August and had visited her twice in Charlottesville. Following Alderman Road around Scott Stadium, I found an apartment complex and pulled into a vacant spot.

The Cadillac needed fuel, the gauge sitting at one-eighth of a tank, but I left it running anyway. Several cars buzzed up and down the road, and there was no indication of Chloe Collinsworth or her Porsche. I punched up the browser on the Cadillac's onboard computer and searched for the admin to Alderman Road Residence Area, which conveniently had a phone number and email listed at the bottom of the page.

The number was hyperlinked on the vehicle display, so I punched that, and on the second ring, a student answered.

"Alderman Residence Area. This is James. How may I help you?"

"James, I am Reagan Sinclair's father and have lost my phone, so I'm using a friend's to call the admin. Can you please pass her a message?"

"Certainly, sir. I'm ready when you are."

"Ask her to meet me in the parking lot in five minutes. I'm driving a black Cadillac Escalade. New car."

He paused, suspicious. "New car. New phone."

"Lost phone. New car. Just tell her I have some questions about Mom."

"Yes, sir. Got it."

I waited five minutes and then wheeled out of the apartment parking lot and pulled into the dorm lot. I saw Reagan standing inside the dorm-glassed windows, staying warm, but still crossing her arms. She was wearing a light green ski jacket, a thick, fuzzy cashmere scarf, and a gray beanie atop her blue jeans and hiking boots. Her reddish-brown hair spilled down her back, and her green eyes locked onto me. She was flanked by three friends to whom she nodded, indicating she recognized me. She bounced down the steps with a serious face and came around behind the vehicle and stopped two feet behind the driver's window, rapping it with her knuckles.

"Anyone holding a gun to your head?" she asked as I buzzed down the window. In the side-view mirror, I could see her inspecting the back seat.

"No. Hop in, Rea," I said. We pronounced her name *Ray* because she liked it better than being named after a president. Melissa had picked the name, not me, but I had agreed with it.

She slid in the passenger seat and immediately looked in the rear.

"Holy shit, Dad, what have you got two AR-15s for? And this car? WTF?"

"Good to see you, too."

"Seriously, Dad. You've got an arsenal in here." She was picking through the detritus and muttering, "Magazines, ammo, night vision, scopes, infrared lasers, and binoculars. Deer hunting?"

"Yes," I said, though I hadn't really studied the contents of the back seat. I had been too busy driving.

"Any dead bodies?" she joked.

I looked at her.

"Oh my God!" she said. "You're serious."

"You might want to check," I said, a brief moment of levity.

Reagan was a tomboy while also being a beautiful woman, the rare combination most guys find appealing. I spent several years fending the boys off until she took over for me. Having a firm sense of her identity and what she believed—God, guns, and justice—Reagan was 100 percent her own person. It was rare to find someone her age that understood what they wanted their life to be about and were driven to achieve that reality.

I drove up Ivy Road and into the parking lot of the Boar's Head Resort, where I sometimes stayed when I visited to play tennis with her. Reagan was a state champion in North Carolina but still wasn't good enough for the UVA varsity team. She drilled with them, though, in hopes of competing one day.

"Take a deep breath," I said.

"Look at you, Dad. You look . . . homeless."

"Might be a good term for me right now."

"I thought you were overseas."

"I was."

"Have you talked to Brad?" she asked.

"Not yet. I came to you first because I'm concerned about you."

"That's not the only reason, though," she said. Not a question. She ignored my comment and said, "I got an invite to Kim Campbell's inauguration. Very exciting. You?"

"I'm not sure. I have to talk to you about something."

"Obviously. Your clothes are retro, even for you."

Her quick repartee was a defense mechanism, and as long as I let it play out, she was typically fine. It was obvious to me by the speed with which she spoke that she was worried about me.

"There are some things going on that I can't explain to you fully, not because I don't want to, but I don't really have the complete picture right now."

"Okay, start talking, and we'll figure it out," she said. It was such a Melissa thing to say. *Cut to the chase and tell me what's happening.*

"I think your mother was killed. I don't think it was cancer."

We locked eyes, and the pain in hers came welling forth. I hadn't intended to be so direct, but we always were when we spoke.

"Dad, how can you even . . ." She had tears coming down her face. Fifteen months, and the sharp dagger of death hadn't dulled.

"I'm sorry. I have discovered new information."

"What information?" She controlled the sobs and regained her composure.

"Her name was on a list of people that had experimental surgery or something else at Fort Detrick."

"She never did that."

"How can you be so sure?"

"I drove her everywhere. I took off from school for September and October. Brad couldn't cope, and you were back and forth."

She didn't mean it as a dig, but that was how it felt.

"I was there almost every day. The staff at Walter Reed got to know me. Everyone except for that creepy new doctor."

"What new doctor?" While I never cared for Blankenship, it was news to me that she had someone else.

"Jensen or something like that."

"Why am I just hearing about this?"

"I don't know. Mom died. You got back. Things were crazy. You left again."

Story of my life, right there.

"Why was he creepy? I mean creepier than Blankenship?"

"I saw him in the parking lot one time talking to some guys. They looked like guys who wanted in the Rangers but couldn't hack it. They had the high-and-tights but were a little soft around the edges."

Reagan had been around paratroopers and Rangers enough to know the difference between a hardened soldier serving his or her country and someone who was serving his or her own self. When she was growing up as a child on Fort Bragg, she would sometimes run behind the formations of soldiers calling cadences at six thirty in the morning and was eventually adopted by several of the units, who also cleaned up their lyrics. She grew out of that phase when she was ten and then went into full tennis-jock mode, but she always checked in with me every day to discuss training, foreign policy, and her plans to do something large with her life.

"Yeah, turns out he wasn't the best—"

"Wait a minute," she interrupted. "There were two days when I had an ACC tennis camp at Chapel Hill. That's the only window."

"When?"

"That was October 25 and 26. I remember it like it was yesterday, because I was so freaked out about leaving her, but she encouraged me to go."

This was slippery ground for Reagan. I didn't want to give her any reason to feel that her mother's death was in any way her fault, but ultimately, she was too quick and smart to not see the potential link. She wasn't there, and her mother was taken. Her eyes fell and her hand came to her mouth.

"Oh my God. Was that when she was taken?"

"I'll check."

"Don't lie to me, Dad."

I paused. "Yes. She was at Fort Detrick then." Then to change the subject, I asked her, "Did Mom say anything to you before she died? Anything . . . strange?"

"Don't change the subject!"

"Rea, it's my fault. I wasn't there, and I should have been. This is one hundred percent on me."

She paused, sighed, and said as Melissa would have wanted her to, "It's on both of us, Dad."

Like a bridge truss, Reagan spread the load of the burden by accepting some of it, but thankfully not all of it.

"Did she say anything to you?" I asked.

"No. I mean, yes. But not really. She said a lot of stuff. We talked about life. You. Brad. Me. The future. The past. Family. Friends. I was there. The doctors were treating her for cancer. It *was* cancer. Maybe Detrick was something real?" She emphatically pounded her gloved fist on her thigh.

"What friends?" I asked.

Her phone buzzed with a text.

"Get that," I said.

"Just Lindy asking me if I'm okay." Like most people her age, she had an ability to know what a text message contained with barely a glance.

Her phone buzzed a few more times, but I continued.

"What friends?"

"All of them. She talked about . . ."

"What?"

"Well, one thing did strike me as odd. She was never that close with the Tharps, but Angie Tharp was a friend of mine when we were kids living at Fort Bragg, so Mom and her mom stayed in touch. Now that he's the secretary of defense, it's kind of a big deal."

My heart began racing. Melissa's warning about Tharp's class—*Brave and True.*

"Go ahead," I urged.

"She said that Donna, Angie's mom, was stressed out about something that her husband said or did. I only briefly poked at it," she said.

Reagan's goal was to one day be the FBI director. The path would take her from UVA to UVA School of Law to the FBI, where she would work her way up.

"What was the issue?"

Reagan's phone continued buzzing, but she ignored it.

"Mom said that Donna said—see the problem here, all hearsay—that Jim was talking to one of his classmates. They had been drinking, and evidently, one of them said something about war with Iran. That Iran needed a regime change or something like that. Any moron knows that wouldn't work, but that's what they were discussing . . . according to Mom, who heard from Donna. You know like the REO Speedwagon song . . . heard it from a friend who heard it from a friend whoooo . . . that kind of thing."

Tharp, Owens, and Estes were all three devout Iran hawks. Campbell was not. She had campaigned on finding a measure to hold Iran at bay while avoiding war. I was at the center of the execution of that policy and had been involved in countless discussions about direction on Iran. The West Pointers would be pushing for intervention early in her term, unless, of course, she fired them right away.

"Okay, but your mom was never unreliable in any way when it came to passing information. She was the last thing from a gossip. So Donna Tharp confided in her that her husband and probably Estes were talking about starting a war with Iran?"

"Something like that, but I wouldn't take it to the bank," Reagan said.

What she didn't know was Melissa's letter to me and her veiled reference to Tharp's class motto. The picture was starting to come together, and I was beginning to feel exposed and vulnerable. I was being pursued by murderous assassins, and here I was sitting with my daughter in an open parking lot.

She looked away, chewing on her lip. No cars were moving in the parking lot. A few people were strolling to their rooms through the cool evening.

"What?" I asked.

"He told me not to tell you, but we discuss everything, right?"

"We do," I said. Fear boiled in my stomach.

"When I talked to Brad yesterday, he said a man named Ben David had approached him to make sure he was okay."

My friend checking on my family—or something else?

"Where's Brad now?" I asked in a sharp breath.

"He had a gig at Mary Washington in Fredericksburg," she said. "He was drinking a beer with his friends when this guy pulled him away."

"Is he okay?"

"Well, he called me. So I'm guessing he is. Who's Ben David?"

"A friend," I said.

"You're in trouble, Dad. You don't have to tell me, but I can help if you do. And Brad will be fine. He sounded totally normal."

I hoped she was right.

"I've already endangered you, Reagan. We need to go. Do you need a weapon?"

"Dad, you'll get me arrested."

"Grab one if you need it," I joked.

She looked in the back seat.

"Like Halloween candy? Just reach my hand in and grab some?"

We shared a brief chuckle, short-lived, but a good relief from the tension.

"Hey, Rea?"

Another sigh. "Yeah, Dad?"

"You're helping me figure this out. Something bad is happening, and you are part of solving it."

She lifted her eyes to meet mine. "You know what Mom always said, right?"

"Good wins," we both said in unison.

I used the remaining one-sixteenth of a tank of gas to drop Reagan at her dorm. She pecked me on the cheek and took one last glance in the back.

"That's some good hardware back there. Whatever you're involved in, my money's on you. Oh, wait. Hang tight."

She jumped from the car and ran upstairs to her room, returning in less than two minutes. She handed me a burner cell phone still in the wrapper and said, "Ditch that guy's phone and this car as soon as you can. And here's my number."

"Thanks."

She pecked me on the cheek through the window and said, "Love you, Dad."

"Love you, too."

I was two hours from Washington, D.C., and two and a half from Fort Detrick. What I really needed to do was talk to Donna Tharp. But I drove to the gas station on fumes and used one of Denuncio's hundred-dollar bills to pay for a seventy-two-dollar fill-up. I then drove north to the small town of Ruckersville, Virginia, pulled into the Walmart parking lot, and set up the new phone while I ditched the owner's in the dumpster. I didn't dare leave it near Reagan's dorm.

First, I unpackaged the phone Ben David had given me and charged it for fifteen minutes using the USB port of the Cadillac. When the screen came to life, I opened contacts and found a number already preprogrammed into the phone. No surprise there. I switched on speakerphone and pressed the number. After the third ring, David answered. My eyes sparked again, causing me to look away from the screen and into the parking lot. *Demon Rain or just tired?*

"Why are you talking to my son?" I asked.

"You're on the run. I'm making sure your family is okay."

His voice was even-pitched and without defense. I paused.

"How is he?" I asked.

"He's fine. I just told him to be careful. I hadn't heard from you, so I wanted to make sure what family you had left was okay."

What family I had left.

"How did you know where he is?"

"He plays in a rock band called Napoleon's Corporal. They advertise their engagements. We may be dear friends, but I know you're not naive enough to think that Mossad has not provided me a full dossier on you."

I had competing instincts tugging in opposite directions. Was he a Good Samaritan helping me as I had helped him in the past, or was there something else at play?

"What do you know about MKNaomi?" I asked. "You mentioned that on the cave floor."

He sucked in a quick breath.

"Ben?" I asked.

"Do you think that's what they want?" he asked. David's voice was the epitome of steadiness in every conversation I had with him over the years. Here, it quivered, if only for a moment. The dissonance was noticeable only because of his prior unflappable consistency.

"The CIA? Maybe," I said. "Remember where I found you?" I was being circumspect because Mossad was listening, and I didn't want to compromise him if his mission to Yazd was off the books.

"Yes," he responded.

"Has the drug affected you?"

"No," he croaked. Again, something in his voice was off.

"Ben, where are you going? Meet me in D.C.," I said.

"I have to go," he replied in a hushed voice. "But okay."

The line went dead before I had a chance to ask him where we would meet. I assumed he could track me on the phone, so I kept it.

I sighed, worried about Brad, mostly. I took the next ten minutes to disable the GPS system and set up the phone Reagan gave me. I texted the number she provided, and it seemed to go through just fine. I looked away, avoiding eye contact with the screen but listening for the sound of an incoming text. As I waited, I tried Brad's phone number three times. Nothing. Then the phone buzzed, and I risked a glance at the text.

```
Here's a pic of Mom and me in the hospital
the last day w that new doc Jensen
Ok, find Brad. Tell him to come to you
Ok . . . ???
```

I stared at the picture, first noticing Reagan's forced smile as she held up the phone, then Melissa's beautiful eyes overpowering her gaunt face. Her smile was genuine and peaceful, communicative, sending love to all of us.

Then I focused on the doctor, at first thinking it was another trick with the screen. My optical nerves flared again. I saw spots, but I couldn't stop looking. I pinched and spread the photo to enlarge it so there was no mistaking the man Reagan said was her doctor.

I lifted my head and sighed, breaking the spell the phone had on me.

This couldn't be true.

I scanned the parking lot. My eyes were momentarily blacked out from staring at the phone screen. A mistake.

Nonetheless, I called Reagan and began turning out of the parking lot as the driver-side window shattered in my face.

24

AT THE EXACT MOMENT glass sprayed in my face from an incoming 5.56 mm bullet fired by an Iranian Immortal team member, Parizad was making final preparations in the above-garage apartment on a farm that straddled the Pennsylvania-Maryland border.

His host returned to the farm to deliver a message from the Gang of Four, as they called themselves. Parizad and his host sat in the comfortable leather chairs of the combination living room and dining room of the above-garage apartment that was actually bigger than many houses. The satellite dish on the top was the primary concession his host had provided.

"The gang is concerned that Sinclair is on the loose," the host said.

"It's almost better that he is. He's right now trying to figure out what's going on. He has very little chance of putting it all together. There are too many moving pieces for him to sort out everything in a day."

"But with the Demon Rain injection, doesn't that make him unpredictable?"

Parizad paused, looked out the window, and then turned back to his host.

"Let me tell you about Garrett Sinclair. He's an enigma and is best left in the wild. Your people couldn't hold him for more than forty-eight hours. He has allies everywhere. Now I have people tracking him, but as long as we keep him on the move, he is little threat to us, and we have near-total visibility on his every move. We know, for example, that he just saw his daughter in Charlottesville and is now making his way north, toward D.C. We're not sure if he's going to D.C. or Fort Detrick. If we can kill him, we will."

"Killing him was always a possibility, but I didn't think that was where we were headed here. It's not what I wanted." His host was nervous.

Parizad looked wistfully out the window again, sipped his lemon water, and smoothed his salt-and-pepper beard.

"You may 'know' Sinclair," Parizad started, using air quotes. "But you have no idea with whom we are dealing. I know Sinclair better than anyone does, except maybe his dead wife. I remember a young Captain Sinclair spying on me in the 1988 Olympics. I was boxing and had every chance to win a gold medal. Every day, we would work out in the yard of our compound. We knew the Americans were watching. Israel. France. British. Many others. But the Americans had a Ranger company and a sniper team up in the apartment building a quarter mile away. We had already investigated this area and thought it was best left alone so that we would know who was watching us. It worked very well. We had microphones and cameras watching them as they watched us. Meanwhile, one of our Immortal cells in America developed a dossier on young Captain Sinclair and his wife, Melissa, and, over time, on their two children, Brad and Reagan."

He took another sip of water, looked through the window at the darkening sky, and continued.

"In our communication with the ayatollah about being watched by a company of Rangers, the supreme leader thought it was best to put on a demonstration of Iranian strength. There was some question whether

I could beat Ray Mercer. I'm pretty sure I would have, but he was older and more experienced. At that age, I was unorthodox but good. I made up for what I lacked in technical skills with strength and brute force. He hadn't really been challenged, and I was eager to destroy the American as revenge for my father's death. I was full of piss and vinegar, but the ayatollah passed instructions down for me to put on a demonstration to the spying Rangers. I followed his orders and redirected the symbolic revenge of combating Mercer to actual revenge against the American military in general and Garrett Sinclair very specifically, an Army Ranger and the eventual commander of their Joint Special Operations Command, the very unit that had killed my father through their own incompetence.

"I had many opportunities to kill Sinclair in the intervening years when I joined the Quds Force under the mentorship of Qassem," he continued. "He taught me it was better to wait, to let the urge build, develop the situation, and find a grand opportunity equal to that of having lost my father. Defeating Mercer would not have had anywhere near the value of what is about to transpire. The total humiliation of the commander of U.S. military special forces. My father would be proud. Qassem would be proud.

"Before the start of the Second Gulf War, Sinclair and I met outside of Basra to discuss limitations. The meeting was short, but I had the opportunity to look him in the eyes, this lone personification of the men who had killed my father so many years ago. I have the proper balance of respect and fear of this warrior. I believe you underestimate him, which is a grave mistake."

He took another sip of water and leveled his eyes on his host.

"Anyway, I promised you some things, and you promised me some things. The problem with these situations is that you have far more to lose than I do. Win, lose, or draw, I am a hero to the Iranian people. You killed my father, and you killed a beloved commander in Qassem, but those are just two of the many transgressions your country has made. With tens of thousands of soldiers planted in the Persian Gulf—the *Persian* Gulf—you continue to misread the situation.

"However, I promised a trade with you, and I will live up to my end of the bargain. I only interrogated Sinclair's wife. It was your men who . . . were the barbarians. It is you who has poked the bear. I helped you capture him, and we put the drug in his system. While I am not done with Sinclair, now it is time for you to live up to your end. It's that simple. It is my turn to collect on the payback. A small attack that will give you the precursor to then attack my country, should your president decide to do so."

"A small attack," the host said, voice croaking and sounding dry.

"Yes. Small by any standard. It is enough to give you the impetus for a hasty strike into Iran and begin to duel with our forces. Your economy is fifty times ours. Your country is twice as big as mine. We have but a quarter of your population. It gives you what you and your neocon friends want. We understand scale."

Parizad smiled at his host.

"I'm not saying what we will do, but a pinprick here gives us the option," the host said.

"Yes. I am prepared to deliver a pinprick. I also understand you have to have deniability, but as we discussed previously, this is good for me in my competition with Ghanni to command the Quds Force. I was, of course, loyal to Soleimani, but Ghanni is a total embarrassment. I keep your secret if you keep my secret."

He slid a folded piece of paper across the table. Ghanni was the placeholder commander who replaced Soleimani as the head of the Quds Force so as to not blow Parizad's cover.

"On this, you will find the three locations that General Ghanni resides. He will be responsible for the attacks that occur tomorrow."

"Attacks?"

Parizad paused. "Attack. You misheard me."

"I didn't mishear anything. You said *attacks*. Plural."

"No. You mustn't be so nervous. Calm down. I have delivered on my side of the bargain. In Iran, we have the concept of Tarof, where we defer to rank in social and bargaining situations. I delivered first on my end of the bargain because of your status in America. It is something that is meaningful in Iran. It is your turn to deliver as I did."

"Remind me exactly what you delivered?"

Parizad smiled and said, "Your experimentation labs in Germany and Japan were about to be uncovered by an American journalist. I put Garrett Sinclair at both locations. There are pictures. I shot him with Demon Rain. His mind is struggling right now with reality, depending upon how long the dart stayed in his system. He is now trying to determine where the threat is. He is a man on the run, and men on the run make mistakes. He's a wanted man by your government. From hero to zero in a matter of days. He is your rival. I have set him up for a mighty fall, as you requested."

His host nodded. "How dangerous is he now?"

Parizad laughed loudly, deep and bellowing. "Praise Allah, man, I thought you knew General Garrett Sinclair. Even if I removed his mind, his body would still be a killing machine, and if I removed his arms, his mind would be a killing machine. Demon Rain is the only hope we have at incapacitating him."

"Some of my team are getting cold feet. In concept, the idea was a good one, but in reality, as the hour draws near, they are concerned."

"*Scared* is most likely the proper word," Parizad said patiently. "It is good for you that I am not as ruthless as my mentor, Qassem, or you would be dead right now. I can say this, however, that I have recorded every conversation with you as the emissary for your group. I have pictures. It is all well documented. This conversation is actively being recorded on both audio and video. While I believe that you are a man of

your word, I have not met the others, so I cannot gauge their trustwor-
thiness. You should be careful that they are not hanging you out to dry,
because I most certainly will if you renege on our deal."

"How many casualties should we expect?"

"Straight to the point. I like it. Minimal, as I said. There will be more
psychological damage than anything else," Parizad said.

"Define *minimal.*"

"When you asked me to get Sinclair on the move and into an embarrassing position, I didn't ask you for specifics. In the military, this is
called *mission orders.*"

His host leaned back and wiped his brow. "I understand. Last question?"

Parizad shrugged. "Sure."

"Why are there pigs in my cattle corral?"

"Pork is a delicacy I don't get to enjoy in Iran. We have a shortage.
Humor my indulgence. They are yours to sell to the highest bidder."

"I checked, and they are still alive. Have you injected them with Demon Rain?"

Parizad smiled. His host was only a partial fool, it seemed.

"So," said the host, "your plan is to try to do mind control on a large
number of people?"

"Just pigs," Parizad said. "Now I must get to work."

When his host departed, Parizad returned to his task at hand by sitting at his command and control platform.

The submarines were on one screen. Flashing red markers indicated
their locations. The next monitor showed Immortal teams collapsing
on the farm to prepare for Parizad's final actions. The third monitor was
connected to multiple drones that were providing security around the
farm. And the last monitor showed the Immortal team near Charlottesville taking up their sniper's perch in the Walmart parking lot. The Immortal team sniper lay in the back of the SUV and sighted through the

scope that was connected to the satellite through Bluetooth technology, giving Parizad the same sight picture the sniper was seeing.

The stolen CIA contractor Cadillac SUV sat at the opposite end of the parking lot. The sniper's crosshairs loomed large on the driver-side window.

"Bring him to me," Parizad said.

25

THE PHONE RANG AS I spun onto Route 29 North and brushed glass shards from my hair and face.

My plan to stay below the speed limit to avoid the police would not suffice with assassins chasing me. A pair of headlights was gaining as I was storming up to ninety miles per hour.

Reagan was yelling, "Dad! Are you okay?"

The phone was on speaker and had tumbled into the passenger seat. I reached across, grabbed the phone without looking at the screen, and said, "Nothing to worry about, Rea. I'll call you soon."

"Dad!"

I shut off the phone as the rear windshield imploded. As part of my training in JSOC, I had received instruction on in extremis driving, which made me a bit more comfortable as I tried to outrace the car closing on my rear bumper. The heavy SUV was slow to accelerate but had a reasonable top speed. I pushed it into triple digits and created some space between the vehicles as I blew through a red light and narrowly avoided a pickup truck pulling a boat trailer. The truck wobbled, causing the trailer to jackknife and the boat to topple into the road.

About a mile beyond the stoplight, which now had traffic blocking the intersection, I turned onto a country road that veered off from Route 29 where I skidded into a 180-degree turn and aimed back at the main road while nudging the nose of the SUV through a small group of trees. Shutting off my lights, I waited for the cluster of cars at the stoplight to ungroup. I used the brief moment to study the two long guns in the back, both AR-15s easily purchased at any number of gun stores in Maryland, Virginia, or West Virginia. Ten magazines of 5.56 ammunition were in the kit bag, and one of the rifles had a nightscope. I tested it, got a decent sight picture, and slapped a magazine into the well. While chambering a round and flipping the selector switch to Fire, I eased out of the SUV and found a good position about fifty meters toward the road. I checked my fields of fire, and there was nothing but a farm angling up to the east. Behind me was Route 29. To my left was north and to my right was the intersection with the traffic jam I had created.

The lines of sight were good from the intersection to where I had turned off the road, and I was guessing that they had watched me or could track me.

I was right.

Another black SUV Escalade slowed into the turn and rolled past me at about twenty-five miles per hour. I let it get about twenty meters beyond me when I started hammering away and sending lead into the tires and wheels. The two rear wheels were flat, as was the right front wheel.

The occupants probably had little idea from where the fire might be originating and were probably ducking and trying to avoid the fusillade. I waited until the doors opened. They did so all at once, spewing forth three men dressed in black who were carrying long guns. I shot the first two on the right side of the vehicle. They dropped to the ground, wounded or dead. The boots I saw beneath the SUV chassis were walking slowly toward the rear of the vehicle. The nightscope on the rifle also showed someone moving in the front seat. I moved the scope back to the boots when the driver's door opened, and another pair of boots joined the calculus. As I was sighting on the first person, the second darted in front of the hood of the SUV and sprinted into the woods toward me.

In sync with the person moving to the woods, the first man lifted his rifle and spun around the back corner of the Escalade. I quickly shot him twice in the gut. As he slowed, I fired two more center-mass rounds at him. He tumbled forward maybe twenty feet from me, and I turned toward the south, where the driver had infiltrated the woods. I reached for my knife and pistol, expecting close-quarters combat.

He was upon me as I turned, blocking my pistol with his left arm and swiping at me with a knife, which I avoided by lifting my left arm and blocking his thrusting arm. We locked for a moment in this position. His face was dark and covered with a thin black beard. He was strong, but I was feeling amped up as a burst of energy surged through me. My mind focused on the brief opportunity he presented when I snapped back my left arm, causing his right hand to thrust forward from the latent isometric pressure.

With his right shoulder dipping in front of me, I raked my knife up against the inside of his triceps and then stabbed his neck. Blood sprayed as I retracted it. He reacted by dropping his weapons and hopelessly grabbing his neck. I left him to die in the woods and checked each of the four. All were dead except one, the second man to exit the vehicle. He was severely wounded, but cognizant. I leaned over him.

"Speak English?"

"Fuck you," he said.

That was better than a yes or no.

"Where's Parizad?"

No answer. I gouged my thumb into his upper chest wound.

"Answer my question."

"Just kill me."

Never one to debate perfectly reasonable requests, I slit his throat with the knife and checked each of my attackers, confiscating phones, wallets, and weapons. I raced to the vehicle, closing the doors as I leaped into the driver's seat and began pulling away. I eased onto Route 29 and then merged into traffic when an opening presented itself.

I was certain I was pinging somebody's tracking device, but I couldn't slow down now. As my adrenaline raced, my mind filled with nakedly murderous thoughts. I noticed three aspects of how my physical response to stress at this moment differed from the way I usually operated, feeling nothing like my thirty-plus years of combat when I had a knack for taking everything in stride while remaining clearheaded. First, my heart slammed against my chest like an old-school alarm bell, incessantly and without hesitation. Next, I was sweating profusely, something that I never did before, even in the intensest combat. Lastly, my thoughts were now fuzzy enough to distract me from the task at hand, which was finding the secretary of defense's wife, Donna Tharp, and learning what she had said to Melissa before she died.

I had never cared for her husband, Jim Tharp, who was an engineer officer for his minimum five-year commitment and had transitioned to private life, where he made his fortune in the dot-com bubble, cashed out at the right time, and then pivoted into a term as the governor of Kentucky, which quickly led to his selection as secretary of defense four years ago. Former national security advisor John Bolton was a shrinking violet when it came to Tharp's expressed views on Iran and other violent actors in the Persian Gulf area.

Tharp was a skilled bureaucratic operator. My mind sizzled with hatred for Tharp. The thought of killing him seemed reasonable. Killing my wife to protect a secret? Did he really do that? I was unaccustomed to the level of emotion fueling my decision-making, and I wondered, what had changed? In the last twenty-four hours, I had ideations of killing the president and secretary of defense. While Fillmore saw me as a rival, I had nothing but best wishes for President-Elect Campbell . . . until I had learned that she may have had complicity in Melissa's death. I wasn't sure how she was involved, but Donna Tharp might be the key to that knowledge.

I dialed Reagan again. The rear view mirror showed promise.

"Dad. What is going on?"

"Nothing, Rea. Can you get me the address for Donna Tharp and text it to my number? Gotta run. Love you."

I hung up and in ten seconds my phone chimed. I opened the text . . . and pushed on the pin Reagan had dropped, which brought up the home. Naturally, it was in McLean, Virginia, along with all the other politicians.

Uninterrupted, I could get there in about ninety minutes, but there was no guarantee I could speak with her. She would be more inclined to talk to Rea, whom she knew.

"Rea, any word from Brad?"

"Not yet. Not answering his phone. Straight to voice mail."

"Keep trying. And please reach out to Donna Tharp and ask her if she'll meet me."

"You're scaring me, Dad."

Reagan didn't scare easily, but this was a higher level of tension than she had ever experienced. She was accustomed to me being in control at all times. There was never anything to fear if I was around. Now there was everything to fear. I had suggested that her mother had been killed, and now I was on the run. Was she in jeopardy?

"Okay, listen, reach out to Donna Tharp and text me where she can meet. And keep trying Brad. Let me know the minute you hear something. Stay inside the dorm."

"Okay," she muttered.

"Last thing, Rea. That picture. You're sure that was in the hospital?"

"Of course I'm sure. It was the day before I went to tennis camp. I wasn't supposed to be in there but wanted to see Mom. And that new, creepy doctor was in there."

"Did he say anything to you?"

"No. He left as soon as I came in. I sat down and snuck a selfie. Why? Do you know him?"

Did I know him? I couldn't honestly answer that question at the moment. Because if the person in that picture had anything to do with Melissa's death—and why else would the individual be in a doctor's lab coat in her room?—then I absolutely had no idea who that person was.

"I don't think so," I said.

"Okay," she said softly. "Be safe."

"Roger that."

I hung up and continued to cruise up Route 29 and then slid onto Interstate 66, headed east toward Washington, D.C. About thirty minutes before the McLean exit, my phone chimed again. Reagan had dropped a pin for a coffee shop in Rosslyn, Virginia, just across from Georgetown.

She texted: *Donna has moved out and is living in Georgetown. Meet her here in 45 min. No word from B. Worried—Love you, R*

I voice texted her, "Love you, too, baby."

Thirty minutes later, I was parked in the strip mall parking lot with fifteen minutes to spare. I used the time to study the wallets and phones of my pursuers. Farouk, Hashem, and Ghazi, all Persian names, if these licenses were reliable. The phones were locked, but texts were scrolling on the screen in Farsi. Both the locked phones and the use of Farsi were protective measures. The weapons were basic AR-15 rifles and Beretta 9 mm pistols. The volume of message traffic smacked of heavy coordination. This was no random team.

Donna Tharp pulled up in a BMW 750i and parked in front of the coffee shop. I was at the far end of the parking lot, watching. I waited five minutes and saw her checking her phone and watch. She was dressed in a cashmere camel-colored coat, a red beret, and leather boots that came up to her knees.

I did a 360-degree observation check and didn't think anyone was following her, though I couldn't be sure. Walking to the coffee shop, I continued to surveil my immediate area until I was inside. I chose a table all the way in the rear and nodded at Donna when I passed her. She followed and sat down facing me as I scanned the small crowd. There were five people scattered at the other tables, all looking at phones or MacBook computers. The espresso machine whined, drowning out the voices.

"Jesus, you look like shit," she said.

Donna was an attractive woman in her late forties. She and Tharp had three children in their late teens, including one set of twins. She had large, brown doe eyes and full lips. When she spoke to you, her eyes locked onto yours. I always liked that about her, though tonight she was wearing sunglasses indoors with a heavy application of makeup on her face. I wondered if she was hiding something. Her scarf covered her neck. Tharp had a reputation as a hothead, and I wouldn't put it past him to smack Donna around. The last time I had seen her was at Melissa's funeral. Her husband hadn't attended. Matters of state, she had told everyone.

"Yeah, well, it's been a rough few days," I said.

"Why all the cloak-and-dagger? What's going on?"

Two men entered through the front door. They scanned the establishment, eyes skipping across us and landing on the menu above the barista's head.

"Did anyone follow you?"

"What?"

"You're going through a divorce with the secretary of defense. Don't be naive, Donna," I said. Melissa and Donna had become friends while they were visiting West Point at the same time when Tharp and I were cadets. She and Tharp, like Melissa and I, had dated for the entire four years of West Point, which had an informal group that provided support to significant others and potential spouses. Melissa, true to form, had dived into that crowd and made friends with the group. There were a few visits where she'd spent more time with the women than she did with me, but I supported her broadening her base because I knew what life would be like for us once we got married. I had lived it as a kid. Always moving. Boxes stuffed in the attic that never got opened, carrying three or four different movers' tags on them from location to location. Without a strong network of support, the task was that much harder. Naturally, Melissa had become the hub of support for most everyone with whom she interacted.

We had mingled with the Tharps semi-frequently when we were living in Northern Virginia on one of my Pentagon tours as the deputy operations officer and before I knew he was a first-class asshole. Tharp was a congressman then, and I'd made the mistake of attending an annual West Point dinner where we were seated at the same table. Donna and Melissa had become close friends. Tharp and me, not so much.

"Yes, that's true, but it's not public. How did you know?"

"It doesn't matter. I need to know about your last conversation with Melissa."

She leaned back in her chair and removed her glasses. The makeup almost covered the greenish bruise, but it was evident. The two men at the table between us and the front door were talking quietly, but one subtly turned his head when Donna removed her glasses. It was difficult to tell if they were making a point not to look at us or were uninterested bystanders minding their own business.

"I'm sorry," I said.

"Don't be. I'm just holding out until after inauguration. Then I'm going public if he doesn't give me what I want."

"That's actually a crime," I said.

"Fuck it. What do you think this is?" she hissed, pointing at her face.

"Worse. He should be in jail, but why wait? What difference does the timing make?"

She looked away and said, "He broke down crying, apologizing and asking me to hold off until after the inauguration. All the parties are happening right now. I think he's at the New Zealand embassy party tonight. After the inauguration tomorrow, this will be front-page news." She pointed at her eye when she spoke.

"He'll deserve everything he gets," I said. Though, if he had anything to do with Melissa's death, I might kill him first. "What did you tell Melissa before she died?"

"What do you mean?" She looked away when she spoke. When she turned her face, the two men looked at her, and it occurred to me that Tharp could be tailing her to dig up dirt. Whether they recognized me was a different matter. The report would probably be something akin to, "She's talking to some homeless guy."

"You told her something you weren't supposed to. Something you were scared about?"

She sighed. One of the men at the table slid his phone under his arm to take a picture. I leaned so that Donna was blocking me but wasn't sure if I moved in time.

"This was right before al-Baghdadi was killed . . ." She looked up and interrupted herself. "Sorry if this is a sensitive topic."

Everyone knew I was absent when Melissa passed. A text appeared on her phone screen, and she entered a series of ones to unlock the screen and looked at the message. She put her head in her hands and sighed.

"Everything okay?" I said.

"Fucking asshole. I've got a PI following him, and he's actually at the party tonight with one of his assistants." She showed me a picture of Tharp wearing a tux and with a leggy blonde in a black cocktail dress walking next to him, talking on the phone.

"Sorry," I said. I gave her a second and then asked her again, "Did you tell anything significant to Melissa? State secret? Anything?"

"Well, I told her lots of things, but the only thing I can think of that would be off-putting to Jim was I told Melissa that I was scared. Scared of

Jim and scared of what I'd heard. I had found this," she said as she pushed a flash drive across the table.

One of the men at the table answered his phone and then looked in our direction. I scanned the crowd again. No threat, but my back was turned to the long hallway that led to the bathrooms and the storage area. The burner phone that Reagan gave me buzzed against my pants pocket.

"Sorry. Continue."

"Everything you need is on there. Emails between him, that crazy bitch Owens, and the weasel Estes. How he got to be secretary of state I'll never know. They're all shitting razor blades now wondering what a new president will do. I hope she fires them all."

I slid the flash drive into my pocket and felt the phone buzz a short burp like it did when someone left a voice mail. I looked down as Donna continued to speak.

"We kept a Ring camera in our study where we put our dog, Bruno, when we went to functions. He's a twelve-year-old Maltese with some health issues. I'd heard Jim mention some woman named Naomi when Owens and Estes came over, so I turned on the camera and recorded him to build evidence of his years of cheating on me. But for once, it wasn't another woman—Naomi had been killed in the Middle East somewhere it seems—"

The men at the table stood when two bullets washed over my left shoulder and bored into the center of Donna's forehead. It was clear she was dead or dying as her head lolled to the side, the energy from the bullets pulling her to the floor, which might have been the only thing that saved me. Her unexpected fall into the aisle tripped the lead man as he was retrieving what looked like a Walther pistol. I snatched her phone from the table and spun quickly to the rear, knowing full well I was running into the teeth of whoever had shot Donna.

A figure dressed in black clothes and running shoes dashed out the back door, which was straight down the hallway with bathrooms and storage closets on the right. I blew through the door before it closed completely and intentionally performed a gymnast roll as two shots zipped above my head.

The man leaped onto a motorcycle and missed on his first attempt to start it, giving me enough time to sail through the air and tackle him. The bike clanged onto the ground as I rolled over the wiry assassin, dislodging his pistol from his grip. It tumbled into the air, where I caught it and trained it on him. He was up quick, and I was tangled in my trench coat. As he was lifting the bike and cranking the engine, I popped up, aimed the pistol, and shot him in the head. The silencer muffled the shots as he fell to the side, and I caught the idling bike before it crushed me. I clicked the Kawasaki Z650 into gear and spun from the parking lot as the two men chased me from around the corner.

I drove from the parking lot on Wilson Boulevard heading the wrong way, horns blaring at me and pedestrians stopping to watch. I leaned into a left-hand turn and then a right and another left before I was passing over the Key Bridge into Georgetown, Washington, D.C. I headed west on M Street past Georgetown University and merged onto Foxhall Road, passed Saint Patrick's Episcopal Day School, turned onto a trail in Whitehaven Park, followed the trail east until I crossed Wisconsin Avenue and let the motorcycle fly from beneath my legs into the ravine. The finely tuned machine whined as it arced into the creek and rocks below. My momentum carried me forward, and I did a forward roll, losing the assassin's pistol and not bothering to slow and grab it. I continued running for another half mile until I passed a wooded area around Edmunds Street.

I stumbled down the steep ravine until I fell into the creek that trickled at the bottom. Lying on the rocks, cold water soaking my boots, I looked skyward as I took inventory of my body in exactly the same fashion as I did after every combat equipment parachute jump. My mind traveled from my feet and ankles to my knees, my thighs and pelvis, elbows and shoulders, and finally my head. Nothing was broken, other than my pride, which was running in low supply at the moment.

I crawled across the rocks to the thorny vines of the banks, cut my hands to the point they were bleeding, and scrabbled my way to a trail about ten meters above the creek. I made my way north about a quarter mile, surprised that there was this much undeveloped green space within Washington, D.C. I knew generally where I was located, which was just north and west of Georgetown University, which placed me in Dumbarton Oaks Park near the Naval Observatory, where the vice president lived.

By my calculations, that put me about a mile from the New Zealand embassy. Donna Tharp had mentioned that her husband was at the inauguration party for Campbell. Would Campbell be there? Was Tharp still there? Could I kill two birds with one stone by infiltrating that party?

My mind sparked with anger and adrenaline, fueling my push through the thorns and vines to the high walls of the New Zealand embassy. There were guards posted in guard towers at the two corners of the wall, which was maybe ten feet high. I backed away, knowing full well that electronic measures for early warning and detection were scanning for me by now.

A gate to the embassy compound opened to the right, and two guards with long guns walked briskly toward the woods. I was burrowed deep into the bushes and trees, smothered in low ground cover. But still, they were twenty meters away and closing toward me.

I pawed the pistol in my pocket and prepared to defend myself.

26

AS TWO GUARDS RAISED their rifles and entered the forest in search of me, the record shows that Parizad was in the large barn of the five-hundred-acre farm, filling his crop-dusting drone fleet with Demon Rain, this batch laden with more sarin liquid than previous concoctions. Parizad was interested in testing the most potent combination of hallucinogenic drug known to man.

The video cameras installed in the expansive space showed Parizad walking among ten octocopter drones arrayed like helicopters on an airport apron. Parizad wore a protective mask and poured a liquid from a milk jug into the tanks of each drone, carefully closing each lid with rubber-gloved hands. He walked to the front of the barn, removed the gloves, and texted: *In position?*

Yes. The pigs are ready.

Parizad had 150 pigs shipped in from Smithfield Foods the previous week. There was a portable, six-foot-high cattle corral two hundred meters from the barn, which facilitated the holding and transportation of the Angus cattle that roamed the farm. The pigs had been separated into the ten holding areas and had been provided corn. There were large, two-hundred-pound hogs and small thirty-pound piglets, with all sizes in between.

Parizad walked back to the drones, started each of them, their eight tiny blades whirring silently in the cavernous space. He opened the application on his tablet and drew a flight plan with his finger around the perimeter of the barren cornfield that was five football fields long and ended at the corral behind the barns. He slid the image for Drone 1 onto the path and watched as the actual drone lifted from the floor of the barn and buzzed through the open doors, then tilted onto the path Parizad had outlined on the application. Keeping his mask on, he walked through an opening in the fence that surrounded the house and the barn and stood on a small hillock overlooking the endless furrowed rows of brown stalks. There was little ambient light, and the stars were brilliant against the black sky. The cattle corral was a series of man-made shapes against the natural terrain.

Repeating this process for each of the ten drones, he watched as each drone followed a different path he had designated. Ten squares with live thermal video streams appeared on his tablet next to the macro view of the cattle corral and the pigs. The drones were programmed to spray at a specific GPS point on the ground. As each drone approached its target, it began releasing an aerosolized mist of sarin gas from fifteen feet above ground level.

Parizad studied the flow rates of the fluids being released. He calculated the distance from which he had launched the drones to their intended spray areas and knew he would need more distance from the objective area. As the drones executed their missions for their designated flight times of thirty minutes, Parizad studied the geography around the intended target area, calculating other supplies he might need. This was the final rehearsal before the attack.

And he listened.

The pigs grunted and squealed high-pitched noises. The Demon Rain blanketed them to the point that within a matter of two minutes, every pig was dead.

Perfect.

The first of the drones buzzed past Parizad and landed in its original location, wobbling as its eight blades lowered it to the dusty plank flooring. The others followed suit as he checked the spray tanks of each.

Parizad looked again at his tablet, now showing an image of the Camp David compound, which was less than thirty miles from the front gate of the farm. He had much left to think about at this point, but his plan was solidified.

His layered approach to attacking the Americans fit well with his long view that a mere act of retribution was a disservice to his father and Soleimani, his mentor. Rather, his plan to create psychological fear and inflict lasting economic damage within the United States—and, by extension, the rest of the world—was a multifaceted juggernaut of defensive and offensive actions.

Mahmood walked into the barn.

"I think that went well," he said, removing his protective mask.

"I agree. Between this and the tests in Yazd, I think we have evidence that we will be successful."

Mahmood nodded.

"Half of the crowd dies and the other half attacks?"

"Something like that. When the drones spray the crowd at the inauguration, those that don't die from nerve damage will be holding their phones up to take pictures. Our hack into all iPhones and Androids will mesh with the hallucinogenic properties to make the crowd do our work for us."

Holding at bay the very people charged with deterring threats to the United States, Parizad was now able to maneuver a twenty-first-century array of forces in the cyber and physical domains to extend the conflict with the United States, seizing upon inner discord and parlaying the Americans' nefarious personal ambitions into a golden opportunity for Iran.

Like any well-laid war plan, Parizad's political demands were well conceived and approved by his country's leadership.

His three other drone operators entered the barn to join him and Mahmood. They were all wearing protective masks.

"First, decontaminate the drones," Parizad said. "Then yourselves."

When they were done with both tasks, Parizad convened his team in the command center above the garage, where they discussed minor issues and the fixes they would implement until the attack.

He thanked his men and issued instructions before retiring to his room. The extensive camera system allowed him to see the guards at the main gate and surrounding his inner perimeter.

He was reviewing his checklist when his cell phone rang.

"We have a problem. Sinclair is in D.C.!"

27

I WAS SITUATED IN the forest that came to a point between three high walls protecting the vice president's home at the Naval Observatory, the Danish embassy, and that of New Zealand, holding my pistol, and steadying my breathing when a General George Patton quote unexpectedly floated through my mind: "Prepare for the unknown by studying how others in the past have coped with the unforeseeable and the unpredictable."

I had put a few things together on my trek through the woods. I always operated on two levels, at a minimum. First, of course, was the basic survival required to stay alive in order to be effective. Second, regardless of when I had seen, read, or heard a piece of information, there was a part of my mind that was constantly synthesizing the nuggets like some artificial intelligence algorithm.

Poet George Santayana had originally penned the oft-misquoted maxim: those who do not remember the past are doomed to repeat it.

My belief system up until Melissa's death had generally been to look at past success and execute some facsimile of what others did to succeed while of course critically analyzing mistakes made and learning from them. The human mind is fascinated by failure and the salacious acts of others. No doubt, others want to be successful, powerful, and rich, but very few are able to piece everything together to prevent failure while achieving success. A large part of success was preventing failure, while also having a clear vision of your desired solution in your mind.

I had been so focused on haranguing myself for fifteen months about missing Melissa's last few moments that I overlooked the most important aspect of what she wanted to leave me. Not only had I not been there physically, I had been so absorbed with guilt that it clouded the very thing she wanted me to understand and execute. I was focused on the failure, not the success.

We had always been a team. She had always helped with the big decisions. Here I was self-flagellating and running on fumes in a stolen trench coat and beanie while carrying stolen weapons and phones as I eyed two men charging in my direction amid the sounds of music and laughter floating over the New Zealand embassy's protective wall.

And a few more cylinders clicked into place.

I had read everything about Project MKUltra run by the CIA and Sidney Gottlieb. It had been an utter failure. They had tried everything and declared the decades-long hunt a failure. It had included hiring Nazi and Japanese war criminals to run labs in Germany and Japan, as well as opening experimentation centers at hospitals around the country, including Walter Reed—where Melissa had been treated.

The locus of activity for Gottlieb's ghouls had been what was called Camp Detrick at the time and later became Fort Detrick, where the U.S. Army Chemical Corps would test new chemical weapons and defenses to known toxins.

The computer chip in the back of my brain was piecing together Melissa's death, the raids in Heidelberg and Yokkaichi, and Parizad's involvement. Whatever drug I had flowing through my system was ebbing.

The optical nerve was sparking less, and I was gaining clarity on my thoughts. The logic was there. Or so I believed. The imagery on the mobile phone was a new layer to consider.

The drug first, then some kind of mind control through an iPhone?

Melissa had known something that she wasn't supposed to. And there was a good possibility that my fellow members of West Point's Long Gray Line, and perhaps even the president-elect, had something to do with her death.

Without the phones, though, the hallucinogenic form of Demon Rain was less effective. Without the techno-drug combination, there was little chance of a breakthrough. Was Parizad sophisticated enough to employ something as elaborate as a techno-drug? I had always considered him a brawler, not a technical fighter. I had figured mind control would be too esoteric for him. So why the wild-goose chase? To keep me preoccupied? If so, *from* what? To set me up? If so, *for* what?

Or was I wrong about Parizad? Had he evolved as a thinker and strategist? It was certainly possible.

Ever since the COVID-19 outbreak, part of my responsibilities as the commander of the counterterrorism task force involved smoking out not only the types of threats that the likes of bin Laden, al-Baghdadi, Soleimani, and Parizad could deliver to the homeland but also the increased likelihood of chemical and biological warfare, whether intentionally or passively delivered.

The unanswered questions were: What wasn't I supposed to see, and what had necessitated killing Melissa?

My mind stormed. Short breaths escaped in misty clouds as my heart raced. I silently pushed my body deeper into the thick underbrush, wriggling my shoulders and arms against the loose dirt beneath me. The number of electronics scanning and probing these woods had probably already sterilized me. Thermal cameras, motion detectors, passive infrared indicators, and an assortment of other early-warning apparatus were monitoring my every move.

"Either a big animal or a person," said one voice in a Kiwi lilt.

The brush broke ten feet from me on either side as they split up. I had used what little time I had to burrow farther into the deadfall. The warmth from the earth beneath a foot of leaves and branches welcomed me. The man on my left crunched the leaves on the forest floor beyond me and circled to his left, toward the Danish embassy's rear wall. The man on my right circled to his right as they performed a typical cloverleaf security sweep, which sometimes left the middle uncovered if they didn't get it right the first time. I breathed slowly and sucked in the earthy smell of decomposing leaves and dirt.

"Fuck it, it's cold out here," the guard on the left said as they circled back to the middle. "Probably a deer."

I remained still for five minutes after the gate clanged against the metal support of the New Zealand embassy fence. Slowly pushing myself up to one knee, I backed away from the sensors and into a small ravine about forty meters deeper into the woods.

Having left Ben David's phone gift in the Cadillac, I retrieved Donna's phone and punched one six times as I had seen her do in the coffee shop. At the top was a text from "Douchebag," whom I guessed to be Jim Tharp, her husband. I punched on the text and then the Call button.

Tharp answered, "Yeah, bitch, you recording this?"

"Hi, Jim, it's Garrett Sinclair," I said.

"What the fu—you boning her? Gotten over your dead wife?"

"I've talked to Donna and know what you're doing. If you want to survive . . . politically, meet me at the parking lot on the west side of Fort Detrick."

"Keep dreaming," he said, but he didn't hang up.

"I know about your plan. You tell me what you, Owens, and Estes know about Melissa's death, and I'll give you the flash drive that your dead wife gave me. Oh, and you're looking good for the hit on Donna."

The truth was that it wasn't he who would be blamed for Donna's murder. I was probably the number-one suspect. I had been the last one to be seen with her. Regardless, I hung up on him as he was in midsentence, responding with some mix of trash talk and disbelief I didn't have time for. I had to figure out how to get to Frederick, Maryland. Tharp would have a Lincoln Town Car and a chase car with at least three or four security guys, and I had no transportation.

I backed into the forest, scanning in every direction. There was one piece of high ground, and I needed to insert Campbell's SIM again and make a call. I retrieved my other phone and exchanged SIM cards, immediately producing two messages, one from a number I recognized as Campbell's and one I didn't recognize. I quickly blacked out the phone and looked away.

The clearing to my front was a lone area of high ground in the deep ravine, an aberration in what was otherwise a slash in the ground. I broke brush and stumbled through the rocky creek before climbing from the depths of the gulley and clawing my way to the military crest of the hill. I was still thirty meters beneath the peak of the terrain feature, which afforded me a view of flashlights swooping through the forest near the embassy. Dogs barked, hot on the scent. I slid around to the south side of the hill, planning my escape, but in the distance, blue police lights cut through the barren trees like a strobe. Both to the north and south were gated homes in elite northwest Washington, D.C.

The SIM card had not been in the phone long enough for Campbell's Secret Service team to home in on me so quickly. The heightened security status due to the inauguration created a higher density of forces—good, bad, or indifferent—that could be leveraged against any possible threat.

Men in tactical vests with rifles bounced through the creek, tugged forward by large German shepherds tight on leashes, clawing through the deadfall. I was in the middle of Dumbarton Oaks Park, a rare rectangular two-hundred-acre stretch of land in Washington, D.C., with police closing in on my position.

I considered evading to either side where the gates and walls were high, but by this point, it wasn't obvious I had the angle to beat them to the wall, and if I did win that particular race, I had no good intelligence on what was on the other side.

The dogs barked louder, sensing my proximity. I crawled to the top of the hill, a barren piece of land no more than twenty meters in width. Trails crisscrossed the plateau, and the detritus of high school romance littered the hilltop. Beer cans, condoms, cigarette butts, and spent lighters littered the trails as I stayed low and thought through my options.

Surrender? Fight? Flee?

Fleeing was looking remote, especially with dogs. The police would tie me to the Charlottesville and Arlington shootings and lock me up immediately. My protestations of a plot against the homeland would be dismissed as the rantings of someone who was not stable. The drug running through my body enhanced all my senses while at the same time clouding my judgment by making me more prone to emotion instead of reason.

Still, I was able to string together enough logic to understand that three West Point graduates were conspiring with Dariush Parizad and that Melissa's death was necessary to their success.

And there were only fifteen hours left until the inauguration of a president who might or might not be complicit.

The dogs were barking in stereo now, beginning to claw up the base of the hill. I stood upright and looked at the phones. There were two voice mails I hadn't listened to yet. One was probably Campbell trying to trick me into turning myself in, and the other might have been spam.

I glanced at the phone long enough to call the unknown number, and it went to an anonymous voice mail. I risked another glance and pressed on Campbell's phone number. She answered on the second ring.

"Garrett!"

A man lunged at me from the west side. I rolled away and dropped the phone as I retrieved the knife I was carrying. There were too many homes in proximity to risk collateral damage with a gunshot. His momentum had made him tumble, so I kicked him in the gut before kneeling and landing a solid right cross on his cheek.

The beams of light were closer. The dogs were louder. The men were close enough for me to hear them talking.

As if this weren't enough, the distant sound of helicopter blades popped in the distance, louder by the second. The airspace had to be locked down tightly, though airplanes were still etching along the sky above the Potomac River a mile away on their milk runs to Reagan National Airport.

I was surrounded on all sides with men and dogs clawing up the hill, and the aircraft above me was about to close the door on any possibility that I would learn what actually had happened to Melissa or be able to thwart an attack on the country.

The man at my feet lay still as I dropped my knife and raised my hands.

28

AS I WAS SLOWLY turning around, my arms raised, watching the world close in on me, video and audio records show that Dariush Parizad was a busy man. Yesterday, he had greeted a new visitor, who delivered a hooded and bound hostage, whom Parizad placed in a cell in the basement of the farmhouse. Now, Parizad took a phone call.

"Between your men and ours, I think we've got Sinclair roped in. He'll be good for at least a few murders," his host said.

"It is careless to call me with this nonsense," Parizad replied and hung up.

Parizad preferred direct confrontation, which was what he sought with me now. His Immortal teams had specific instructions to either kill or, preferably, capture. There was no in-between, and the capture would lead to a mano a mano resolution.

Parizad flipped on the body cams that his Immortal operatives wore and watched as they attacked from two directions. Parizad's hands visibly shook as his men ascended the hilltop. His view was an erratic mishmash of dirt, sky, arms, and legs until one of his men stood atop the hill and lunged.

The plan emphasized detention, which was why they didn't unleash the dogs. His phone rang again, distracting him from the melee.

"Yes," he said, frustrated with the distractions.

"I'm five minutes away. We need to meet," the voice said.

Parizad walked down the steps and onto the front lawn of the estate. Parizad appreciated his anonymity but disliked having to endure the comings and goings of his host. The car drove up the long driveway with its lights out, a measure of secrecy.

His host exited the black Town Car from the driver's door while another car idled by the street.

"What do you know about Sinclair having more information than he should?"

"I told you, he's a resourceful man. You should not underestimate him."

"He wants a meeting in an hour or so near Fort Detrick. Do you know anything about this?"

"How would I know?" Parizad tightened. He wasn't happy. Less than fifteen hours until execution, and he was having to deal with an unprecedented level of meddling.

"I'm just covering all the bases."

"I'm not a base," Parizad said. "And I don't require covering."

Parizad considered killing his host, but whoever was waiting in the car would notice his absence. Parizad could kill them, as well, and then the next level of supervisors or concerned parties would come running, all inside the execution window of his operation. That was how the bureaucratic mind operated. If after a reasonable time you haven't heard from your boss, call around and figure out what was happening. All those texts and phone calls would eventually lead to the next level. And the next.

"I can send one of my teams to back you up for your meeting," Parizad said. It would give him insight into what was happening anyway. He could spare the manpower. There was no threat to the farm so far, and he couldn't see the Intelligence Community moving fast enough to discover either his location or intentions. In twenty-four hours, everything would be gone from this location, anyway, except the dead pigs.

And there was no chance they would find the hostages his resident Immortal team had been keeping at the farm for the past few days.

"It's not my meeting, but that might be good, as long as they keep their distance. We will have layers of protection."

"Sinclair may be captured before he ever gets to a meeting."

"Yes, we know his location, but the police are slow in responding, so we are still planning the meeting on the off chance it does happen."

Parizad nodded. "Okay, then, the trade is I will tell you the entirety of my plan that will give you the catalyst for your full ground war and invasion against Iran that you seek. In exchange, you will give me access to Sinclair if you capture him."

"That's a deal."

They walked into Parizad's above-garage command center.

"Please, sit."

His host sat at the command terminal and looked at the four monitors.

"On your left, you see an Iranian submarine patrolling well off the shore of New York's Long Island. This is our rescue vehicle. We will use a helicopter to take us there."

"What helicopter?"

"That is not your concern. I haven't asked you for one, and I don't need one at the moment."

Parizad pointed at the next screen. "This screen shows Fayetteville Street in downtown Raleigh. We have an explosive device that will attack the rally that is being conducted in support of the new president, who is, as you know, a former governor of North Carolina. This next screen shows Fort Detrick. There will be an attack on the unauthorized storage of sarin gas if anyone attempts to disrupt my plan. This last screen shows my hostages. They will remain unharmed as long as I am provided free escape to my submarine."

"So the attack on Raleigh, is it?"

Parizad nodded. "It is a pinprick."

"I appreciate your transparency."

"Never underestimate the general," Parizad said.

"He's made some mistakes."

"Or has he?" Parizad asked. "What may look like a mistake to you could be an intentional ruse. Be careful. I've said all along that he was the one person that could disrupt your plan. He's no fool, nor is he my responsibility."

"Stopping Sinclair from disrupting our plan is the entire reason for all of this," his host said, waving his hand around the room.

"Then let's get to work."

The host nodded and exited the apartment, entered the car, and drove back to the end of the driveway. Parizad messaged his Immortal team watching the mouth of the driveway and told them to stand down.

The East Coast submarine had always been a throwaway given the density of U.S. vessels patrolling in the Atlantic. If they found that, it would confirm that the host was leaking information. The bomb in Raleigh was a pure fabrication.

The hostages, however, were very real.

Parizad looked at the monitor. The hostages were tired and drained. Captivity could seem like days or years, even for the new addition. He wondered what these captives were thinking after being bound and hidden away.

He walked into the basement and followed a small tunnel into a carpeted underground playroom that the host's children or grandchildren most likely used. The adults could lock the kids in there and let them play for hours. He opened a side door into a work and laundry area closed in with cement walls like a workshop. It was connected to the barn with a fifty-meter walkway, essentially a tunnel.

He opened the door to one of the small rooms adjacent to the tunnel and stared at one of the hostage's feral eyes and gagged mouth, white teeth clenched against the cloth tightened around the mouth and neck.

Parizad nodded and closed the door and checked in on the new addition, who looked the same. He had no sympathy. One was a soldier; one was a child. So be it.

Wild eyes looked up at him. Alarm or anger? He wasn't sure.

They would die with the attack; that was their fate.

29

THE HELICOPTER BLADES SMACKED against the sky above me. Dogs snarled as they lunged against the taut leashes of their handlers. Men dressed in black-and-brown tactical clothing came barreling up the hill, brandishing pistols, rifles, and knives.

I was surrounded. If I ducked, though, they might all kill themselves with gunfire.

If they wanted me dead, any of these men could have killed me, or at least tried. The only effort so far had been the initial man lunging across the well-trod terrain, but suddenly a man handed his leash to another and lifted his rifle.

The helicopter blades resonated louder against the night. A spotlight shined brightly on us, as if we were theater actors on stage. I could now clearly see the faces of my pursuers. They were not D.C. police or, for that matter, any official law enforcement that I could determine. Rather, they looked like Parizad's men, the Immortal sleeper cells we had studied and feared would be present on that fateful day they were operationalized.

A rope dropped from the helicopter, which I just now focused on. I recognized the signature chop of the Black Hawk's blade. This wasn't a police helicopter. It was the Beast.

I grabbed onto the lifeline and tugged hard with my weakened arms. My pectoral muscles clenched as the helicopter slowly lifted. I gritted my teeth, knowing that there was no time for weakness. Mental and physical strength were required most when a reasonable person could expect them least. As I looped the rope around my feet, I was running on fumes, surrounded by armed assassins and ferocious dogs.

A rifle emitted flame from a weapon muzzle as I ascended into the sky. Something bit at my leg, most likely a bullet that had found its mark. The helicopter banked to the south and sped into the Potomac River corridor, heading west. I held on using an S-turn in the rope between my feet to lessen the strain against my tired arms. We flew below the tips of the trees and just barely above the water.

The rope was slowly elevating into the helicopter. The Beast carried the jungle penetrator lifesaving system that allowed for the crew to retrieve wounded from the battlefield. The winch-and-pulley system was slowly pulling me into the aircraft. The crawl of the device was painfully slow. My grip was weakening. My hands were tired, my arms at muscular failure, and my legs were giving out. The slipstream and rotor wash beat me against the side of the aircraft as I felt hands pulling me inside.

I rolled inside the helicopter, and the crew chief shut the door. He was wearing a space-age crewman's helmet, which prevented me from seeing his face. I did, however, recognize Joe Hobart wincing in pain in the cargo hold of the Beast. He slipped a headset on me and said, "We've got you, sir."

I swallowed dry spit and said, "What's wrong?" The grimace on his face indicated pain.

"Just some stitches," he said.

"Where to, General?" McCool said.

"Anywhere an F-15 won't put a missile up our ass," I choked out.

"Roger," she said.

"Undercover?" Hobart asked.

I looked at my clothes. Trench coat, beanie, a week of stubble, muddy, hollowed out, and probably a wild look in my eyes.

"Yeah, undercover," I said. Then, "On second thought, Cools, let's go to Frederick. Fort Detrick. Strip mall parking lot on the west side. I'm supposed to meet Tharp there."

"The SecDef?"

"Yeah."

"Roger that."

"How'd you break into the airspace?"

"I flew the Gold Top missions for a stint a few years ago. Used my old call sign and got in. Getting out is a different story," McCool said. Gold Tops were the secretary of defense's administrative helicopter fleet full of Black Hawk VH-60s that were tricked out with the executive package and painted gold on top, presumably to avoid being errantly shot down by air force pilots.

"So he might know you're here?"

"Maybe. It's not like he tracks helicopter flights, but if he's got people looking for an anomaly, he will find out."

We flew above the river, passed over the falls, and stayed below the treetops for about thirty minutes when McCool and her copilot, Rogers, turned north and wound her way through farm fields and forests until she flared the Beast and brought it in for a soft landing in the rolling hills straddling Catoctin Creek. She taxied along the dirt runway and steered the helicopter into a large hangar with two Cessna single-propeller airplanes parked to the side, noses pointing out. She had landed at a county airfield that had no air traffic control or maintenance personnel this time of night. There could be the random aircraft owner or mechanic tidying up, but there were no obvious signs of life. Whether the U.S. Air Force had tracked our movements was a different story.

"A friend keeps his airplane here. Said we could use his hangar," McCool said.

"Roger. Tell him thanks," I said.

At the far end of the hangar were large storage tanks, a boat on a trailer, a pickup truck, and some black fifty-gallon drums.

The rotors wound down and finally stopped. Hobart, Brown, and McCool helped me off and walked with me to an office in the hangar. There, they had set up a makeshift medical area with an elevated litter, IV bags, and assorted drugs, needles, and gauze. They laid me on the stretcher, and Hobart limped over and began cutting my pants leg.

"Gunshot wound," he said. His left arm was in a sling, and he used his right hand to inspect my wound.

McCool came into the room and removed her helmet. Jimmy Rogers followed her. They were wearing their olive flight suits and carrying their aviator helmets. The room spun around my head. My hands were blistered raw from holding on to the rope and pulling at thorny vines. Bursts of pain exploded in my brain as Hobart cleansed and tended to my wound.

"You need rest, sir," McCool said.

"We need to talk," I said, my garbled, croaking, dry-throated words not carrying the conviction of their meaning. "It's ten p.m. Inauguration is in fourteen hours."

"Rest first," she said placing a hand on my arm. "If only for thirty minutes."

"I have information. We have to act now. The phone. Demon Rain. They work together."

"Give me thirty minutes of sleep, General, and then we can talk."

"What if I don't?" I asked.

She smiled weakly. "You will." McCool put her hand on my arm and leaned into my ear. "You're wanted by the police in Virginia, Maryland, and D.C. The FBI, CIA, and DoD contractors are after you. Intel tells me that Iranian sleeper cells have activated. Trust the team like we've trusted you."

"I have to be in Frederick in an hour."

"Thirty minutes, General. We've got a car here. They'll wait."

My mind spun and swooned into and out of reality. I didn't know whether it was the drugs that had been coursing through my system from Yokkaichi or something new that Hobart might have injected into me.

"Where are Van Dreeves and Jackson?" I asked.

"Get some rest. That's an order. I'm the pilot in command," McCool said.

There was something comforting about her voice, her presence. I was glad to be surrounded by friends and teammates. People I knew and trusted. I had told Tharp to meet me in two hours, which was about an hour ago, maybe more. Thirty minutes in the woods and thirty minutes in the helicopter.

I slid into unconsciousness, knowing I couldn't allow myself to miss the opportunity to meet with Tharp. He held the key to Melissa. Melissa held the key to Parizad. Parizad was planning something.

I faded, blacked out, and then awoke. It might have been five minutes or five hours. My mind was foggy. McCool was hovering over me.

"Sir. Let's go. You gave me thirty minutes. I'm getting you to Fort Detrick," she said. "I sent Joe up there to get eyes on. I'm driving you, but first we've got new clothes for you in the bathroom. You've got ten minutes."

I walked to the bathroom, ran the shower hot, scrubbed off the muck from the creek while avoiding Hobart's patch job on my leg laceration, and pulled on a change of clothes that McCool had grabbed from my go bag in the Beast.

Emerging from the bathroom, I followed McCool into a black Chevy Suburban SUV. She handed me an MRE and said, "Eat this on the drive."

I didn't argue and wolfed down the spaghetti and meatballs MRE, notably the only combat ration that was remotely edible. My mind was still groggy from the lack of sleep, despite the unconscious thirty minutes I had snagged at McCool's urging. As I ate, McCool's brow was set in a permanent worry, as if she knew something that the rest of us did not. She was a smart woman. West Point, Rhodes Scholar, flight school, and combat veteran pilot with a Purple Heart earned when Taliban machine-gun rounds had severed a fuel line leading to her left engine, which had burst into flames, causing her to shut it down and fly to a hard landing in the Hindu Kush. One of the bullets had exploded in the cockpit, shrapnel buzzing everywhere and slicing her neck. I saw the white line of the scar as she stared intently ahead toward the road.

"So, here's the deal, sir. You're wanted in Maryland, D.C., and Virginia for murder, treason, and about a dozen 'lesser crimes,'" she said. "Like I was saying, there's every manner of good guy and bad guy looking for you."

"Where's Van Dreeves?" I asked, ignoring her comments.

"He was wounded badly in Japan, and last I heard he was in the hospital system somewhere," she said. She didn't sound convinced.

I thought about that for a moment. McCool was the unofficial keeper of tabs for our team. Plus, she and Van Dreeves had an affinity for one another. There was no chance that she didn't have clarity on Van Dreeves's status.

"What aren't you telling me?"

She kept her eyes on the road. Her hands gripped the steering wheel so tight her knuckles were white.

"I've lost him, sir."

"Lost Randy? Like he's dead?"

"Oh God, I hope not. No, I took him to the U.S. military hospital in Yokkaichi. He was wounded badly in the action at the target. I had to get you, Hobart, and Brown on the C-17 medevac. Everything was happening so fast. Jackson was dead. I lost my crew chief. You and Hobart were hanging by a thread. I didn't know what to do, so I stuck with the bulk of my team, because I figured that was what you would have done. Be where you can make the most difference. I've called a million times to check on Randy, and no one can tell me anything. I have a friend who's a nurse at the hospital there, and she said he was checked out by a doctor in Japan and put on a private flight. I checked at Walter Reed, and there's no record of him."

She was near tears but held them back.

"How did Jackson die?" This was news to me.

"It was quick. Gunshot to the head. We were on exfil with you from the Yokkaichi house, and a stray round punched inside his crew door as he was laying down suppressive fire."

"When will we do the memorial? Has anyone notified his parents?"

Jackson was from Philadelphia and born to two public school teachers who had protested when he, after leaving professional football, decided to join the army, and then protested some more when he joined the Rangers, and then went completely off the rails when I had selected him for Dagger. I could tell that their concerns weighed on him. Every time I spoke with him about his parents, he would cast his eyes downward and say, "Sir, this is just what I want to do. They wanted to be teachers, and I wanted to be a soldier. It's as simple as that."

Calling them would not be an easy phone call, especially because the details would be sketchy and insufficient to satisfy their rightful desire for information.

"I've got someone working that," she said.

I nodded, trusting her. Now for the million-dollar question. "How did you find me?"

She let out a small grunt. It was somewhere between a sigh, a laugh, and a moment of relief. The weightiness of what was transpiring weighed on her; that was obvious.

"The chip I gave you. It was the SIM card from your burner phone. You know, the one you used to communicate directly with the president-elect?"

I immediately understood her displeasure with me. Our team was built upon trust and open communications, regardless of rank. I had hidden this piece of intel from her and the rest of the crew, which on its own was not unusual. Given the chemistry of our team, though, I probably should have shared the information.

"I should have told you," I said. "But she asked me not to."

"That's probably because she's been tracking you, too."

I processed what McCool had just said. "How do you know?"

"When I took the phone from you, I had two guys suddenly appear when I got back to Washington, D.C. They had been following me. I've got an ex who is Secret Service. I texted him a picture, and he said that my followers were an outsourced team they used when presidential travel required a surge. I was busy taking care of Hobart for a day, so I had a friend of mine from UVA track you."

"A blonde?"

"You saw her?"

"Yes. Wasn't sure if she was friend or foe. Chloe Collinsworth?"

"Friend. Yes."

"Why would Campbell want to track me?"

"Why does anyone stalk anyone? Obsessed? Worried?"

I didn't have time to tell McCool that I thought Campbell and/or the West Pointers might have played a role in Melissa's death, because McCool's phone buzzed.

"Brown's got something," she said. Her fingers played with the phone screen as she divided her time between looking down and looking up at the road. "Shit."

She showed me the phone.

I had never been one to complain about a picture of me, other than the fact that one existed. I couldn't recall where this photo of me had originated that was now projected high definition on her phone screen. The faded photograph captured a menacing look with my eyes narrowed and glancing to my left. My Ranger and airborne tabs were visible on my left shoulder. A helicopter was beyond me in the distance. Tossed hair, longer than I can remember it ever being, curled across my forehead. Tan and brown hills climbed into the distance behind the helicopter. My teeth were clenched in a quasi–Clint Eastwood "Make my day" grimace. Maybe Iraq? Afghanistan? It didn't matter. Obviously, some soldier had snapped this photo either before or after a mission, and now it was broadcast around the world.

The words beneath it read: General Goes Rogue: Possible Link to Terror Plot.

30

TWO THINGS I SHOULD have realized before this all started: The gift from Campbell was more than a friendly invite inside the ropes of her campaign; it was a tracking device. And the Heidelberg and Yokkaichi missions were bogus errands in support of a deadlier plot partially referenced in the news segment with my photo.

A million scenarios ran through my mind as to why the president-elect would want to know where I was at all times, but I couldn't escape the notion that the tracking and the plot were connected. I was being set up to take the fall for something, possibly a chemical attack on the United States. It didn't take a brain surgeon to understand that the inauguration now fourteen hours away was a prime target for mass casualties.

But why me? I was nothing but a loyal servant to the nation, despite some murderous thoughts about whoever might have played a role in killing Melissa. Heidelberg and Yokkaichi had checkered pasts as CIA chemical test hotbeds. I was on two deniable missions with my limited crew—three if you counted the Yazd Province raid.

We pulled into the same strip mall parking lot next to Fort Detrick where I had been cornered by the military police and the Immortal team.

"There," McCool said. She pointed across the parking lot to a black SUV and separate black chase car. "Hobart has eyes on with the sniper rifle from the opposite direction."

She handed me an earbud for our communications system, which I plugged into my right ear.

"Two guards covering the wood line." Hobart's voice was crisp.

"Roger. This is the secretary of defense we're dealing with, so be prepared for other threats. Air, long distance, especially from the fence line fifty meters to the east."

"Roger. Plan?"

"I'll walk to his car, get frisked, and probably get in. If they drive away with me, don't block their exit. I'll deal with it."

"Don't like it. Stay outside," he said.

"Worst case, I'm inside. Maybe only way to get intel."

"They can lock you in."

"Understand. Humint is important here. Might be the only way."

I was done debating the plan. The food and coffee perked me up marginally. I felt sore, not tired, which I took as a good sign. The news report had gone a long way to clearing the fog from my mind, like a marine layer burning off at noon, realizing I was now the face of terror to the nation. Between avenging Melissa's death, stopping a terrorist attack, and clearing my name, the stakes could not have been higher.

With the recognition that the president-elect of the United States knew exactly where I was and that the secretary of defense was awaiting my arrival across the parking lot, I dumped all but my one weapon in the front seat and exited the Suburban, saying to McCool, "See you in a few."

She nodded, still hiding something behind her worried eyes. Maybe it was the simple fact that there was an all-points bulletin on national television regarding me and that I could soon be arrested. Regardless, I walked across the empty lot wearing the new clothes with the old duster and beanie, believing that Tharp and his team would be looking for me in this clothing. The wind gusted with an icy bite. The air smelled of pine forests and tree sap. The cold asphalt resonated through the soles of my worn boots. Presidential inaugurations signaled change, and now, more than ever, my sense was that the quiet night and the icy breeze were a harbinger.

Knowing full well I might be detained, I approached the SUV and stopped when two men exited the chase car. Hobart had spotted two in the woods and now there were two here. They had extra people, plus whatever was in the secretary's car.

"Hold up, General," one of the men said. "We are coming to you." They walked toward me with weapons carried low. Each man held a pistol and walked with purpose. The man on the left was white, tall, and broad shouldered. The man on the right had a medium build and was of Asian descent. As they closed on me, Hobart whispered in my earbud, "Have them in my sights."

"Hands up," the tall guy said as his partner stopped and leveled his pistol at me. The tall guy walked toward me and stuffed his pistol in his belt as he frisked me, again missing the knife in my boot. As he came back up, he leaned forward and whispered in my ear, "You're a dead man."

His stale breath poured over me, and I got the sense that he had been awake for a couple of days. His eyes were tired, and his hands shook as he felt me up.

"Roger that," I said, avoiding provoking him.

The lead guard removed a set of flex-cuffs and restrained my hands, cinching them down an extra notch just to make me feel the pain, but I didn't give him the satisfaction of revealing he had cut into my wrists.

"Tough guy, huh?"

He led me to the SUV and opened the door.

Secretary of Defense Tharp sat in the middle row of the vehicle. The left seat was jacked forward to provide access to the third row of seats, which the second guard used to enter and position himself behind me. The lead guard shoved me into the back, causing me to stumble forward. The rear guard grabbed my shoulders and pulled me into the middle seat as the lead slid in beside me and closed the door.

"Hello, Garrett," Tharp said. "I understand you killed my wife. Thanks for doing that. The nosy bitch was becoming a problem."

"Your hit man did that," I said.

"Not mine, but a minor technicality, don't you think? They were aiming for you, a well-publicized threat to the country, but they missed and poor Donna was the unfortunate recipient of the bullet."

He had given the matter some thought, but I was hardly paying attention. I had a gun to the back of my head and one in my side. The SUV was idling, and the Dodge Challenger in front of us had plumes of exhaust coming from the tailpipes. They were prepared to move. My hands were tied together and hanging over the edge of the seat. The exhaust bump through the middle of the vehicle brought my knees higher than normal. I felt my boot top with my bound hands.

"Windows look bulletproof," Hobart said in my ear.

"Let them know that if they leave, I'm following," McCool said.

I ignored McCool's comment and said to Tharp, "She was your wife. She loved you and supported you." Like the turtle on the fence post, Tharp believed that he had risen to his exalted position solely on his own genius. People like him ultimately failed at some point in time, even if it meant being alone when they died. People in power had enough "friends" to sustain them until that fateful moment when they could no longer do any good for the hangers-on.

"We're not here to talk about her. You asked for this meeting. It's generous of me to give you a few minutes. Luckily, I had other business to attend to up here, anyway."

I turned and stared at him when I said, "I bet. You, Estes, and Owens have something going on."

A cloud passed over his eyes, but he was a skilled practitioner of the art of deception.

"We've always got something going on, Sinclair. The real question is, do I turn you over to these guys and later on stumble across you and claim to be a hero? Or do I let you go hang yourself? Both are equally appealing."

"You should kill me," I said. "I know what you're up to with Parizad."

He flinched. His eyes batted twice, and his left cheek twitched. "Parizad?"

"Yes, Mr. Secretary. The Iranian successor to Soleimani that your department is charged with confronting. You sent me on a chase around the world to keep me from seeing what it is that you're doing and to implicate me in your crimes."

It was a stab in the dark, but it was what I had been able to piece together. The West Pointers were planning something, maybe a consolidation of their power. The vast and far-reaching muscle of the Defense and State Departments, coupled with that of the CIA, made for a potent brew, whatever the endgame.

The tenor of his voice changed.

"Killing you *is* looking like the best option," Tharp said.

I wondered about the thugs who were protecting him. They were most likely rejects from the military that enjoyed being near the center of the flame. The man to my left nudged his pistol into my side. The man behind me pressed his pistol into the back of my neck.

"Look at you, Sinclair," Tharp said. "You always were that straight arrow, but now you look like a fucking homeless bum. Anyway, what is happening is much larger than you, and even if I told you, which I won't, you couldn't stop it. It is what this country needs, though, to bring it together. That much I know. All right, guys, dump him in the woods. Your call on what happens to him."

On that, the guard on the left opened the door and pulled at me while the guard in the rear pushed against the back seat. I already had the Blackhawk special ops knife open and slicing through the flex-cuffs. I rammed an elbow into the nose of the guard behind me—blood sprayed everywhere—as I spun out of the vehicle and kicked the tall guard's pistol out of his hand. I was sure that Hobart and McCool were watching and that Tharp was a paper tiger. I doubted he carried a weapon.

Two whispers cut through the night, which had to be Hobart firing on the guards along the edge of the woods. A bullet pierced the handle to the driver's door of the SUV, then two more spiderwebbed the window. McCool was laying suppressive fire.

"What the fuck, Sinclair?" Tharp shouted. "Drive! Drive!"

That was the Tharp I knew. Leave his men behind to save his own ass. Estes and Owens were no different.

The guard lunged toward me, and I stepped aside, shoving the top of his head into the guard with the broken nose, who was again trying to exit the vehicle. Several shots rang out, and tires hissed as the driver, sealed in his seat, attempted to pull forward but bumped into the chase car parked in front. I grabbed the back of the guard's head and smashed his face into the side of the SUV, denting the rear fender. As the man dropped, the broken-nose guard was squeezing out of the back of the rear seat. When his head popped out, I landed a solid right cross on his temple. He fell like a shot quail.

The driver was turning with his pistol in his left hand as I stepped out of the way of two shots pinging off the frame.

Tharp shouted, "Go! Go! Go!"

I lunged inside and swiped the knife across the driver's gun hand, causing the pistol to fall at Tharp's feet. I reached in and grabbed it to prevent him from hurting himself and aimed it at the driver.

"Crawl across the seat and step out, now," I said calmly. He slid over the console and opened the passenger door. By now, he knew there was more than just me involved in this ambush. He stood quietly by the open door. The one thing about bad leaders was that their troops never went the extra mile for them.

I turned to Tharp, who was visibly shaking.

"Okay, tough guy. Let's go before you piss your pants," I said. "Step out of your door. If you try to run, you'll be shot."

"You're making a big mistake, Sinclair," he croaked.

"Made several already. No biggie. Let's go," I said.

I kept the pistol aimed at him as McCool pulled around to the opposite side. Her window was down, and she had a pistol trained on him.

"Hey, big guy," she said. "Need a ride?"

He looked over his shoulder at me and then at his driver, who was still standing outside the passenger door, maybe calculating the odds. Hobart appeared, holding his rifle at the ready, aiming at the chase car, opening the door, and dragging the driver out. He flex-cuffed both men and piled them in the back of Tharp's Suburban. Then he took his knife and stabbed the tires of the chase car. He flex-cuffed and loaded the two unconscious guards in the back seat of Tharp's SUV and took the fobs to both cars, locking both.

He came around to where I was standing with Tharp and mumbled, "Fucking child's play," as he snapped a pair of flex-cuffs on Tharp. He led Tharp to the back hatch, lifted it, and dumped him in the back, then tied another flex-cuff around his ankles.

Tharp was screaming, "Hey! Hey!"

Hobart said, "Save it," and blindfolded him before he shut the hatch door. He turned to me and nodded. "Good job, boss." Then he jumped in the back seat as I slid into the passenger seat next to McCool. The entire operation had taken ten minutes.

We dropped Hobart a mile down the road at his car in a different strip mall parking lot. He jumped out, and once he was in his car, we drove back to the hangar in silence. We had operated together enough that we knew better than talking in front of a captive.

Fatigue washed over me as the adrenaline ebbed, but I continued to think through the possible permutations of what was happening. If

Tharp, Estes, and Owens were teaming up and potentially working with Parizad, I knew what the play might be.

We pulled into the hangar, parked next to the Beast, and shut the door. McCool and I carried a squirming Tharp to one of the empty offices in the hangar, dumped him on the floor, and then huddled in our makeshift command post two doors down.

"Good job, team. Not much time. I'll question Tharp, but you guys heard what he said. The key, I think, is when he said, 'It's what this country needs to bring it together.'"

"External threat," Hobart said.

"Who is the gravest threat?"

"Iran by a long shot. Russia and China are red herrings," McCool said. "Nukes oddly keep us safe."

"Roger that."

"Parizad," we said in unison.

"Right. You guys think creatively about what might be going on." I turned to Hobart. "Joe, Donna Tharp heard that douchebag talking about invading Iran, I think, based on what she and my daughter said. Make some calls. How many carrier groups do we have in the Middle East? Airplanes? Troops? What's the Eighty-Second Airborne doing right now? Ask all the hard questions."

I turned to McCool. "Sally, pull the thread on where Parizad is. My money says he's in America or Europe. Same thing. All the hard questions. Inauguration Day is D-Day. Eleven hours."

I limped into the room with Tharp, removed his blindfold, and kicked him in the ribs. My rage burned brightly. I didn't know if it was the drugs or the passion, but I missed Melissa more at that point than any other since her death. But now I was thinking, was it not her death but her disappearance? I knew that I had buried my wife, or was it someone made to look like her?

"Tell me what you did with Melissa."

FEINTS AND RUSES HAVE been a part of warfare since the beginning of time. Like magicians, commanders pretended they were doing something over there so that they could distract their opponents and do something over here. While trickery is basic, it also works repetitively because the best deception plans played to the fallible human minds of the decision-makers and their biases.

So far, there was no app or system that could leach out bias, belief, fear, or passion from decision-making, providing openings that creative opponents could exploit. There was Eisenhower's head fake at Calais because the Germans believed that the Allies would cross at the nearest point between the British Islands and the European continent. And Alexander the Great when he invaded what we know as present-day Pakistan. General Magruder at Yorktown. The list was long.

I looked at Tharp lying on the floor and thought about every speech he had ever made about wanting a ground war with Iran to overthrow the government. I was certain he would fight to the last American citizen who wasn't a family member of his, and maybe even those, if necessary.

His position was in stark contrast to that of Campbell's, who preferred leveraging the elements of national power—economic, diplomatic, informational, and military—to achieve her vision of a stable Middle East.

Was Tharp on a rogue mission with Estes and Owens to start a war with Iran? If so, they would need a provocation and an ally. If Parizad was involved in this, it could only be related to the fact that he saw an opportunity for the grand vision he pursued. His was not the schoolyard taunts of "the Great Satan" and "Zionists." Rather, Parizad was a skilled planner that required tactile administration of his plan. He was never a Muhammad Ali–style trash talker. He quietly and efficiently planned his fights, entered the ring, adapted to the changes, and secured victory. He would be on hand and nearby if this were something in which he was involved.

We had less than eleven hours to determine the plan—provided there was one—and to prevent what I was sure would be much grander than anyone could imagine.

But first—at least this time—Melissa.

"Melissa knew about your plan because Donna told her. You had to get rid of Melissa first because Donna would be too obvious. You bought her silence after you killed Melissa as a show of force, correct?"

He squirmed on the floor in his shiny silk tuxedo and black Italian shoes. He had salt-and-pepper hair that fell just over his ears. His eyes were narrow, and his nose was bleeding, though I hadn't hit him there. Maybe Hobart had gotten a shot in when he tossed him in the back. The dust from the concrete was turning his tux gray, and he looked like a throwback to disco days as he squirmed on the floor, attempting to alter his entirely inescapable predicament.

I pulled up a gray metal chair and extracted my knife from my boot. The blood coursing through my veins felt electric. I was on fire. Maybe the Yokkaichi drugs were still in play, though I didn't blame them for my hand putting the edge of the blade against Tharp's pasty face and hissing, "What. Did. You. Do. With. Melissa?"

Blood trickled down his cheek from the small incision, curling into his mouth as his lips moved.

"I've got nothing to do with that," he said. His voice was high-pitched and filled with fear. His gold West Point ring winked in the dim light. I put my knee in his chest, pinned him to the floor, lifted his bound wrists, and flattened his left hand on the cement. Sliding the knife into the notch between his ring finger and his middle finger, I began sawing into the skin.

"You're fucking crazy, Sinclair! Oh my God, stop it!"

"What did you do with Melissa?" I asked. "I'm done wasting time."

"Okay, okay," he muttered. "Holy fuck. Okay."

I didn't stop.

"I said I'd talk!"

I hit bone.

"She knew, okay? She knew. My cunt wife told her."

I stopped.

"I knew that. What did *you* do?"

I began sawing into the bone. Blood was oozing through the etchings and engravings of his class ring in rivulets.

"Fuck, fuck, fuck!" he shouted. "It's Parizad, okay? Parizad."

I stopped sawing but kept the knife biting into the bone. "Where's Parizad?"

"I don't know!"

I resumed sawing and could feel that I was over halfway through the bone, so I just finished the job. His finger flopped off his hand, and the ring spun into a pool of blood, a better metaphor for his class I had never seen if what I believed was happening was true.

"Oh my God!"

His wail pierced my already hypersensitive hearing. He flopped beneath my knee as if he were being electrocuted. His perfect life was being dismantled as he watched, both literally and figuratively.

"Looks rather odd, don't you think?" I asked him. I put the knife on his left pinkie finger and said, "This will probably be more aesthetically pleasing."

"He interrogated her," Tharp spat. "He fucking interrogated her."

"So you provided her to him?"

He didn't respond, nor did I saw off his pinkie. I had other plans. Finally, he nodded.

"The cancer wasn't real. The doctor wasn't real. Right?" I said.

He said nothing but finally nodded again.

"What poison?"

He sighed. The pain was probably severe, though he chose not to look at his hand. The reality of missing even a finger might send him over the edge.

"Botulism," he said.

"The doctors and the treatments were all part of the plan. Not doctors at all."

"That was Owens's people! Not me!"

As if that made his eventual outcome any different. Having confirmed what had been percolating in my mind, I transitioned to Parizad and the imminent threat.

"What does Parizad have planned?"

He paused, so I lopped off his pinkie. It lay there next to his ring finger, providing fresh blood to the spreading pool.

"Oh my God, you're going to kill me, aren't you?"

I said nothing. He turned and looked at me. My eyes were locked onto his face, looking for the tell.

"A small attack. That's all."

His eyes were fluttering, and I thought he might pass out, so I cut the ties on his ankles and wrists. He pushed himself up, blood draining from his mangled hand, and stumbled back against the wall.

"You're fucking crazy, Sinclair."

No argument there.

"Where is he?"

"You'll never stop him. It's too late, Sinclair. Let me go, and I'll make sure nothing happens to you." Tharp was always a master at overplaying his hand and underestimating his opposition. Perhaps he thought I was participating in a deception. His relative freedom seemed to energize him, despite his missing digits.

While he could easily kill his wife, I could easily kill for mine. He didn't have the capacity to understand the depths of the love that Melissa and I shared, nor could he possibly have any regard for the selfless sacrifice it took to serve the nation and not himself. He was a useless fool drunk with power.

"Where?"

"There's no time, Sinclair. Now let me and my fingers the fuck out of here!" he shouted and ran toward me.

I sidestepped him, and he fell forward into the knife, or that was what I later said, but whichever version of events actually happened, the knife found his heart and stayed there as he fell to the floor. I flipped him over, retrieved my blade, and said, "One down."

I wasn't sure how many were left to go, but I knew there were at least three, possibly four. Estes, Owens, and Parizad needed to be stopped by any means necessary.

And possibly President-Elect Campbell.

I opened the door with McCool stepping forward, fist raised in preparation to knock, Hobart grimacing behind her while scanning over my shoulder.

"What happened?"

"He tried to escape," I said. "And ran into my knife."

"You killed the SecDef?"

"Self-defense."

"He's missing two fingers," McCool said, stepping around me and kneeling next to the gory scene.

"He tried to escape before I could get to the others."

"What did you learn?" Hobart asked, unmoved by the carnage.

"He played a role in killing Melissa. Parizad has a plan to strike America. He's in the country."

"Killed Melissa?" McCool said, turning away from Tharp's body.

"Yes. It wasn't cancer. Botulism delivered slowly over time. They tortured her for two days until she confessed she knew their plan. That's the video we saw."

"Fort Detrick makes sense," McCool said. "It's where Projects MKUltra and Naomi were centered. There are stores of bio and chem weapons still on hand. Even LSD. It's all still there from sixty years ago when the CIA was experimenting on them."

"Right," I said, leading them out of the room.

"We've got three missions," I said as we sat in our windowless makeshift command center with three chairs and a desk. There was an assortment of phones and weapons scattered on the desk. My protégés peered back at me, perhaps still reeling from the dead VIP in the room across the hall in this random airfield hangar in central Maryland.

"When we blow this thing open, a dead douchebag will be the least of our worries. But I realize that both of you have full careers ahead of you, and if you want to exit stage left immediately, no harm, no foul. I'd almost prefer it."

"Almost," Hobart said, the corner of his lip moving fractionally upward.

"What's the plan?" McCool asked.

"Find out the rest of what happened to Melissa. Stop Parizad. Get Van Dreeves back." I pointed at McCool. "We really don't know what has happened to him, do we?"

She looked away and muttered, "No."

"We make our money on simple missions. Clear guidance. Flexible execution."

"True," Hobart opined.

"The good fortune here is that I think it all overlaps. Tharp said that Parizad has a limited strike planned. We've got Tharp's phone right there. Let's use his thumb to open it and see what we can dig out. But before we do that, I have to tell you something about Demon Rain. I think I was injected with it. You and Randy probably got most of it out with the EpiPen and quick removal of the arrow. But it has done something to my optic nerve. I see stars, like I've been hit in the head."

They both listened as I continued.

"But the kicker is that I think it works in concert with a mobile phone. Remember all the dead bodies and mobile phones in the cave and Heidelberg? I was making a call right after I escaped and was staring into the phone when an image appeared. It wasn't real, but it was convincing."

Hobart spoke first. "So don't stare at a phone."

"Classic, Joe," McCool said. "I think the larger point is it could be tied to mass deployment of the drug."

"Roger," I said.

"Speaking of which, we should check these phones." Hobart snagged each of the phones we had cleared from the wounded at the parking lot and went to see which one would unlock. He was gone for a few minutes, during which time McCool's phone buzzed. She looked at it and said, "Useless," then stuffed the phone in her cargo pocket.

Hobart returned. "Got it."

He started scrolling through it, but handed it to McCool, who was second in line behind Van Dreeves to be handling our communications and deep web enterprise. Brown and Rogers were guarding the exterior of the building while we churned away at the intelligence.

"Give me a few minutes," she said, snagging the phone with both hands, upon which ensued a series of swiping and pinching motions. A few minutes later, she said, "There's nothing obvious, but there are a series of texts and phone calls with someone he had logged in here as 'DP.' Could be David Petraeus. Could be Dariush Parizad. The tenor of the texts are meetings, nothing more. There's a reference to you." She pointed to me. "'GS meeting in two hours.' That was four hours ago. If it's Parizad, he replied, 'Finish.'"

"So he was going to kill me. Another self-defense argument," I said. "Check this flash drive from Donna Tharp."

McCool plugged it into the computer and began scanning the contents.

"Lots of video of Tharp with other women. Some documents and transcripts. Something here about Estes and Owens . . ." she said after a few minutes.

Meanwhile, Hobart had been going through all the information he had collected based upon my earlier instructions and broke into the conversation.

"Boss, we've got a third carrier battle group just off the Horn of Africa. Two are in the Persian Gulf. DRB 1 is spooling up at Fort Bragg. CENTCOM has just asked for the 101st Airborne Division to be prepared in case of an attack. Eighteenth Airborne Corps has a warning order to begin 'X-hour' sequence." The division ready brigade, or DRB, was in its final countdown of days and hours until takeoff with three thousand paratroopers to deploy to a combat zone.

"And Fillmore," McCool continued.

Fillmore.

In all the tumult, I had forgotten that General Fred Fillmore, the CENTCOM commander, was the one who had ordered the Heidelberg and Yokkaichi missions.

My classmate. My friend.

"Fillmore is just following orders from Tharp, I'm sure," I said. But the words rang hollow. "Tharp and Estes are pulling together a show of force in the Middle East. They're using Fillmore to get into position to invade Iran," I said.

"Maybe," McCool said, unconvinced.

"Fillmore repositioned the sub hunter planes from CONUS to the Middle East based upon intel on the Iranian subs in the Persian Gulf," Hobart said, reading something from his tablet.

I thought about that for a moment. Another text pinged on McCool's phone. She looked at it and shook her head.

"Van Dreeves?" I asked.

"No. Minor bullshit."

I had never known McCool to let minor bullshit fluster her, but I figured the gravity of the entire situation weighed on all of us.

Returning to Hobart's point about the submarines, I asked, "So what subs do we have on hand here?"

"Limited. Mostly in Jacksonville, Florida. Some in Hawaii, a few in California."

"What about SOSUS? What are they picking up?"

SOSUS was an acronym for Sound Surveillance Systems, placed primarily in the northern Pacific and Atlantic oceans to track submersibles and submarines.

"A few weeks ago, there were five Iranian subs tooling around the Gulf. Nothing since then, and nobody knows where they went."

"Do we have any SOSUS in the Southern Hemisphere? South Africa, Indonesia, Malacca Strait, Panama Canal, anything?" I asked.

"I'm not sure, but if those subs aren't in the Gulf, are they here, off the coast?" McCool asked.

"Think like Parizad. We've studied him. He knows strategy and tactics. He can land a left jab, hook, right cross, you name it. He can put a thumb in your eye and go for the occasional low blow. He paces himself to last the duration of the match to fight again, and he does. He doesn't think punch by punch or fight by fight; he thinks in terms of a career. His legacy. He taunts emotionally, punches physically, outlasts you psychologically," I said.

"So he's nearby, and he's got a plan that hits us on several levels. How's that work?" Hobart asked.

"If Tharp and team want to invade Iran, then they need a catalyst. Parizad would want to control the catalyst, make an offer of some minor thing."

"Why wouldn't we be seeing any of the moving pieces?"

"Because Owens is in on it. She's as much of a hawk as Tharp and Estes. CIA is consuming the intel, processing it, and ultimately delaying it. Someone in there has the answer as to what's going on, but it will be over before we can figure it out."

McCool was being uncharacteristically quiet. She typically engaged in these brainstorming sessions.

"Thoughts, Cools?"

"I'm processing, sir. We have a dead SecDef twenty feet away. People will know he's dead soon. They'll be pinging his phone." She held up the phone in her hands.

"Good points, but we're moving forward. What's our solution here? Remember: Melissa, Parizad, Van Dreeves. We have to resolve those, or we fail. The nation fails."

She nodded.

"Melissa was poisoned, possibly tortured. We have the video. She knew Tharp wanted war with Iran, and they let Parizad torture her," McCool said. "Van Dreeves disappeared in the medical system. The same system that routed Melissa to Fort Detrick and Parizad. I expect that's a connection."

I snapped my fingers and said, "Good point. Could be the same fake planted doctor."

"Let me see that phone," Hobart said. McCool was slow to give it to him, but she relinquished. Hobart tucked his head down and began poring through the phone.

"I don't know how to say this, sir," McCool began. "But when you buried Melissa, were you, you know, sure it was her body?"

I remembered seeing her in the hospital. The viewing at the memorial service. I had closed the casket. I saw her, but of course, her eyes had been closed. There were no dimples or smile. It was Melissa, but it wasn't. Her soul was somewhere else, definitely a better place than a world that could have tortured her. I had been an empty vessel, harangued by guilt that she would never let me bear. I saw her sometimes, hanging there in my mind's eye, coaching me, guiding me, but that was different from her fully joining me with her spirit.

Or maybe she wasn't available to come in.

Was she possibly alive?

The doctor had signed the death certificate. But what doctor? The fake plant? Another?

But, no, I never had a DNA test done.

"The person in the casket certainly looked like her," I said.

"You know what they call that nowadays, right?" McCool said. "Deepfake. It's mostly online and with images and apps, but who is to say it can't apply here?"

I said nothing.

"Oh my God," McCool said. She had been talking to me and scrolling through the flash drive that Donna Tharp had passed to me. "Speaking of deepfake, here's that video again of Melissa. But this time, it's not Parizad interrogating her."

"What?" I said. I snapped my head toward the monitor and saw the exact same video we found in the Heidelberg raid, except the man torturing Melissa was the doctor in the photo that Reagan had texted me.

I was still wrapping my mind around this when Hobart looked up and said, "Tharp has DP's number on his Find My Friends app. DP shows up about forty miles from here near the Pennsylvania border, just north of Camp David."

"That's worth checking," I muttered, still stunned by the picture on the computer monitor. "Again, Melissa, Parizad, and Van Dreeves are our priorities."

"I'd add a few more," McCool said. "Owens and Estes and whoever this prick is on the screen. I'll focus on them, and you guys can hit the location in Tharp's phone."

I knew the prick but still couldn't believe what I was seeing.

"Hang on," Hobart said. He fidgeted with the phone for a second. A moment later, McCool's phone dinged with a text. McCool looked at her phone in Hobart's hands, her eyes lighting with surprise.

"Why did Tharp have you on text, Sally?" Hobart asked.

32

THE LAST THING I needed at this moment was to lose trust in McCool, but that was exactly what happened.

Major Sally McCool had spent two years in the Pentagon in between combat tours, working as a military aide to the secretary of the army and, before that, as a pilot in the Twelfth Aviation Battalion, the secretary of defense's Gold Top wing of Black Hawks. First, she flew the secretary of defense everywhere local, such as Camp David. After that assignment, she carried the secretary of the army's bags and got to meet all the important decision-makers during that year. She claimed to have hated it, but no one truly despised those jobs. She was a witness to history and sniffed the intoxicating fumes of power. She was inside every decision that her principal made and sometimes, if only rarely, contributed to the content.

"What gives, Sally?" I asked.

"We worked together in the Pentagon," she said. McCool was smart and crafty and certainly no shrinking violet to my and Hobart's suspicions.

"He was SecDef then. You worked for SecArmy," Hobart said.

She looked away and then back at me. "No. I flew Tharp when I was with the Gold Tops and *then* worked for SecArmy. It was a tough two years. Tharp and I got to know each other when I was flying. Said he liked my voice. He couldn't see me, because I was in the cockpit, and he was riding, but of course, I was communicating with him. Come to find out, he had a condo in the same building I was living in. Where he stayed when he wasn't at his McLean mansion. There's a Starbucks on the ground floor. We'd bump into each other early every morning or late every evening. I didn't recognize him at first, and we just chatted. He was a good-looking older man. Yes, he was married, but I was going through my own bullshit. I was out of my element and my league, it seemed. And he didn't clue me in that he was an asshole, though I should have known better." She paused, looked away, and then continued. "We had a thing. It was done. I knew nothing about this." She waved her hand across the room.

"Did you know about Melissa?" I asked.

The question cut within her like an icy wind through a T-shirt.

"No! Oh my God, sir. No. Fuck no. It was a fling. We had sex. That was it."

I felt betrayed either way, perhaps irrationally. What she did in her private life was her business. She was smart, beautiful, and sexy. I understood why Tharp or any other man would desire her. Still, she was better than Tharp. I was disappointed in her choices more than anything.

"Why didn't you mention this?" I asked.

"Excuse me, sir. I don't tell you every guy I screw," she said.

"A tad defensive. I'm talking about in the last few hours since I met with him."

"What would I say? 'Oh my God, you just killed a guy I banged'? Please, sir. Trust me. It was sex. I didn't break any bond between us."

The conversation had taken on the air of a marriage headed toward an irretrievable impasse. Trust had been broken, or had it?

"I didn't read everything, but it's just a bunch of 'Where are you,' 'That was awesome,' 'I'll be right down,' and so on," Hobart said.

"Give her the phone, Joe," I said.

I looked at McCool and said, "You're in charge of that. I want you to look at it and see how far back it goes and tell me anything you want to tell me. If you don't have anything you want to say, that's fine. We will drive on like this never happened. If there's something that can shed some light on Melissa, Parizad, Randy, or the man in the new video, then let me know."

She took the phone as if it were radioactive.

"Shit. That's just like you," she whispered. "You could have gone all nuclear on me, but no, you give me the phone and restore trust. Fuck," she muttered.

"We've been through too much, Sally. If you had a fling with Tharp, I don't care. If you can think of anything he did or said that can help us here, then I care."

She looked me in the eyes. The corners of her mouth were down-turned, her eyes clear and moist.

"I knew none of this. I had a thing with him. That's it. And I'm sorry I didn't mention it when you met with him. I didn't know how to handle it, but you're right. It's material to what's happening."

I nodded. "It's okay. We will do this just like we always have. Sally, you're in charge of logistics. Joe, you're support. I'm assault."

I broke the team into our basic components to simplify execution. There was no option other than to go head-to-head with Parizad and the West Pointers, who had made clear they preferred a ground war in Iran to root out the theocracy.

"We have to confront the more immediate threat, which is Parizad. If there's some type of trade-off, Parizad comes first and it is here. It is one a.m. on Inauguration Day. We need to scout the farm, gather intel, and follow the intel. Same plan as always. Go where the intel takes us."

"We are three people. Parizad's got sleeper cells. The West Pointers have armies of contractors and operatives in the CIA, State, and Defense," McCool said. "One thing I did hear Tharp talk about was how he had a group of private contractors that would 'take care' of problems for him."

"Probably the guys we dealt with at the parking lot," I said.

"REMFs," Hobart said. "Cakewalk."

"To the extent that our theory is true—that the West Pointers are trading with Parizad—then we can expect them to pull out all the stops to keep their plan on track," I said.

"That's been true from the onset," Hobart added.

I nodded. He was exactly right. Our mission was to deter exactly these types of threats. Ever since the Intelligence Community disasters of 2016, the president had created and tasked the Joint Special Operations Command, JSOC, and more specifically Dagger, to be uniquely plugged into all the intelligence pipelines. Sending me on the Demon Rain missions seemed to be more of a distraction than anything else. Mind control hadn't borne fruit sixty years before, but it seemed possible today. My optical nerve was still flaring, and my mind was fuzzy at times. Sounds of helicopters blades and bullets whizzing past me juiced my adrenaline and made my thoughts race. Too often in the last twenty-four hours, I had focused on Campbell—not the West Pointers—as the cause of Melissa's death. Was my anger at Campbell legitimate or messaged to me somehow? I had a new focus and little time to sort it out prior to the largest mass gathering since the COVID-19 outbreak.

And still, the mass of people in the Iranian cave, the group in Heidelberg, and a similar setup in Yokkaichi were all indicative of some kind of mass illusion or murder, or both.

"It's a head fake, maybe," I said. "What do we know about Ben David's whereabouts?"

"That seems like a century ago," McCool said.

"He escaped. Why would he do that?" Hobart added.

"What are the odds Parizad turned him?"

"What are you saying, sir? You trust him as much as you trust us," McCool said.

"Not quite, but close," I replied.

"He was in the cave, almost dead," Hobart said. "What we know is that Parizad has always operated on several levels. Maybe he needed Ben David off the grid like he needed us off the grid. Dagger and Mossad were the two entities that could get in his way. So part of his plan is preventing failure, as you tell us, sir, and the other part is offensive action: aerosolized poison; submarines. That's what we know. So the question is, how do you spray poison? What do you spray?"

I nodded.

"I think it's pretty obvious what the target is: inauguration. If Demon Rain is as powerful as we've seen, then he can kill tens of thousands," McCool said.

"How does he get past all the defenses?" I asked.

"Low, slow, small," Hobart said.

It made sense.

"And with the cell phone aspect," I said. "There's a hack out there that will have everyone who is both poisoned and holding their phone up filming the event do something terrible."

"I know we discussed it briefly, but it seems so . . . abstract," McCool said.

"Have to believe it's real," Hobart said.

"Okay, so, Joe, you and I head up to the Find My Friends location, and Sally, you're command and control back here, collecting intel and analyzing. If we need extraction, grab Rogers and Brown from guard duty and come get us. You've got the location."

"Yes, sir," she replied.

It was rare that she would resort to a curt, official reply, but knowing her the way I did, she most likely felt horrible about me having cast any shade on her integrity.

Hobart and I loaded our weapons and ammunition in the SUV, powered up the navigation, and plugged in the latitude and longitude, which turned out to be near Emmitsburg, Maryland. Only fifteen miles from Gettysburg, Pennsylvania, Emmitsburg was believed by some to have been Robert E. Lee's intended target, but a fire had destroyed half the town a few days prior to the advance and negated any logistical advantage the Confederates might have derived from seizing the town.

We made the forty-five-minute drive in typical fashion: silence. Along the way, we veered around the outskirts of Frederick and Fort Detrick, passed split-rail fences, tunneled along stretches of dark two-lane roads, and slowed when we neared the flashing indicator on the navigation application.

Crossing a short bridge spanning a narrow creek, we climbed steadily out of the draw and onto higher ground when I said, "Slow down, Joe."

I reached into the kit bag in the rear seat and placed a pair of night vision goggles on my head. Hobart parked in a small gravel pull-off and shut the lights.

"Looks like a farm. Cattle. Horses," I said. The animals were milling in the darkness on the east slope of the hill. "Let's park off the road and come up midway through the property and use the Black Hornets."

McCool had secured the case of Black Hornet drones in the cargo hold of the Beast when we'd left Yokkaichi. We took a few minutes securing the gear, exited the vehicle quietly, and began breaking brush through the low creek bed until we veered off at about four hundred meters. We snaked beneath the log fence and set up the drones on a small hill. There was a house in the far distance and a barn about two hundred meters closer to us. In the goggle display, the green-and-black shades showed a light emanating from the barn.

"Let's get the Hornet into the barn," I said. Then I texted McCool: On location.

Hobart flew the Black Hornet drone up the slope to the barn, which was maybe four hundred meters away. The drone's range was a mile, but we found the image was better at closer ranges.

"Lights," Hobart said.

The drone feed on Hobart's tablet showed a cavernous space that was brightly lit. Men dressed in black with long rifles were walking among dozens of large drones. They were pouring a liquid into a payload container on each drone.

"Low, slow, small," Hobart whispered.

He was referring to the fact that the number-one threat commanders in Iraq and Syria faced was from "low, slow, and small" drones. To date, they were nearly undetectable and could fly via GPS coordinates, which meant electronic countermeasures would not be effective.

A man walked into the center of the barn. He was big and broad shouldered. His black hair and beard were thick. His arms strained the seams of his long-sleeve black shirt. Thigh muscles pushed at his cargo pants. He spoke, issuing instructions and pointing at the drones. His charges stopped and looked at him as he spoke.

It had been just a week since I had seen a fleeting image of Parizad, but there was no doubting who he was.

"Hostile," I said. I immediately texted McCool: Jackpot.

She had not replied to my first text, and I didn't wait for a reply here. I imagined she was busy prepping the Beast.

"Roger," Hobart replied. "Trucks."

Two semitrucks with container trailers moaned up the long driveway to the barn. The men began loading the drones into the backs of the two trucks. We counted a combination of forty rotary and fixed-wing drones being ferried into the truck trailers.

"Inauguration," I said. This had to be Parizad's headquarters. Perhaps we had lucked into his command and control nexus.

"Shoot the drivers?" Hobart asked.

I thought about that. It wasn't a terrible idea, though we didn't have near the intelligence we wanted for the other aspects of the operation.

"Make them go into lockdown? Stop the trucks?" I said.

"My thoughts."

Hobart was already piecing together his SR-25 sniper rifle with night vision scope. He slowly clicked the magazine into the well and chambered a round. He moved about ten meters away to a location that gave him a clearer field of fire. We were communicating by our earbud communications system.

"Execute," I said, taking control of the Black Hornet via the tablet. I steered the drone to give me a vantage on the cabs of the two trucks to provide Hobart battle damage assessment. Hobart's first shot zipped from the suppressed muzzle. The man in the cab slumped over. Another shot. Another dead driver.

"Two dead," I said.

"Others?" Hobart asked.

At that moment, there was a buzzing noise as light as hummingbirds' wings above Hobart. My mind cycled with rage again. The whirring of a drone. The spin of a helicopter blade. The whine of an airplane turbine. My adrenaline pumped as I thought about Melissa and Campbell, drawing a direct line between my wife's death and the president-elect.

The drone coughed as it flew over Hobart and sprayed a mist into the air that settled like a heavy morning dew, drawing me back to the moment. *Demon Rain,* I thought.

"Pro mask!" I hissed.

Hobart rolled away and scrambled to pull on his protective mask carried in a pouch in his rucksack. I pulled on mine, also, but was concerned that the drone had dispensed its contents before Hobart had realized what was happening.

The crack of rifle fire snapped overhead. Two men rushed from behind me, their boots crunching dried leaves. In my transition to put on the protective mask, I had removed my goggles and ceded any night vision advantage.

I pulled a pistol from my right cargo pocket, but one of the men was on top of me before I could fully engage the weapon. A fist landed across my face, snapping my chin to the left and breaking the seal of the protective mask. I kicked the man in the stomach as he lunged toward me, his mask magnifying his eyes. Rolling to my right, I was able to dodge the knife in his hand and gain the advantage by spinning to one knee and retrieving my boot knife in one motion.

I plunged the knife into his neck and tugged against his windpipe as I ripped his mask from his face. His eyes were wide with fear as he flopped on the ground and bled out. I moved toward Hobart, who was limping. His protective mask was ripped, and blood was running from his face onto his chest. A dead attacker lay behind him, but the man who had never needed my help was suddenly helpless. What was happening to my team?

"Yazd," he groaned, falling toward me with his rifle hanging from a snap hook on his outer tactical vest. He was referring to our mission a week ago in Yazd, Iran, where we saw the huddled mass of dead people. Keeping my mask on, I lifted him into a fireman's carry and jogged down the hill as I called McCool.

"Sally, we need you," I barked. Leaning forward with the heavy weight of Hobart on my shoulders, I pulled the phone from my pocket and risked a glance to see if McCool had responded. She hadn't.

"McCool, now!"

I entered the creek and submerged Hobart fully in the cold, tumbling waters to decontaminate him. I scrubbed his clothes and cupped the water in my hands to wash his face and hair, willing the chemicals from his body. I scrubbed his outer tactical vest and his rifle hooked into the snap link by a three-point sling. Once done with Hobart, I laid him on the bank next to his weapon, removed my mask and stowed it, then submerged myself in the frigid stream and repeated the process. Soaking wet, I lifted Hobart over my shoulders and began making my way toward the SUV we had parked a half mile away when finally, McCool's voice cracked over the radio. I heard the reassuring vibration of the Beast in the background as she spoke.

"Ten minutes out. Send coordinates," she said.

I popped out the other side of the creek, climbed the bank, and found an adjacent farm field, where I lay Hobart on the open ground and retrieved an infrared beacon from my cargo pocket. I switched it on, checked its pulse by lifting my night vision goggle to my eyes, and looked at my location using the smartphone.

"Infrared beacon at the following location," I said, and then I read the grid coordinates. "Possible chem."

"Roger," she said.

If she didn't arrive soon, Hobart could die of hypothermia if not his wounds. A moment later, I heard the distant chop of the Beast. I used the minute I had to pull on my gloves and check his wounds. His cheek beneath his left eye was bleeding from a knife cut, and his breaths were short and choppy. He had an abdominal wound, as well. The cold air was bone chilling against the wet clothes, but the upside was that blood flow was restricted, which kept Hobart from bleeding out for the moment. When he began shaking violently, I removed an atropine injector from his medical kit and plunged it into his leg.

The Beast landed twenty meters away, and Brown jumped through the open cargo door wearing his protective mask. He unfolded a body bag to use as a makeshift medical litter and helped me carry Hobart to the cargo bay, where they had fixed a litter in place. We put him on the stretcher and strapped him, stopping the zipper at his neck so he could breathe. Brown laid a heavy wool blanket over him and gave me a thumbs-up.

Then I hopped off and ran from beneath the whirring blades.

"Sir!"

"I'm staying. The threat is here. Take care of Joe," I said.

After a moment, the Beast lifted off the ground and spun to the south. I stayed low and still for five minutes, assessing my surroundings. I collected Hobart's rifle from the creek bank and moved back into the woods on the farm side of the stream. I moved north so that I was above the position from which we had been operating. Crawling through the mud, I peered to the south and saw four men on all-terrain vehicles buzzing around their two dead comrades and, more importantly, the rest of our equipment. I slid back below the military crest of the slope and continued north, using the stream as a handrail guide for navigation. At the north end of the property, there was a series of metal gates that made up a cattle corral. At first glance, there were no animals in the corral. But then, from fifty meters away and lifting my goggles to my eyes, I saw the bodies of dozens of pigs huddled in the corners of their pens.

I stopped and sucked in my breath. Was it possible Demon Rain *wasn't* a mind control drug? Or were there two compounds, one an advanced form of chemical weapon that could kill on contact? I thought of Hobart and said a short prayer in my mind. I whispered into my earpiece, "Sally, test the chem."

"Roger," she replied instantly.

I backed away from the dead pigs and moved south again, taking up a position where I had a good angle on the barn and the trucks. I still had Hobart's rifle and my knife and pistol, but little else. Hobart had taken two shots with the rifle, so I checked the magazine and counted out eight bullets. I quietly snapped them back into the magazine, reseated it, and chambered a round.

I had little time to stop Parizad's unspeakable attacks against the inauguration.

I low crawled to a better firing position, extended the bipod, and sighted on a new group of Parizad's Immortals, who were placing their dead on the four-wheelers. They were wearing protective masks, also, which indicated they were prepared for the mission. This was not a low-rent operation.

With two shots, I killed two. A third looked up when the first two fell, providing me an opportunity to put a bullet in his chest. Three down, one to go. With the first two Hobart and I killed, the total was five. How many did Parizad have here?

The fourth man stayed low and crawled into a firing position. He stopped moving when I drilled two bullets into his spine. Five shots, three bullets left. I resealed my protective mask and slid on my gloves before carefully moving toward the four-wheeler they had parked out of the range of the aerial spray.

I heard a whirring sound above me and reached for my pistol when I realized it was the Black Hornet Hobart had deployed earlier. I found the tablet in the basket of the ATV and saw it had fourteen minutes of dwell time remaining. Maneuvering it to a landing, I connected it to its charger and placed it in the ATV cargo hold along with the intelligence haul. I studied the phones in the ATV basket and saw Farsi texts scrolling across the screens, confirming my suspicion that these men were Iranian sleeper agents. The wounded continued moaning behind me. I wanted to eliminate them as a communications threat, but I didn't want to reenter the contaminated area or waste ammunition, so I forged ahead, pulling the ATV to a stop about a hundred meters from the barn, where I watched the activity and thought about the pigs, the chemicals, Parizad, and how it all came together.

A common tactic the night before a large operation was to consolidate your forces, gain face-to-face contact with your team, ensure everyone understood the plan, and rehearse.

I thought of my team, especially McCool, Hobart, and Van Dreeves. They were scattered, but had never failed me, ever. And of course, there was Melissa, my forever teammate. Melissa's gentle smile and kind eyes hovered in my mind, pushing away the horrible images I had seen on the video of her torture.

What were the connections between Parizad, Campbell, and the West Pointers? Had Parizad been working for Campbell? Or had Melissa confessed a salacious secret about Campbell during her interrogation and the West Pointers blackmailed the president-elect for incumbency in her administration?

Holy shit. Was that their play? Why else would the incoming president be keeping her three primary appointments from the previous regime?

And now, kneeling in the mud behind an ATV, staring at the dim lights on the top floor of a large farmhouse, I tried piecing it all together. The Demon Rain, the sleeper cells, the West Pointers, and the president-elect. My team had raided three chemical weapons facilities in three countries, finding evidence of mass execution like the Jonestown suicides.

Were we less than ten hours away from a weapon of mass destruction? Had the West Pointers traded to Parizad an attack on U.S. soil as an entrée to attack Iran?

And was Melissa actually dead? I didn't dare give myself any hope that she was alive, for to relive the pain and anguish of losing her and the subsequent guilt of missing her death would nearly kill me. I had a duty, though, to my children, and if Melissa wanted anything in this life, it was for her family to be happy. I was as committed to Brad and Reagan as I was to this country.

Brad. I hadn't spoken to him in a couple of weeks, which was not unusual, but Reagan had mentioned he'd been absent from her, as well.

I had been so consumed by guilt and my job leading my team that I had missed so many obvious clues.

Why had Ben David been checking on Brad? And where was Van Dreeves? How had my team, which had endured so many missions, suddenly fallen apart?

I couldn't make sense of it all, but I knew enough to continue forward in search of the truth.

Could I stop these attacks and learn the reality of what truly happened to Melissa? Knowing that I still had Campbell's tracking chip in my boot, I doubled down on discovering the truth. Frankly, it was all I could think about, so I removed the Black Hornet from its charger, saw I had thirty minutes of dwell time, and pushed it into the air.

As it approached the barn, the video stream showed the two trucks still parked in the long driveway that led up from the county road. Several men were huddled and conversing, some punching at their phones, others speaking into radios. I was seeing and hearing both groups on the other end on the communications devices I had lifted from the ATV basket. In the seat console where I had placed the phones and radios, texts pinged and radios belched. I slowed, silenced the devices, and proceeded at full throttle.

I had two options. I could go with the full-throttle approach I was employing or back off and move with stealth. There was always a tipping point in a fight where audacity and violence of action trumped assessment and stealth. There was no mathematical formula for determining which course of action to choose; rather, experience and instinct typically ruled the day. Like a surgeon making an on-the-spot decision to alter the plan upon finding an unexpected tumor, or a pilot choosing to switch from autopilot to manual in a storm, my instincts told me to attack, though they may have been amplified by the drug that had coursed through my system.

Approaching the barn, I lifted the rifle and pistol as I leaped and let the ATV strike the gathering like a bowling ball headed toward a group of pins. I popped up to one knee and began firing at the scrambling men with Hobart's silenced SR-25 sniper rifle, charging as I did so. There were maybe six of them consorting, and I killed half with my first shots by the time the hammer fell on an empty chamber. I rushed them, dropped the rifle, and fired the pistol at close range until it, too, was out of ammunition and they were on the floor of the barn.

Spinning 360 degrees, I scanned. My mind was counting. Two dead at our initial position. Four dead from the counterattack. Six dead in the barn. Two drivers lying next to open truck doors. Fourteen total. Had they been two teams of seven? Seven teams of two? And what was the most likely number and combination of the men remaining? How long had these men been in the country? Months? Years? How had our intelligence missed them? Too many questions, too little time. I leaned over and checked the faces of my victims.

Parizad wasn't among them. I grabbed two fresh pistols from the dead, checked their magazines, and charged the weapons, then tried McCool.

"Cools, you there?"

Nothing.

Tried her again. Still nothing.

The lights high above buzzed with static. The trucks were still idling, so I began to move along the near wall toward the gaping barn door. Tractors and combines were parked on either side. Bales of hay were stacked in the rear. I crouched behind a snowplow when footfalls thundered from outside.

Two men were speaking in Farsi in rushed tones. The truck engines revved. A third voice joined the conversation. The conversation centered around one person, whose voice I instantly recognized.

Parizad. The Lion of Tabas.

After a minute of silence, I looked around the corner and saw Parizad's back to me. I raised my pistol, but he stepped forward and began to follow the two trucks that were now moving down the driveway. Soon, he was beyond the door, and I had no shot. When the trucks roared into the distance and silence ensued, Parizad turned and reentered the barn, pistol drawn. He looked at the stack of dead bodies and ran a hand along his beard. I had never seen him less than confident, but the look on his face was a sign that his plan was in jeopardy.

He quickly exited the barn and left my field of view. I waited a minute and moved to the edge of the barn door, listening. The only sound remaining was that of the buzzing lights, and I wasn't sure I would normally have heard it without heightened senses. The whirring and the buzzing made my mind race.

After another minute, I spun around the corner with my pistol raised. My heart slammed against my chest like a rivet gun. I still had my night vision goggles looped around my neck and lifted them like a pirate searching for land. A light winked across the field a quarter mile away from above a garage in the farmhouse.

Crouching low, I rushed along the inside of a split-rail fence that followed a quarter-mile gravel road to the garage. The cold air burned my lungs. The clear night was like a portal for the stars to blaze down upon me, heightening my sense of exposure, but I pressed ahead. I'd ditched the duster when I'd carried Hobart to the Beast, and the chill knifed through my polypro shirt but melted against the heat of my headlong rush into the den of the Lion of Tabas.

A light above the garage flicked off as I approached the farmhouse from its eastern side. I angled away from the fence into the field, found an old trailer, and knelt behind the wheel. The automatic garage door began to raise. I used the noise as cover to close on the side of the garage and spin inside next to an idling Buick Enclave. A thumping noise was coming from the back of the Enclave, but I was too busy noticing that Parizad wasn't in the driver's seat.

He stepped in front of me and landed the hardest punch I have ever taken across my left cheek. I saw stars and flew into the back of the Buick, denting the fender. My optical nerve flared. Bright white light strobed in my eyes, blinding me.

"Sinclair," he barked and continued in on me as I had seen him do a thousand times to sparring partners in Seoul. I lifted my left arm as a powerful descending blow landed on the side of my head. I blacked out for a second but had the good instincts to roll away from the next punch first, which shattered the side window of the Buick. Chunks of glass sprayed as Parizad retrieved his bloody fist and lifted it again.

By now, I had no idea where my pistol was and had little muscular control from my shattered nervous system. If this were an Ultimate Fighting Championship bout, there was a good chance the ref would have called it already, an even better chance that they would have never let me in the ring with him.

Whether he let me up or I managed to evade his next couple of punches was uncertain, but I found myself standing, squaring off with him in the open bay of the other half of the three-car garage. We circled in the spotlight of the overhead fluorescent lights of the garage door opener. His eyes were demonic, red veins pulsing through the whites. He commanded the rhythm, holding his left hand high in standard boxing pose while keeping his right hand cocked near his chin like a cannon.

Two quick jabs with his left hand stunned me and stood me straight up, the perfect target for his blistering fast right cross that on any given day should have killed me but for some reason only spun me around, dazed. By now, I was seeing at least three of him, my hands trying to block the middle version. I hadn't taken a beating like this since mandatory plebe boxing at West Point when I'd fought Jimmy Kurtz, the Golden Gloves champion from Iowa, in the validation box-offs. I ended up losing with a split decision in that fight, both of us bloody and exhausted at the end.

Somehow, I managed to land a couple of quick jabs on Parizad despite my dizziness. Two powerful right crosses blew past my face as I pulled back just out of reach and regained my balance. I powered a left hook into the side of his sturdy head, cracking my knuckles but satisfied with the blow. He stumbled and came back up with a flurry, having taken harder punches in longer fights. He connected with a straight left jab, and even though I had seen this move several times from behind the sniper scope in Seoul, the fake right cross caused me to blink and turn my head to the right, directly into a crushing left hook he already had aimed at my jaw.

I dropped like a shot quail, and the lights went out.

Literally.

The automatic timer on the garage door lights hit the five-minute mark, because suddenly we were thrust into complete darkness. Parizad's boot whizzed past my fuzzy head. I turned away and slid under the chassis of the idling Buick as Parizad's boot crushed into the lower section of the door, following the scrapes of my back on the cement.

The heat of the exhaust thrummed against my face as I reached into my boot, extracted my knife, and snapped open the blade. A pistol ratcheted and fired three times quickly under the chassis in the spot where I had been before I'd slid out of the back end. I raced to where Parizad was leaning over and spraying beneath the vehicle, and I lunged for his neck as he turned toward the scuffle of my boots.

The thumping from the rear of the Buick grew louder, but I remained focused on staying alive.

My knife glanced off his massive deltoid, causing his pistol to skid onto the concrete, but he turned into me with a flurry of punches as if he were hitting an invisible speed bag. The forward momentum put me on the defense, taking away my previous momentary opening. He was living up to his billing as an Olympic boxer and then some.

My eyes had adjusted to the darkness by now, and I imagined his had, as well. Weak starlight skidded in through the gaping garage door and the open side door that his momentum was pushing me toward. I backed into the opening, giving myself an egress. My left heel caught against the threshold, and I stumbled backward into the breezeway between the garage and the house.

The door slammed in my face, and suddenly, the Buick fishtailed out of the garage and roared down the driveway. I ran around to the front, chasing the car as it sped away. Heavy breaths escaped my bruised lungs. My face stung. My leg ached. But all the pain was washed away by what I saw.

The dim light fell onto the departing car from above the garage façade. Peering out at me from the dusty rear window was either a ghostly apparition or Brad's face, his eyes pleading to me across the gulf of pebbles and dirt.

33

I WATCHED HELPLESSLY AS Parizad sped away with my son clawing at the back window of the Buick, as if he knew what fate lay ahead not only for him but for mankind.

I had briefly wondered why Parizad would leave me alive when I had made it to the heart of his operation. The only reasons I could conjure were that he had already delivered the execute order and he had everything he needed, including Brad. Either I stay away or Brad dies. The way I saw it, Parizad would kill Brad either way. I couldn't allow that thought to disrupt my execution right now.

I loved my son. He was my firstborn and had aced every class he had ever taken. After graduating from Chapel Hill, he joined a rock band and played the East Coast bar scene between Fort Lauderdale, Florida, and Ocean City, New Jersey. Napoleon's Corporal was an '80s and '90s cover band that mixed in some of their own music. Brad was a sensitive soul, and for Parizad to kidnap my son as part of his plot intensified my drive to defeat him even more, if that was possible.

I did the only thing I knew to do. Execute.

I turned on the lights in the garage and grabbed the two pistols lying on the floor, then crashed through the door to the house and swept each room on the bottom floor until I was convinced that no one else was there.

On the way back out, the light was still shining from a window above the garage. I entered the side door and carefully climbed the stairs, charging across the top landing into an open living, dining, and kitchen area. I turned and raced along a hallway into a bedroom and then checked the bathroom. The bedsheets were rumpled, and a toothbrush sat on the bathroom counter. The closet had two shirts hanging from a single rod.

I moved back into the main living area, where there were four computer monitors. Three had blacked-out screens, and one showed a split screen of two holding cells. One cell was empty, and the other had a person huddled in the corner. These were detainees. I moved the mouse of the main terminal and the other three screens jumped to life but asked for passwords.

A scratch pad with random notes in Persian characters was next to the mouse. This was Parizad's command and control unit. I stared at the monitor showing the huddled prisoner and recognized the markings on the wall, a diagonal line through four perpendicular lines. It was the same as those in the video where Parizad had questioned Melissa.

The huddled figure was turned away from the camera, so there was no way to tell who it might be. My mind raced with all the possibilities, straining to hold them at bay so that I could think more clearly.

A movement in what had to be a closed-circuit camera caught my eye. It was a timer counting down.

A bomb.

I was standing on a bomb. This was why Parizad had left so quickly. He didn't want to be anywhere near the explosion when it happened. The remote switch was probably in his vehicle. He could destroy all the evidence right here, including me.

Where was the bomb, though? The numbers cascaded down like an avalanche gathering steam, though I couldn't make out what any of them were. I considered that I had been in the garage, the above-garage apartment, and the main floor of the house. That left the upstairs, potential basement, and maybe something connected to the barn.

I ripped the hard drive out of the stack terminal and slid it into my cargo pocket before racing into the house, finding the basement door, and navigating my way along a long tunnel to a series of rooms, doors open, except for one that had a locked steel door. Adjacent to the locked room was an open cell, probably Brad's. Parizad had snatched him from this cell as leverage to slow me down. I fired the pistol into the doorknob until it flew off in an explosion of sparks. In the back corner was a person turned away from the gunfire.

I ran to the timer and saw that it was counting down from two minutes, numbers falling atop one another, time slipping away. I turned the shoulder of the huddled figure and saw Van Dreeves, eyes vacant and hollowed.

"Randy, we've got to go," I said, suppressing all kinds of emotions.

I lifted him the best I could and dragged him into the hallway and up the stairs. He eventually gained his footing as I was talking into my earpiece.

"Cools," I said.

No response.

By my math, we had maybe thirty seconds to escape whatever that timer was meant to ignite. Scurrying past the photos and paintings on the wall, my periphery caught pictures of someone I recognized and his family.

This was General Fred Fillmore's family farm. I'd known that he had a Maryland connection, but given our friendship, I had not considered him a threat. I had never considered that he would partner with Parizad, if that was what was happening here.

I got about fifty meters from the front porch when we fell into a ditch where the cattle grate was cut into the driveway. The entire house erupted into a massive fireball like a miniature nuclear explosion. Shingles and debris zipped above us as I covered Van Dreeves with my body. The heat from the blast licked at my face like a demon's tongue. After a few seconds, I risked a glance and the left side of the house was in flames. The garage was still intact, but perhaps not for long.

"Cools, this is Dagger Six," I said. Again, no answer. I felt my ear for the micro communications device and realized that one of Parizad's punches had knocked it loose. My mind locked onto the fact that two Mack Trucks' worth of drones and chemical weapons were headed to Washington, D.C., to attack the inauguration in eight hours. There was time to stop this aspect of the attack, provided we could find the trucks. Whatever else Parizad had planned was most likely already under way.

So many thoughts sprinted through my mind like race cars buzzing around a short track. I was glad to have found Van Dreeves alive, if that was what we could call his present state. But I was disappointed I had let myself believe that there was a chance Melissa was alive. And Brad. Oh my God, my son was with Parizad.

The only option now was to succeed.

I checked Van Dreeves again, who had a weak pulse.

"Randy?"

He looked at me with weak eyes. "Boss. Damn, that was some explosion."

"Glad you're alive," was all I could muster.

"Me, too."

"Did you see Brad?"

"Brad? No. WTF?"

"He was in the other room. Parizad has him."

"Jesus."

For a moment, I had nothing to offer him, distracted by the fact he wasn't Melissa or Brad. I had tucked away the forlorn hope that she had been secreted away and all my efforts would be rewarded. I had no way to communicate externally with the rest of the team, but I did remember the ATV full of phones and radios back at the barn. I left Van Dreeves in the ditch and jogged to the barn, where I had loosed the four-wheeler on the Persian sleeper cells. Instead of looking for the phones of the dead guards, I angled toward the two dead drivers Hobart had shot initially. Each had a phone. I unlocked both using their thumbs and carried them back to where I had stashed Van Dreeves.

"Whatcha got, boss?" he asked. His eyes were weak, but he hadn't lost his optimistic bent.

"Phones. I can't reach McCool."

"Give me that," he said. He reached out with a weak hand as I gave him the phone. A trembling thumb pressed the phone app and then a series of numbers. He placed it on speaker as it rang through to voice mail.

"Be cool, leave a message," her voice mail said.

"Hey, Sally, VD here. Come get us, babe. Dropping you a pin."

Maybe they *were* an item.

He manipulated the map app on the phone and dropped a pin at our location. Within a minute the phone rang, and McCool's voice came across muffled by the speakerphone and background noises of people shouting.

"Ohmygod, ohmygod, Randy, you're okay!"

"Never okay, only awesome," he said.

"You got the boss with you?"

"Yeah, I saved his ass, but we got to get rolling. Look for the big-ass fire burning. Best to be gone before the cops get here."

"Randy, we are blocked in the hangar by police cars with flashing lights and guys aiming rifles at us. If I were outside the hangar, I'd go vertical, but I can't get out without wrecking the Beast."

"Ask them what they're doing. Tell them you're with JSOC security for the inauguration," I said.

"I'll try, but they don't look like they're talking. Shit. I gotta go," she said.

We waited ten minutes and called five times but got no response.

"Want to update me, boss? I've been in a cell. These CENTCOM ya-hoos moved me from Japan to here on a C-9 Nightingale," he said. The Nightingale was a medical evacuation airplane used to ferry troops from combat zones to airfields such as Ramstein in Germany or Joint Base Andrews in Maryland for quick evacuation to hospitals. Most patients didn't usually end up detained in farmers' basements.

I recapped the last forty-eight hours for Van Dreeves, who nodded and listened.

"Some wild shit," he summarized.

"All that and we're really nowhere better than when we started. Parizad's got two truckloads of drones with Demon Rain, which I'm convinced is chem and not some mind-altering thing."

"The mind control thing could be horseshit," Van Dreeves said. "Misdirection."

"Not totally, but I understand. There's sarin gas, too."

The fire had not swept across to the detached garage yet, and I remembered Van Dreeves was not only a first-class operator but also our resident expert computer geek.

"Let's try something," I said, helping him up. We walked up to the garage, the house already a giant bonfire with unbearable heat. It was only a matter of minutes before someone from a nearby farm would call 911, if they hadn't already. I helped Van Dreeves up the steps as he clutched his gut where he had been wounded. I sat him down at Parizad's desk and slapped the hard drive back in.

"Can you do anything with this?"

"I can try," he said through gritted teeth. The pain from the gunshot

302 A. J. TATA

wound to my calf reminded me that we had all been wounded in some fashion in the last week. He booted up the computer and played with the keyboard and the mouse as I watched the fire consume more of the house and crawl toward the garage.

In the distance, a red flashing light sped from the town of Emmitsburg, maybe seven miles away. We had five minutes, but I didn't want to pressure Van Dreeves. He knew the deal.

"Got something," he said.

The four monitors popped to life. On the left was an image of the coast of California. Next to that was a display of the Gulf of Mexico and Atlantic Ocean coastlines. Next was a static image from a camera fixed to what had to be the Washington Monument. It looked down on the National Mall, where the crowd was already camping out for the historic inauguration of President-Elect Campbell. In a few hours, there would be over a million people packed tightly into the area witnessing history.

"What's up with the coastline shots?" I asked.

"Over a hundred targets. See these red dots in Cali, Texas, Louisiana, et cetera?" he asked, pointing at the two screens.

"Roger," I said. "What are they?"

"I know the ones in Cali are oil refineries, so I imagine the others are also."

"Submarines," I whispered. "Iran used part of its unfrozen assets to build submarines carrying cruise missiles. Remember that strike on the Saudi oil refinery that was in the news with little explanation? It must have been a rehearsal. Those cruise missiles had come from a sub, which was—well, is—classified. We never released that information."

"Looks like the countdown is on, which puts it right at inauguration time," he said.

"This will be a simultaneous strike," I said. "Chemical weapons most likely at the inauguration itself, plus a strategic blow against our refineries. My guess is those are the largest. A psychological blow against the inauguration. Real impact economically and reinforce our vulnerabilities psychologically."

A crackling noise crawled up the roof as the flashing red lights bounced along the county road.

"Let's go!" I said, lifting Van Dreeves from the chair. We stumbled down the stairs together, our wounds biting at us the entire way. The flames were engulfing the breezeway roof, singeing my hair as we fled out the back. Van Dreeves was struggling, so I lifted him again, and we made it to the back of the barn as the fire trucks pulled close to the garage.

I didn't want to take an ATV because of the noise, but I knew we had to vacate the area if we were to stop what Parizad had planned.

Van Dreeves swiped open the phone to hear McCool's voice. "Twelve minutes out."

We jumped on an ATV and sped away to the northeast, gave wide berth to the corral full of dead pigs, and found a two-track that entered the streambed and popped out the other side. The fat, knobby wheels bounced and spun until finally making purchase up the opposite bank and delivering us to the adjacent farmer's field near where I had delivered Hobart to McCool earlier.

McCool flared the Beast and landed long enough for us to board, Brown helping us slide onto the metal flooring. He slammed the door shut as McCool lifted into the sky and said over the internal communications system, "Where to, boss?"

Her question made me discount the fact that she had removed the seats from the Beast and had a stack of green containers that looked like they held Stinger missiles. I could ask her about those later, I assumed.

The hangar was burned, I assumed, and I was a wanted man. Hobart was in the rear, giving Van Dreeves half a hug, which was as much emotion as I had ever seen from him. We each had headsets on, and I surged with pride knowing my team—save Jackson—was back together.

We faced an incalculable attack, but if anyone could stop the very worst of it, the six of us could.

"Wait one," I said.

I retrieved the SIM card from my boot and placed it in the latest iPhone I had snagged from one of the dead drivers. My fingers were cold, and the helicopter was chopping through turbulence. I dropped the tiny rectangle of plastic and silicon, but Van Dreeves saw what I was doing and snagged it from the floor for me.

With the card finally in the phone, I dialed Campbell's burner.

"Garrett, what is happening?" No preamble. No niceties. All business. It was nearly four a.m., meaning she was eight hours away from her inauguration.

"Major terrorist attack about to go down on your inauguration. It's Dariush Parizad, and at least three members of your cabinet are involved."

"Not my cabinet."

"In eight hours, it is."

"You can't be serious. Your picture is all over the news!"

"Get the Secret Service to get you to Camp David. Give us clearance to get in there, and be there in an hour," I said.

"I can't do that! I'm not president yet!"

"You have a detail. They'll figure it out. You must. You will."

"Garrett—"

"Tharp, Estes, and Owens killed Melissa. Do what I say, now!"

It was unlike me to be so emotional, but I was still conflicted on whether or not Campbell was involved in killing Melissa.

"What!?"

"You're wasting time. The largest attack on our economy is going down in eight hours. We are completely out of position. Five Iranian submarines are off our shores. Come to Camp David. Don't bring anyone but Admiral Rountree from CENTCOM. We must defend, now."

She hung up, which I took as an "I'll be there."

"Cools, go to Camp David," I said through my mouthpiece.

"Whaaaa," she said. I appreciated how my team could keep their cool and sense of humor during stressful moments. That trait made us stronger.

McCool banked the Beast to the west and zeroed in on the presidential retreat.

"Been there, done that," she said. "But we need special clearance to enter that airspace; otherwise, we get a Stinger missile up our ass."

"Campbell's working it out," I said.

If the West Pointers were in on this plot, there was no way to trust the administration's team or anyone else. Campbell had to make this happen. Plus, I wanted to look her in the eyes and ask her about Melissa.

We passed the farmhouse blaze to our south and sped to the west. We couldn't have been more than ten minutes away.

"Nothing yet," McCool said. "Shit. I'm getting pinged by radar."

Hobart and Van Dreeves looked at me. No one wanted to go down in a blaze of fire, especially without solving the problem at hand.

"Unidentified Black Hawk, state your intentions," a male voice said over the communications system.

"This is Major Sally McCool, U.S. Army, flying JSOC Pave Hawk with Beast nomenclature, requesting landing at Camp David," McCool said.

A tense moment ensued before the controller came back, "Landing denied. Exit airspace immediately. Two U.S. Air Force F-15s will escort you. If you do not comply, you will be shot down."

34

WHILE WE WERE STARING at two F-15 Eagle jets on either side of the Beast, Dariush Parizad was meeting with Mahmood, his longtime confidant and lieutenant, in the barren parking lot of an Alexandria, Virginia, Walmart. The early morning was crisp and still. The subtle wash of security lights dotted the black asphalt.

Mahmood had been forced to drive one of the two Mack trucks when the drivers had been shot. In the back of both trucks were forty drones apiece with enough modified sarin gas to kill tens of thousands of people.

An Immortal team member had driven the other truck to a Home Depot lot in northeast Washington, D.C. The plan was to use the northeast location as a stationary launch platform, being just three miles from the National Mall. Mahmood's task was to pull onto I-395 and head toward the Fourteenth Street Bridge over the Potomac River where it would drive slowly and Parizad would open the rear doors, allowing the drones to buzz from the truck in motion like releasing paratroopers over a drop zone. From there, it was a short mile to the Mall, where a million people were already gathering.

"Mahmood," Parizad said. "You and I will deliver these drones to the president's platform. Nothing can stop them. We will kill the country's leadership with one swarm. Each truck has drones with the hallucinogenic form of Demon Rain and separately some with the sarin gas weighted mixture. The sarin will kill, and the techno-drug will have the crowd do as we wish."

"We have lost the element of surprise, Commander," Mahmood said. "And I am not an expert at driving this truck."

"You did fine getting to the rally point. The other truck is in position at a stationary launch platform. We are in position sooner than I preferred, but no plan is perfect. We are still in good shape."

"The submarines?"

"They already have the order to execute at inauguration hour," Parizad said. "Simultaneous attack."

"What is next for us?" Mahmood said.

"We live to fight another day and relish our victory. My car is undetected," Parizad said, chinning toward the Buick. "Arshad has instructions on receiving us in Florida and then backing out of the country the way I came in."

"What about the hostage?"

"The kid? We put him in the cab. Strap a suicide vest on him and make it look like father and son are in on this attack."

"I'm good with this plan."

The two men performed the hand-to-forearm warrior clasp, bumped shoulders, and hugged.

Parizad walked back to the Buick and drove to the northeast D.C. Home Depot to put eyes on the driver passing cordoned areas with U.S. Park Police already working shifts, checking people in through the entry points and patrolling the local areas.

The reconnaissance reassured Parizad of this portion of his plan. His goals were to kill the thousands of dignitaries seated and standing on the western front of the U.S. Capitol where the new president would be taking her oath of office.

Mahmood's truck would be the first wave, and depending on the battle damage assessment using the cameras on the surviving drones, Parizad would either reinforce success with the second swarm on the steps or conduct a deep flanking maneuver and hit the middle of the mass of people there cheering on their new president.

At the same time, hundreds of cruise missiles were to attack dozens of oil refineries, crippling the thin energy infrastructure in the country.

This one-two punch was akin to Parizad's signature move: left jab, deep right fake, left cross haymaker.

After rehearsing the drone operation with the Immortal team member in the Home Depot lot, Parizad returned to Mahmood's location in Alexandria, near President George Washington's home at Mount Vernon.

He parked his vehicle behind the store, where there were several trailers backed up to loading bays, awaiting cargo. There was no sign of life as he passed quietly behind the colossal store. The video cameras were recording him, but everything would be over by the time the FBI began pursuing the leads to dissect what happened.

He parked behind a batch of green dumpsters in a small parking area covered by tall pine trees. Crawling into the back seat, he lay down and set the alarm on his phone. He wolfed down a box of Pop Tarts that Arshad had placed in the Buick and drank two bottles of water to rehydrate. He needed caffeine but needed sleep more.

Crossing his arms across his chest, Parizad thought about his mother and sister back in Tehran. Smiling, he knew that they would be proud. The ayatollah. Qassem. Everyone. He had worked for years to put this plan in place.

The roar of the Lion of Tabas was about to be heard around the world.

35

OUR LIFELINE TO CAMPBELL buzzed in my hand.

"They're going to shoot us down," I said calmly.

"As well they should," Campbell said. "But I've gotten clearance, and a friend has instructed them to escort you to Camp David. I'm on my way. I'm bringing whomever I wish, and I have extra security."

"That's fine."

"I don't need your approval, General."

She hung up, and I said to McCool, "Camp David. ASAP."

"Roger," she said.

We landed at the Camp David helipad, and after some discussion about refueling versus shutting down, we decided we needed the mobility, so McCool repositioned to the small refueling pad, making way for Marine One.

Hobart, Van Dreeves, and I stepped off the Beast looking like the cover of *The Red Badge of Courage*. It would not have surprised me if we were arrested on the spot; in fact, I braced for it when four bulky Secret Service agents manhandled us up against the wall, stripping us of phones and even my boot knife. We had left the more obvious weapons in the helicopter.

The agents then put metal handcuffs on us, and I figured this was it. Campbell had led us into a trap. She was being inaugurated and didn't need this distraction.

"Garrett," she said as we were perp marched into the helipad terminal. No presidential cabin for us. Campbell was seated in a large conference room with four more bodyguards. She was dressed in blue jeans, a Meredith College sweatshirt, and running shoes. Hardly inauguration attire.

The brutes shoved us into chairs at the table and drew pistols before clasping their hands in front of them in fig-leaf pose. The men stood directly behind us while the other four guards were directly behind Campbell. I recognized one of the men. Carson. He was the marine that had provided the seat belt cutter when I was strapped to the gurney in the Fort Detrick chemical test facility. I wondered what device he might have to help us this time.

To Campbell's right were General Fillmore, CIA director Owens, and Secretary of State Estes. The West Pointers.

"Madame President-Elect," I said. My nod and weak attempt at a slight smile took a notch off her hard-assed demeanor. I had played quarters with this woman in college and still believed I had some cachet with her.

"I'll give you thirty minutes to tell me what you need to tell me, but this is my team going forward. President Davidson was kind enough to let me borrow them in the name of a smooth transition," she said. "We just found Secretary Tharp's body south of here. You're the primary suspect. Donna Tharp was killed in a coffee shop in Arlington. You're the primary suspect. CIA safe houses in Heidelberg and Yokkaichi have been raided. Missing from those safe houses are all the stockpiles of sarin gas. Hitler never used what he developed. And Hirohito shut down his operation after slinging tons of it at the Chinese. Point is, they both had leftovers.

"You are the only person who has been to both of those places in the last week. Your fingerprints are all over General Fillmore's farm a few miles to the north of here. We found the missing stockpiles of sarin and a bunch of dead pigs. Only one container has a broken seal, and its volume analysis shows that the only missing sarin is that which was used on the pigs. Dariush Parizad has been seen in the D.C. Metro area. That's what I know," she said.

Clasping her hands in front of her, she grimaced and demanded, "Now tell me what you know."

Nodding, I said, "I understand, ma'am."

Before I could say anything further, Owens said, "As the president-elect said, President Davidson provided us to the incoming team to ensure a smooth transition of power. It seems you're a major threat to that, General. Out of deference to your dead wife, I presume, President-Elect Campbell has given you the slightest of openings here. Use it wisely."

I understood now, I was totally fucked. The Praetorian Guard of Estes, Owens, and now Fillmore were there to defend their plan and themselves.

Fillmore? My classmate and friend.

Had he been blinded by the potentiality of being the chairman of the Joint Chiefs of Staff? Had he openly lent his family farm to Parizad as a staging base for his attacks? Betrayed a classmate?

Even more, they were ingratiating themselves to the incoming president in hopes that they would remain in place long enough to enact their crazy plan to invade Iran, or, more likely, Melissa had given them Campbell's secret. Typically, we worried about enemy attacks during changes of command, but here were three West Point strategists who were exploiting that seam from the inside out.

"My team and I went on the Heidelberg and Yokkaichi missions on the orders of Director Owens and General Fillmore," I said.

"That's not true," they both said in unison.

"What I have discovered is that General Fillmore, in his pursuit to become chairman—"

"Which he will," Campbell interrupted.

"Yes, ma'am, in his pursuit for that position he has made a deal with Estes, Owens, and the recently deceased Tharp to allow Parizad a small attack in the United States in exchange for a strategic opening to have a ground war in Iran."

"That's not true," Fillmore, Owens, and Estes said in unison. At least they had rehearsed.

"If it were true," Campbell said. "we've stopped it. We found the sarin at General Fillmore's farm. He arrived shortly after the fire started and immediately alerted all the authorities. His alertness also led to your capture and your team's. You're in handcuffs now. The real threat has been eliminated."

I tried to understand where she was going with the line of total bullshit, but it seemed that she was in lockstep with her coconspirators. Had Campbell made a deal with this crew of hawks? Did she really want a war with Iran?

"There are two Mack trucks with close to a hundred crop-dusting drones filled with sarin gas arriving in D.C. right now. Your inauguration is the target."

The Secret Service men surrounding the room were getting fidgety. They knew a crock of bullshit when they heard it. The question was, which crock were they nervous about?

"That's not possible," Owens said.

Campbell raised her hand to silence the CIA director.

"There's no missing sarin gas. Don't you see, Garrett? There is no threat. Parizad has disappeared. He's on the run, most likely already headed back to Iran."

Nodding again, I said, "That's entirely possible, but in my best estimate, that's not what is happening. I saw the trucks. The drones. The sarin."

Van Dreeves followed up. "If I may, ma'am, I'm Master Sergeant Randy Van Dreeves."

"I know who you are, Sergeant Dreeves," she said.

Van Dreeves looked down and then back at her. "That's Sergeant Van Dreeves. The *Van* is part of my last name."

"What in the fuck does she care for, man?" General Fillmore shouted.

Campbell snapped her head toward Fillmore. I immediately understood what she was doing.

"Fred, let Randy continue," I said quietly. I kept my eyes locked onto Fillmore as Van Dreeves spoke, anticipating a reaction.

"The Iranians have five Akula-class submarines, which they call Warriors, each with a hundred cruise missiles patrolling the Pacific Ocean, Gulf of Mexico, and Atlantic Ocean. Their targets are the energy infrastructure of our country. They intend to kill thousands at your inauguration, true, but they also intend to destroy our energy infrastructure, leaving our country without its leaders through the crisis. The Iranians have found a billion barrels of new oil in their northern provinces, and in ten minutes, this attack can flip us from independent to dependent on oil from the world. In particular, Iran."

Campbell's expression didn't change. However, those of the West Pointers did. Fillmore's eyes widened. Estes looked at Owens. Owens stared hard at Van Dreeves and said, "What. The. Fuck. Are you talking about? The Iranians don't have Akula-class submarines!"

Campbell looked at me and said, "See the problem we have here? Everything you're telling my team is just not true. But their bravery is. Is that all?"

Their bravery is true? The West Point motto. The class Melissa warned me about. *Always seek . . . Brave and True.*

Fillmore was frozen in time, his eyes staring at the far wall.

"If there's nothing else for me," Campbell said, "I'd like to return. I've a big day ahead. Less than seven hours." Turning to the assembled team, she said, "There are vehicles to take the rest of you back." And then, dismissively waving her hand in our direction, she said to her security, "You know what to do with them."

As she left, Owens said, "I'd rather fly back."

"No, Samantha, I need some time to think," Campbell said. "A lot has happened in the last several hours. You, Fred, and Bob can sort this out."

Owens's face hardened, holding back multiple biting invectives, I was sure. She didn't yet work for Campbell and wanted to at least hang on for a bit longer.

When Campbell departed, Carson, the commando who had helped me two days ago, walked her to the door and returned when the helicopter departed. As he came back in, he retrieved his pistol, aimed it at me.

Van Dreeves muttered, "Shit."

Owens, the queen among her peers, said, "I'm in charge now. Lock them up."

The four-member SEAL team that had been standing beside us moved forward and yanked us up from our chairs so that we were standing.

"Take them out back and do your thing as far as I care," Owens said. "We've done far worse at our black sites."

There was nothing the CIA wouldn't stain, even Camp David.

Owens turned to Fillmore and said, "We launch at noon. It will be nightfall in Iran by then. I want planes, missiles, and the Eighty-Second fucking Airborne in Tehran by daybreak tomorrow."

Carson grabbed my handcuffs and said, "Sorry, sir," as he slid something heavy into my pocket.

"No problem," I said.

The bracelet released at the same time that Carson and the other SEALs moved into the center of the room with pistols drawn, aimed at Estes, Owens, and Fillmore.

"Hands where I can see them!" they shouted.

"I'm doing no such thing. Now lock them up," she demanded.

"Now," Carson said.

"How dare you?!" Owens said.

I reached into my pocket and retrieved the Glock that Carson had placed there. I aimed it at Owens from maybe fifteen feet away and said, "Never bring a purse to a knife fight. Lock them up, team."

In unison, the SEALs snapped the handcuffs on the protesting West Pointers. Admiral Tom Rountree stepped into the room and said, "We don't have much time."

I took a second and walked up to my classmate Fred Fillmore, whose shoulders were shrunken inward. His face was wet with tears. His mouth was contorted downward in a sob. I lifted his chin with the pistol barrel.

"Look at me, Fred."

He opened his eyes. They were bloodshot and moist.

"I trusted you, classmate. You deal behind my back with these assholes for what? The chairman job? All you had to do was ask me to make a call, buddy. Instead, you stab me in the back. Melissa's dead, and Brad is a hostage to the guy you've been talking to at your farm the last few days. Thanks, buddy fucker."

I flicked the pistol barrel up, which snapped his head back, causing him to stumble into a burly SEAL, who latched onto him. Estes and Owens gasped at the mention of Brad's name.

"Steadfast and Loyal, assholes," I said as the SEALs marched him and the others outside. The bond between West Point classmates was typically unbreakable, and I was offended that Fillmore had not only broken that pledge of friendship and loyalty but worked against me and my family.

It had become clear to me that Melissa's deathbed note—*Always seek. Be Brave. Be True*—was her way of warning me about Estes, Tharp, and Owens. I had been gone when it dawned upon her that they were conspiring against her and she couldn't trust any form of communication to warn me other than her cryptic letter. Nor would she have wanted to endanger Brad or Reagan by telling them. Melissa—brave, true, steadfast, and loyal to the very end.

We followed them out, jumped in a large golf cart, and buzzed to the presidential cabin, where Campbell awaited. In the cabin was a small command post obviously set up by Admiral Rountree.

Two large-screen televisions were piping feed from drones somewhere above Washington, D.C., as they made cloverleaf patterns in small circles starting from the Mall and working outward. It could take forever to find the two trucks using this method, but it was better than nothing.

President-Elect Campbell was standing in front of the fireplace, arms crossed. A Revolutionary War musket hung on the mantel with a powder horn on one side and a drum on the other. A tattered Betsy Ross flag was framed above the musket. Except, as it turns out, this was *not* the president-elect.

"Directly before coming out here, President Davidson agreed to have me sworn in in private. I'm the president and have control. When Tom here showed him the intelligence, he understood that there needed to be continuity of power throughout the day."

I nodded. It was a good move, and Davidson was probably more than happy to relinquish control so he could blame Campbell if everything went south.

"You guys can use this as your command center. The chopper is coming back around to get me, but I wanted to tell you two things, Garrett. I had nothing to do with Melissa's death. My God, I'm horrified at the thought of what that brute Parizad did to her and what those assholes put her through! Interrogation. Torture. Drugs. My God." She pointed in the direction of the helipad. Near tears, she said, "Melissa was my best friend. There's nothing—I mean nothing—I wouldn't have done for her."

"Thank you," I said. I didn't believe her.

"The second thing is, I'm driving on with the real inauguration, even if it's only for show. It's an important message we send around the world. The bit about the sarin was true. There's no evidence that anything is missing."

"Ma'am, you can't be serious."

"A million people, Garrett. Maybe two million. First woman president. First big event post-COVID-19. This is too huge. You ever have a million people come to support you? We've doubled the numbers of law enforcement and radars. We've got some special drone-catching bullshit. I'm comfortable we've done everything we can."

"I advise against this," I said.

"Save that for when you're chairman, which I'm offering you, by the way. Fillmore's been up my ass for months."

"I respectfully decline. I could never work for a president who so blatantly ignores my advice," I said.

"Then solve the problem," she said. "I've handed you the equivalent of John Wilkes Booth and his coconspirators the night before they killed Lincoln. Figure the rest out. I don't want anyone to know how terrible my judgment was on this gang of criminals that President Davidson had working for him."

"Parizad has Brad," I muttered.

She stepped back and placed her hand on her chest. "Your Brad?"

I nodded.

Her hand covered her mouth, but then something glinted in her eyes. She firmed up and pointed at me.

"Save him and save this country, Garrett, goddamn it."

"I need to focus on finding him," I said.

"Do both," she said. "It's the same mission."

"Well, there is no need to double down on terrible judgment, is there, to let people die out of your own stubbornness? We've still got time to put out the warnings and do the event inside."

"And send a million plus packing? Deny the world the opportunity to see me being sworn in? It's a hugely important symbol, Garrett. You of all people should know that."

"You're risking your own life and that of the entire leadership of the country," I said. "And that of my son!"

"Don't you dare leverage Brad against me. I risk my life every day I step outside. Crazy assholes that don't want a bitch president. Inauguration Day will be no different. You have full authority to leverage NORTHCOM, SOCOM, all the COMs to do whatever you need. Stop these attacks, if they are real. I'm not changing anything. You find Brad, you stop this thing."

I said nothing.

"And after that, do what you want with those traitors. You know the penalty for treason. Sometimes a brass verdict is best."

I said nothing again, though I was pretty sure the president had just recommended killing two members of her cabinet and a general.

With that, she departed.

I didn't waste any time arguing with her. I figured I could always make a last-minute appeal, though the crowd would already be unwieldy if it weren't already. Certainly, there was a tipping point where it wouldn't be possible to clear everyone out of the target area.

"Tom, get the CNO on the line," I said. Within a minute, he had the chief of naval operations, Admiral Skip Bunch, on speakerphone.

"Skipper, here's General Sinclair," Rountree said.

"Admiral, we've got five Iranian submarines patrolling off California, Texas, and New York. They have cruise missiles with intent to strike energy facilities like oil refineries."

"Thought you were in jail," Bunch said.

"Not yet. We are at D-Day, and H hour is noon eastern. Inauguration. Get your sub hunters in the sky and do what you can."

"You don't give me orders, Sinclair."

"Skip, do what he says. President Campbell just gave him full authority."

"I'll do it for you, Tom, not for some wanted felon."

"Awesome," I said. "Once you unhitch your ass from your ego, get me someone who can talk to your commanders going after the Iranian subs."

"Fuck you, cowboy," he said.

I took that as a compliment and replied, "Teamwork makes the dream work," and hung up. "You might need to patch some things up with him, Tom," I said.

"You think?"

I turned to Van Dreeves and Hobart, neither of whom were used to standing around. As it was, they both were stripping and rebuilding the pistols Carson and the other members of the SEAL team had given them.

"We need McCool ready to launch on the trucks when we find them. We go as a team."

"Roger. On it," Hobart said, picking up his phone.

Turning to Rountree, I said, "Now we search."

"Kind of hard to sit around with our thumbs up our asses," Rountree said.

"Want to join me with the Three Stooges?"

"Love to."

We took the golf cart to the helipad and saw that the SEAL team had the West Pointers in the stress position, sweating them. They were cuffed and holding their hands out in front of themselves.

"Perpendicular!" Carson shouted. He might have thought he was back in BUD/S, but I didn't care after their betrayal. Estes was looking particularly weak. They were all probably anxious judging by the furrowed brows, profuse sweating, and yelps. Fillmore was openly sobbing.

"Lighten up, Fred. At least you made four-star general," I said. "Carson, I need to talk to these people individually. I'll be across the hall. Drag them in one at a time."

I entered a pilot briefing room about half the size of the conference room. The Secret Service and pilots most likely commiserated here as they planned their presidential flight missions.

Carson rapped his fist on the door and dragged Fillmore in, dumping him on the floor. Fillmore looked up at me and said, "Garrett, please. I didn't know."

"Take his cuffs off," I directed Carson. He understood I wasn't going to fight a bound man.

With his hands free, Fillmore pushed up from the ground and tried to open the door, but Carson was standing on the opposite side holding the door shut.

"Turn around," I said.

As he slowly rotated toward me, his face was a torturous combination of downturned mouth, wide eyes, and trembling lips. He held his hands up in front of him as if I were going to shoot him.

"Who knew about Melissa?" I asked. "This is not a game. You answer me truthfully, you live. You lie, you end up like Tharp. Parizad is doing his thing, so all we have to discuss is Melissa."

"Please. Please. I didn't mean to. Didn't want to."

"But you did. That's what matters. Sometimes we want things in this life so bad we do things we don't mean or want, but we do them and then we have to pay the consequences. Be held accountable. So tell me."

And he did. Every bit of the story. I stood there stoically receiving the information, visualizing my beautiful, strong wife being abused, all because Donna Tharp had confided to her friend out of distress, had told her the plan as she had heard it.

But Donna hadn't known everything.

When he was done, I told Fillmore, "Come closer."

I was standing in the middle of the room. He shuffled his feet like he had just aged twenty years, which maybe he had.

"Defend yourself," I said.

He threw his hands up in his face like a boxer on the defensive. My mind boiled with rage after listening to Fillmore tell me everything he knew about Melissa's death. I clenched my fists, gritted my teeth, and reared back to punch Fillmore into oblivion.

But it didn't feel right. I dropped my fist and pushed him back.

"You're not worth my energy, Fillmore. Get the fuck out of here."

Carson brought Estes and Owens in separately. Their stories aligned nearly perfectly with what Fillmore had said. The bottom line was that they actually did want to start a ground war in Iran and believed that they needed a provocation. The conspiracy theorists about 9/11 being an inside job had propagated the myth that the United States was looking for an entrée into Iraq, but this one wasn't a myth.

Combat wasn't a theory. The bodies stacked up, and eventually people grew tired of listening to the daily drumbeat of death, tuning out the conflict as they proceeded to go about their daily business.

While nothing was ever proven with respect to that war, here was documented evidence that four or five people who wanted to see how war might play out in Iran had almost made—even still might make—it happen. I pictured Owens, Fillmore, and Estes sitting like the observers of the First Bull Run battle in the Civil War, under their parasols on a high bluff while watching American troops die in house-to-house fighting. No rose petals here or ever.

I left the SEAL team in charge of the West Pointers and whatever fate might lie ahead for them. Collectively, they understood they were doomed, which was good enough for me. For their role in what happened to Melissa, I should have beat them each to a pulp, but I felt her voice inside me telling me forgiveness was the better path. I trusted her more than I trusted my own instincts at the moment. I was a barbarian without her comforting love and support. My skills as a commander and a warrior were considerable, and there would have been no stopping me had I pummeled Fillmore. But I was a warrior, not a murderer. I had come close enough to that line with Tharp, who it turned out deserved what he'd gotten in return.

Campbell was right about one thing. If I found Brad, I found Parizad.

When I got back to the cabin, it was 5:00 a.m. We still had nothing. At 7:47 in the morning, Hobart said, "Jackpot."

36

BY 7:54 A.M., WE were aboard the Beast heading to a Home Depot parking lot in northeast Washington, D.C.

"What's in these containers, Cools?" I asked, remembering to inquire about the stack of four long, rectangular boxes she had secured to the back wall of the aircraft.

"Stand by," she said.

"A D.C. Metro police officer is moving to the location," Van Dreeves said. "Home Depot manager said whoever is parked there never got approval, so he called the cops."

"We need to beat the cops there," I said.

"Roger. Moving the Reaper drone over the location. Meets the description we're looking for," Van Dreeves said.

"So do a million other trucks," I said. "Watch it."

"Sally, we have to get over the target ASAP before the locals check it out or make him move," Van Dreeves said.

"Nine minutes out," McCool said. "Just got clearance from the Freeze."

The Freeze was slang for the Flight Restricted Zone, or FRZ, in Washington, D.C., which was monitored constantly and used lasers to warn pilots away. Flying in the FRZ got a quick response from air controllers and lasers and, if ignored, the U.S. Air Force.

As if to emphasize the point, two F-15s leveled off above us, prepared to shoot us down if we made one wrong move toward the White House or the now assembled throng of maybe two million people ready to welcome the first woman president. Every street was filled with cheerful well-wishers. We had less than four hours to neutralize a major threat to them and our democracy.

"We can fast rope into the parking lot, if necessary. What do we know about others on the ground?" I asked.

"No knowledge," Hobart said.

"Okay, we go in as if Parizad is armed and prepared to defend. Key is keeping that back door shut. I don't want anything to allow for the release of that gas or liquid anywhere."

"Dagger, this is Frogman," Rountree said into the headset. He was still at the Camp David cabin.

"Go," I said.

"One Iranian sub found and destroyed off Cortes Bank, southwest of Los Angeles," he reported.

"Roger. Closing on OBJ time now," I said.

"Roger, out."

"How about VD and I go in. You C2 from up here," Hobart said. "Lots going on."

"Agree. Execute."

McCool slowed over the top of the Home Depot. A single police car was pulling into the lot, unaware that a terrorist with a truckload of drones filled with chemical weapons was parked in the lot. Brown dropped the fast rope, and my two men buzzed into the parking lot. Hobart approached the truck from one side, Van Dreeves the other.

I was concerned about the cop seeing my guys with long guns in the parking lot.

"Hover low between the cop car and the truck," I told McCool.

She maneuvered the Beast until we were hovering about ten feet off the ground and the police officer had buzzed up his window and was turning away from the violent turbulence.

"Got him," Van Dreeves said.

Hobart ran around to the rear of the truck and opened the doors. He closed them quickly and turned the locking bar.

"Oh my God," he said. "Dozens of drones. Have to move this truck. It's a dirty bomb. Even if a single drone doesn't fly, it's a truck full of crop-dusting drones filled with some kind of poison."

"Roger. You and VD move the truck. We will escort you."

"Roger. Nowhere close by to take it," Van Dreeves said.

"The chemical geniuses at Fort Detrick should know what to do with it. That's ninety minutes away," I said.

"Ninety minutes we don't have," Hobart added.

"Let's head to Detrick, and then we can regroup from there."

Ninety minutes turned into two hours with the traffic, and we were still only halfway up I-270 with another twenty miles to go when Rountree contacted me again.

"Two more subs. One in the Gulf and one in the Atlantic. Think they've got another one in the Gulf. Stand by."

"Roger."

"Break, break. Dagger, this is Frogman. Reaper has picked up a suspicious truck moving west on I-495. It momentarily got on the GW Parkway. No trucks allowed. Cops had them move off the road and reported it in. It's turning from 495 to 395 North."

"Roger, that's it."

I said to McCool, "We've got to go after that. No time to get the team."

"Copy all," Van Dreeves said.

McCool spun the helicopter and nosed over to nearly two hundred knots until we were zipping up I-395, passing over the Pentagon and a golf course.

"Frogman, call Park Police, Arlington, everyone. They need to block routes into the city."

"Wilco," he replied.

"Bingo," McCool said. "Mack truck headed north just turned off 495."

"Get low in front of it. Not sure the cops are going to make it in time."

Traffic was moving slowly, but the truck was weaving aggressively onto the shoulder and crossed into the HOV lanes, breaking the red-and-white-painted bars intended to prevent northbound traffic from entering when the southbound lanes were open.

Parizad wasn't this stupid. GW Parkway. North on the southbound lanes. Drawing attention.

"Get low," I said. "I don't think it's him. We still have thirty minutes to inauguration. This is a fake."

McCool spun around and played chicken with the truck, then pulled up before a head-on collision.

"Looks like some crazy guy with a suicide vest on," she said.

"Shit. The Immortals. We didn't kill them all." Then to Rountree, "Where are we on blocking the Fourteenth Street Bridge? I think this is a decoy. Immortal team member is wearing a suicide vest. Could be a dirty bomb. Could be the drones. But my guess is this is a fake. The vest might explode if he goes below a certain speed."

Like Parizad's signature boxing move, this truck was the feint with the right cross. Somewhere else was a roundhouse left hook coming at Washington, D.C. Parizad's boxing opponents rarely saw it, and we hadn't, either.

"D.C. and Arlington are reporting good copy on 395 blockage," Rountree said.

"Okay, keep the Reaper on him, but think about where he might be. He knows his plan is coming apart. What's his play?" I said this as much to myself as I did to Rountree.

"I'm looking at a map of Northern Virginia right now," Rountree said.

McCool pulled up high so we could see all the arteries.

"Sir, I'd take U.S. 1 up through Alexandria. It's where all the truck traffic is because they can't use the GW Parkway."

"We got a police report of a dead truck driver in an Alexandria Walmart dumpster. Truck is missing," Rountree said.

"Okay, that confirms Route 1. Let's go."

McCool flew us to Crystal City and began working her way south along the Jefferson Davis Highway, or U.S. Route 1. "Bingo," she said.

We had ten minutes until inauguration. Hobart and Van Dreeves were moving a truck full of chemicals out of harm's way. This was up to McCool and me.

"What do you have?"

"Truck pulling up the ramp to I-395, gaining speed. The roadblock doesn't look like it's fully set up there yet. Just a couple of cars deeper on the bridge."

I saw what she was talking about. The HOV lane roadblock was about a quarter mile into Virginia, but the police had set up everything else on the bridges over the Potomac, not realizing all Parizad needed to do was open the back and release the drones from a mile away.

The truck moaned up the ramp and slowed as it approached the police cars. Cops were in front of the roadblock on the bridge, waving down the driver as if he might be lost.

"Garrett," Rountree said, his voice somber. "San Francisco oil refineries on fire. Direct hit. Over fifty cruise missiles at ten targets. Second sub found in the Gulf. Destroyed."

"Jesus," I muttered. That accounted for the five that we knew about. Were there more? The navy had risen to the occasion. It was a tall order to find five submarines in deep water.

"The sub came into San Francisco Bay and detonated. It was a nuke."

So that was the plan. Dirty up the ports, destroy the oil refineries, and kill our leadership. Parizad had built redundancy into his scheme, and here we were at the inflection point, with McCool spinning the helicopter around so I could see into the cab of the truck. The cops were holding onto their headgear and waving at us to go away. The Potomac River rippled beneath the powerful rotor wash.

Inside the cab was a large, hulking man driving the truck. He looked familiar and was possibly the sparring partner of Parizad's that I recognized from thirty plus years before. Next to him, my son, Brad, sat, bound at the wrists, a hostage. Brown dumped the fast rope out, and I slid onto the roof of the truck, which was now idling in front of the police cars. The driver had exited the vehicle and was lifting his hands in an "I'm so confused" manner toward the police.

I shouted, "Take him! Terrorist!" But the rotor wash was too loud and allowed the big man to shoot both cops with a pistol he brandished quickly from his hip. I jumped from the roof and tackled the man, who shrugged me off. He was every bit as big as Parizad, maybe even bigger. He threw me against the police car, which I bounced off, came up spinning, and landed two solid kicks into his midsection. My wounded leg bit at me, but I pressed ahead. He stumbled back from my kicks, and then Brown shot him twice in the chest.

I jumped into the cab. Brad yelled, "Dad!"

"Stay still, son," I said.

He was wired with a suicide vest. This was Parizad's last line of defense. Use my son as a means to distract me. Fortunately, over the past twenty years, I'd seen my share of suicide vests. After a few seconds of assessing the wiring, I went to work and carefully removed it.

Turns out Parizad wasn't all that great at rigging the vest.

"Let's go, son," I said.

I carefully pulled Brad from the cab of the truck and lifted him into the helicopter that McCool had lowered onto the bridge. Brown was manning the machine gun and keeping an eye on the trailer behind the cab.

With Brad safely on the helicopter, I picked up Mahmood's pistol and ran to the back of the truck and began climbing up the vertical locking bar of the trailer when the door swung open, pushing me out over the river. I dropped the pistol to hang on with both hands, my feet flailing in the sky over the bridge. The door bounced off the hinges and ricocheted back toward the open trailer, where I came face-to-face with Parizad, who was standing in the center of the trailer surrounded by buzzing drones.

I landed inside the floor of the trailer, tumbled over a couple of drones, and bounced to my feet as two drones darted into the sky.

Parizad thundered toward me as I rolled to my feet and prepared to defend against another onslaught of iron-fisted punches. I backed against the thin wall and narrowly avoided a searing right cross that dented the metal frame. In response, I bounced two uppercuts off Parizad's abdomen while his left hook glanced off my head. I tried to slide in either direction, but his bulk was blocking me.

The trailer sounded like the middle of a hornet's nest. The drone propellers were buzzing at max velocity, ready to follow their GPS waypoints to attack their designated targets on the Capitol steps and in the audience. As Parizad and I traded punches, the doors were fractionally open, and the drones bounced off them like birds against a window. I became concerned about the amount of sarin gas in the truck. It was a hazard just sitting here. If we put a missile through it, the chem hazard might persist for years.

Parizad was clearly stalling as he backed to the door. He shot out two jabs and stepped back through the tilted drones that had bounced off the door. Those in the back had lifted, obviously on a timer to fly out of the truck in sequence.

The doors had to remain closed. Given the size of the spray tanks on the drones, maybe as large as an old-style coffee can, the two drones that had escaped seconds before could kill a thousand people, at least. The Beast's blades beat against the sky somewhere nearby. I felt my right ear and was glad to still have my communications device.

"Outside in thirty seconds," I said.

"Roger," she replied.

As Parizad missed with a right cross, I landed two solid punches to his face that made him stand up straight. His abdomen received my boot heel with all the force I could muster. He doubled over, and I pursued the momentum by bringing my knee up into his face, causing him to stumble backward toward the doors.

To prevent him from falling through the doors and opening them wide, I sprang behind him and pushed him toward the interior of the trailer. His sheer mass was steadfast, though, as he regained his footing and bearings, and smiled.

"Sinclair," he said through bloody teeth. His black eyes looked above me as drones bounced against the doors, opening them wider with each charge. I popped him twice in the face, but he didn't seem to notice. He lifted his arms and roared as he charged me, tackling us into the doors, opening them wide.

McCool was hovering twenty meters from the back of the trailer with Brown at the machine gun mounted in the crew door, spitting heavy 7.62 mm bullets at the drones, chipping the ones he hit to pieces, but also releasing liquid sarin gas into the truck.

Parizad and I tumbled onto the concrete road and continued to roll. He'd gotten his wish for a mano a mano duel with me and for the doors of the truck to open, unleashing his drone attack on the inauguration.

He barreled at me, eyes filled with rage. I remembered the sweeping foot drag I would do turning a double play as shortstop, where I would glide a little to my left, drag my right foot along the outer edge of the base, and then rocket the ball to first base with my right arm. I simulated that move as Parizad charged me by treating him like any number of runners trying to take me out of the play so that I couldn't make the turn.

I slipped to my left, dragged my right foot, tripped him, and rammed my right fist into his face as his eyes followed me. He tumbled headlong into the guardrail, the only thing separating us from the freezing waters of the Potomac River fifty meters below.

Parizad held on to the rail, his feet dangling above the water, his hands slipping until they finally released. Brown continued to chip away at the drones inside the truck. I waved at him to stop and ran to the back doors, closing and locking them, trying to avoid the chemicals on the floor and keep them from leaking onto the street. It appeared there were over thirty drones chipped up and tilted onto their sides. A few were still bouncing against the door.

That meant at least four or five were en route to their targets. They could kill five thousand to ten thousand people, including the entire leadership of the nation. More D.C. police arrived at the scene on the Fourteenth Street Bridge. I ran to them and shouted through the window of the first car, "Secure the truck! Call the hazmat team!" The officer nodded and said, "Roger that," and I ran toward the truck, where I then signaled to McCool to land and pick me up, which she did. Swarming into the sky were F-15 fighter jets and a company of Pave Hawks representing the JSOC quick reaction force.

Once on board, I put on the headset and said, "Brown, kill Parizad hanging from the railing there."

As we lifted up, Parizad fell into the river, arms dangling, legs pinwheeling.

"Put as much lead onto where he went in as possible!"

"Sir, I counted five drones that escaped. Have eyes on right now. They're all making a beeline for the inauguration," McCool said.

Brown emptied two belts of machine-gun ammunition into the river where Parizad had entered as we sped across the water with the Mall in sight.

"Those boxes?" McCool said. "Drone guns. Thought we might need them."

I looked down, and Brown had already opened and armed them like a good combat crew chief.

"Simple. They're like a bazooka. Aim and pull the trigger when we're close enough," Brown said.

We closed on the trail drone, its eight small rotors powering it through the sky twenty meters behind the one in front of it. Brown switched crew doors and lifted the device. It was a SkyWall Patrol drone catcher. It looked exactly like a Stinger missile with its long green tube and trigger mechanism.

Brown fired and a metal cylinder rocketed from the bore. The cylinder contacted the drone and deployed a net and parachute, which carried the drone into the river. I fired and hit the trail drone.

"Two down, three to go," I said. The problem was obvious. We had four drone catchers and five drones.

Brown and I repeated the process and eliminated the trail drones, leaving the lead as the only threat we knew about. We passed over the golf course on Hains Point, and shortly, the Capitol was in view. The throng of people was moving, responding to the threat. By the time we caught up with the lead drone, we were over I-395. The bridges were packed with people and police.

"Sir, I'm on final warning with the air force tool who says he's shooting us down," McCool said.

"Tom, can you do something?" I said, hoping Rountree was still monitoring.

"Roger. Have been on it. You're cleared. He's rogue. I'll reinforce."

"Can we use the rotor wash to push it down?" I asked.

"We can try," she said. "Narrow corridor."

We were approaching the Rayburn House building and finally had the room to maneuver on the drone above the U.S. Botanic Garden. The crowd was scattering in all directions, which of course meant that they weren't going anywhere, because there were so many people on hand for this historic inauguration.

McCool crabbed the helicopter to artfully use the massive rotor wash to block the forward momentum of the drone. We passed above the large glass atrium of the main building and then finally countered the forward progress on the back side of the complex adjacent to the massive crowd and less than fifty meters from where the president was standing.

McCool lowered the helicopter, forcing the drone down, but it darted and moved as if it were thinking on its own. McCool couldn't keep up with the quickness of the drone even though she was doing an excellent job keeping it within a cone of pressure from her rotor blades. The plan, such as it was, had been to force it into a free fall, but this was a stubborn commercial-grade outfit made for the harsh climates and conditions of crop-dusting.

I searched the inside of the Beast to find only an aviator's kit bag and a body bag, which I scooped up.

"Keep going. You're doing great," I said.

"I can't see it. Brown's keeping me on it."

About twenty meters above the Botanic Garden pool, I leaped at the drone with the body bag, not unlike a flying squirrel, and tackled it, feeling the blades chipping away at the bag, fighting me back. I landed in the shallow water, hit the concrete bottom, and then surfaced to where I was standing chest deep in the pool.

The drone floated in front of me, one propeller spinning in defiance, driven to continue its mission. I scooped it into the body bag and in seconds had it muted and neutralized. I was surrounded by Park Police, Secret Service, and anyone else in the D.C. Metro area authorized to carry a gun that day.

McCool pulled away and fled the airspace, saying, "Boss. It's a shit show down there. Looks like you've got it covered."

Yes, I loved my team.

But my mission still wasn't complete.

37

THANKS TO PRESIDENT CAMPBELL'S insistence, I lay in a Walter Reed hospital bed in the same room where Melissa had allegedly died of cancer. I stared through the windows, watching the sheer curtains flutter in the winter wind. The afternoon sky was slate gray. Crows perched stoically on the barren tree limbs, watching the hospital.

A day had passed since the showdown on the Fourteenth Street Bridge with Parizad. It wasn't clear to me which was more contested: my fight with Parizad or those dueling to take credit for "capturing" me. At the end of the day, the FBI had been given the credit, though they had been the last on the scene.

One of the concessions that Campbell had made for me was to have the FBI quickly investigate Dr. Blankenship. His Harvard Medical School degree and position as a Walter Reed physician didn't add up in my mind. Turned out, he had been drafted into the CIA over ten years ago to work assassination programs and in particular the development of poisons that could replicate natural death.

Parizad had paid the West Pointers $20 million for the access, half of which they readily gave to Blankenship to eliminate a threat to their plan. Parizad had never trusted the West Pointers, as he shouldn't have, or Blankenship, so he relied upon his longtime partner to do the ultimate dirty work.

Fillmore had served as the intermediary for the Ring Knockers, meeting with Parizad several times at his family farm, with Owens, Estes, and Tharp especially adept at keeping someone between them and the problem.

Demon Rain coupled with mobile phone technology showed nefarious promise as a mind control technique, and now the CIA was flush again with experiments. MKUltra and MKNaomi lived on.

As for Parizad, divers did not find a body at the bottom of the river, and there were no reports of a giant, drenched Persian running through the streets of D.C. or Northern Virginia. I didn't discount that he was still alive.

Reagan, McCool, Van Dreeves, and Hobart had all been in to see me, sneaking me chow and other things they thought I might need. Even Brad managed a visit as he recuperated in another wing. Other than his pride, he was uninjured.

Now President Campbell sat by my side with two hulking Secret Service agents flanking her.

Hobart was concerned about my safety and had provided me a pistol and knife, which I held under the sheets. The Secret Service had checked everywhere but beneath my ass, where I had uncomfortably stowed the small Glock and my knife.

My optic nerve still sparked, and when one of the Secret Service agents turned on a small handheld gadget intended to mask conversations from recording devices, it made a whirring sound that sent me straight back to the cave, Heidelberg, and Yokkaichi. The sounds were similar to this nearly imperceptible whirring, and my ears buzzed and optical nerves flared. The white dots were sparkling as if I'd been hit on the head. I lost focus as my hand gripped tightly on the pistol beneath the sheets.

"Garrett, thank you for what you did," President Campbell said.

I said nothing as I slid my hand to the side to lift the weapon. I moved the pistol incrementally given the hawkish stares of the Secret Service agents.

"I want to emphasize to you again that I had nothing to do with Melissa's . . . not being here anymore," she said.

I missed most of what she said and said nothing in response. Reagan had finally gone through all her mother's belongings and found an old, tattered diary from college. Searching through it, she'd found the lines:

> *Oh my God. Kim told me she might have killed Patricia. It was*
> *all a mistake, of course. A drinking contest. Alcohol poisoning.*
> *But she's freaked out. Patricia is in the hospital in an alcohol-*
> *induced coma. Extra prayers tonight.*

"And I want to offer you the chairman position. You have more than earned it."

My hand began to raise slowly. I shook my head as I looked at her, white dots and static filling my vision.

I continued lifting the pistol.

"Garrett?"

I closed my eyes, fighting the unnatural pull I was feeling.

I love you.

There. Melissa's calming voice finally intervened.

I love you, she said to me. My shattered soul had no fuel left to hate or kill. I dropped the pistol into the mattress softly and opened my eyes, moist with tears.

"I got you situated in this wing. Now make good use of it," she said.

I nodded. She squeezed my hand. I let her.

The door closed after she departed, and I drifted to sleep.

Sometime in the middle of the night, the door opened, and two sets of footfalls made their way toward my bed.

I creased one eye open as Ben David and Dr. Blankenship entered the room.

"Doctor, Ben," I said. "So good to see both of you. Please have a seat."

Blankenship was wearing a long white lab coat as I had seen him wear on my visits with Melissa sixteen months ago. His white hair was coifed, and his eyes were downcast as if bearing bad news.

David had credentials around his neck and wore a lab coat, as well, just as he had done in the picture Reagan had taken of him. His face was more wizened than I remembered. He had no problem locking eyes with me. Years of lying and tradecraft had made him the best in the business, by a long shot.

"Garrett," David said. "I wanted to personally thank you for pulling me from that cave in Yazd Province."

"Anything to help an old friend," I said.

He nodded and smiled, confident. Blankenship looked less sure, though I was certain he was no neophyte in this business.

"I'm sorry about Naomi," I said.

David's eyes flickered with fire, but he quickly, almost imperceptibly recovered by smoothing his face and creating a distraction.

MKNaomi was different from Ben David's Naomi. Further research by the Israeli Defense Forces showed that David had married an Iranian woman name Naomi. She had been the second person out of the tunnel in the Gaza Strip attack and was summarily slaughtered by the Israeli Defense Forces that had allowed the Mossad agent safe passage.

Ben David had turned. He wasn't escaping Hamas, he was leading an attack. The coded "88" was a trick to confuse the Israeli Defense Forces into a slow response. With my unwitting help, it had nearly worked.

David's utterance on the floor of the cave was not a warning about MKUltra but what he believed might be his last words. Sometimes the simplest explanation was actually all the evidence you needed. We found him alive in a cave of dead people. He was holding a Quds Force coin and whispering the name of his wife, the two things he held most dear.

Friendship, feigned or real, often served as blinders. Xerxes, it turned out, was the perfect nom de guerre for David. The King of Persia was teamed with the Lion of Tabas.

I saw the syringe weighing in his pocket. My guess: it was either botulism, like he had given to Melissa, or cyanide.

His quick eyes caught my glance.

"Well, then, shall we get on with it?" he said.

"Finally, your medical school put to use. Your parents would be proud," I said. "But tell me, how did you do it?"

"Does it matter?" he said.

"I guess not. But since we're here, humor me. I just want to know what you did to Melissa."

"In my part of the world, an eye for an eye is a fair deal," he said.

"Are you in on it with him?" I asked Blankenship.

He coughed and said, "I'm here as part of a routine follow-up."

I chuckled and redirected my attention to the man who was intent on killing me.

"Tell me, Ben," I said. "When did you turn on your country? On me?"

David smiled. It was the same half smile he had given me when he was staring at the Mediterranean Sea and we were drinking coffee at the Ritz-Carlton seaside café.

"Never," he said.

And I understood. He was always a double agent. He wasn't a Mossad member who had infiltrated the Quds Force; he was just the opposite. He was a Quds Force member who had infiltrated Mossad.

"Gaza," I said, "was an attack, not an escape."

"Dariush and I always said we should never underestimate you," David said.

He reached into his pocket, producing the syringe, which he clicked twice with a long finger. Blankenship leveled a pistol at me, evidently part of his routine follow-up procedure. David stood and lowered the syringe toward my neck.

"Naomi was second out of the tunnel. I saw her cut to pieces by machine-gun fire during your failed attack," I said.

He blinked, most likely remembering the moment when he was leading the attack on the Israeli outpost. The needle stopped long enough for Hobart and Van Dreeves to rush from behind the curtains on the far wall.

They quickly disarmed Blankenship as I snatched David's wrist like a cobra strike and rolled off the bed. I plunged the needle into his neck and lowered him to the floor as he gasped all the way down.

"An eye for an eye," he muttered on the way to the floor. I put my knee in his chest and held the plunger in his neck until he stopped writhing. He died with a sudden jolt as if shocked by electricity. Evil escaping the body.

Hobart flex-cuffed Blankenship and led him to the basement parking lot, stowing him in the back of the newly rented SUV. They returned for David and removed him in the same fashion.

I didn't feel any better, but justice had been served.

I lay back down, retrieved a new burner phone Campbell had given me, and called her.

"I made good use of this room. Thank you," I said.

"You're welcome," she said and hung up.

Once my adrenaline ebbed, I drifted to sleep. In the middle of the night, a hand touched mine.

"Garrett," she said.

Her voice was soft and musical, bringing back a rush of memories too precious to consider for too long before breaking my heart all over again.

A light wind crossed my face. The gentle caress of Melissa's hand.

"Garrett, I love you," she said.

As I opened my eyes, she shimmered like a desert mirage, standing above me. Her dimples and smile, jade-green eyes, and clear countenance were all there.

"I love you, too, Melissa," I croaked.

The curtains fluttered, and I looked at the open window, only to turn back to find Melissa had vanished with the wind.

ACKNOWLEDGMENTS

THANKS AS ALWAYS to my editor at St. Martin's Press, Marc Resnick, and his editorial assistant, Lily Cronig, for their unwavering support of my work. Marc is a great mentor and I'm thankful for his friendship and guidance. Ken Silver's production team is the absolute best. Thanks to Sara and Chris Ensey for their spade work in copyediting *Chasing the Lion.*

I appreciate Scott Miller and Trident Media Group for their steadfast dedication to my writing career, now fourteen books strong. I'm also thankful for the broader author-thriller community. It's a supportive group of talented writers and I am blessed to be among their ranks. I also appreciate the advice and assistance of my writing coach, Kaitlin Murphy-Knudsen. She makes me a better author with each book.

Thanks to my dad, Bob Tata, for his mentorship in life and support of my writing career. I also appreciate the patience of my two children, Brooke and Zach, the support of my brother, Bob, and his wife, Anne Ferrell, and the steadfast encouragement from my sister, Kendall.

Finally, thanks to Laura and Snowy for being by my side every day reading drafts and making everything better.